ILLUSION

ILLUSION

A NOVEL

Frank Peretti

HOWARD BOOKS
A DIVISION OF SIMON & SCHUSTER, INC.
New York Nashville London Toronto Sydney New Delhi

 Howard Books
A Division of Simon & Schuster, Inc.
1230 Avenue of the Americas
New York, NY 10020

First Howard Books hardcover edition March 2012

HOWARD and colophon are trademarks of Simon & Schuster, Inc.

For information about special discounts for bulk purchases,
please contact Simon & Schuster Special Sales at 1-866-506-1949
or business@simonandschuster.com.

The Simon & Schuster Speakers Bureau can bring authors to your live event.
For more information or to book an event, contact the Simon & Schuster Speakers
Bureau at 1-866-248-3049 or visit our website at www.simonspeakers.com.

Designed by Davina Mock-Maniscalco

Manufactured in the United States of America

10 9 8 7 6 5 4 3 2 1

Library of Congress Cataloging-in-Publication Data
Peretti, Frank E.
    Illusion : a novel / Frank Peretti.—1st Howard Books hardcover ed.
      p.   cm.
    1. Husband and wife—Nevada—Las Vegas—Fiction. 2. Accidents—Fiction.
3. Hallucinations and illusions—Fiction. 4. Psychological fiction. I. Title.
    PS3566.E691317145 2012
    813'.54—dc22   2011040115

ISBN 978-1-4391-9267-2
ISBN 978-1-4516-1735-1 (ebook)

All scripture quotations are from King James Version of the Bible. Public domain.

To Barbara Jean, my beloved for forty years.
Only the Lord God could have brought me such a woman.

chapter

1

Mandy was gone. She went quietly, her body still, and Dane was at her bedside to see her go. The ICU physician said it was inevitable, only a matter of minutes once they removed the ventilator, and so it was. Her heart went into premature ventricular contractions, stopped, restarted momentarily, and then the line on the heart monitor went flat.

It happened more quickly than anyone expected.

She was an organ donor, so she had to be removed immediately for procurement. Dane touched her hand to say good-bye, and blood and skin came off on his fingers.

A nurse wheeled him out of the room. She found a secluded corner out on the fourth floor patio, a place with a view of the city and shade from the Nevada sun, and left him to grieve.

Now, try as he might to fathom such feelings, grief and horror were inseparably mixed. When he wiped his tears, her blood smeared his face. When he tried to envision how she gladdened whenever she saw him, how she would tilt her head and shrug one shoulder and her eyes would sparkle as she broke into that smile, he would see her through the blackening glass, crumpled over the steering wheel, the deflated airbag curling at the edges, melting into her face.

A handkerchief made careful passes over his face below and around his eyes. Arnie was trying to clean him up. Dane couldn't say anything; he just let him do it.

The smell under his robe found his attention: sweat, antiseptics, gauze, bandages. His right shoulder still felt on fire, only, thanks to the painkillers, on fire somewhere else far away. Not a serious burn, they told him, so he kept telling himself. The bruises ate away at him, little monsters sequestered against his bones, festering under all that blued flesh in his side, his right hip, his right shoulder. It hurt to sit in the wheelchair; it hurt more to walk.

He broke again, covering his eyes to ward off the vision of her hair crinkling, vaporizing down to her scalp, steam and smoke rising through her blouse, flames licking through the broken glass, but it remained. Oh, God! Why? How could He change her so instantly from what she was—the woman, the saint, his lover with the laughing eyes, wacky humor, and wisdom of years—to what Dane had just seen perish on a bloodied gurney behind a curtain, sustained by tubes, monitors, machines? The images replayed. He thought he would vomit again.

Arnie brought the pan and a towel close under his chin.

He drew in a long, quaking breath, then another, then centered his mind on every breath that followed, commanding, controlling each one.

Arnie put the pan aside and sat close, silent.

Dane gave his weeping free rein; there could be no stopping it even as his bruises tortured him with every quake of his body. The moment passed, not in minutes but in breaths, thoughts, memories, wrenchings in his soul, until somewhere in his mind, just slightly removed from the visions, the soul pain, the hospital smells, and the painkillers, he took hold of what he already knew.

He could hardly place the breath behind the words. "I am just so much going to miss her."

Arnie blew his nose on the same handkerchief he'd used to clean Dane's face. "You may never finish saying good-bye. Maybe that's okay." He cleared his throat. "If it were me, I could never give her up."

Dane noticed the move of the breeze over his face, the warmth of the sun on the patio. Birds flitted and chattered in the arbor. Mandy was about things like that.

"I suppose there were many who loved her," Dane said. "But it was my arm she took to go to parties; she wrote her love notes for me; she chose to share my future when I didn't even have one." His vision blurred with fresh tears. "How did a guy like me rate a woman like her?"

Arnie touched him on the left shoulder, the one that wouldn't hurt. "That's the stuff you wanna remember."

Arnie Harrington, his agent but mostly his friend, a little on the heavy side, still had some hair but not much, and had to be as old as Dane but didn't look it. How he found out there'd been an accident Dane would have to ask him later. It was only now that Dane fully recognized he was here.

He drew a breath to calm his insides and touched Arnie's hand. "Thanks for coming."

"Got a call from Jimmy Bryce over at the Mirage. He thought it was a rumor so he called me. I suppose I can call him back, but it'll be all over town by now."

"Guess it'll be in the papers."

"Guess they're already writing it. I'll handle all of that."

"I'd appreciate it."

Dane followed Arnie's gaze toward the Las Vegas Strip, where every structure, object, entrance, and electric light vied for attention. It was no great revelation, but after all the years he and Mandy worked here, all he could see, all he cared to remember was the woman who remained real in such an unreal place. "I got way better than I deserved."

"Well, yeah."

"Forty years."

"Like I said . . ."

"Forty years . . ." The fact came alive as he lingered on it and salved the horrors from his mind, at least for now. With no effort at all the unfaded image of Mandy first setting foot in his life played before his eyes, the dove girl sitting in the front row who caught and held his eye . . . to the swelling, carnival sound of a gilded merry-go-round.

chapter

2

Whatever that organ-grindy tune was, Mandy had heard it so many times that day that she could sing along, with some harmony—"Da da da daaahh, tada da da bup booda WAA!"—as she clasped the silver anklet around her ankle. It cost her fifteen bucks, her limit for the day not counting an upcoming chicken basket from the Spokane Junior League booth. She and Joanie and Angie were looking through the old Shoshone Indian's wares when the wings of two silver doves glinted in the sun and caught her eye.

Doves. Her favorite. She raised them. Bonkers, Maybelle, Lily, and Carson were even now strutting their stuff in their cages over in the Poultry Barn, basking in the glory of two blue ribbons and a red.

Doves. In the Bible, a symbol of the Holy Spirit.

And Joanie, her best friend since first grade, loved it. "It's perfect! I love it!" Of course, she was still hyped out of her mind from her third ride on the Chair-O-Plane. Right now she loved everything.

Mandy let the anklet hang with a gentle curve about her ankle, the doves on the outside, and straightened, clearing her blond hair from her face with a brush of her hand and flip of her head. She repositioned her headband, tresses properly in place, and looked down. All she could see were the flared bottoms of her faded jeans and the toes of her sneakers. "Well, *guy*, you can't even see it."

"That's okay," Joanie hinted.

She hitched up the leg of her jeans to expose the anklet—worn over her white crew sock. Yeah, it looked dumb.

"You should've worn a skirt and sandals," said Joanie.

Mandy made a face at her. This was the county fair. She was helping her dad show his llamas, she was showing her doves, there was straw to pitch, feed to carry, poop to scoop—and ride the Chair-O-Plane in a skirt? Right!

"But doves," said Angie, enraptured. Angie was a new friend from college, usually half on this planet and half not, depending on the moment. "It's you, Mandy. Free-spirited, always flying somewhere."

"Yeah?" said Mandy, admiring the doves once again. "Way cool." Dumb she could do.

All around them was the carnival at the Spokane County Interstate Fair: the faithful, ever-turning merry-go-round putting out all that music; the ring toss, bag toss, ball toss, and dart toss booths making it look so easy; the crowds, kids, cotton candy, cheap prizes, stuffed toys, whistles, and windmills; one crying kid with one addled parent every hundred square feet; the rap-rap-revving of the gas engines that kept the rides spinning, lurching, tumbling, heaving; the screams—oh, Mandy and company had done their share of that already. What's the carnival without screaming?

Like the screams coming from the Freak Out right now, getting louder with a touch of Doppler effect every time the huge pendulum swung through an arc and the eight kids riding it got another wave of adrenaline and nausea. The sights and sounds made Joanie unreasonable. "We gotta try that one!"

"Time check," said Mandy, willing to consider it.

Joanie had a watch. "Oh, yeah! It's, uh, ten to one."

The Great Marvellini would be doing his amazing thing on the North Stage at two. Magic! Mandy did not want to miss that.

"I'm going for that chicken basket," she said.

"Right on," said Joanie.

"Where'd they get the chicken?" Angie asked.

Mandy broke into the County Fair Weave, a bent-kneed scurry she'd first developed as the After Church Weave and then the School Hallway Weave. It got her through crowds quicker—supposedly—and worked even better if she used her hot rod noise. "Brrrrrroooom!"

"Whoa, wait up!" came Angie's voice.

Mandy checked over her shoulder. Joanie was in her slipstream, and Angie was catching up. The Spokane Junior League Chicken Basket booth was just across from the grandstand. Mandy made it into the line with Angie behind her and Joanie in third place, hopping, trying to get her sandal back on. Score two points for crew socks and sneakers.

Joanie secured her sandal and scanned the menu chalked on a blackboard. "I think I'll take a look around."

Angie was already scanning the booths for something grown without chemicals. "Where you wanna meet?"

Mandy wiggled her index finger toward the North Lawn, a grassy common with picnic tables under the trees. "I'll grab us a table."

Joanie and Angie turned and the crowd swallowed them up.

Mandy got her basket soon enough, the chicken still steaming, along with a diet soda in a Styrofoam cup, plasticware, and two paper napkins. Just like last year.

She made her way onto the North Lawn, looking for a table. The place was busy with late lunchers, so she opted for a grassy spot in the shade of a honey locust tree, a good place where she wouldn't get stepped on. She sat, her back against the tree, her basket in her lap. A clock on the end of the Corn Dog booth said five after one. If she and her friends could cram their lunch down and get to the North Stage by quarter of two they could hopefully get a seat up close. She could take in the one-hour show and get back to the Sheep and Goat Barn to give Daddy a break with the llamas. Sounded like a plan.

The Great Marvellini. She smiled as she chewed, amused. With a name like that and a gig at a fair like this, he probably wouldn't blow her away. But then again, a chance to watch a real magician didn't come often, and if she could just keep up with him, see how he did his loads, switches, and misdirections, that would be so cool. Would he tear up a newspaper? She could tear up a newspaper and restore it whole, and do it so smoothly it still had Joanie and Angie guessing. Rope tricks she didn't care that much about. The cutting the rope in half trick was fun, but ehhh . . . who didn't do that one? But . . . oh! Back-palming cards! Now, that still had her frustrated. She could do one card in front of a mirror or a few friends, but twenty cards at once, in front of a big crowd? If he could do that one and do it well, now, that would blow her mind. She'd been practicing—

Oh! The tree moved, bumping her head, shoving her forward. She looked back; did something hit it, a car or a golf cart or something? Weird. She turned forward again—and saw white cloth with little blue flowers in her peripheral vision.

She stayed motionless, as if a bee had landed on her. She blinked. She rubbed her eyes, then opened them again.

Freaky. Very freaky.

Somebody'd thrown a cloth over her, something white with a pattern of tiny blue flowers. It covered her down to her knees, and with one movement of her arms she realized it had sleeves and she was wearing it.

Her chicken basket was gone. So was her drink, her paper napkins, her plasticware.

Her mouth was empty. She'd been chewing on chicken . . .

Bare feet. She looked about for her sneakers and her white socks, but nothing.

Not just bare feet. Bare legs. She raised her right foot: the anklet was gone. Her fingers shot to her earlobes. Empty.

But not just the anklet and earrings. She gasped with a little squeak as she distinctly felt the prickling of the grass against her bottom, the scratch of the tree's bark against her back. Her hands shot down to secure the cloth, keep it down, keep it tight, don't let it move . . .

She checked herself, one side, then the other, top to bottom, front to back, frantically finding out just how much of that cloth she had to cover herself.

"Augh!" she cried out, then stifled herself so no one would look. Unbelievable! She was wearing a hospital gown, those embarrassing things they make you wear for physicals and operations and stuff.

She squirmed and wormed, planting her feet on the ground and her back against the tree to elevate herself and make sure everything was closed up back there. Any extra she wrapped tightly around her, holding the outside layer. Now she was scanning the commons, her hair, with no headband, whipping about her face. Somebody had to be watching this, having a really dirty laugh. Did anyone else see what happened?

The people sitting at the tables were eating, talking, paying her no mind. The people . . .

What happened to the fat guy sitting at the second table with half his butt showing? What about the two ladies in the pink Take Off Pounds Sensibly T-shirts eating salads? Where'd they go, and how did they move so fast?

She must have been sleeping quite a while. Her eyes went in search of the clock on the end of the Corn Dog booth.

No clock. Different booth, and this one sold . . . it took her a moment . . . Vietnamese food. *Vi-et-na-mese?*

She looked a careful, second time at the faces around the commons, the people sitting at the tables. *Nobody* looked the same. Not even the tables. They were blue; they used to be green.

She carefully pulled in her feet and got them under her.

Was she in a different place? She twisted to make sure she was still under the tree. This one was bigger. It was a honey locust, but a lot bigger. Where was the smaller one?

A couple walked close by, and the guy gave her a quizzical look. She was about to return his look stretched out of proportion when it occurred to her that her own stare might have started it.

Smile, Mandy.

She smiled. He gave her a halfway, "it's cool" smile, then looked to see where he was going.

She looked down at herself. No, crouching under a tree in nothing but a hospital gown and staring holes through everybody didn't blend.

She'd better find Joanie and Angie.

Unless they were the ones who did this to her. But they never pulled weird pranks like this.

Maybe this was a drug trip. Somebody slipped her some acid in that diet soda. She'd never done drugs; she wouldn't know what to expect.

She stood, keeping her back to the tree as she prepared the gown for walking in public. Blades of grass tickled between her toes. Any other time that would have been fun.

Daddy taught her to stop and think when they used to go hunting. He'd say, "What's the first thing you do when you're lost?" and she knew the answer from the last time he asked her, "Stop and think."

She eased away from the tree. She could walk. She could breathe. Her eyes were working fine—well, lying to her, but at least they were in focus. She stepped across the grass, taking a few jabs in the feet from twigs and stones—those were real enough—and made it to the asphalt walkway that ran between the booths.

All the booths were different. New frames, new signs, new locations, and . . . and the Junior League Chicken Basket had changed to the Shriners' Barbecue. She could feel her stomach tightening and her hands starting to shake.

Daddy used to tell her, "When life gives you lemons, make lemonade."

"I'm having fun," she said out loud so she could hear it, rubbernecking in the middle of the walkway with people passing on every side. "Just going nuts here and having fun."

She caught a sideways glance from a lady but smiled back. "It was a girl! Seven pounds, five ounces! It went great!" The lady kept going.

The asphalt was hot under her feet and hurt with every step. Mandy bore the pain, stepping in any shadow she could find, searching the booths: Curly Fries. Mexican Grill. Huckleberry Ice Cream. Crab Cakes. Breaded Tenderloins.

No Joanie. No Angie.

She passed a little dispenser with a picture of a hand on it: Hand Washing Station. Wow. A place for people to wash their hands, right out in the open. But it took two hands, and one of hers was indispensably occupied.

Then came the Tobacco Free Zone. Where? Everywhere, or just there?

Huh. Since when did some of the boys start wearing really short hair, even butch cuts? Instead of an Afro, a black kid had no hair at all. Was that *in*?

She walked back toward the carnival rides, past Oklahoma Funnel Cakes, Elephant Ears, A Taste of Italy, Gyros Gyros Gyros.

The organ-grindy tune from the merry-go-round had changed. She made herself look: it was a different merry-go-round.

She came to the end of the food booths and turned two complete circles, one hand holding her gown, the other holding her hair away from her face and shading her eyes as she scanned the crowd.

Her friends were gone like they never existed.

She tried to fend it off, hold it down, but this *feeling* kept turning her stomach, shortening her breath, making her hands quiver: the Disneyland Freak-Out. She was little, with Mom and Daddy at Disneyland, and all she had to do was look away to watch Pluto go by and the next moment she couldn't see them anywhere, only strange people, strange feet and legs and strollers and other kids, and no one looked at her and no one knew her, and she didn't know them, and she'd never known such loneliness before, like dangling over death, so much so that she screamed for Mom and Daddy . . .

Her hand went over her mouth. This felt *just like it.*

Strangers. All these people were strangers. Even the buildings, the booths, the trash cans, the signs . . . all strangers.

At least the layout of the fairgrounds looked the same. She hurried through the carnival toward the livestock buildings. Her feet hurt, again and again. She couldn't avoid the small pebbles, bits of trash and straw, and the heat, always the heat at midday with so few shadows. She was starting to limp, about to cry.

She passed three guys with long, snaky hair, tattoos all over their arms and backs, and their pants falling down, showing a pair of underwear falling down, showing another pair of underwear.

"Oh, Jesus, what have I done?"

She was drawing more stares now. Hobbling, fighting panic, her hair constantly in her eyes, she was getting noticeable and couldn't help it.

A guy walked by with a funny plastic thing in his ear, talking out loud to someone who wasn't there— ". . . well, how about four? You leave the kids off and then I'll swing by . . . no, no problem."

She asked someone, raced to the building labeled Camelid Barn, and found llamas content and quietly munching in straw-lined aluminum pens.

At the far end, a rancher on a raised platform, microphone in hand, was giving a llama lecture to a small crowd.

She'd never seen him before. She scanned the faces of those minding the animals. She once knew most of them; now she didn't know any. She hurried among the pens reading the names: Johnson Sisters. Bingham's Llamas. Sunrise Ranch. Lotta Llamas. No one she knew or remembered. She looked up and down, peering, searching through the people, pens, and long furry necks. She climbed to the second rail of a pen and searched again.

"Daddy?" she called.

She didn't see him. A kid about twelve turned and looked in her direction, but only because she looked so out of place in here.

An answer was all she wanted. "Daddy?" Louder. "Arthur Whitacre, are you here?!"

Now the llamas were checking her out with huge brown eyes, starting to get nervous. That didn't sit well with the owners, who were checking her out as well.

"Has anybody seen Arthur Whitacre?" Her eyes were blurring with tears and she couldn't help shaking.

"Oh, what have we here?" somebody said.

A gentleman from the Sunrise Ranch, in plaid shirt and rancher's hat, approached, extending a hand to her. "Miss, why don't you get down from there?"

She didn't know him and she didn't come down. "I'm trying to find my father!"

"Shh, now just take it easy. We'll find him. Just come on down before you get hurt."

She stepped, nearly fell, from the railing. He reached and steadied her but she didn't appreciate his touch and brushed him off.

"Arthur Whitacre! I'm looking for Arthur Whitacre!"

A nice, curly-headed gal in an Alpaca Acres T-shirt hurried to help, but just repeated his name, "Arthur Whitacre?"

Don't play dumb with me! "Yes, Arthur Whitacre! The Wooly Acres Ranch! He had four llamas!"

Miss Alpaca Acres looked around the room, bewildered. Another lady joined them, the really fat one from the yarn spinning display. "Who's she looking for?"

"Arthur Whitacre?" said the gentleman.

"He had four llamas!" Mandy repeated.

"There's nobody here by that name," said the gentleman.

The rancher who'd been doing the lecture arrived. She had to tell him the same things all over again.

"Are you sure you're in the right building?" he asked.

She stared back at them, aghast. Such unbelievable, total knownothingness. They could have been mannequins, dream people.

"Daddy . . ." slipped in a hoarse whisper from her lips. She turned away from the strangers and toward the huge room to look just one more time, hands trembling, barely gripping the paddock rail. If only she could see him. If only he were working close to the ground, spreading straw or checking hooves, and would finally stand up straight and appear chest and shoulders above the pens, billed cap on his gray head, feed pail in his hand. If only she could see him smile big and wave at her and she could run to him and let him put his guarding arm around her and pull her close for just a moment . . .

Then everything else wouldn't matter. She would have been home, even in this place.

"Please don't be gone," she whispered. "Please, dear God, don't take him away, not him, too!"

She was crying, really crying, and she didn't care who noticed even as gentle hands touched her shoulders and the strangers came close.

"Where'd you come from, sweetie?" asked the gentleman.

"Is there somebody we can call?" asked Alpaca Acres.

Mandy came away from the railing and let them gather around her. They were less strangers now and she needed them.

The fat lady asked, "What's your name, sweetie?"

"Mandy Whitacre—and my father's Arthur Whitacre, and we had some llamas . . ."

She could see them looking her over, reading something in what they saw.

"Mmm," said the rancher. He was looking at her bare feet and her hospital gown. "She might have gotten out of the . . ." He jerked his head toward the west.

The gentleman seemed to understand. He nodded, then spoke kindly, "You don't worry now. We're gonna get you some help."

"We sure are," said the fat lady.

The llama lecture rancher took a little gadget from his belt, touched it, and it lit up like a tiny color television. He rubbed his finger across the screen, and the picture moved. Little numbers and letters appeared like a keyboard on the screen and he started touching them as they made soft, musical beeps.

It was enough to scare her. "What's that?"

He looked up at her, strangely interested in her question.

She asked him, "What's that going to do to me?"

The four exchanged looks and nodded little yeses to each other.

chapter

3

Mandy sat on a hospital gurney, bare feet on the linoleum floor, trying not to wrinkle the white sheets. She had a robe now— *Thank You, Jesus and Spokane County Medical Center*—and under the circumstances she was deeply grateful. It even had the hospital logo stitched on it.

She was in one of those through-the-door-and-down-the-hall examining rooms every hospital and doctor's office has, the one in which the smiling nurse takes your temperature and blood pressure, asks you some questions, tells you the doctor will see you shortly, and then leaves you to sit for a while. She could hear some occasional stirrings from the hall outside, a nurse or doctor walking by, some muffled conversations, sometimes the low rumble of a passing gurney or cart. It was a big, busy place out there with lots of people waiting their turn, just as she was.

I should be safe. Unless this was like *Planet of the Apes* and she was Charlton Heston, the astronaut who landed there, and all the apes thought *he* was the weird guy.

Like that lady sheriff's deputy back at the fairgrounds. "Honey, we're going to take you to the hospital just to make sure you're okay, all right?"

It made sense at the time. Something had to be wrong with her head and she was desperate.

But it was a little heavy riding in the back of a police car with no handles on the doors and a cage between the front and back and a big shotgun mounted on the dash. . . . She didn't have anything against cops, at least not yet, not personally, but plenty of her friends did, and maybe for good reasons: Mayor Daley's cops during the Democratic National Convention in Chicago, and those kids at Kent State getting shot, to name a few.

The lady deputy was named Rosemary and she talked a little bit, but Johnny, the big Hispanic guy who drove, hardly said a word except on the radio, something about "transporting subject for police hold."

Subject. She was a subject. And "police hold" didn't sound like help.

She fidgeted, dried her palms on her robe, stood up because she was tired of sitting. *I've got to call Daddy.* He'd be looking for her by now, getting worried. Joanie and Angie—wow, they'd be ready to skin her.

She touched the soft surface of the gurney. It was really there. She was really here. There were no boogie men or aliens or armored apes standing around trying to jab her with big needles or suck out her brain. She could recite the opening of the Declaration of Independence and the opening lines from the Gettysburg Address. Two plus two was four. Eight plus eight was sixteen. Eight times eight was . . . um . . . sixty-four!

"Mandy Eloise Whitacre," she recited, "January 15, 1951, 12790 North Lakeland Road, Hayden, Idaho, 83835. Arthur and Eloise Whitacre—Eloise passed away March 12, 1965. I graduated from Coeur d'Alene High School in 1969. Sophomore at North Idaho Junior College working toward a major in theater . . ."

There was a gentle knock on the door and it opened. Two nurses came in—at least she figured they must be nurses. One of them, a nice-looking lady in her forties, was dressed in dark pants and a comfortable blouse with pockets and had a stethoscope around her neck. She could have been somebody's mom. The young, pretty one was wearing blue pants and a flowered top and had long hair done up in braids. Neither wore a cap. The younger one was pushing a little wheeled stand with a . . . Mandy didn't know what it was. A TV? A typewriter? Both? How could it be so small and flat and be either one?

The mom-looking nurse said, "Hi, Mandy. I'm Dr. Fried, but you can call me Angela, and this is June."

Mandy shook Angela's hand, actually looking at it. It was warm
and real. "Mandy Whitacre."

"Go ahead, sit down," Angela said, indicating the gurney. "Make
yourself comfortable."

Mandy settled back down, again trying not to crinkle the sheets.

Angela left the door half open—Johnny the cop was standing just
outside like a wall, watching everything—then came close to Mandy,
looking her in the eyes and with a gentle hand to her chin to turn her
head, either side of her face. "So, what brings you here today?"

"The sheriffs."

"June's going to take your blood pressure, okay?"

Mandy was staring at the really flat TV hinged to a really flat
typewriter as June wrapped the cuff around her arm. "Okay."

"Do you know where you are right now?"

"Spokane County Medical Center."

"That's right."

June pressed a button on a small white box; the cuff squeezed
around Mandy's arm all by itself and red numbers began blinking on
a little machine. Now Mandy stared at that.

"And why do you think they brought you here?"

Mandy's mind went dead in the water. The question wasn't hard;
it was the answer that was tough.

"One-forty over eighty," said June, removing the cuff. "Pulse is
one-ten."

Angela nodded with a smile and touched Mandy's hand. It was
trembling a little. "It's okay, Mandy. You're safe."

Mandy drew a deep breath, let it out, and tried to relax.

"That's the stuff. Now hold still, just look at me." Angela took
an eye doctor's instrument from her shirt pocket and shined it into
Mandy's eyes. "Try to keep them open just a little longer . . ." Then
she took another instrument and looked in Mandy's ears. With a
gentle hand and soft words, she turned Mandy's head, lifted her hair
aside, and checked behind both ears. "I'm just looking for any bruising, any damage to your head."

June was typing on the little flat typewriter.

"What is that?" Mandy asked.

June skipped a beat trying to understand the question. "What is
what?"

Mandy pointed. "That thing you're typing on."

Angela rotated the stand so Mandy could see it better. "This thing right here?"

Mandy nodded, amazed at the words and lines and little blinking spaces on the screen—and there was her name in tight little letters as clear as a bell. It was like television, only much better.

June put a little white thimble over Mandy's thumb and another gadget on a wheeled rack showed the results in more red numbers: 95, 97, 96 . . .

Angela saw the numbers and typed those in. "This is a computer. You've never seen a computer?"

June stroked a little gadget over Mandy's forehead and said, "Ninety-eight point six."

Now Mandy had to check that thing out. "Did you just take my temperature?"

June smiled. "Sure did."

"No thermometer?"

"That's what this is."

Mandy reached out and touched, then tapped the edge of the computer screen. It was real under her fingers.

Angela was watching her. "Mandy, have you had any drugs or alcohol in the past twenty-four hours?"

This was worse than *Planet of the Apes*. This was *Planet of the Weird Hospital of the Future* . . . or *The Time Machine Gone Crazy*, or . . .

"Mandy?"

"I need to call my father."

"Can I ask a few questions first?"

Mandy slowed her words down. "I need to call my father. He's going to be worried about me. He doesn't know where I am."

"We'll call him, but we need to be sure you're all right first."

Nobody ever *listened*! "I need to call him *now*!"

Johnny, still stationed just outside the door, gave her a corrective parent look, his weight shifted in her direction.

"All right, Mandy." Angela reached into her pocket. "Here you go." She handed Mandy a little plastic square thing, folded like a clam.

Mandy held the thing in her hand, turning it over, exploring, trying to understand it. She was getting that sinking feeling she got in school when she didn't know the answer to a test question—and she could easily sense that Angela was playing the prof.

Angela reached over and opened the little clam. Inside were tiny buttons like an adding machine and . . . was that a television in there? What was this, another computer a whole lot smaller? Mandy felt totally stupid.

Angela asked, "Have you ever seen one of these?"

"Maybe on *Star Trek*. You know, 'Kirk to *Enterprise*!'"

Angela reached over and took it from her. "What's the number?"

"Parkway three-seven-one-two-zero."

Angela and June looked at each other.

"Parkway?" asked June.

Angela asked, "You wouldn't have another number we could try, would you?"

"That's the only number we have."

Angela shrugged with her eyebrows, tapped on the little buttons, and handed the thing back.

Mandy didn't know what to do with it—was her dad going to pop up on that little TV like Captain Kirk?

Angela mimed holding a phone to her ear. Mandy put the thing up to her ear.

Oh. Wow. This was too much.

Right away she got a rude squeal and a voice: "We're sorry, the number you have called is no longer in service. Please check the number and try again."

"The number was wrong," she said, staring at the little buttons.

"Press Off."

Mandy obeyed.

"Now press Talk and try again."

Mandy pressed Talk and listened. Dial tone. She entered the numbers again, watching them appear on the little screen. *Wow.*

"We're sorry, the number you have called is no longer in service. Please check the number and try again."

Mandy thrust the little plastic clam/*Star Trek* communicator back at Angela. "I need a real phone, one I can dial with!"

Angela took it from her hand. "Sweetie, this *is* a real telephone. It's a cell phone, right?"

You expect me to know that? Mandy couldn't sit. She was on her feet before she noticed, shuffling about the free floor space like a nervous fish in a very small bowl. "A cell phone." *Yeah. Riiight!* Like everybody and his mother and his uncle and brothers had a cell phone! She wanted to bite somebody. "Where'd you get it?"

Angela gave a little shrug. "I bought it. You've never seen one?"

"No. There's a lot of stuff I've never seen before, everywhere I look. It's like I've gone into the future or something."

Angela paused just a moment and her tone changed ever so slightly. "Mandy? What year is it?"

Mandy looked at her, looking for a sparkle in the eye, an up-turned corner of her mouth. "You serious?"

Angela just tilted her head with an apologetic air and waited for an answer.

"It's 1970," said Mandy. "It's September twelfth, 1970."

"Who's the president?"

Oh, come on! "Nixon's president!"

"Okay."

Now June was typing on the computer.

She is messing with me! "Nixon's the president. Spiro Agnew's vice president. You want to know the Speaker of the House? John McCormack!"

"Mandy . . ."

"And Nixon ran against Hubert Humphrey and Humphrey's running mate was Ed Muskie and I don't do drugs and I don't drink and I never have!" Now Mandy was crying; she couldn't help it.

"All right, Mandy, all right."

"I'm not crazy!"

Johnny leaned in. "Everything okay in here?"

Who invited you? "I'm fine, thank you!"

He just kept that same old steel expression: Mr. Wall. *Don't try to get past me.*

Angela whispered something to Johnny and then closed the door to only a crack. Then she sat with Mandy and put an arm around her shoulder. It felt good, warm and human. It gave her permission to cry, so she just let go. She needed to.

Angela spoke close to her ear, almost in a whisper, "Sweetheart, we're your friends. We want to make sure you're all right and we want to fix whatever's wrong, but we need your help. We need you to help us help you. Do you understand?"

Mandy's nose was running, but June had a tissue right there, just in time, and then another one for her tears. Mandy used both, received a third, and then nodded.

"Now, we're going to do all we can to contact your father; we'll get some people working on that right away and they can be doing that while we're working with you, but right now we have to ask questions and do some tests and do all we can to isolate the problem. Will you help us do that?"

She wanted to trust them. She nodded again.

June remained seated at the computer, typing away while Angela asked Mandy a whole string of questions:

Full Name: Mandy Eloise Whitacre.

Age: Nineteen.

Address: Mandy could recite it without a hitch.

Next of kin: Her father, Arthur, and there was also her aunt Josie, her dad's sister who lived in Seattle. June typed in all the phone numbers and addresses.

Height: Five-four.

Weight: 108.

On any medications? No.

Any allergies? None that she knew of.

Any past surgeries? No.

Medical problems? She fell off a horse once and sprained her ankle.

When was her last menstrual period? Just finished it last week.

So not much chance she was pregnant? No chance at all, since she'd never had sex.

Was she in school, working? She was attending North Idaho Junior College, pursuing theater, and working in the research library to offset her tuition.

"And when did everything become different? Do you remember what time, how long ago?"

That was easy. Mandy recounted the whole story, throwing in lots of details just to show her mind was sharp.

Angela listened, nodded, then asked, "Do you remember being in any accidents where you hurt yourself, where you may have hit your head?"

"My girlfriends and I went on some rides at the fair."

Angela perked up a little at that. "What kind of rides?"

"Uh . . . the Tilt-a-Whirl, the Chair-O-Plane . . . and that thing that looks like a hammer on both ends and the cars tumble around while the big hammer spins—you know what I mean?"

Angela stepped back and looked her up and down. "Have you ever heard of a CAT scan?"

"I don't think we went on that one."

"Well, I'm talking about—"

"I'm kidding. But can I ask you something?"

"Shoot."

"What year do you people think it is?"

Angela looked around the room until she spotted something. "Let me show you, and you tell me what you think." She stepped over and moved an IV pole that had been half covering a wall calendar, one of those charming calendars with a Norman Rockwell painting for each month. She pointed at the precise date. "Today is right here, September seventeenth, 2010."

Mandy studied the calendar. The year 2010 was printed plainly over the month. No doubt she could touch that calendar and it would really be there. She was a little surprised at her own reaction, a strange, incredulous chuckle. Why shouldn't it be 2010? By now they could have told her she was on Mars in an experimental futuristic city under a huge plastic dome with artificial weather and that would have fit in just fine with everything else. "What's a cat skin?"

chapter

4

FIERY WRECK KILLS MAGICIAN

Mandy Eloise Collins, best known as the witty and offbeat wife and partner of Dane Collins in the magical duo Dane and Mandy, was killed yesterday and her husband, Dane, injured when the Collins's car was sidestruck by another motorist, also killed in the crash. Dane Collins, riding in the passenger seat, escaped and was subsequently injured trying to rescue his wife from the burning vehicle. . . .

The news story went on recapping their career, identifying the drunk driver, quoting a police spokesman, covering the lesser details, blah blah blah. Dane could read only so far before the real world with its real pain returned, overrunning the stupor of the painkillers and the drug-induced oblivion of the previous night.

The photo was difficult enough. Arnie sent the *Las Vegas Sun* some promo pictures and an eight-by-ten for them to crop, resize, whatever they wanted, but of course it was the wrecked BMW that made the newsy photo, caved in on the driver's side, gutted and charred throughout. The seats were reduced to misshapen steel and wire frames, and the floor was burned down to the metal. Half the roof was gone—that was how the rescue team got Mandy out.

Dane let the paper fall to his lap as he sat on the edge of the bed. Yeah, there was that sick, crushing feeling again, the head-bashed-against-concrete, immovable, immutable cruelty of the real world. *Good morning, Dane. Glad to have you with us.*

Earlier, by now another world away, he woke up by gradual degrees and found himself in a place that could not have been real, only a dream he didn't have to believe. No, this didn't have to be a hospital room. He wasn't really hurt. The pain was only sunburn and maybe a charley horse here and there.

And any moment, Mandy would walk into the room, look down at him, and say, "Wow, that was a close one!" And he would say, "Yeah, sure was," and then they'd take each other's hands and thank God together that they made it through another one. God was taking care of them just as He always did. *Remember that spinout we had on Donner Pass the winter of '73? Got away without a scratch. Hey, what about that fall you took from the stage in Pittsburgh? If that nice gentleman had not been in the front row for you to land on . . .*

But the sorrow was, he continued coming around. His eyes roamed in small circles, then greater, and everything he saw he discovered for the first time and then remembered: the bed in which he lay, the remote that raised and lowered the bed, the call button for the nurse, the television on the wall, the food tray waiting for breakfast or his next dose of pills, the graduated drinking mug with the hospital's name on it, the happy face to miserable face pain chart, stripes of sunlight coming through the slatted blinds, and the flowers. Everywhere, the flowers. The room smelled like a florist shop—or a funeral, either one.

Oh, right. He'd had visitors bringing bouquets, loving words, comforting touches—on his left side only. Bouquets stood on the shelf, the sill next to the bed, the windowsill, even the floor below the window.

The daisies. Ernie and Katelynn Borgiere brought those because Mandy always liked them. Ernie was a stage magician in the classic style. Some of Mandy's favorite dove tricks she got from him, and he was honored.

The red roses, pink lilies, and purple asters in the tall basket came from Pauline Vitori, musical director for Dane and Mandy's six-week run at the Las Vegas Hilton. That engagement was five years ago, Dane and Mandy hadn't seen her in all that time, but she was here yesterday, teary-eyed and bringing a bouquet so big it had to sit on the floor.

Chuck and Cherry Lowell, Dane and Mandy's pastor and his

wife, were there for a great part of the day and brought the dozen roses and baby's breath. The card read, "For a grand lady at the close of a great performance."

Preston and Audrey Gabriel sent roses and a heartfelt letter. Preston, a veteran magician and innovator of magic, was the wise old man in Dane's life. Now hosting a television show on A&E, he was making quite a name for himself debunking phony psychics and faith healers. He was always good for a deep discussion.

Carnations. Orchids. Lilies and birds-of-paradise. Greens shooting out of the vases and baskets like splashes. Ribbons. Cards.

So yesterday really happened.

Didn't it?

Then Arnie arrived with a fresh change of clothes to replace Dane's bloodied and burned ones, and handed Dane the morning paper.

Guess it did.

Dane went back to the photo and studied the car's blackened frame, broken windows, collapsed steering wheel. It was time to face it. What happened, happened. No option, no escape, no denial. It happened, and the sooner he came to grips with that, the sooner he could learn to live with it. He studied the photograph until his stomach turned and his hands shook.

Arnie took the paper away from him. "That'll be enough for today."

He sank forward, elbows on knees, hands over his face, sitting on the edge of the bed, recovering, breathing. He didn't cry this time, he didn't know why. Maybe his whole body was tired of crying. He just ached, felt sick, felt as if he could never eat again. He wanted to stay in the dark behind his hands.

"You need help tying that shoe?" Arnie asked.

Dane let his hands drop from his face and the light of today's world flood his eyes. He reached down, but stopped and grimaced halfway.

"Let me do it." Arnie knelt down and tied the shoe, which was just as well. The other shoe took Dane a painfully long time.

"So what'd they do with the car?" Dane asked.

"Police have it. I talked to the insurance agent. It's all in the works, don't worry about it." Arnie stood. "You all set?"

Dane nodded. He'd had his talk with Dr. Jacobs, the primary

physician. He had his plastic tote bag with the hospital logo containing his patient discharge instructions, a bottle of painkillers, a bottle of cream for his burns, and a prescription for more of either one if needed. He was dressed and now both shoes were tied. "Let's do it."

Arnie pulled a wheelchair over.

"I don't need that."

"Does it hurt to walk?"

"Everything hurts."

"Then ride in style, my man. Your insurance is paying for it." Arnie gave him a hand hobbling into the chair. "Oh, Chuck said he and Cherry could get all these flowers over to your house."

"Aw, that'd be great."

"You've got more flowers there, by the way, all over the front porch."

What could Dane say to that? He could only shake his head and feel as if he could cry again.

"So we'll put her in low and away we go," said Arnie, pushing Dane toward the door.

Going home, but without her. Dane could feel the bittersweetness already.

A lady in a white coat came to the door before they got to it. "Dane?"

Oh. He recognized her immediately: Dr. Margo Kessler, head of the emergency room, a lovely lady in a plain sort of way, somewhere in her late forties, with blond, neck-length hair cut in a practical, fuss-free style and running shoes for all the standing, walking, and running she had to do each day. She was there when the medics brought him and Mandy into the ER; she was there in the ICU when Mandy passed away; she was there through the whole thing, cool and efficient with her duties, warm and personal with her patients. "Oh, looks like I just caught you going out the door."

"Slowly, but definitely."

"I'm so sorry. I wonder if you might have a few minutes?"

"No problem."

Arnie took his cue. "Didn't they have some coffee down the hall?"

"Espresso, cappuccinos, lattes," said Kessler with a smile. "They should be open by now."

"My kind of place."

"I'll bring him down to you," said the doctor.

Arnie stepped to the door. "Dane, you want anything?"

"Later maybe."

Arnie headed down the hall.

"Need help?" Kessler asked, then helped Dane wheel back so he could face her as she sat in the room's single chair.

He spoke first. "Thank you, Doctor, for everything."

"You're most welcome. And I'm very sorry things couldn't have ended better. If you or someone could let me know what your funeral plans are—when you have them . . ."

"Well, it won't be a funeral. I think I'll just have a private crema-tion and then we'll do a memorial service. How long does this organ procurement thing take?"

"That should be complete by now. I'll check into it. And thank you."

"Thank Mandy."

"Yes. Thank Mandy." Change of tone. "So. You're heading for Idaho?"

"It's where we were headed when we were hit. We made an offer on a ranch up there in Mandy's old stomping ground. I'm going to stick with the plan, go up there, and close the deal."

"Where in Idaho?"

"Hayden, up in the panhandle."

"Are you retiring?"

"Well . . ." He would have had an answer for that yesterday morning as he and Mandy were packing the car: *No, just looking for a change.* But now, "Good question." For the first time he thought about it in today's terms. "We finished our run at the Horizons Hotel and we hadn't booked anything else. We just wanted out of town, just wanted some time to think, pray, check out our life and where we were going. It was like a change in the seasons. We could feel it." But yesterday's dream was fading now; he could feel it turning away from him like a mailman with nothing to deliver. He was losing any reason to complete the thought even as he spoke it. "So it was time to move on, see what else there was. At least that was the plan."

"Do it. Get that place up in Idaho. Spend some time there, and look at everything from a whole new perspective."

Dane digested that a moment. It felt right. "May as well."

Her chair must have been uncomfortable, the way she shifted in it. "Well I won't keep you. Just wanted to see you before you left, see how you were and extend my condolences . . ."

"I appreciate it."

"And . . . if I may put on my physician's cap one more time. You have your meds and prescription from Dr. Jacobs."

"Right. One or two every six hours, not to exceed six in twenty-four hours."

"Very good. Only as needed, okay?"

"Right."

"Because I need to tell you something." Now she looked up as if the next thing to say was on the ceiling somewhere. Her hand drummed the arm of the chair and she drew a deliberate breath again. Dane felt nervous for her and for himself. "It has to do with the combination of medication and severe trauma such as you've experienced—are *still* experiencing. We've seen this before in rare cases, and since your case is very much like those cases, I wanted to give you a heads-up."

Dane was listening, not yet following. Waiting, too.

Dr. Kessler finally continued, "Well, how has your mental state been? Let's just get right down to it here. Have you had any nightmares, recurring dreams, um, flashbacks of the accident?"

He was glad she asked. "Yes. Every time I close my eyes and sometimes when my eyes are wide open. I slept last night because I was doped and that's the only reason."

Dr. Kessler nodded. "Mm-hm. That's normal. That's to be expected. But that's why I'm bringing this up, so you won't be alarmed. You see, especially in a severe post-traumatic stress situation, the stress and the injuries coupled with the medication can produce, um . . . delusional disorders, mild hallucinations, especially concerning the loved one."

"I'm trying to stay with you here . . ."

"Reliving the accident?"

"Oh, yeah. Over and over again."

"Expecting Mandy to come into the room . . ."

"I'm going to do that until I die."

"You might think you hear her voice; you might even see her, or think you see her."

Dane could imagine it, and he smiled. "That would be nice."

Dr. Kessler matched Dane's sad and whimsical smile. "I suppose, but it would be a hallucination and something we'd want to know about."

"If I could take a pill that would bring Mandy back, if only for a moment . . ."

"Well, it wouldn't be just the pill. There could be a head injury or a stress-related factor, that's what I'm saying."

Dane mocked disappointment . . . sort of. "Right."

"So Dr. Jacobs may not have warned you about this, but that's because it's not listed in the literature and because hallucinations produced by this medication only crop up in severe post-stress situations, which is what you have."

"So . . ."

"So if you think you see Mandy or someone who really looks like Mandy, or you think you hear her voice, anything like that, please let me know." She gave Dane her card.

"Because if I see things and hear things that aren't there, I might be crazy?"

"No," said the doctor. "You might be in danger."

chapter

5

By her second day at the Spokane County Medical Center, Mandy was willing to believe she wasn't in the company of aliens—or any other creepy, time-warpy, *Twilight Zone* sci-fi creatures. The CAT scan machine looked as if it *could* have sucked out her brain, but it didn't. A nurse named Carol took a sample of her blood, and that wasn't weird—she used a real needle. Leaving a urine sample in a little jar was tricky, but she worked her way through it. She even got a few meals, a warm, clean bed, and good old down-to-earth questions about insurance.

Midmorning, June took her to a nice sitting room just off the main hallway, where sweet lovin' Johnny the cop was waiting for her. She sat in one comfortable chair and he sat in another comfortable chair directly across from her so he could keep an eye on her.

Now, in addition to a modest pair of scrubs and a robe, she had slippers that slipped right on and slipped right off. She had to dig into them with her toes so they'd stay with her when she walked, but it was so much better than being barefoot, and as for the scratches and cuts on her feet, June had taken care of those.

She was there to wait while the doctors got the results of all the tests and decided what to do. Wait there with Johnny watching her.

And watching her.

"Hi," she said just to see what he'd do.

"Hi," he said back.

He was a big guy with a gun and a radio and handcuffs and he knew it. It was like staring down a guard dog.

There was a box of Kleenex within reach. She reached. He watched her, his eyes full of warning.

"Got to blow my nose," she told him. She blew and wiped her nose and he seemed okay with that.

She reached for another Kleenex and this time it didn't bother him so much, so he didn't mind or notice the extra Kleenex she took at the same time and hid in her robe's collar behind her head. She snorted a little, trying to clear her right nostril, scrunching her nose around. He looked at her but didn't seem to find that exciting.

She took hold of one corner of the tissue in her hand and squished and twisted it into a point. Then she fed the point up her nostril, sucking in air to help it along. She pushed, she snorted, she drew long and deep, even threw her head back a little. The Kleenex looked as if it was going clear up her nose.

Now Johnny was scowling, paying full attention.

She sucked the whole thing up her nose and then brought her empty hands away from her face, palms visible so he could see them, and gave a little hum of satisfaction.

Ah. She had him. He was looking at her with intense, head-tilted suspicion, and hadn't noticed how she stashed the Kleenex down her robe sleeve.

Now for the final effect. She winced in pain, shook her head to jar the Kleenex loose, then brought her hands to her right ear, dug in with her right finger, and found the end of the Kleenex—from behind her head. With a little grunt or groan with every tug, she pulled the Kleenex from her ear a little, then a little more . . . then a little more . . . and finally free, letting it hang from her fingers. "Whew!" She sighed with relief.

He actually smiled a little and wagged his head. Well, that was progress.

"Mandy?"

Ah, Dr. Angela appeared in the hallway, a folder in her hand, which had to be the results. She was smiling, which made Mandy smile—for a moment.

As the doctor came into the room, two security guys in navy blue shirts and gray slacks—their name tags said Bruce and Dave—came in with her and not just to visit. With put-on smiles they walked like actors on a stage and took positions on either side of Mandy, close enough to invade her space and make her cringe. As for Dr. Angela's smile, there was something phony-professional about it, as if she'd taken it out of her doctor pocket and stuck it on just for the occasion.

She could have lent it to Johnny. As he stood to give the doctor his chair, he went back into wall mode, eyes on Mandy, all business. Mandy may have gotten a faint smile out of him a minute ago, but now his face was back on duty and there was nothing to like about him.

"So . . ." said Angela, flipping the file open. "Things are going in the right direction for you."

Mandy leaned forward, waiting.

"First of all, we have good news as far as your medical condition. All the tests came back negative. No drugs, no alcohol, no brain damage or injury to your head. All your vitals are just fine. The only problem we still have is . . ." She looked in the folder at a page that had nothing to do with medical tests. Mandy could see her home phone number among a flurry of notes. "You've given us names and phone numbers and we've tried to contact these people and as far as anyone can tell"—she looked straight into Mandy's eyes—"there are no such persons, no such phone numbers, no such addresses. Besides that, there's no Mandy Whitacre on file with the Department of Motor Vehicles. The Social Security Administration has no record of a Mandy Whitacre with your Social Security number. There's no Mandy Whitacre enrolled at NIC—and it's North Idaho College now, not North Idaho Junior College. Your insurance company . . . well, they were bought out in 1995 and don't exist anymore as a company."

It had to sink in a moment. This learned doctor could not possibly be saying such things. *Lies. How in the world?* Somebody just wasn't thinking. Mandy looked right back into Angela's eyes. "And no Mandy Whitacre sitting right in front of you? I know my own name, Doctor!"

The doctor was flustered. "We know it seems real to you, but we can't verify any of it."

"As if I don't know my own name and my own father? How dare you say such a thing to me!"

Angela raised her hands for a truce. "That's not for me to decide, that's what I'm getting to. It was my job to check you over physically, to make sure you don't have a medical emergency, and now that's done and my part in this is over."

Mandy looked at Johnny, Bruce, and Dave. "So why are these guys still standing here?"

"There are some other people you still need to see."

"And they're going to make sure it happens, is that it?"

"They're here to keep you safe."

Well. Enough of this. "I'd like to leave now."

Dave put a hand on her arm. She slapped at it. "Get your hands off me!"

Bruce took her other arm. Outrage! She reefed and twisted against their grip as her indignity built to a scream. "Let go of me! *Let go!*"

Angela—dear, lying, off-her-ever-loving-nut Angela—came in close, speaking softly, trying to defuse the situation. With what, more lies? More branding *her* a liar?

"Mandy, listen to me."

She glared at the doctor, every muscle in her body pulling, straining against her captors. *Check my heart rate now, you witch!*

Angela kept trying. "You have no clothes, no shoes, no money, no ID. Do you want to go back out there with nothing but those scrubs? How long do you think you'd last?"

"Long enough to go *home!*" The thought made her cry. She twisted and fought some more because she doggone *felt* like it.

Angela got right in her face—*close enough to spit on*, Mandy thought, but didn't. "If you want to go home, then stop this, right now! Stop."

Mandy didn't relax but she held still, angry breath gushing into and out of her nostrils.

The doctor spoke quietly, slowly. "You are here on a police hold, which means by law you have to stay here at least twenty-four hours for evaluation, maybe longer, until everyone is satisfied you won't be a danger to yourself or anyone else—"

Of all the stupid! "Well, what—"

"And . . ."

"—do you think I'm gonna do—"

"AND—are you listening?"

Mandy listened.

"There are people who will help you, they'll listen to you and try to figure out what's going on. But they'll need to see that you can control yourself and conduct yourself safely around others, which means . . ." The doctor indicated Mandy's situation at the moment, like a raging animal in a net. "If you want to get out of here, you'll behave yourself so nobody has to restrain you. Does that make sense?"

Make sense? This was just so ridiculous! This really was *Planet of the Apes* and she really was Charlton Heston the astronaut and she was the weird one, not them, and nobody could see that.

But why would they, and what could she do about it anyway? These were the rules of the game, like it or not. She was the one in the complimentary scrubs and borrowed robe, and all she had in the world was what she knew but couldn't prove. She wasn't the doctor with the totally true and trustworthy folder in the big, intimidating hospital with Johnny, Bruce, and Dave working for her.

Play the game, girl. Do your time. Show them you're okay.

She gave up and covered her face to shut out these people and this insane, impossible world.

Dave and Bruce relaxed their grip but didn't let go.

"Bruce and Dave are going to take you to another part of the hospital and get you checked in."

She rose to her feet, ably assisted. "What part?"

"Behavioral Health. Don't worry. They're great people."

chapter

6

"Hi, Mandy. I'm Bernadette Nolan, from Health and Human Services. How are you?"

Mandy squared up the deck of cards she was playing with, set them aside, and stood to shake hands. Bernadette, a young lady with fiery red hair in big, beautiful curls, took the only other chair, on the opposite side of the table. She did it so professionally, as if she'd said "Hi" and "I'm Bernadette Nolan" to a zillion souls before this, maybe at this very same table in this very same little room with no windows except for the one in the door.

Mandy answered, "I'm clean," which was about all she could say for sure. The Behavioral Health Unit had loaned her soap and shampoo for a shower and a toothbrush and toothpaste for her teeth and took them back when she was finished so they couldn't become a means to harm anyone, including herself.

"You look great," said Bernadette, opening a valise and pulling out a writing pad and some forms.

Right. Clean, but with no way to fix her hair and wearing nothing but hospital scrubs and another pair of those one-size-almost-fits-all slippers. Mandy sent a message with her face: *Oh, come* on! She thought better of it and stowed the look, but not before Bernadette saw it.

"Go ahead. Say it."

Mandy looked into those friendly green eyes. "*I* look clean. *You* look great." And Bernadette did look great. Nice jacket, cool jeans, slick pumps.

Bernadette nodded, even chuckled. "I'm the one in the civvies and you're the one in the scrubs."

"Right on."

"How does that make you feel?"

"How should I feel? You weren't locked in your room with a camera trained on you. You didn't have to take a shower with Nurse Baines watching you. You got to fix your hair this morning and pick out your own clothes. You even get to wear a bra because nobody thinks you'll use it to hang yourself." *Mandy, you're getting angry.* "But you do look great. And I like your lipstick."

"Thank you. It's called Deep Blush."

"It goes with your complexion."

"So how do you usually fix your hair?"

"Oh, straight, with combs and sometimes a clip. I have some headbands, they're kind of a trip—hey, I made a rhyme!"

Mandy had no grudge with Bernadette and Bernadette was sweet enough. They talked—maybe a little testy at first, checking each other out—but they got on a roll, and every once in a while Bernadette would jot a note on her writing pad or circle an item on a form. Mandy settled within herself that Bernadette was only doing her job; it wouldn't be fair not to like her.

"So," Bernadette finally said with a little clap and rub of her hands, "let's do the questions and the games. What's my name?"

"Bernadette."

"Do you remember my last name?"

Mandy had to work a bit. "N . . . Nolan?"

"Right. And you know where you are?"

"Behavioral Health, Spokane County Medical Center."

"And what year is it?"

Mandy had to think about that one. It depended on who you asked, so she asked, "Is it 2010?"

"That's right," Bernadette answered, but she jotted something down. "And when were you born?"

"January fifteenth, 1951."

It was fun watching Bernadette trying not to react. She looked at Mandy and smiled, studying her a bit. "Do *you* think it's 2010?"

"That's what I'm told and that's what I'm seeing."

"But you were born in 1951."

"That's right."

"That would make you . . ." Bernadette had to work it out on her pad. "Fifty-nine. Are you fifty-nine?"

"No, I'm nineteen."

She chuckled. "Does that puzzle you at all, your being born in '51 but you're only nineteen?"

Mandy threw up her hands. "I am *completely* puzzled!"

"That's good. That's actually very good." Jot, jot. "Okay, I'll give you three words: cadillac, zebra, purple. Can you say them back to me?"

"Cadillac, zebra, purple."

"Can you count backward from one hundred by threes?"

Oh-oh. Mandy and numbers didn't get along. She counted down as far as fifty-two before Bernadette let it go.

"What were the three words I gave you?"

"Cadillac, zebra, and purple."

"How about the days of the week? Can you say those backward?"

Mandy felt nervous about that one, but they tumbled out just fine.

"Got a favorite TV show?"

"Carol Burnett. And Daddy and I always watch *Gunsmoke.*"

"On DVD?"

"Uh . . . no, Channel Four."

Jot jot. Hopefully she jotted something positive.

And it went on and on.

"Spell the word *world* backward."

"Explain what happened yesterday. What do you think should have happened?"

"Can you tell me my name again?"

"Can you name the last four presidents?" Jot jot.

"What were those three words again?"

"Can you give me two different definitions for the word *right*? How about the word *bit*? How about *left*?"

"What do people mean when they say 'A rolling stone gathers no moss'?"

Mandy had no trouble answering the questions and doing the

thinking, but it was getting tedious. She never thought to pick up the deck of cards; she just noticed she was shuffling them as she spoke.

"What do you think people mean when they say 'When the cat's away the mice will play'?"

Brrrriiiip! Riffle shuffle on the table. "When the authority figure is absent, people push their boundaries and see what they can get away with."

"What about hallucinations or delusions? Have you experienced anything like that?"

Brrrrrriiiip! Riffle shuffle off the table, hands in the air, like a skilled cardsharp. "You mean, besides thinking I'm living in 2010?"

"Well, aren't you?"

Fffffoooot! Waterfall, the cards cascading through space from her raised right hand into her waiting left. "You think I'm living in 2010 and think I'm from 1970. I think I'm living in 1970 and think I'm living in 2010. That's the difference."

Jot jot. "Wow. Does that scare you at all?"

"Very much."

"Do you feel afraid right now?"

Ribbon spread, the cards spread out across the table like a long ribbon, perfectly lapped and spaced. Mandy had to pay attention to the cards for a moment, it looked so good. "I'm making lemonade."

"Excuse me?"

Mandy gathered the ribbon, squared the deck, and looked Bernadette in the eye. "What do you think people mean when they say, 'When life gives you lemons, make lemonade'?"

Bernadette nodded. "Got it." Jot jot.

"Daddy told me that." She spread the cards into a ribbon again, all facedown except for two in the middle faceup, the king and queen of hearts, side by side.

"You're very good at that," Bernadette observed.

"Daddy showed me."

"You must practice a lot."

"Sure."

"Do you ever feel the need to do something over and over until it's perfect?"

"Practice doesn't make perfect. It makes better. Daddy told me that, too."

"How about worry? Do you worry a lot?"

Not until yesterday, she would have answered, but her eyes were locked on a memory: Daddy in his Gonzaga T-shirt, sitting with her in the kitchen, teaching her how to shuffle a deck of cards and do a ribbon spread. She didn't ask for the emotion; she didn't even expect it, but now her throat was tightening up and tears were filling her eyes.

"You miss your father, don't you?"

Mandy just looked at her, the tears overflowing onto her cheeks.

"Sorry."

Mandy wiped her tears with one hand and gathered the ribbon into a deck with the other. She shuffled the cards and spread out the ribbon again, faceup except for one card facedown in the middle. Her voice quivered and she couldn't help it. "He didn't know a whole lot of tricks, but he got me started, and he always told me, 'Don't worry about getting perfect, just keep getting better.' And he wasn't just talking about card tricks."

"Those were wise words."

Tremors of emotion made it hard to talk. "He was a guy trying to raise a teenage daughter all by himself, and he did it." She lifted one card at the end, starting a wave, and flipped all the cards over as the wave swept through the ribbon. "That's why I don't want it to be 2010, because if it is, then my daddy might be dead and that's why nobody can find him." With that, she couldn't talk at all.

Now all the cards were facedown except for the king in the middle, all by himself.

Bernadette offered her a Kleenex to wipe her nose.

Mandy blew and wiped and then steadied herself, at least enough to speak. She tried not to sound angry, but doggone it, she was. "Maybe you should stop asking me all these find-out-if-she's-crazy questions and just ask me what I want."

Bernadette glanced at the form she was marking with little underlines and circles.

Mandy covered the form with her hand and would not let Bernadette look anywhere else but into her eyes. "Ask me."

For a moment, something a little more human came back to her through those green eyes. "Mandy, what do you want?"

She felt so tired of being not herself but a question, angry at that stupid form that was supposed to be her, bitter toward the people who acted so concerned but locked her up and went home at night. "I want to go home." She tapped on Bernadette's form and on her writing pad with all the little scribbles. "Write this down: I don't know what's wrong with me and I'm sorry I don't know what year it is, but Bernadette Nolan can drive her purple Cadillac through a zebra on her way home and all I can do is sit here feeling scared and alone and embarrassed until somebody will just let me be who I am and go home. I didn't ask for this and I don't want to hurt anybody and I don't want to hang myself. I just want to go home. I want to go home to my father!"

And that was the end of the questions and games as far as she was concerned. She dropped her gaze and settled back in her chair, looking down at the ribbon of cards. Sure was a nice ribbon. She did that well. She did a lot of things well—not perfect, but pretty doggone well, and Daddy would be proud. He always was.

Bernadette made one more little note on her form, then put everything back in her valise, double-checking the table, the chair, and the floor to make sure all her pens and pencils were accounted for. "Mandy, I really appreciate your time. This was a nice interview."

"Sorry I got upset."

"That's no problem at all. You were being honest."

"You really are a nice lady."

"Thanks. So are you."

"So how'd I do?"

"Oh, we'll let you know. I'm going to talk with the other DE and then—"

"DE?"

"Sorry. Designated examiner. That's what we call ourselves. The other one is Karla Harris, and she'll be coming by tomorrow to talk with you."

"About . . . ?"

"About you, pretty much the way I did."

"I hope I get an A."

"Well, like your father said . . ."

Mandy eased a little and smiled.

"I wouldn't worry too much. Just be yourself." Bernadette threw her a wink, then rose to leave. "Karla'll talk to you, and then she and I will talk to each other, and we'll see where we go from there. By the way"—she scanned the ribbon of cards, passing a pointing finger over them—"are you going to tell me where you put the queen of hearts?"

"She's in your pocket."

"In my . . ." Bernadette didn't believe it.

Mandy guided her with a gaze and a nod toward her outside jacket pocket. Bernadette reached in, and her professionally pleasant face clouded with amazement when she found something. She withdrew her hand, and there between her fingers was the queen of hearts.

This felt so good. Bernadette held that card up, looking dumbfounded. "How did you do it?"

Now it was Mandy's turn to put on a professional face and withhold an answer to a direct question. "Oh, I'll let you know. We'll see."

Bernadette shook her head with a smile, laid the queen next to the king, and went to the door. An orderly let her out, and the door clicked shut.

Mandy stared at the queen; she touched the card with her index finger and moved it in little circles. These cards were sure cooperative. They seemed to fall right into place like a little drill team under her command. There was nothing special about this deck, nothing rigged, no short cards or gaffs. It was just one deck of cards Nurse Baines brought her from the activity room. It had only one queen of hearts.

That was what had her puzzled. The Queen in the Pocket trick needed two queens, one to plant in the pocket and one to vanish from the deck. Mandy stared at the cards, trying to remember.

How *did* she do it?

chapter

7

The black Lexus entered the parking lot of Christian Faith Center with the inertia of a yacht easing into a marina, rolling up the first row of parked vehicles, then down the next row, then up the third, then down the fourth, chrome wheels lazily rotating without blur, brake lights mostly on, the turning engine barely audible. There were plenty of empty parking spaces by about the seventh row, but the Lexus didn't go there, not without its occupants viewing every occupied space first.

The driver called himself Mr. Stone, an apt name for a man whose face looked like he just woke up from a nap on a bed of pea gravel. He was blond, masked behind black sunglasses, and well dressed in black. He drove with his left hand, and with his right hand he held a digital camera propped in the open window, discreetly recording every license plate of every vehicle.

Mr. Mortimer, his associate in the passenger seat, made a near opposite: handsome, Mediterranean, dressed in expensive black. He was also using a digital camera, capturing every license plate on his side, the back ends of the cars reflecting and distorting in the lenses of his designer shades.

The Lexus moved steadily, efficiently, recording every vehicle, and finally came to rest in a parking space of its own. Stone and Mortimer got out, put on a personable, respectful demeanor, and headed for the church doors.

A nice lady with a white corsage greeted them in the foyer and handed each a folded bulletin: In Loving Memory of Mandy Eloise Collins. A voice came through the open doors to the sanctuary, what sounded like a testimonial: ". . . always remember her wonderful sense of humor, her way of finding the up side to just about anything . . ."

They smiled at the lady, then strolled to a large display, a collection of photographs from the life of the deceased set up among bouquets of flowers in baskets, stands, and vases. Memories. Great moments. The men smiled, nodded to each other, pointed and acted in every way like two old friends of the deceased now remembering how great it was to know her. "Hey, remember that?" "She looks great, doesn't she?" "Now, that illusion baffled everybody!" "Is that her mom and dad? She really takes after her mother, doesn't she?"

And with an appearance of fondness, love, and whatever else would make the act seem natural, Mr. Mortimer took out his camera and started recording the photographs: Mandy the teenager, straight-haired and tie-dyed; Mandy no older than twelve, sitting between her mom and dad with a new puppy; Mandy in her high school talent show performing the Chinese Sticks illusion; Mandy at eighteen, in jeans shorts and One Way T-shirt with four white doves perched on her arm.

Mr. Stone made his way through the door into the sanctuary. Neither he nor Mortimer was a churchgoer, but the venue was not unfamiliar, comparable to a theater or Vegas showroom without the lavish theme and decor. Pews were arranged in a fan-shaped room sloping toward a central stage set up for a band and possibly a choir. On the back wall was a large cross and above that the words "Jesus Is the Same Yesterday, Today, and Forever." At front center stage was a diminutive Plexiglas pulpit where the minister delivered his sermons. At the moment, no one stood there. The voice was coming from an attractive young woman down in front, probably a friend in show business, speaking into a wireless mike: ". . . and I will always smile and laugh when I think of Mandy. I know she'd want it that way."

She set the mike on the edge of the stage and then bent and gave a hug to a silver-haired man in the front row, recognizable as Dane Collins, the bereaved husband. From this position in the back of the room, Stone could catch only a glimpse of Collins's profile before the man looked forward again, but Stone determined to get close enough, perhaps during the reception following, to study the face and get to know it.

A video began to play on two large screens on either side of the stage. Stone gave it his full attention because it was a collection of scenes from Mandy Collins's life. The first clip was a grainy, scratchy film—the original had to be Super 8—of Dane and Mandy, two kids barely in their twenties, performing on a truckbed before what appeared to be a company picnic, pulling white doves out of sleeves, from under silk handkerchiefs, from an audience volunteer's hat, out of nowhere. Stone noted Mandy's hair in curls, medium length, and her figure youthful, slender.

As the video played in the sanctuary, Mortimer continued recording photos in the foyer and noting when they may have been taken: Dane and Mandy's wedding in June 1971—beautiful bride, long hair in graceful waves and lacy ribbons; Dane and Mandy with his folks and her father, 1975, Mandy looking about the same.

Stone edged halfway down an aisle and found a seat as he watched a grainy VHS recording from somewhere in the 1980s: Mandy in an evening dress, hair magnificently coiffed atop her head and jeweled earrings dangling, drawing laughs from an audience as she fumbles with two narrow tubes, a glass, and a pop bottle on a table. "Now, you put this tube over the glass and this tube over the bottle and they will magically trade places . . ." The tubes go out of control, producing a bottle where the glass should have been ". . . Oops! You weren't supposed to see that! . . ." then producing bottles, bottles, and more bottles. "No no no, let me try that again!"

Mortimer recorded a 1990 photo of Mandy in jeans, shirt, and baseball cap with her aging father and two llamas. Mandy was thirty-nine at the time and still looked great: big smile, engaging eyes, neck-length haircut.

Somehow the video historian found a clip of Dane and Mandy appearing on *The Tonight Show Starring Johnny Carson*. That had to be prior to 1992. Mandy could have been entering her forties or still in her late thirties; it was hard to tell.

"Now, I've seen you do this," Carson was saying, sitting behind his host's desk and holding a Rubik's Cube. "And of course there's a magician's way of solving it instantly, a magical effect, but you can solve a real one—"

Mandy, in the chair closest to Carson, gave a playful nod, "Uh-huh," which got the audience stirring and squealing. Dane sat in the next chair, exuding full confidence. Ed McMahon sat to his right.

"How long does it take you?"

"Depends on my fingernails."

"Well, how are they?"

She looked. "About right."

"Less than a minute?" Carson offered her the cube.

Mandy rolled her eyes, but the audience cheered and goaded her and she took it from him.

Carson, a magician himself, assured the audience there was no trickery involved; the cube was genuine. He said "Go" and clicked a stopwatch, the audience counted down as her fingers became a blur, and she held up the solved cube, every side totally one color, in thirteen seconds. Not a world record, but good television.

Mortimer was especially interested in the family photos, the informal shots of Mandy the gal: Mandy and Dane on a fishing trip, holding some admirable salmon they'd caught; on a bike trip, although the helmet and sunglasses made Mandy's features hard to see; a later promo photo commemorating Dane and Mandy's thirtieth year in show business presented plenty of detail: the laugh lines around her eyes, the subtle lines in her face, the glint of white in her blond hair. The big-eyed smile was still there, just as in the photos of Mandy at eight, at twelve.

The video was a mother lode of information showing facial expressions, mannerisms, vocal tones, reactions. In an HD clip from only a few years ago, Dane was levitating Mandy a good twenty feet above the stage at the MGM Grand when she suddenly woke up from her magical hypnotic state, looked at the stage lights, and observed, "Boy, talk about dead bugs!" and produced a portable hand vacuum from nowhere. Her playful smile came through the video as well as it must have reached the back rows in that theater, and the rest of the illusion was a well-timed, well-planned catastrophe for her husband.

Mortimer finished up by surreptitiously recording the signatures in the guest book. It didn't take long.

Stone finished up by requesting a copy of the video from the tech in the sound booth.

They stayed for the reception afterward, but only long enough to apprise themselves of Dane and Mandy Collins's circle of friends and peers. They slipped out quietly, before they could be noticed enough to be introduced to Dane Collins.

chapter

8

Dane limped off the plane at Spokane International and found this once-familiar piece of ground where Mandy grew up was suddenly, strangely unfamiliar. He and Mandy came to visit regularly until her father passed away in '92. After she sold the ranch in '98 they still returned simply because it was Idaho and Mandy loved Idaho. When they came here recently to scout out a new place to call home, it felt like home.

But this trip felt entirely first-time.

He'd bought one ticket, packed one bag, carried only one boarding pass. There was no one to wait for while going through security and no one to wait for him. He had no one to meet in any particular place when he came out of the restroom and no one to keep in touch with by cell phone; he bought only one Starbucks coffee and a blueberry muffin for only himself. There was no one to watch their stuff while he walked around and no one to walk around while he watched their stuff; he went through doors first with no one to open them for.

While waiting for his one bag to slide onto the carousel, grief overcame him as it often did, on a schedule all its own, unpredictable, unavoidable. Maybe it was standing here alone, picking up one bag. Maybe it was the memory of her calling her dad from this very spot to let him know they'd arrived. Maybe there was no reason at all. Grief just came when it came, worked its way through, and receded quietly until the next time. That was the way it worked.

On the other side of the carousel, Mr. Stone and Mr. Mortimer stepped through the waiting bodies to pluck up their bags. They had shed the cool, pretentious look of Las Vegas and put on duds that said laid-back, outdoorsy Idaho, but they weren't feeling it yet.

Dane's rental car had a GPS. He punched in the address of the Realtor in Hayden, Idaho, and the route popped up on the screen. I-90 most of the way, very easy. He remembered it from the last time they were here.

The last time, *they* were here. *They* were on their way to close the deal when the wreck happened.

"Well, let's get it done," he said to himself and to her as he turned the key in the ignition.

Mandy had had a better room the past few days, thanks to Bernadette, who recommended it, and Dr. Lorenzo, who okayed it. It wasn't a whole lot different from the room she had in intensive: the bed was a mattress on a wooden box with no metal parts, the light fixture was a breakaway design that would not bear the weight of anyone trying to hang herself, and the door could be locked from the outside only. Two nice differences were that the bed had no restraints installed and that Nurse Baines and Dr. Lorenzo saw no need to lock the door—as long as Mandy kept it open and gave them no cause to decide otherwise. So she had moved up in the world, sort of, with a bit more freedom and trust, but at the same time, anyone standing at the nurses' station could take just a few steps away from the counter and see right into her room.

Well, it was a hospital. What didn't they know about her?

She twisted and buried her face in the pillow. Was it really crazy to be Mandy Whitacre? Could she, should she ever, *ever* allow herself to think that her entire life, everything she had ever been and known, was only a delusion? How could that be? She couldn't have made up her mom and dad, the schools she went to, the friends she had, the ranch, their church, getting saved and baptized, raising her doves, learning and showing her magic, grilling hamburgers in the backyard with the youth group, taking classes at NIJC. All of that was real and every day was a new discovery, something she never thought up before she got there. Life happened to her and she lived it.

She sighed. Okay, then. She really was Mandy Whitacre, and nobody was going to change that.

So what about waking up in the year 2010? It was easy to make up a wild sci-fi explanation, something like an *Outer Limits* episode: some wacky scientist at the fair was showing off a time warp generator and she'd accidentally walked into its vortex and been transported forty years into the future. It made a great explanation. Everything she was experiencing fit right into it. The only problem was, it was loony above loony.

So, could it all be a delusion? Could she really have imagined and made up things like a CAT scanner, computers, cell phones, flat TV screens, Google (she still didn't know what that was), and little square plastic things that put out music without playing a tape or a record? She couldn't have imagined Dr. Angela and June and Dr. Lorenzo and stony Nurse Baines. She couldn't have conceived of the questions they asked and the words they used, and how her whole world could shrink down to this sterile, hypercontrolled cluster of little rooms.

Or . . . could she? She'd always had a creative imagination. She liked making up stories. Had she slipped a gear and put herself into a story she was making up? Maybe she'd slipped a gear and put herself into her own magic trick, the queen imprisoned in a stranger's pocket.

She rolled onto her back and stared at the flat, white ceiling, featureless except for the hangingproof light fixture. Could she be imagining that light fixture? Was it part of a delusion? It looked real enough. How could she tell the difference?

Well, she would start with what was real. Daddy was real. The ranch was real. Maybe she was wrong about the dates, but she knew where home was, and that would be the place to sort all this out—not here. In this place, she was crazy; at home, she was Mandy Whitacre and nobody there would look at her funny or jot down little notes or make her take pills. And she didn't have to be afraid. If she could get home, she could have all the time she wanted to work out this mess.

With her eyes focused on the bare white ceiling above her—in other words, on nothing in particular—Mandy's mind drifted over memories of homecomings throughout her life: getting off the school bus and walking along the white paddock fence that bordered North Lakeland Road and always noticing the height of the hay in the field: short, taller, ready, then mowed short again; short, taller, ready, then mowed short again. It was a long walk when she was in the first grade wearing a dress, tights, and Mary Janes. The walk was shorter when the hayfield became the llama pasture and she was wearing fishnets and a skirt to her midthigh. By the time the white fence was replaced and the llama pasture divided off for some horses, she was in an embroidered blouse, flared jeans, and sandals and didn't think about the distance; she was driving a Volkswagen Beetle and too busy thinking about everything else.

The mailbox grew a little more rust each year and went through several sets of reflective, stick-on letters and numbers: WHITACRE, 12790. From there the gravel driveway with the potholes and rain ruts went up a hill between two pastures toward the big white house with the gabled roof and wraparound veranda. Every time she walked or drove up that driveway her line of sight would clear the crest of the hill and she would see the dove house Daddy made for her out of a secondhand tool shed they brought in on a trailer, then the horse barn, and across the alleyway from that, the smaller barn for the llamas. The last thing to peek over the brow of the hill would be Daddy's machine shop, with the old tractor parked alongside . . .

Dane wore his sunglasses to drive, checking out the city of Spokane as he drove through on I-90. On the left was downtown, with its classic brick buildings and modern vestiges of the 1974 World's Fair. To the right, on a hill overlooking the city, were the hospitals: Shriners Hospital for Children, Deaconess Medical Center, Spokane County Medical Center. He looked back to the freeway. He'd had quite enough of hospitals, they only brought back all the memories . . . although the Spokane County Medical Center caught his interest for no particular reason. He looked back once.

* * *

Above Mandy, the ceiling went blue, like a cloudless summer sky. She blinked. Still blue. Maybe she'd been staring at all that white too long. Her eyes fell toward the wall . . .

She saw—she didn't think she was imagining it—a white paddock fence running along a two-lane country road, the uncut grass obscuring the bottoms of the posts and reaching past the first rail; a gravel-lined ditch between the fence and the road shoulder; a robin perching on a fence post.

She did a double take, then sat halfway up, resting on her elbows. Her lazy stream of memories had come to a close at the old tractor next to the machine shop. This white fence was here without her remembering it, and so was the robin until it flew away.

She tried to relax the very interested look from her face as she peered past the white fence and out the doorway to the nurses' station, now sitting in the high grass of the pasture.

Freaky. Not scary, freaky. How was her acting? Convincing? She couldn't let them find out about this!

Rolling onto her side and passively resting her chin on her hand, she took in the double exposure, or more like a double *location*, two places sitting right on top of each other. Three aspens with white-striped trunks and quaking green leaves stood in the community area—she could see them through the wall.

It was all so lovely and so much what she wanted to see that she was captivated, not frightened. She lay there quietly, motionless for several minutes, just watching the grass wave in the breeze and the robins, blue jays, and finches flit about in search of worms and wild seeds.

The vision faded. The blue sky surrendered to the white ceiling, the grass faded from the nurses' station; the white fence and the white-striped aspens dissolved as the walls of her room became solid . . . almost. Maybe it was Mandy's eyes not used to the darker room after being "outside," but everything in the room looked dimmer, and the edges of things—the edge of the doorway, the edge of the counter at the nurses' station, the edges of Tina, the nurse now standing there—were shimmering, as if Mandy were watching them through little heat waves.

Things sounded different too, muffled, as if she had her hands over her ears, which she didn't, with a low, rumbly hum like a big appliance whirring away somewhere deep under the floor. And there was a smell—pungent, like singed hair, like something burning. She crinkled her nose.

Trying to relax and not look weird in any way, she sat up and swung her feet down to the floor. The floor was cold linoleum, but now it felt soft and warm, as if her feet had come to rest on a thin, fuzzy carpet. Looking down, she marveled at how the floor gave a little under her feet, as if it had turned to rubber.

She looked fine, not dim, not wavering. The edges of her legs, arms, and feet were sharp and clear, and stood out in stark relief against everything else. So she was there, but everything else was only *sort of* there.

Well. Maybe this was good news. Maybe it meant she was real and the room, Tina at the counter, the hospital—and Dr. Lorenzo and Dr. Angela and Bernadette and the tables and chairs and pills and yucky sandwiches and scrubs—might not be.

She could live with that.

But she'd better be careful.

She reached for her slippers—they looked like they were submerged under weak, wavy tea, so she reached just an inch at a time until she actually touched them. They were soft and spongy, but didn't dissolve her hand or zap her with a lightning bolt. She took hold of one and it blinked on, crisp and clear, as real as she was. The other slipper did the same. She slipped them onto her feet and, looking casual, rose from the bed. The doorframe gave under the pressure of her hand, warping like an image in a fun house mirror. She withdrew her hand, and it wobbled back into shape again. Nurse Tina kept working behind the counter and didn't look up. Mandy waved at her, smiling.

Tina didn't seem to notice.

Nurse Baines jostled behind the counter, digging out some charts and looking like she hated it. The nurses' station was shimmering like a mirage, and so was Nurse Baines.

Well, Nurse Baines was no game player, no sir. If there was one way to find out for sure . . . She had to hurry, before she woke up and the dream was over.

She didn't rush but she did stride briskly up to the counter. "Nurse Baines?"

Nurse Baines looked at Tina and asked, "What happened to Forsythe?"

"Who?" Tina asked.

That was a perfect response to make Nurse Baines angry. "For. Sythe. The chart I asked for?"

"I asked Carol to make a copy."

Mandy jumped in place. She waved a little wave.

Well, Nurse Baines could have been ignoring her.

"Nurse Baines!" Mandy called.

"Well, you see this?" Nurse Baines slapped a red filing folder on the counter. "When you get that copy, it goes in here and the folder goes back on the shelf—under F. We clear?"

"Yes, ma'am!"

The electronic lock whirred and the big double doors swung open. Clive, from billing, came in with some paperwork, tossed it on the counter, then turned and went out the doors while they lingered in a programmed pause—and Mandy stood and stared down that long, open hallway illuminated with sunlight through a row of big windows. Through those windows she could see the tops of trees lining the parking lot and some of the city beyond that, the whole, big, outside world. The doors began to swing shut. Three-quarters open. Half open.

Mandy stood there. Oh, that beautiful hall! That beautiful outside world!

The ranch. Home. Daddy.

She looked at Nurse Baines. At Tina. Were they really ignoring her? She could see Tina's coat on a hook in an alcove near the doors.

The doors were still closing, closing . . .

She made a timid movement toward the alcove . . .

Oh, God help me! She grabbed for the coat. It was wavy like everything else, dim and fuzzy as if Mandy were seeing it through a tea-stained window. She grabbed hold. The coat felt like warm plasticine in her fingers. She pulled it toward her—

The coat broke through the tea-stained window and shimmering heat waves and became clear, crisp, and real in her hands.

Almost closed.

"I'll bring it back, I promise!" she called, dashing through the narrow opening a millisecond before the doors would have clamped on her foot.

chapter

9

In Hayden, Idaho, Dane signed his name to a good-size check and slid it across the desk to the Realtor along with all the duly signed papers. A handshake, warm wishes, and a welcome, and he was out the door with the papers and the keys in his hand.

He got in his car and made a left turn onto Howard, a four-lane that would take him back to I-95, the corridor that connected Coeur d'Alene and Hayden with the northern reaches of the Idaho panhandle and the Canadian border. His new ranch was maybe twenty minutes away, traffic allowing, which it probably would.

Only two blocks up the avenue, he happened to pass a minivan full of high school kids going the other way. He didn't notice them, they didn't notice him, and as he turned onto I-95, they pulled into the parking lot of the Realtor's office.

"All right, here you go." Doris, the most talkative of the five teenagers, slid the side door open and pitched her own seat forward so Mandy could climb out.

Mandy stepped down to the parking lot, careful not to lose her slippers. "Thanks, you guys!"

"See ya 'round!" "Good luck!" They all waved and drove off, some of the nicest people Mandy had had the pleasure to meet since the day she suddenly quit knowing anybody. She waved, she smiled, they disappeared around the corner . . .

And the smile fell from her face. It was just another lie anyway, another act on top of the one that got her here: "Hi, I'm a nursing student and my boyfriend and I just had a terrible fight so he drove off and left me to find my own ride home. Which way are you going— can you give me a lift? Hey, far out!"

It got her a ride clear out to Hayden, even though those kids were only going as far as Coeur d'Alene.

She felt soiled, so much that she couldn't pray.

Maybe she should have kept trusting the miracle just as the apostle Peter did when an angel sneaked him out of prison right past the guards. It seemed she'd just played out her own version of that story, walking in a weird dream or vision right through those double doors, down a stairway to an outside exit, and safely to a quiet residential street several blocks from the hospital where she "came to herself" just as Peter did. Everything snapped back into *real* and there she was, standing on a solid sidewalk on a solid street with solid houses, still dressed in her blue scrubs, goofy slippers, and borrowed coat, with no clue what to do next. It was a miracle.

Finding the kids in that van at McDonald's was a miracle, too, a van with an empty seat going clear to Coeur d'Alene, driven by a bunch of kids who bought her story and drove the extra miles just to take care of her. It had to be the hand of God—but she lied to make it happen.

She slouched, weak with shame.

So what if she'd trusted the miracle and told the truth? "Hi, I just escaped from the mental ward at the hospital and I wonder if you could give me a ride home? It's out of town—way out of town." Maybe they would have said yes anyway because they were angels God had sent. Maybe they would have had a complete change of clothes for her, too, just her size, including a decent pair of shoes, and maybe they would have taken her to North Lakeland Road and it would have looked just the way it was supposed to look and not . . . like this.

She looked up at the real estate office. This was the landmark that caught her eye, that made her tell her friends-for-the-moment they could let her off here. The two-story farmhouse had new siding, new windows, a new roof, perfect planting beds, and a paved parking lot where the front yard used to be, but she knew this house. Her best friend, Joanie Gittel, used to live here. They met when they started first grade and waited together at the bus stop right across the road. Howard Road.

Mandy looked across the four-lane street. There was a city bus stop where her school bus stop used to be, and a sign on the corner: Howard Way. The name of the cross street was North Lakeland Avenue. She could have guessed that from the name of the realty that had moved into Joanie's house: Lakeland Realty.

Her mind came to a standstill. All she could do was look, and look again, but nothing clicked. There was no figuring it out, and right now God wasn't helping her.

She went to the curb, looked both ways just as Mommy and Daddy always taught her, and hurried across with the first opening in the traffic. The bus stop was a small shelter with a concrete bench, a trash can, and a posted bus schedule. She sat on the bench and looked back across the street.

She remembered. Mrs. Gittel would watch from that front door until the bus came, and wave as it carried Mandy and Joanie and thirty other kids away for the day. *There used to be an old garage right next to the house where Mr. Gittel kept his '57 Ford, and there used to be a big apple tree in the front yard—Gravensteins. Daddy built the bus stop that used to be here and even put a cedar shake roof on it.* She remembered it being about the same size, but she was remembering it through a child's eyes, so it was probably smaller. *There was no sidewalk then, only the gravel shoulder, the ditch, the white paddock fence, and the hayfield.*

She stopped, troubled at herself. She was *remembering.* She was thinking words such as "then" and "used to be."

She got to her feet, reining in her thoughts, putting on the mental brakes. This wasn't the real now, this was some kind of delusion, and it would break, it would dissolve away and this whole nightmare would be over. She just had to find her old mailbox, her old driveway . . .

No! She stomped her foot. Not her *old* driveway, her *driveway*! Not her *old* mailbox, her *mailbox*! And the bus stop that Daddy built was sun-bleached and leaning a bit, but four, five . . . however many days it was ago . . . it was here, and there was no four-lane street and the Gittels' house was still their house and it was gray, not forest green.

She hurried up the sidewalk along the two-lane avenue that

North Lakeland Road had become, holding her hand to the side of her face to block her eyes from seeing concrete, asphalt, parked cars, businesses. No, they weren't really there. She was on her way home, and there was a hayfield—she could imagine it so clearly—and a white paddock fence and hay cut short and a ditch where little frogs floated with just their eyes and noses out of the water, and a field with Daddy's horses and a paddock with llamas watching her come home with those big brown eyes.

She tried to run but could only shuffle-run in the slippers. Cars passed on her left and they were so close, so noisy. She smelled their rubber and exhaust and the oily stench of the pavement, not the old smells—no, the *smells*!—that used to—no, that still *did*!—bring her joy as she walked this *road*, not this *street*: cut hay, wildflowers, apple blossoms.

She shuffle-ran until she was gasping, but the concrete sidewalk never ended and she never found the mailbox. She dared to lower her hand and look, hoping, trying to have faith, but there was no driveway, there were no pastures or fences, no big house on the hill. She looked back, down that long white ribbon of concrete, and saw the Gittels' house appearing as small as it always appeared from the Whitacre mailbox. She looked up the hill, across acres of blacktop, over curbed islands of lawn and young planted firs, past rows of automobiles and gaggles of moms, kids, and grocery carts, and saw an Albertson's grocery store, a Hancock Fabrics, a Starbucks, a Rite Aid, and a thrift store.

And they wouldn't go away, no matter how hard she tried not to believe in them.

And this was the dream, their new adventure?

Dane shut the ponderous, hand-carved front door then leaned his back against it, suddenly bereft of any reason to move. Under his feet was the slate tiled foyer, and just ahead, the sunken living room with red oak floor, cathedral ceiling, and large pane windows with gorgeous views of mountains, forests, fields, a Dutch-style barn, and a pond big enough to be called a lake. The former owner had done well and grown ambitious in his latter years; the house came to forty-nine hundred square feet altogether. The kitchen was sized for entertaining, with an elongated center island and surrounding counters and cabinets; a dual access staircase led up to an open office overlooking the great room and a master suite boasting cathedral windows, a stylish double-vanity bathroom, infrared sauna, whirlpool tub, walk-in shower, and walk-in closet. There were two other bedrooms and a full, unfinished basement, a blank slate he and Mandy could have utilized any way they wanted.

Yes, a big, beautiful home for big, beautiful dreams: a theatrical management company; research and development of new effects and illusions; a Christian kids' magic camp; some books, some memoirs, some articles, and why not some horses or anything else they had yet to imagine, for this would be a new season in their life, a promised land far from Egypt, a fresh garden for new ideas grown their way.

At least that was the idea.

There was no chair, no furniture at all to sit on, so Dane sank to the tiles with his back against the door, taking up maybe three of the forty-nine hundred square feet. He could hear the air moving against the walls. The sound of his own breathing traveled along the wood floors, high ceilings, and huge windows and came whispering back to him like Noah's dove after her first mission: there's nothing in here. The dreams never made it through the front door.

Why did I even—

The answer came quicker than it took to think the question: because it was going to be he and Mandy. She was going to be carrying plans and sketches down those stairs to show him; they were going to try some new French recipes in that kitchen; she was going to be napping under that window, dancing with him on the red oak floor, combing through that closet for her other glove, walking out in the morning light to feed her doves in that barn; they were going to make love in the starlight coming through those windows.

But now his eyes fell on the silver urn in his hands and he knew. Of course he knew.

She was the dream. The house was just a frame around the picture.

No wonder the house felt so empty.

Just like him.

* * *

They were real—Albertson's, Rite Aid, Hancock Fabrics, Starbucks, all of them—real. She touched the concrete, the stonework, the windows; she pulled open the doors and looked inside. She could feel, hear, smell them. She could see her pitiful reflection in their windows. She was here, they were here.

Which meant, as near as she could explain it, that she was lost, really lost, hyperlost, even to herself. She could see the reflection of a walking body in the glass, but what was it, and when, and where, and who was in there? Certainly no one she knew.

Mandy Whitacre lived here from 1951 to 1970.

The girl in the blue scrubs and the coat that didn't fit, with her slippers coming apart, didn't. She couldn't have.

Mandy Whitacre had a father, nineteen years of a wonderful life, a home.

The crazy-looking girl in the glass didn't.

No father. No Daddy waiting for her, no Daddy standing there with her.

Whose daddy? Whose father was he in that other place, that other time, if not hers? Whose memory had she stolen? Had he ever existed at all?

There was one thing she knew. She didn't want to know it, but she did. Everything in her mind had gone adrift like a drowning swimmer, kicking, struggling, not touching bottom anywhere, but this one thing had never budged from the time she stepped out of that minivan, and now, bigger than ever, here it was: He was gone. No lemonade today; there was no Daddy.

The girl in the glass was starting to shake and stare back at her with crazed animal eyes. *Oh, they are going to lock me up for sure!* She'd better hide.

Her mind did not record how she got behind all those big buildings, back on the blank side of the thrift store where there were no windows or signs, just steel loading doors and steel people doors and heaps of flattened cardboard boxes and packing materials strewn around big metal Dumpsters. Her first awareness, the first thing she knew she could know, was that she was huddled against one of the Dumpsters holding pieces of crumpled cardboard up against her face as if that would muffle the sounds she could not contain. She wailed, she quivered, she cried, begging God without words, pouring out anguish without thought. She didn't breathe, she gasped in anger, pain, fear, and despair, shaking but not caring, not knowing, not knowing, not knowing . . .

"Oh, God, oh, God, oh, God!"

She didn't hear a car pull up. She didn't hear a car door open and close. She hardly felt the touch on her leg. When she did, she grappled for more cardboard trying to bury herself, wriggling and wailing something like *no no no*. She heaped the panels on top of herself, curling up, trying to hide under them.

It was a lady's voice; it sounded so faint on the other side of the cardboard. "It's okay, I won't hurt you!"

A hand patted her foot. She dared to peek from under the cardboard and saw a lady with an angelic face. The lady was on her knees, eyes full of concern, reaching to touch her.

Mandy—if that was her name—shied away, but the angel lady touched her cheek. "Shhh . . . it's just me. Can I sit down?"

Mandy didn't answer. She just stared, her eyes streaked and burning, her breath still broken into sobs.

The angel lady sat down next to her, right on top of the torn-up cardboard and packing material, and drew close, arm extended to embrace Mandy's shoulders. Mandy wasn't sure, not at all, but the arm got around her. Mandy wasn't sure, not at all, but the angel lady wrapped her other hand gently around her cheek.

Before she knew it, before she could think about it, she'd buried her face in the angel lady's shoulder, she'd clutched for her very life to the angel lady's arm, and she was still crying but now it was different. Someone was holding her, someone could hear her crying, and now she was crying about that, too.

The angel lady never stirred, and her embrace never faltered. She just stayed right there, holding Mandy, whispering comfort, patting her arm, until Mandy, exhausted, cuddled against her like a child, head against her shoulder, sad, reddened eyes looking at nothing in particular.

"I'm sorry," Mandy said at last, her voice a low, quaking whimper.

The angel lady gave her a handkerchief. "Don't be sorry."

"I didn't mean to be a bother."

"You're not a bother. You're somebody in trouble."

"Whoa, yeah."

"My name's Mia. I work right here at the thrift store. What's your name?"

Her name? Should she lie again? The truth could lead to another truth and another and then she'd be back in the hospital. Then again, she was back here sitting on the cardboard next to a Dumpster because the truth had abandoned her. If she didn't know what the truth was, how could she lie?

"Eloise," she said. That would be true enough for now.

Mia touched Mandy's toes, now protruding through the end of a road-weary hospital slipper. "Eloise, would you like a pair of shoes?"

chapter

10

Mr. Stone and Mr. Mortimer had gone rural, renting a small farmhouse in northern Idaho for enough money to send the owners to Europe and, if need be, Mexico and, if need be, Hawaii. They'd left the black Lexus in Vegas and were driving a green Dodge four-wheel-drive SUV; they'd doffed the black suits and were decked out in jeans and flannel shirts. Mr. Stone had found himself a John Deere billed cap, while Mr. Mortimer was reliving a childhood dream under a cowboy brim.

The house sat on a green hillside, huddled among old-growth firs and facing the pastured valley below. The front window provided a pleasing view of the valley, the fields, a winding creek, and particularly the high-end ranch house across the valley on the opposite hill, the one purchased two weeks ago by their man of interest, Mr. Dane Collins.

They'd rearranged the living room, turning the couch to face the front window while allowing floor space for a spotting scope and two long-lensed cameras—one a video, one a still. They had snacks and a thermos of coffee stationed on the coffee table and a computer open on a TV tray. Today's plans included getting online with a portable satellite linkup—not difficult—and then scouting out better vantage points for observing and eavesdropping on that ranch house—difficult. They would probably carry out that part of the mission that night.

Mortimer was taking his shift at the window when he was alerted. "Hold on, who's this?"

He went to the spotting scope; Stone went to the video camera.

A white Toyota Rav4 had pulled up the paved driveway and parked under the carport. A small, roundish lady in blue sweatshirt and jeans got out, lifted what appeared to be bags of groceries from the rear compartment, and headed for the side door of the house, the one that led to the kitchen.

"No . . ." said Mortimer. "Not yet."

Stone glanced over the photos taped to the wall. Some they took at the memorial service, mostly photos of photos; others were easily available promo shots of Dane and Mandy; some, like the few they had of Shirley Morgan, were the sneaky, surveillance kind: telephoto, shallow focus, shot through trees, from behind cars, often partially blocked by objects or people's backs. "Shirley Morgan," said Stone. "Grounds manager. She came with the place."

Dane was on his cell phone, pacing in the kitchen of his big, empty house when Shirley came in with the groceries. He waved hi, she proceeded to put the milk, bread, oat flakes, and paper towels away while he drifted into the breakfast nook. "Seattle. Is that what you said? Seattle?" He made a frustrated face at Shirley, who made a sympathetic face back. "Listen, I can look at a map, but I don't think Seattle's on the way to Idaho. I mean, I drove all the way up here from Vegas and I never passed through Seattle."

He'd bought some cedar patio furniture in a fall close-out at Ace Hardware in Hayden: four chairs, two deck recliners, and an oval table with a hole in the center to support an umbrella. The recliners were in the den; the table and chairs were in the breakfast nook. The store couldn't find the umbrella. He got a good deal.

He sat in one of the chairs. "Well, I thought your truck was going to take the same route." He listened, he sighed. "Okay, tomorrow. I can sleep on the floor one more night. Mmm, it's all right. 'Bye." He switched off his cell phone and clipped it back on his belt. "The load's in Seattle."

Shirley laughed derisively. "Wasn't it supposed to be here Monday?"

"Well, they had somebody else's load they had to drop off in Seattle first. Funny how they left out that little detail."

"I won't need the air mattress for a while."

"I thank you, my back thanks you."

"I got you the soap and shampoo. What about laundry soap?"

"There was still a box in the laundry room and . . ." Dane looked down at the clothes he was wearing. "I don't have a lot of laundry."

Shirley placed some envelopes and catalogs on the granite counter. "All your friends are finding you."

"You can toss those women's catalogs."

"Okay." Ka-foom! Into the wastebasket in the pantry. "I'm moving all the hanging baskets into the greenhouse today, and then, if it's okay with you, I'll shut down the irrigation pump and blow out the sprinkler lines."

"Blow out the . . . what?"

"The yard sprinklers. I use compressed air to blow the water out of all the pipes and heads so they won't freeze."

"Oh. Right."

"And I should take the tractor in to get all the fluids changed next week. You'll want to get that done before we have to plow snow."

Oh. He hadn't thought of that. "When does it start snowing?"

"Depends. Middle of November usually, give or take."

Dane nodded. It was now the second week of October. The mornings were getting crisp, and the leaves were turning. Pretty soon he'd be experiencing *that* aspect of living in Idaho.

"I don't have any warm clothes."

"No boots either."

"No."

"Ah. That's something you need to do, just take a trip into town and do some shopping."

"Yeah, I guess, when I'm feeling up to it . . ."

She leaned, resting her elbows on the counter—she was so short it wasn't much of a lean. "If I may . . ."

"Is it that obvious?"

She nodded. "You're dragging so much you're scuffing the floor. You need to get out of here and just do something. Go into Coeur d'Alene, look around. There're some malls, there's Eddie Bauer, there's Inland Outfitters . . ."

* * *

And there was the Pendleton Wool Store on Sherman Avenue in the heart of the town, one block up from the lake, two blocks over from the big resort. It was an embracing little store that made him feel warm just going in the front door.

"And just what are you looking for?" the nice lady asked.

He had no clear answer, and he felt like a fool. What the heck was he doing in here? What was he doing in Idaho? "Uh . . . I guess I need some warm clothes for winter."

She got him started on the basics: socks, gloves, a casual, not-too-fancy sweater that had pockets and zipped up the front, two hats: a wool cap—without a ball on top—to wear out in the yard, and a very male western hat for looking studly. He picked out a scarf to go with the hat, something that would give him that rugged, Louis L'Amour look once he got a hefty, fur-collared coat. "I'd try Borris's Western Wear for that," she said. "Up on 95. And if you need long underwear, try Inland Outfitters. They have a whole line of polypros, a lot less bulky. And boots, too—and I don't mean galoshes, I mean a man's kind of boot."

So there, he'd done some shopping after a whole lot of traipsing. He stepped out onto Sherman Avenue with the western hat on his head, the gloves on his hands, and the rest of his new stuff in a shopping bag, feeling as much better as new stuff could make him feel, which wasn't a whole lot.

The wind moved up the street, fluttering the leaves still on the ornamental trees and scattering those on the sidewalk, and there was that October chill, a little warning nip on his face to trouble him, *Are you ready? Are you ready?*

"No," he answered.

He knew where he'd parked his newly purchased, low-mileage, extended cab Dodge pickup with four-wheel drive—his replacement for the BMW—but he just plain didn't want to go there. That rig, just like the hat on his head and the bag in his gloved hand, struck him now as so much a part of this whole reefing, wrenching, uprooting change that he'd only made worse by moving here in the first place. What in the heck was he thinking?

The cold wind nipped at him again. No, he wasn't ready. He might never be.

The wind swept the heat from him; he could feel the cold

through his light jacket, his *Vegas* jacket. Fine, he would go pick up a coat, maybe some long underwear and boots, and then head back home to his big, stupid, empty house.

"Hey, meester! Vould you li-eek to see a treek?"

The tacky street Gypsy with her card tricks. He'd seen her across the street earlier, flourishing those cards and accosting people for tips. He'd managed to avoid her until now.

She fanned the cards, then held them like a fan, undulating in a standing dance, her long skirt trailing after her hips, and her arms making snaky moves. She thrust the cards toward him, her bracelets jangling. "Seelect a card, eenee card!"

This was so bad. The Spanish blouse and secondhand shawl, the cartoony flowered head scarf, the cheap jewelry and stage makeup as thick as a mask—in October, in Coeur d'Alene, Idaho? From here he could see maybe four people out on the street, certainly en route to somewhere indoors. No one was lingering on the sidewalk benches, and the eating establishments had pulled in their sidewalk tables and chairs. Maybe this town didn't have any busking ordinances, but for this poor girl's sake it should. She was in sandals. She wasn't wearing a coat, only her costume. Her hands were red from the cold, and a drop was forming on her nose.

Oh, all right, he felt sorry for her. He pulled a card from the fanned deck.

She waved her hand in front of his face in a magical, hypnotic gesture, "Do not let me see eet! Study zee card! Write eet een your my-yeend!"

Six of clubs.

She'd squared up half the deck and directed him with a witchy finger to place his card on top. As he stood there, drawing upon his dwindling patience and getting a bit cold himself, she went through the routine, shuffling, counting, flashing cards around. He knew the trick, and she wasn't doing it very well. The six of clubs was in the stack of cards she placed in his hand, not in the five—actually, four— she kept.

"Now"—she backed away for the big finish—"I haff not touched you, no?"

"No."

"Tell me eef you feel somezing." She tightened her lips, got buggy-eyed, and flexed the cards in her hand with an audible snap. "Zere! Deed you feel zat?"

Well. What would he want his subject to say? "I think maybe I felt something, yes."

"Look!" She spread out the five cards faceup—except now there were only four. "Oh, what ees zees? I have only four cards!"

He could have acted more surprised. "Oh, well, look at that."

"I have dawn eet! I have sent your card to yoo!"

He raised an eyebrow for effect and looked down at the deck in his hand.

"Look through zem! Now!"

He fanned through the cards, all facedown except . . .

"Hey!" The six of clubs, faceup among the others.

"A good treek, yes?"

He smiled at the cards in his hand, then gave them back. "Yeah. Good trick." He turned to leave.

She had a can on a lanyard around her neck, and gave it a little shake, jingling some coins. From the sound he could tell business had not been good.

He reached for his wallet. "Aren't you getting cold out here?"

That must have made her think of her nose. She dabbed it with a corner of her shawl. "I do not my-yeend." Her other hand was holding out that can expectantly, and her eyes were full of hope.

He fumbled his gloves off, then pulled out a twenty and dropped it into the can.

Her eyes got big—they looked even bigger under all that eye shadow. Obviously a twenty was a new experience. Maybe paper money was a new experience. "Ohh! Sank you! Sank you, sir!" She was starting to hunch her shoulders and cross her arms against the cold.

"Better call it a day. You're going to catch pneumonia out here." He turned to walk away.

"Oh, but wait!"

Now he'd done it. She was following him. "Vould you lie-yeek to see anozair treek?"

He wanted to say no without slowing or turning around, but that would have been mean, and here she was all by herself and the Bible always had something to say about caring for the poor, and . . . He stopped. She caught up with him, wielding that deck of cards and looking up at him with imploring eyes. Blue eyes on a Gypsy!

"I know anozair! You weel love eet!"

He studied her face under all that makeup. She was very hard not to like, and so young. He shouldn't be encouraging this. "Gal, you really need to find another line of work. You shouldn't be out here on the street all by yourself."

She must have been very hungry, too. She was starting another trick already. "Zees ty-yeem you just touch a card, eenee card . . ."

He held up his hand. "Wait."

"Eet ees a good treek!"

He grabbed his wallet and fished out another twenty. "Let's do that other one again."

That befuddled her. "Oh, meester, I cannot—"

"Do the same trick twice, I know. But . . . if I may . . ."

She was looking at him warily, her weight shifted away from him. He planted the second twenty in her tip can. She still looked suspicious.

"Your fingers are getting cold, aren't they?"

She looked at her hands and gave a little shrug of denial.

"I could see the steal when you were counting." He looked up and down the sidewalk. There was nobody close enough to see or hear anything. "The rest was okay—well, you drew a little attention on that double undercut—don't watch what you're doing so much, look your audience in the eye, get them to look at you and not the cards." He reached tentatively for her hands. "May I?"

She didn't say yes, but she didn't say no either. He showed her a better dealer's grip, moving her fingers into position around the deck—her fingers were like ice. He showed her how to fan out half and control the first card returned on top of the selected card. He adjusted her little finger as it held a gap in the cards near the back of the deck. "When you set up the break—I know it's cold out here, but try to use just the tip of your little finger and don't let me see it. You see there? Tilt the pack up toward my eye level so I don't see it, and watch for the people on your right. Use your right hand to cover. Now . . ."

Slowly, one step at a time, he guided her hands through the moves. "Okay, try the count again, and move in deeper with the right hand. That's it. Right hand covers the steal. Oops, don't let that edge hang out. Try again. Keep that left hand moving so it draws the heat. They'll tend to watch the hand that's moving. There, that's it!"

He took her through the routine up to the finale, the selected card mysteriously transferred into his hands. She'd have plenty of homework to do, if she did it.

But now her eyes were tearing up as she slowly shuffled the cards. He hurt her feelings. "You okay?"

She just nodded. "I am veree sankful, sir!"

"I hope I haven't offended you."

She shook her head emphatically. "Oh, no, no sir! I am just so glad zat you cared . . . to show me. Eet ees just as my faw-zere used to show me."

"Well, I showed you the trick, but . . ." He hesitated. "But, uh . . ."

She was listening, her eyes on him. And she was shivering.

"You need to get home, you're freezing. You live around here?"

"I am staying at—"

"No, no, don't tell me. Never tell a stranger where you live. Uh . . . oh, brother, just hold on a second." He dug into his bag and pulled out the wool sweater. "Here." He draped it around her shoulders. It was big on her, but right now that was a good thing. "Listen, I gotta go. You're getting cold and I have some more stops to make, so just let me tell you for your own good—I'm being honest, okay? This . . . this gig is all wrong. You're going to freeze out here and the season's over—if there ever was one."

She just listened, dabbing her eyes and pulling the sweater close around her.

"You need to get some indoor gigs, maybe kids' birthday parties. Kids are always having birthdays and parents talk to each other so they'll be your best advertising. You work as an independent contractor, you set up your own gigs, you do your own payroll and taxes. It's great experience, it can be good money—not great money, but good money, and steadier than this. Warmer, too. But you need another persona, a better shtick. This, this Gypsy fortune teller thing, the costume, the accent . . . it's not marketable. Moms and dads won't want you around their kids and the businesses—the fun zones, right? Chuck E. Cheese, a theme park, a, a family center—they aren't going to want you in their establishment because you're not . . . you're not 'family,' you know what I mean? You represent deception, dishonesty, maybe a little bit of temptation, you know?"

She looked as if she were trying to be brave even as tears came to her eyes again.

"No, no, please, I'm all for you, you understand? I want you to come out of this thing a winner. But the other thing about the Gypsy shtick is . . . well, it just isn't you. You're just not wearing it well. You need to be yourself. Find who you are and be that, and then—"

He saw a city police car coming their way down Sherman. "Do you have a permit?"

"A permeet?"

"Did you get a permit from the city to be out here doing business on their sidewalk?"

That stung her. "I didn't know about zat."

"Ehh, you don't look like it." He went for his shopping bag again and produced the wool cap. "Better put this on, right now." He put it on her, covering most of her head, her scarf, and her face. "Take this bag and walk with me."

She picked up the shopping bag and walked alongside him, face toward the storefronts as the police car passed by.

"I don't know what the rules are in this town, but you'd better find out. You don't want to get in trouble with the cops. But I was starting to say, magic isn't just tricks. It's a whole experience; it's a story, an adventure that draws people along. You're not going to hold people's attention as long as you're performing in fragments, just, you know, tricks. Did you notice how you had to run after me? The people see you do one trick, they think you're done, they move on, and you get nickels and dimes instead of dollars. And you think they're going to spread the word about you? They need to see a show, something to hook 'em and make 'em stay even if it's only five minutes long."

He stopped and looked into those eyes. "Listen. I wish you the best. But keep learning, and . . ." He indicated her Gypsy outfit. "Don't settle for this. You find . . . find the real person inside you, the one God made. I think people will like her."

She thought that over a moment, a strange sadness in her eyes, and then she stopped and shed the sweater. "Sank you so much. I should go."

"No! No no, you keep the sweater, keep the hat."

She pulled off the hat. "No. I cannot be owing to you."

"No! Keep 'em. Please. I'm going. I don't want anything else from you. I'm just . . . I'm going. End of encounter."

She looked at him, the tears starting to streak her makeup. "Are you sure?"

"You're going to take good care of them, right?"

"Always."

"All right then. Square deal."

She worked on that a moment, but apparently the cold—and now being able to protect herself from it—persuaded her. With a quaking sniff, she pulled the sweater back around her body and the hat back on her head. "Sank you," she said in a feeble Gypsy voice. "You are so very kind."

"I'm so sorry if I hurt you."

"No, no, eet ees not you. You have not hurt me. You have helped me. Sank you." She gave him a little bow.

"You're very welcome," he said.

"You are right. Eet ees cold. I should go home now."

"Yeah. Yeah, that's good. Get warm."

"May God bless you."

"And God bless you, too."

"Sank you again, so much." She gave him a polite bow and started up the street, wiping her eyes, quickening her step to get away.

He watched her go until he thought he might be staring and looked down at his shopping bag, hanging open. He grabbed it up. Much lighter now. He looked up the street again, but she was gone.

chapter

11

The girl who called herself Eloise stepped quickly, keeping her face toward the storefronts and away from the street. That was all she needed, another run-in with the cops, and dressed very, very far from normal—as usual! So much for playing a Gypsy. She was playing embarrassed now, and vulnerable, and awkward, and . . . well, naked wouldn't be that far off. This didn't feel much different from that day on the fairgrounds. She hung a left and took the first cross street to get off Sherman.

Who was that guy? Out of nowhere, in no time, he hit all the right buttons to make her cry: he gently touched her, taught her, reminded her of her father, told her to find the real person inside. And she didn't even get his name!

Keep walking, keep walking. . . .

She found any excuse to scratch her neck, brush her hair from her face, hold her cap on her head, anything to block a view of her face from the street.

A few blocks north, a right turn, two more blocks, and she made it safely to Sally and Micah Durham's place, a halfway house run by the nicest family on the planet and her home for the past two weeks. She felt safe once she got inside the door—"Hi, it's Eloise, I'm home!"—safer once she chucked the Gypsy outfit, and safest of all after a shower where the Gypsy face went swirling down the drain.

Standing in front of the bathroom mirror in a white camisole and blue jeans from the thrift store—*God bless them!*—she looked at her washed face, now a blank slate, a blue-eyed question. Who was she? Who should she be? Mandy Whitacre was a fugitive from the nuthouse who might or might not be who she thought she was and would do best not to talk about herself; the Gypsy Girl was only a role and a not-so-great idea, since she wasn't family-friendly or even legal on the streets.

She'd better just stay with Eloise.

Eloise was nineteen, born January 15, but in *1991;* she was young and pretty. Her hair, now towel-dried and tousled, was cut short, layered, and colored brown. Her reflection in the mirror looked troubled because she was.

She claimed she had no family and was running from an abusive boyfriend she would not name and preferred not to talk about. She had no ID, no driver's license, no way to prove who she was . . . but no one could disprove it either, so far. The Durhams and the two other girls staying here knew she was holding out on them, not telling them everything, but for now that was okay. She could talk about things when she was ready—which she supposed would be never.

Eloise knew about computers, DVDs, CDs, cell phones, digital cameras, and MP4 players—at least, that's what she wanted people to think, so she was faking it until she really did know. She'd been catching up on who was president, where the latest wars were happening, what some of the popular songs were, and what TV shows people were following. She noted that only older folks used words like "bummer," "far out," and "heavy trip," and only as leftovers from their younger days. "Cool" was still around, but now "like" and "I'm like" got stuck in everywhere, at least as much as "you know" used to be.

Eloise, like the other girls, was supposed to be looking for work if not employed, but—of all the years to land in!—2010 was a bad year for job-hunting, especially for a girl who'd been majoring in theater and was mainly skilled—well, maybe not so skilled after all—in magic. She could type but knew nothing about computers (her little secret); thanks to the father her other self must have had somehow, she could fix things around the house, knew quite a bit of carpentry and plumbing, could give a car a tune-up if it wasn't built too long after 1970, was a good cook, and knew how to take care of horses, llamas, and poultry, including doves. She was good with people and, she figured, could do fair to middlin' as a waitress, a housekeeper, a live-in domestic, a ranch hand, a cook, a bottle washer, a feather duster . . . just give her a job!

But besides there being so few jobs available, there was one nagging little hitch she couldn't get around, and she ran smack into it every time she was handed a job application: that little blank space on the application that required her Social Security number. Mandy, born in 1951, *thought* she had one, but of course Mandy born in 1951 thought a lot of things that weren't necessarily so and were best not talked about. Eloise, born in 1991, did not have a Social Security number, and since she had no ID, driver's license, or even a birth certificate, she had no way of getting one. Too bad—*bummer!*—because it would have to be Eloise who got hired.

Too bad the Gypsy Girl idea didn't work out. She didn't need an application or a Social Security number for that, just a can with TIPS written on it.

Who was that guy? What if he was right about everything?

She cleaned up the shower, put her towel in the laundry basket, gathered up her toiletries—courtesy of the Durhams, *God bless them!*—and went to her bedroom, a nice room with two beds for two girls, but occupied by only herself at the moment. Her deck of cards was lying on the dresser, banished from her life for, oh, forty minutes or so, at least until she reached for the box once again, pulled out the cards, and started shuffling them from her right hand to her left in an overhand shuffle and a three-way cut; reviewing how to do a double undercut, left hand to right; controlling the top card, controlling the bottom card, retaining the top stock—all the things Daddy first showed her and she knew since she was in junior high . . .

Now, what did the man on the sidewalk show her? *Cover the break. Be more subtle. Watch that right side, don't look at the cards so much when you shuffle them . . .*

She sat on the bed and went through that card trick again. And again. And again. Her hands were warm and fluid, and the cards were so obedient. . . .

"No way!" Darci, a lanky blonde fresh out of jail for drug possession, had the best expression on her face a magician could hope for: eyes wide with the white showing, mouth dropped so far open you could see her fillings. She was holding the deck of cards in her hand and had just discovered her selection, the three of hearts, faceup in the middle of the deck.

"How did you do that?" squealed Rhea, a cute and hefty Hispanic who'd just fled from an abusive husband. She was the hairdresser who cut and colored Eloise's hair for free.

Ah, what a feeling! Eloise smiled, receiving her cards back, lithely shuffling them and doing a waterfall, just milking the moment. That trick had gone so well.

So the guy on the street was right. Now she wanted to remember the other things he told her.

"Okay," said Sally, still applauding. "Let's get going on dinner."

Sally and her husband, Micah, had been youth pastors at the same church that ran the thrift store, but they saw the need for a half-way house and mentor home for young women and opened up their place. Micah went to work for a graphics firm to keep everything afloat; Sally spent the days counseling and loving the girls back to wholeness.

The house had its daily routines, rules, and requirements, and each girl took her turn with every chore according to the rotation chart on the kitchen wall. All three helped prepare dinner, but two—tonight it was Darci and Eloise—branched off each night to set and clear the table and do the dishes.

Usually Eloise preferred to do the cooking, but this evening something happened with the silverware and . . . forget about the cooking! It started innocently enough with the worship music playing on the stereo—uh, the home entertainment system. Like much of the worship music at the church and in this house, it was a catchy tune she'd not heard before, and it got her dancing a little, which spread to her hands as she set the first knife on the table with a graceful little flick of her wrist. The knife slid on the tablecloth and came to rest perfectly aligned beside the plate and, she noticed, right on the beat of the music. *Freaky coincidence. Wild.*

She moved on with jazzy grace to the next place setting and set the next knife with the same jazzy flourish of her wrist. Sliiiide . . .

ding! That knife lay down even and straight as if she'd trained it to do so, and once again, on the beat of the music. Was there something about the music? Maybe it was giving her just the right rhythm and moves to plant the silverware. She started singing along with it, feeling it out, mostly ta-da-da-da-dee-ing because she didn't know the words, and pitched the other three knives.

Sliiiiide . . . ding!

Sliiiide . . . ding!

Sliiide . . . ding!

Darci had been around Eloise long enough. She didn't find such behavior unusual. She just kept setting out the plates, salad bowls, and glasses.

What about the spoons?

On the next circuit around the table, Eloise tried something much chancier: sliding the spoons in against the knives from a sideways direction.

The first spoon tumbled and went crooked. *All right, it's a normal world, the expected happened: it didn't work.* She straightened it, then addressed the four other spoons in her left hand. "Okay, guys. See how he's lying there? Just for grins, let's see you do it."

She dropped the next spoon slightly to the right of where it should be, no more than an inch above the table, and with a musically motivated rotation of her wrist.

The spoon skittered along the cloth and came to rest perfectly aligned with the knife. Eloise let out a squeak.

Darci looked at her.

"Sorry."

She tried the next spoon. Plunk, skitter, ding! She almost made another noise, but held it in.

By the time she was setting out the forks she was really getting the hang of . . . something. The last fork slid about four inches sideways and was crooked, but straightened out as it came to a stop beside the plate.

Now, this was heavy.

12

Nine-thirty. Dane sat in his four-for-sixty-while-they-last patio chair, his computer glowing at him from the super-sale patio table with the hole in the middle, and let his thoughts and fingers amble where they would. This was it, he figured, the grieving process. As he thought it, he wrote it, and he found it helped.

> She was still beautiful, I kid you not. Yes, she was fifty-nine. Her eyes kept the crinkle that smiling had put there; her hair was mostly blond from a bottle; the sun had deepened her freckles and coarsened her arms and back.
>
> But there was nothing like seeing her sitting at breakfast with the morning sun at her back and her hair a corona about her head; nothing like the curve of her hips, as smooth as a classical phrase whenever she draped them with a dress, framed herself in a doorway, even pushed a grocery cart. There was nothing like the pleasant roundness of her breasts under a sweater or her body against mine, that close to no other for forty years.
>
> Was I happy? You bet I was happy.

Nine forty-five. Eloise sat on her bed in the soft light of her bedside lamp, flipping a quarter, part of that day's earnings.

"Heads," she called in midflip. She caught the coin, slapped it on the back of her hand, uncovered it . . .

Heads.

She flipped it again. "Heads."

Heads.

"Heads."

Heads.

"Heads."

Heads. She put her hand over her mouth to keep it quiet.

Pretty lucky.

No, extremely lucky. Her last toss made fifteen heads in a row.

She didn't know how she did it other than just wanting it to happen, like touching the coin without really touching it.

And I suppose I should be honest with myself while I try to understand what happened in Coeur d'Alene today. A part of being lonely, I suppose, or perhaps needing to be needed, or perhaps for no particular reason other than her being a fledgling magician and my being . . . what? The wise old mentor? I just couldn't stay out of it, I couldn't keep my mouth shut.

Dane had to pause a moment, sit, think, and try to make sense of himself. He thought of calling Dr. Kessler but put that thought aside. What happened to him that day could have happened to anybody, trauma or no trauma, and he'd ended his pain medication days ago. It had to happen. She was a magician and . . .

It could be what Dr. Kessler was talking about.

Oh, come on!

He decided to pour himself another cup of decaf from a little coffeemaker he bought just to buy some time. When he sat down and faced his computer again, his thoughts hadn't changed.

All right, I'll admit it: She reminded me of Mandy. Her shtick was silly, ill-timed, ill-located, poorly done; her outfit was hodgepodge, the makeup was stagey, and I could tell she didn't believe it herself. . . .

But how many people, young or old, would have taken

such a chance, gone out on such a narrow limb, just put it all out there the way she did? Mandy was one of the few I've ever known.

Maybe he *should* call Dr. Kessler.

Oh, it was over now. He'd probably never see her again. It was an interesting phenomenon, looking into that girl's eyes and . . . he must have subconsciously loaded his own memories into what he was seeing. That's why the eyes looked so much like Mandy's used to look when she was troubled, when she was trying to figure something out, when she was fascinated. The voice, too, so much like Mandy's when she was goofing around, trying to do a stagey accent . . .

So what's Kessler going to do if I do call her, charge me by the hour and send me a bill?

Forget it. Today's over, she's gone, it was a unique grieving experience, something to remember with interest, maybe write about, maybe share with another widower someday to compare notes.

I wonder . . . what if . . . ?

Eloise tried it. She set the quarter to spinning on the top of the dresser and then watched it . . . and watched it . . . and watched it . . . and as long as she stayed with it, somehow connected with it, it never slowed, it never wobbled. When she "let go," the spin decayed and the quarter wah-wah-wobbled down to a stop. She stood it on edge, flicked it with her finger to set it spinning again, and this time, with her eyes and will locked on it and her body unconsciously leaning along, she made the spinning quarter move toward the rear of the dresser and back to the front, then back and forth again, then in a circle, then in a square. Upon her command—or whatever it was she felt or did, she wasn't sure what it was—the quarter wah-wah-wobbled down and settled—ker-plink!—on the dresser.

She rubbed the side of her face, thinking, trying to deal with this. Was it really happening, or was it from the same bag of insanity as thinking Nixon was president and the war in Vietnam was still going on?

The last girl to use this room left a tennis ball on the dresser. Eloise grabbed it. What to do?

The room was carpeted, not a great place to roll a tennis ball. All the better.

She placed it on the carpet and watched it.

Hmm.

Maybe if she watched from the other side . . .

Ehh . . .

Well, maybe if she watched it and gave it a nudge . . .

It rolled slightly, bumping on the nap of the carpet until it came to rest looking tired and discouraged.

She got down on her elbows and knees, her nose inches away from it. "Come on now, Burt. Look at all that wonderful open space in front of you. Where's your sense of adventure?"

She tapped the ball with her finger and it rolled, bumping against the nap . . .

"Come onnn!"

It bumped against the nap, bumped again, rotated a few degrees more . . . and kept rolling. She crawled and followed it, her nose inches away, willing, commanding, feeling, whatever might work. "That's it, Burt, that's it! Keep goin'!"

It kept rolling, faster now, until it bumped into the wall and started coming back.

She backpedaled, drawing it after her, making it roll, and it followed her like a baby chick after its mother. *Wow, if that guy I met in town could see this!*

What was that on the wall?

She stopped and looked. The tennis ball bumped against her knee and stayed there, forgotten.

The white paddock fence. She could see it projected on the wall . . . no, she could see it *through* the wall. The wall was thinning as if turning to glass, and just beyond it, just outside the house, was the white paddock fence, dimly visible in the night. Beyond that, the green pasture stretched like a dark expanse, and in that expanse stood the three aspens, fragmented shadows against the starry sky, leaves trembling.

Eloise froze right then and there, still on her knees, enraptured, not taking her eyes off it. She did not want to lose this.

The vision widened and clarified before her and beside her as the other walls of the room dissolved and she was no longer in a bedroom but outside on a clear night on a two-lane country road that vanished over a rise in one direction and dipped into an expansive, restful valley in the other. She stood slowly, turning, taking it all in. The stars above were brilliant, like diamonds on black velvet; she could recognize Perseus, Cassiopeia, Aquila, Hercules, and the Big Dipper, and all around her the forested hills traced a black, sawtoothed bite out of the sky. Here and there on the hillsides were the nighttime stars people had put there: mercury vapor lamps burning blue over driveways and barnyards, bare little bulbs on back porches, and the orange glow from the sleepy-eyed windows of ranch and farm houses. The night was so quiet; no town noise. A dog barked; another replied. The birds had all turned in.

Just off the road from where she stood, a mercury vapor lamp illuminated a heavy wooden gate spanning a driveway. The driveway went up a hill between two white-fenced pastures, and at the top of the hill, nestled among charcoal evergreens, were the glowing cathedral windows of a house. She could just make out the angular roof, gables, and stoney facade, but the sight drew her in as if she were seeing a memory, something from a beautiful dream. It looked—it felt—so much like home, only . . . better.

Was this heaven?

Of course I have to wonder how this house would feel, how real, how complete the dream would be, if Mandy were here to grace the rooms with her spirit, her charm, her tasteful touch. She would know where everything should go, how the living room should be arranged, how the walls should be adorned, and . . .

Dane paused to savor the feeling: a sweet and gentle joy he knew from mornings with Mandy, sitting at breakfast with Bibles and coffee; the sense of completeness whenever she returned home from shopping, getting her hair done, running three miles; the way he felt when he would sit beside her in church and she would place her hand on his hand . . .

How home, any home, used to feel when she was there.

He looked around the empty kitchen, and just now, in this one special moment, it didn't feel empty. It felt . . . right, so right that time stopped and he fell silent and motionless, listening, sensing, almost expecting her to come through the archway into the kitchen with a little item on her mind: news of the day, who'd called, whether she liked the cut of her new costume, where the camera might be so she could capture the fall colors.

Slowly, as if approaching a timid animal, he rose from his chair and moved by careful steps toward the kitchen, wanting to walk into that sense of her presence, that deep and wondrous something that had settled in the room. *Mandy?*

She wanted to go through that gate and up that driveway. She wanted to go inside that big, beautiful house. Maybe it *was* heaven. Maybe the answers to all that had befallen her would fall together if she could only go there.

She smelled something smoky, like burning leaves on the slow, cool breeze.

The telephone rang, and against the silence of the house its warble was jarringly loud and obnoxious. Dane instantly resented the interruption . . . *but wait.* The rings came in pairs. It was the phone down at the gate.

What if it was she?

Mandy?

No! The, the girl, *you know, the girl I met today* . . . the . . .

Maybe you should *call Kessler* . . .

He stopped in midthought, hand on his face. *Oh, brother.* Not only was he being ridiculous, he was also arguing with himself.

And the phone was still ringing.

He picked it up. "Hello?"

She was back in her room, so suddenly she stumbled and dropped against the bed. The walls were back, the warmth of the house enveloped her, the light from the bedside lamp made her squint.

* * *

"Hello?"

He could hear the sound of the outdoors coming through the phone from the gate intercom, but nobody answered.

"Hello?"

He hung up. Weird coincidence. If it happened again, he'd have to have the gate system checked. But who would he call to do that? Shirley would know, he'd have to tell her if he remembered, maybe he should write it down, maybe he should call Kessler, but the moving van was coming tomorrow so maybe he'd better open that gate and leave it open. Was there a way to get a truck down to the barn to stash all that magic stuff? Should he worry about protecting the floors? Did he want any more coffee? . . .

A zillion little realities tore him away from the *moment*, whatever it was. He sat once again at the table in the big, dead-quiet, empty kitchen and stared at the words on his computer. Maybe he should make a list of everything that needed to be done. Good idea. He opened a new file and tapped in the heading: Things to Do.

Yes, everything felt normal again. *Whoopee.*

Hallucinations, Eloise thought. That was something Bernadette and Karla asked her about. Did she ever have any hallucinations or delusions?

Well, duh . . .

She sank to the floor, her back against the bed, the tennis ball on the floor beside her. She absentmindedly rolled the tennis ball under her palm, scanned the walls around her, the dresser, the nightstand, the lamp, and the bed, all solid and really there, and then she sighed.

Well, yeah, sure, she was crazy. Not that she'd had much doubt about it, but finally, sitting on the floor in a cozy little room where she was safe, she accepted it, and without fear. She was a little surprised how calm she was, but crying and freaking out were behind her, an old debt she'd already paid to this problem. There was no point to them now.

She made the tennis ball land on the tip of her finger and spin there, perfectly balanced, until she let it stop.

chapter

13

A digital photograph of the Gypsy Girl popped up on the computer screen. She was hurrying up a sidewalk in a downtown district, one hand clutching a sweater closely about her and the other toying with a wool hat she was wearing. She was looking away from the street and her face was not visible.

"Yeah, I'd say she's hiding her face," said a male voice from the computer. "Look at 23."

Stone tapped the right arrow key until Gypsy Girl 23 scrolled onto the screen. This photo was zoomed in closer. The girl was looking down, her profile mostly obscured by her street side hand. She was yanking a scarf out from under the wool cap.

"Most of the shots show the same behavior," said Stone, speaking to the computer.

"Wonder what he told her."

Mortimer, binoculars in hand, divided his attention between the satellite conversation in the farm house and the Collins ranch house across the valley where a moving van had finally arrived. As two movers wearing back braces muscled a sofa from the van through the front door, he glanced over at the computer. Stone had pressed the right arrow key and scrolled number 24 from offscreen to center. Now the girl's eyes and nose were visible, but the makeup still disguised her.

"Whatever it was, it ruined her day. She got out of there," Stone remarked.

"Hoping no one would see her," said the voice. "Not too friendly an encounter."

"He did give her the hat and the sweater," Stone said.

"And a tip," said Mortimer.

"And she's a magician," said the voice on the computer, "which definitely makes her a person of interest. But was there any indication that they knew each other? Remember who we're talking about here."

"None that we could see," said Stone. "I think he was just being generous to a busker."

"How old would you say she was?"

"Hard to tell. Twenties, thirties. But what if . . . ?" Stone and Mortimer looked at each other, and Stone went ahead. "If this is the subject, can she be young enough not to know who he is?"

"What if she hasn't met him yet?" asked Mortimer.

"*That* young?" the voice said. There was a long silence followed by a muttered "Incredible."

"Sir?" Stone inquired.

"Parmenter would have to rework the protocol . . . see if anything matches. This is way beyond our projections . . ." Another pause, and then the voice commented, "But if she hasn't even met him yet, we'd be downright lucky, wouldn't we?"

Splosh! Eloise dipped the long-handled window mop in the bucket of soapy water, then soaped and squeegeed the front window of the Real Life Ministries Thrift Store. Only one more pane to go, and then she could move on to sorting out the donations for the day, price-tagging and hanging up the new clothes, and making sure the children's toys were arranged on the shelves by age group.

The job was fun. Mia and the others were great to work with, and it was a sweet arrangement: girls from the halfway house—today that meant herself and Darci the former jailbird—put in hours at the thrift store, and in exchange the thrift store helped meet the needs of the halfway house with clothing, food, and whatever else might come through the donation door that was useful. So Eloise didn't earn dollars, she earned safety, well-being, and time to figure things out. Such a deal!

She squeegeed the last window, then stopped to look at the girl in the glass looking back at her with clear, expressive eyes. The girl was still a bit of a hobo, she supposed, still a little lost in a strange world and working through some heavy sadness besides, but she was getting there; she was digging her way out. She was getting to know herself, settling on those things about her that were true and likable no matter what world she thought she was living in. She had friends, and that made her world real enough to touch with her heart, and that made all the difference. She was wearing clothes of her own choosing: a warm jacket she'd earned with her labors and the wool cap the mysterious man on the street had given her. Before long, she hoped, she would find a way to actually make some money and pay for the things she needed.

Which got her thinking about her current plan and that tattered black derby hanging inside the store. When did that come in? It looked like something Emmett Kelly would have worn, a little bashed in, old but proud. If it fit it might be perfect.

And what was that term the mysterious man used?

"I know what an independent contractor is," said Mr. Calhoun, leaning on the counter, looking as if she was trying to sell him a quilting club membership or spring-wound fire alarms.

"So you wouldn't have to pay me like an employee. I could start out just making tips."

He looked away from her and took more interest in how things were going in his coffee shop. All around them, McCaffee's Sandwich and Coffee Shop was in full swing. The coffeemakers were pounding, grinding, and squirting out espressos, lattes, mochas, frappuccinos: his wife, Abby, and their two young employees—Megan with the coffee-stained apron and black curls, Myron with enough rings in his face to hang a shower curtain—were taking orders for coffee and sandwiches and hustling them out to the tables as if their jobs depended on it, which they probably did. "The way I see it, any money you take out of here is money I don't get."

"But I might bring in more customers and they might stay a little longer and buy more."

Mr. Calhoun's bald head was getting little sweat beads on it.

"Look, people come in here to grab a bite and talk business, play some chess, work on their computers. They don't want to stop what they're doing and watch card tricks." One look around the room told that story: the place was noisy with chatting customers, and almost every other table had someone tapping and clicking away on a computer. At one table in the center, two guys wearing their billed caps backward were playing a game of chess. "You used to be the Gypsy, right?"

"I bagged that idea. It didn't have family appeal."

"So"—he waved his finger at her new outfit—"what's this, Charlie Chaplin?"

She'd claimed that tattered and dented derby hat from the thrift store, along with some baggy trousers, an oversize black suit coat, and cloddy shoes. A little makeup to stubble her face, sadden her eyes, and redden her nose completed the character. "Hobett."

He made a face at her face. "Hobett?"

"A girl hobo."

"A girl hobo with whiskers?"

She shrugged. "It's funny. And what's a hobo without whiskers?"

He granted her half a smile. "Cute."

"And I do new tricks now."

He looked around the room again, antsy and preoccupied. "Tell you what, I'll give you a coffee and muffin, on me. It's the best I can do for you."

Sad news. She pouted a clownish pout, but then doffed her hat with a salutary flourish. "You're a sweetie."

"I'm telling you no, did you catch that?"

She nodded. "No. I mean, yes, you said no."

He tapped on his wife as she hurried by. "Abby, give her a muffin and whatever coffee she wants. Hate to see someone go hungry." Then he turned back to Eloise and aimed his finger at her. "But this is it, all right? You don't come back, not with this, this hobo thing or any other thing. All right?"

"Yes, sir!"

"All right."

When Abby came back behind the counter, she was sympathetic. "I think your outfit is really cute."

"Thank you."

"What would you like, honey?"

Eloise asked for a blueberry muffin and a sixteen-ounce double-shot decaf mocha. Abby prepared the order herself. Eloise told her, "Thank you so much," and she really meant it.

"You're very welcome. Go ahead and take a table."

She was in a costume for no particular reason now, but this was an artsy kind of place with theater posters on the walls and a musicians/artists/yoga/herbal remedy/colon health bulletin board; looking weird was no big deal. A few folks looked her way, but were immediately satisfied—oh, a hobo. Okay.

She found a table in the center of the room and settled in for a consolatory meal that would end soon enough, but hey, she was going to enjoy it. Her first bite of the muffin was hot, moist, and flavorful; a blueberry burst inside her mouth, spilling its sweetness. The first sip of the mocha topped off the muffin so well she closed her eyes, held it in her mouth, and savored it before swallowing it. This was joy, just enough to close out the talkers and planners, the tapping computers, the chess players, the periodic moan of the front door, and her little dark cloud of disappointment.

When she opened her eyes, she noticed a little girl at the next table sitting in her daddy's lap and looking at her—not staring, looking. She was four, maybe five, with golden curls in blue ribbons, a blue dress that matched, and big blue eyes. She was munching on a cookie, had crumbs on her cheeks, and must have found Eloise to be the most engaging thing she'd ever seen.

Eloise looked back, drawn to those eyes. The little girl was comfortable with that, so neither thought to look anywhere else. While all around them the talking and tapping, the sipping and chewing, the serving and paying rattled on in isolated clusters, she and the girl visited, getting to know each other without a word. *You see me, don't you, little girl? I'm really here, a somebody. I fit into your world and that's okay with you.*

Eloise smiled, head tilted, and gave the girl a little wave with her fingers.

The child pressed close against her daddy's chest but never looked away, and she smiled a teeny bit.

Now her daddy was smiling at the exchange as he took a sip from his coffee. Mommy was smiling, too, watching her daughter.

A mommy, a daddy, and a safe and loved little girl. Eloise felt an ache and a warmth at the same time. She could have cried, but something in the little girl's eyes drove the tears from hers: wonder.

Yes, that was it. Wonder. What Eloise—or Mandy?—used to feel when looking at a flower, cradling a dove chick in her hand, or sitting out on the tractor watching the wispy clouds at the very top of the sky.

Misdirection. Eloise fell into it, just had to do it. She took a long, slow bite from her muffin, drawing the little girl's eyes to her comical face while her free hand found some quarters in her pocket—props left over from the Gypsy's fateful day. A quick load and she was ready. She waved a little wave again, but this time a quarter appeared between her first two fingers. She stared in wide-eyed, clownlike astonishment.

"Oh-ohh," said the mommy.

The little girl stared. Maybe she got it, maybe she didn't.

Eloise closed her fingers, opened them again, and there was a second quarter between her second and third fingers.

"Where'd that come from?" the daddy asked the girl, and now she smiled as if to say, "Hey, what's going on here?"

Eloise waved up a third quarter, then vanished all of them, rotating and showing her empty hand. Mommy and Daddy did some quiet little claps. The little girl just watched.

Eloise's eyes followed an invisible quarter buzzing by. She snatched it from thin air, put it in her mouth, and drew it from her ear.

Clap clap. The girl smiled with one finger in her mouth.

For no more than a second, Eloise wondered if she should be doing this in Mr. Calhoun's coffee shop when he told her no, but she bumped that thought. This wasn't a show, this was making friends.

The little girl was watching, expecting.

Eloise set the quarter she'd taken from her ear on the table and flicked it with her finger, making it spin.

The girl craned to see, wide-eyed, watching, munching another bite of cookie.

Wonder. It was beautiful to see.

Make it quick, Eloise.

She shooed the quarter away with a little jerk of her finger and away it went, spinning around the table, circling the salt and pepper shakers.

Now Mommy and Daddy were starting to get wonder in their eyes.

She gestured "come here" with her finger and the quarter came back around and stopped a few inches shy of the table's edge, still spinning.

Now two guys—they looked like college types, in clothes that cost a lot but were made to look like they didn't—halted their conversation and started watching the quarter spin. They exchanged a look and kept watching, two more friends, two more human beings touching her life as she touched theirs. What a feeling.

The little girl was looking up at her daddy. *Oh-oh, got to get her back!*

Eloise bent low, her nose just above the table, and mutely beckoned to the coin. It advanced a few inches and stopped. She beckoned again. It backed up.

Come on, now, she mimed in clownish gestures, *don't be a wuss!*

The quarter wavered, inched forward, backed up, came forward again . . . slowly . . .

She placed her index finger against the edge of the table, beckoned and cajoled, and finally . . . the quarter spun onto her fingertip. She lifted it slowly aloft, spinning and balancing on her finger.

Now, that got a response! Mommy and Daddy, the little girl, the college guys, and now the guys playing chess all watched in disbelief and delight.

Oh, brother. Where do I go from here? Call it quits before I get in trouble?

They were applauding now, and she had the little girl back.

Top it, top it, top it!

She mimed for the daddy to hold up his finger. He laughed, a little nervous about it, but he stuck up his index finger. She steadied his hand with her free hand and brought the quarter down.

It was like lighting a candle. The quarter passed from her finger to his and he held it there, astonished, looking at the quarter from different sides, watching it spin all by itself.

"Hey, check it out!" somebody said.

"What? How's he doing that?" said a lady at a table close by.

"*She's* doing it!" said the man sitting with her.

The little girl was enraptured. She reached for the quarter as if it were something truly magical, then shied away. Eloise mimed an open palm, and the girl's mother reached and helped. The child held out an open palm. The father brought his finger down, and the quarter hopped into the little girl's palm. Kerplop! It lay flat, happy, harmless, and hers.

Eloise closed the little girl's hand around the quarter and pointed, miming, *It's yours!*

There was a circle of laughter and applause from the four nearest tables, enough to make some of the computer tappers look up. A few heads turned from the front of the place.

Oh-oh. Now Mr. Calhoun was watching. So was Abby. Would they be mad or amazed? They weren't smiling yet.

Well, she'd better be sure they were amazed—and that she had the crowd. It felt a little nutty, something between a ray of hope and a flying leap, but she stood and pulled Burt the Tennis Ball from her coat pocket.

The folks she had were all hers, watching every move she made, expecting something.

She perched Burt on the tip of her finger and gave him a spin. He spun there, never slowing.

How about the little girl? Was she ready? Was she trusting? Eloise mimed for her to point her finger upward.

The little sweetie looked at her daddy. "Go ahead," he said, and she pointed her finger in the air.

Eloise approached slowly, all smiles and adventure, and brought Burt in for a gentle landing on her fingertip.

This child was going to handle the rest of her life just fine: she held her finger still and let Burt spin while the friends sitting closest, joined by friends a few tables out, applauded and cheered.

And oh, the triumph in her eyes!

Eloise brought her own right hand close and the little girl let Burt hop back onto Eloise's finger. Eloise raised her right hand and let Burt roll down her arm, over her shoulders, down her left arm, and then— ta-da!—he spun on the finger of her left hand as she held him high.

Applause and even a few whoops.

Now the clatter and chatter were dropping off table by table, talker by tapper, sipper by muncher, as the circle of quiet attention rippled outward. Folks were leaning, looking around heads and bodies, curious.

Mr. Calhoun was watching; she could feel it.

She let Burt roll back to her right arm and out onto her right index finger again. More applause, but it was time to move on. She let him roll across to her left hand one more time and then, after bringing both left and right hands together and letting Burt twirl on both fingers, she jerked her hands apart and let him fall.

He bounced on the floor, and bounced on the floor, and bounced on the floor as she watched, following him with big nods of her head.

But he wouldn't stop bouncing, and folks were catching on, laughing, marveling. Her look-away deadpan would have made Jack Benny proud, and it got laughs.

Enough of this bouncing. She reached on a bounce to catch Burt—he curved sideways and she missed. She grabbed at him again and he zipped from her grasp. She chased him, groping and grabbing while he bounced between the tables, and finally netted him in her hat. *Well, there!* She was in charge again. She put her hat down on her table with Burt under it and began her next trick, materializing playing cards in her empty hand.

The folks watched her produce a card, then two, then a full hand of them, and they applauded politely, but their eyes were straying and she noticed. They were looking at her table and laughing.

Burt! He was trying to get out from under her hat, wiggling it around, making it crawl blindly around the table and bump into things. The hat was heading for the table edge!

She dove for it, but too late. The hat hung over the edge and Burt dropped free, bouncing—Wow! What a bounce!—into a high arc over the room and dropping toward an older patron's cup of coffee—a patron who wasn't paying much attention, by the way. The crowd followed the arc of the ball with a unanimous "Whoooooaa!"

Burt was dropping right on target when the old guy looked up just in time to see the ball plop into Eloise's hand, inches above catastrophe.

Whoops! Hollers!

And broad, mock relief from the Hobett. She wiped her brow,

plopped her hat back on, then tossed the ball over her shoulder, intending to bounce it off a kick of her heel.

She did it. The ball went flying, arced over the heads of the patrons . . .

And bounced off Mr. Calhoun's head.

Everybody in the place, as one, saw it happen, and everybody howled.

The Hobett stood there horrified, hand over gaping mouth, while Burt came bouncing back and cowered behind her feet, peeking out, quivering with fear. Now the folks were shouting, some shrieking with laughter. Amazement, astonishment, and wonder filled the room. She had the crowd.

But . . . did she have Mr. Calhoun? He was glaring at her, and whether he was acting or serious, he still pointed at the door. "Out!"

Play it. She doffed her hat and bowed repeatedly, backing toward the door.

Burt just sat where he was, undecided.

The Hobett made it to the door, but missed Burt and started looking around for him.

Mr. Calhoun advanced on the tennis ball, about to pick it up.

The Hobett whistled, and Burt scurried to her, struck her big-booted toe, and bounced high over her head. As he came down, she doffed her hat just in time for him to land on her head and replaced the hat just in time to keep him there.

One final bow to a wildly applauding crowd, and she was out the door.

Eloise could still hear the cheers and applause from McCaffee's as she hurried down the sidewalk, emotions in a blender. *I blew it, I did great, they love me, he hates me, it was unprofessional, it was inspired. . . . Oh, dear God, can't I do anything right?*

"Hello? Oh, miss! Could you hold on a minute?"

Should she stop? Was it a cop?

Her shoulders were sagging as she turned to face the music.

It was Abby Calhoun, hurrying toward her, smiling, eyes sparkling. "I never caught your name."

Well, Abby was smiling. Maybe it was safe to tell her. "Eloise Kramer."

"Roger—Mr. Calhoun—told me to run after you."

"Is he mad?"

She looked ready to laugh. "I think he is a little mad, yes."

She deflated, the air sighing out of her.

"But he'd like to talk to you . . . about your proposal?"

Eloise breathed in again and squared her shoulders.

chapter

14

SATURDAY NIGHT, 7–7:30 P.M.,
enjoy . . .
ELOISE "The Hobett" KRAMER
Magician Extraordinaire
Astounding.
Astoundingly Funny.
Bring the Family.

It wasn't her name up in lights, just colored marker pen on white copy paper with some of Roger Calhoun's tacky artwork, taped to the front window of McCaffee's. But that little poster struck Eloise as a page that could turn to a new chapter in her life, and she could feel it to the bones.

Seven to seven-thirty. Half an hour. She could remember thinking, *Only half an hour?* Now, cooped up in the women's restroom in the back of McCaffee's, reddening her nose and dotting her face with black whiskers, mumbling to herself one final time the order of illusions she'd planned, all she could think was, Half an hour! How was she going to fill half an hour?

"This isn't my idea," Mr. Calhoun had said. "It's Abby's idea and I'm going along with it, so okay, I'll give you half an hour and it better be good."

She worked and worried and sweated away the hours in her room at Sally and Micah's until she was ready to eat her pillow, trying to remember and rehearse illusions in the correct order and the right style to hold a coffeehouse crowd, and all she had to work with were two tennis balls—she drew smiley faces on them—a deck of cards, and a batch of quarters.

The doorknob rattled.

"Just a minute!" she called.

It was noisy out in the restaurant, so there was a crowd. Whether they were willing to become *her* crowd was one big question mark. Had any returned from yesterday? Had any word gotten around so there'd be new faces? Was there anybody out there who would, you know, like her in the first place?

She was already sweating. She sniffed herself. Her deodorant was working.

She leaned against the sink and bowed her head. "I'm going to do this. I might make a total fool of myself, but I won't turn away. Here I am with whiskers on my face and tricks in my pockets and . . . and somebody needs to use the restroom. Well, You know what I would have said."

She assumed the Hobett's personality, face, and body, double-checked her goofy smile in the mirror, and stepped out. With a tip of her hat to the lady waiting outside, she slipped past and flopped into one lone chair in the corner to await her cue. She caught the eyes of a couple sitting at the rearmost table and gave them a disarming, clownish smile. They smiled back. It helped.

Her hand was trembling. She wouldn't be able to hold her cards . . .

"Okay, uh, here we go, then. . . ." Mr. Calhoun had stepped to the center of the floor. He and his crew had crowded the tables a touch toward the walls to allow Eloise a few additional square feet. Now Mr. Calhoun stood in that space looking terribly self-conscious. "For the next half hour we're gonna have, uh, Elaine . . . what'd I say? Elaine? Eloise! Eloise Kramer. She goes by the name Hobett 'cause she's a girl hobo, and, uh . . . okay. Here she is."

He wanted to get out of there in no small way, she could tell. He was clearing the floor, face set resolutely toward the safe zone behind the counter.

He'd forgotten. Burt the Tennis Ball was right in his hand and he was walking off.

Great start. *Wonder if he's going to count this one against me?*

She waved at him and he finally saw her. Unhappily, he turned around, went back to the center of the floor, dropped Burt, and cleared out. Now it was just Burt out there, bouncing all by himself with everybody watching.

She leaned forward, eyes on Burt, touching him without touching him from back in the corner. *Come on, Burt. Come on . . .*

His bounce had been decaying, but now, somehow, it gained energy and he kept bouncing, right there in that one spot, up and down, up and down, just as high every time. The people were catching on, starting to giggle to each other. Some of the guys at a front-row table were starting to bend down and search from side to side for wires, strings, the gimmick.

Okay. We have 'em, for now. Got to time this right. Okay . . . now!

She high-stepped out, moving past tables, bodies, faces, and started clapping her hands in time to Burt's bounce. With some whimsical, clownlike persuasion she got the folks clapping along. It would have been so much better with music but there wasn't time to set that up and Mr. Calhoun was at the limits of his niceness anyway.

Get going, get going.

She'd rehearsed this dance with Burt so many times. As she swooped in and let him roll up one arm and down the other, from left to right hand and around again, then let him bounce and weave through her legs in sync with her dancing, she went on pure faith that each move would pop up in her memory when she needed it, and at every crisis moment there it was: *Kick Burt off your heel, catch him in your hat, swing your hat over your head and dump Burt out, let him bounce on top of your head, bounce from head to kicked heel and back again, elbow to elbow, keep those legs shuffling, weave, baby, weave, let him bounce straight up and down from the floor, do your circle dance around him while you get his buddy, Baxter, from your pocket.*

Now the hard part. She got this to work a few times back at the halfway house, enough to take the chance here. She kept her eyes on Burt, her head nodding to follow his bounce, then held Baxter at just the right height for Burt to contact him at the top of his bounce. Bump! Baxter bounced upward, Burt bounced downward, Burt bounced off the floor at the same moment Baxter fell back from his bounce, they met halfway: bump! Now they were bouncing in a perfect column, Burt off the floor, Baxter off Burt, bump, bump, bump!

She had the crowd. They were in that zone where they didn't laugh or applaud, they gasped, marveled, bent, and craned, trying to figure out how in the world . . . !

For this one moment when Burt and Baxter were doing most of the work, she could look at the faces. The college guys were back and had brought girls. Mia was there, along with Rhea, Darci, and the Durhams. They were marveling, too, but so happy, so proud.

Enough of bouncing Burt and Baxter. She plucked Baxter from the air, then Burt, then struck a pose, a ball in each hand. Now the applause came, wild and excited.

Time for the spinning quarters. Megan brought out a small round table, and Eloise went to work, materializing two quarters between her spread fingers and giving them a spin on the table. The quarters danced together, spinning around the table like a pair of figure skaters. It looked great, but . . .

Ehhh . . . only the closest tables could really appreciate the trick. The people seated farther back were having to stand, crane, try to see what was going on.

Bummer! Too small. The energy from the crowd was sinking like a bad air mattress. She was going to die up there.

This better be good.

Come on, come on, spread it out. Make it big. She got amid the tables, reached behind a lady's ear, and brought back a quarter—she rolled her eyes a little: *Riiight, as if you've never seen that one before.* She set the quarter on the lady's table, flicked it to get it spinning, then let it spin onto her fingertip and held it up for all to see.

Ah, they were amazed again.

Keep it close, right before their eyes. . . .

She went to the other side of the room and picked out a cute, buzz-cut ten-year-old. With clownish gestures she had him hold out both hands palm up, then place one hand atop the other, palm to palm. She mimed, *Now lift your top hand away!* He lifted his top hand away, and there was a quarter in his other hand. She got it spinning, perched it on the end of his finger, and now he was feeling great, a magician himself.

She pointed to the shirt pocket of one of the college guys. He checked, and there was a quarter. She perched it spinning on his fingertip, and he and his buddy immediately began studying it inches from their noses. They passed their hands around it, feeling for wires or strings; the buddy got out a pocketknife and held it close to feel for magnetism. Nothing there. They looked at her and she just shrugged a showy shrug: *Beats me.*

A fourth quarter came from the shoe of an older lady three tables back. The lady had long fingernails, but the quarter managed to stay on the end of one without slipping off. Now those folks back there had something to watch.

She pulled a quarter from her nose and milked the gag, wiping it on her coat sleeve and trying to get it to quit hanging and dragging from her fingers by an invisible "string." Everybody was laughing so hard it made *her* crack up. Finally she got it spinning on a table. One of the college girls sitting there was brave enough, and Eloise passed the spinning quarter to her upraised index finger. That got a response; the girl held her hand high to show everyone. She and her friends were totally enchanted.

Following Eloise's lead, they all held their spinning quarters high like the Statue of Liberty and then gave them a little uptoss and caught them in their hands.

The tip can. Good idea.

She grabbed her can labeled TIPS from the counter and passed it around to collect the quarters, blowing kisses as everyone applauded. Hopefully they'd get the hint for later.

Okay, these nice folks were still hers.

She brought out the deck of cards—and her heart sank. She'd learned a lesson from the quarters routine, which was a heck of a time to learn it: the card tricks, like the quarter routine, would have worked fine for one table, just a few people at a time, but what about all the other folks in the room? Boy, they didn't call it close-up magic for nothing.

She smiled, fiddled with the cards, fanned them, shuffled them. . . .

She did a waterfall, cascading the cards from one hand to the other, then switched hands and did it the other way.

She kept raising her feeder hand higher so the cards would drop farther to her other hand. It was getting *very* sporty.

The folks were still watching, still with her but only because they were expecting something.

She held her hands higher and waterfalled the cards in front of her eyes, one hand to the other, that hand to the other, over and over, her hands wider apart each time.

Could she do it? Would the cards do it?

Even though the cards had to be a blur to everyone else, as they flew past her nose she could see each card in perfect detail. She could touch the card's edges without touching them, sense its weight, feel the air swirling around it, hear the little slap as it landed on its fellows in her lower hand. Was all this just part of being crazy? She had no time to think about it. The folks were waiting and she needed something.

She held her hands close together, palms up, deck of cards in her right hand. Eyes locked on the cards, she flexed the deck, building the tension.

She let them riffle loose, they sprang into the air in a stream and flew in a little arc to her other hand. *Fffffflipppp!* And that quick, it was over.

She made them arc again, from left to right, right to left, left to right, back and forth, then started spreading her hands, widening the arc. When her hands were two feet apart she started getting gasps and oohs from her audience.

She extended her hands out past her shoulders, and the cards sailed higher in a fluttering arc. Her eyes, her mind, every nerve ending in her body were locked on the cards, feeling, knowing, energizing. *Flipflipflipflipflip* the cards riffled out of one hand; *plaplaplaplaplaplap* they landed in the other.

When her arms were spread wide and the cards were soaring through an arc high above her head, over and back, over and back, she held the pose and the ta-da moment came. The audience applauded, cheered, whistled. They loved it.

She riffled off the last card, it sailed through the air after its fellows like the caboose on a train and landed in her other hand—plap! Her fingers, quivering a little, wrapped tightly around the deck as she wilted with relief. She made it clowny, but she wasn't kidding.

While the folks were still shaking their heads, cheering and clapping, she caught a quick glimpse of Mr. Calhoun. He wasn't smiling, but only because he was too dumbfounded.

She was trembling, but it wasn't nervousness as much as raw adrenaline coursing through her, the power, the energy, the pure *psych* of being in this place in this moment, and now she wanted more.

The coin toss routine was next, mixed in with some cool surprises. *Just remember, Eloise, reach out, make it big, draw them in.*

She produced a quarter and zeroed in on a grandfatherly-looking gentleman at a front row table. . . .

She sat on her bed in her room at the Durhams', dazed with exhaustion, too excited to sleep. It was going on ten o'clock. She was still in her Hobett outfit, her hair was matted from sweating under her hat, she hadn't even washed off the whiskers, and now many of the little black dots were smeared.

She'd emptied the contents of her tip jar on the bed and counted out the money: $312.75. Now *she* was the astonished one. *Of course,* she told herself more than once, *you won't do this well every night.*

But making $312.75 in a half hour was quite affirming, to say the least, and she couldn't stop replaying the evening in her head.

She could have kept going, but wrapped up her show right around 7:28 P.M. with a big finish and a final bow. Having nowhere to go to get "offstage," she let Hobett talk in a goofy, bummish voice she borrowed from Red Skelton—one of her favorite TV shows only weeks ago—and visited with people. They loved her show, loved her, shook her hand, raved up one side and down the other, and—happy, happy, happy—they dumped tips into her tip jar hand after hand, the coins clinking, the bills . . . well, all that quiet was nice to *watch* for sure.

"Do you do birthday parties?" a mom asked.

Was the pope Catholic? "Sure!"

They found an available date—for Eloise that was easy enough.

"Oh, and what do you charge?"

She scrambled around her brain for a figure and blurted out, "Fifty dollars."

Sold. It was a date.

And then she thought—what was she going to do for a bunch of little kids? And how was she going to get there? She didn't have a car or even a driver's license.

Roger—he said she could call him that—finally got a few minutes with her after most of her public had gone out the door. "That was good," he said. "Gooder—better than good." He was still a little dazed and having to adjust. "What are you doing next weekend?"

He offered her half an hour on Saturday and half an hour on Sunday. She took it.

And she could walk to McCaffee's. It only took about twenty minutes from the halfway house.

Mia, Darci, Rhea, Micah, and Sally gathered around her at the house and had a little celebration with apple juice and Oreo cookies. They were all blown away and just couldn't believe what they'd seen, and all of them voiced the same sentiment: Eloise Kramer would not be a "hobo" for long.

Of course, the question came up as it always did, and probably should if she was doing things well: "How did you do that?" And she just shrugged teasingly and said it was a trick.

And now, sitting by herself in her room and thanking God for a great evening, she faced that question once again: *How* did *I do that?*

chapter

15

SATURDAY AND SUNDAY NIGHT
October 16 & 17
7–7:30 P.M.
Enjoy the incredible
ELOISE "The Hobett" KRAMER
Magician Extraordinaire
Astounding.
Astoundingly Funny.
Bring the Family.
You won't believe your eyes!

Now the poster was larger, done with poster paints, featured a digitally printed, taped-on, color photo of Hobett doing the Rainbow Bridge—her name for her new card routine—*and* it appeared in the front window on Monday. Roger was becoming a believer and Eloise was becoming a performer, which turned out to be good news and, well, challenging news.

Okay, great, I get to perform, but . . . what? I need new stuff!

With the kind and loving indulgence of Mia at the thrift store and Sally Durham's offer to drive her until she could get a license, she went to work full-time on new material, anything she could think of, starting with what in the world to do for a kid's birthday party.

There were twelve kids, ages six to eight, sitting all over that living room as if they'd been thrown in there, party hats on their heads, cake crumbs and ice cream on their faces, laughing like adults breathing helium.

The spinning quarters worked great because they were so magical and the room was small. Burt and Baxter not only bounced among the kids, driving them wild as the kids tried to grab them, they also sat on a little table up front through the rest of Eloise's act, upstaging her at key moments.

Card tricks? Too slow for this bunch. She opted for an old standby, balloons, and made balloon doggies, giraffes, dinosaurs, and anything else she'd learned from books and videos just that week. Of course, a balloon let loose in the room and guided to zip right by the kids' heads—and bonk Eloise right between the eyes—kept things lively, and with just the right kind of attention she could make some of the balloon creatures move.

October 16, at 7:00 P.M., McCaffee's was full and folks must have heard about the spinning quarters; they seemed a whole lot more attentive, even moving in closer to see for themselves what their friends were so gaga about.

October 17, at 7:00 P.M., a whole new set of folks came through the door, which was cool; Eloise could do all the same stuff, which meant she could get better at it.

Of course, every gig led to more gigs, and Sally Durham, a real saint, continued as Eloise's chauffeur, taking her to every one.

Gerry Morris's eleventh-birthday party: these kids, mostly boys, were tougher to please, and the goofier she got the less they bought it, so she eased back on the goofy and played mostly herself. They loved the quarter pulled from her nose—apparently they were into snot and boogers and such. Eloise discovered she could stretch a balloon's neck and make it hum "Happy Birthday." If she'd played it on her armpit that would have gone over just as big. A creative milestone.

Melinda Flowers's ninth birthday was just-us-girls, and Eloise loved it. She ventured boldly into new territory for this one: she reddened her cheeks instead of her nose, left off the whiskers, and came as a semiclownish girl in a fluffy white blouse with a red scarf, black shorts with loud, flowery suspenders, and red-and-white-striped knee highs. It was her first performance working under her own name and her first time working with flowers, making them appear in her hand, in little girls' hands, and best of all, in little girls' hair. Boys wouldn't have cared for that trick, but *every* girl had to get a flower. She could have filled the whole time just doing that.

THIS WEEKEND!!!
FRIDAY, SATURDAY, AND SUNDAY NIGHTS!!!
7:00 P.M.
McCaffee's Proudly Presents
the Incredible
ELOISE KRAMER
Magician Extraordinaire
Astounding.
Astoundingly funny.
Bring the Family.
You won't believe your eyes!

Wow, check out the poster printed by a computer graphics geek whom Roger knew, with a full-color studio photo of Eloise striking a pose and tipping her hat!

At seven, and not from seven to seven-thirty? Well, Roger had come to the point where McCaffee's was "proudly presenting" her, and the half-hour rule had loosened to a guideline with only one qualifier: "Don't wear 'em out."

No dates? Roger was assuming, not really saying up front, just kind of hinting that she'd be doing her show at McCaffee's every weekend, you know, if it worked out, if she was up to it. You know.

What happened to the "Hobett"? Well, sometimes she was the Hobett, sometimes she wasn't. Sometimes it was funnier to play it mute, sometimes it was better to yak it up a little.

And the exclamation marks!!! To think that Roger actually used them!!! He wasn't that excitable a guy!!!

Friday night the place was packed. Saturday night Roger had to ask people to come back for a second show, at eight-thirty. Sunday night, a family reunion filled the place at seven and Eloise had to do a second show again. By the end of the weekend she was exhausted . . .

To the tune of $1,785.25.

Jacquie Palmer's sixteenth birthday was like a whole new thing and like, Eloise was like, *Hey, I'm like almost on the same level* and she wore like, regular clothes instead of doing the hobo and some of her accessories were like, from the mall and not the thrift store.

Oh, and now she was charging like $100 and it was like the moms and dads didn't even mind.

Far out.

She did her seven-o'clock show at McCaffee's on October 30, then dashed up the street to do the Elks' Halloween Bash—now, that *had* to be delusional—but the $1,000 check was real enough.

Halloween Night at McCaffee's? Roger tried to wring every possible use out of the holiday, decorating the place and dressing up like . . . well, a chef all in white with a big paste-on mustache, a pillow on his stomach, and an arrow through his head. Whatever. Abby dressed up like Julia Child but nobody got it. Megan and Myron dressed up like each other. The place was filled with all sorts of weird-looking people. Eloise didn't go in for spooks or sorcerers; she just kept it fun, from this planet.

Her costume? She went as a girl from the 1970s.

Monday morning, November 1, Dane took the silver urn from the mantel, held it to his chest, and faced the living room, taking a special second look at every detail.

"I put the love seat upstairs, but apart from that, everything fit just right, even Mom's old pump organ. I might change the rugs," he said quietly, intimately, as if talking near someone's ear.

He went into the kitchen and stood quietly, his gaze passing over the counters, the cupboards, the sink, every feature. "Everything from the other house is here. The cookware's in that lazy Susan and the cereal's in that corner, just like in the other house. See that? There's your coffee machine. It just brewed its twenty-five-thousandth cup of coffee, can you believe it? And there's the marble countertop, just like you always wanted."

He walked through the breakfast nook, spending a moment commenting on the view of the barn and the leaf-strewn hillside rolling gently down to McBride's Pond, where willows, now mostly bare, were emerging from the lifting fog, their reflections mirror-smooth in the water.

The bedroom was a lovely place, decorated as Mandy would have had it, and he'd been diligent to make the bed every morning. Their wedding photo was on the dresser in its usual place. His favorite picture of her, taken just two years ago, was on the nightstand.

Mandy's clothes were where she would have had them. Her blouses were arranged in the closet by color, her dresses by occasion, her shoes in neat rows on two shelves. He'd set apart one end of the closet for her costumes, each one an icon of a memory: this pink dance outfit was from their three-week stint in the Philippines, this blue gown from their time in London, and this black formal for the award ceremony at the Magic Castle in Hollywood.

All the drawers and compartments of her jewelry case were unchanged, and every piece of jewelry in its place: he bought her this necklace for their thirty-fifth anniversary, this ring to replace the one she lost when they were working the cruise ship. She used to keep an anklet with silver doves on it in this little drawer.

He sat in a wing chair near the windows, one of the matched pair they picked out at least eighteen years ago. "Anyway, that's the house. It's where I'm staying for now, and I notice it doesn't bring me any more joy than that little apartment we had in Van Nuys, and it's easy enough to figure. You were the joy, Mandy. No matter where we were living, you were the joy. I'll always remember that."

He went downstairs, put on a jacket from the entry closet, and took the urn outside.

The valley was heading into winter. Frost had withered the flowers, blackened the fallen leaves, and now lay thick and crusty in the hollows and dark places. The lawn crunched under his feet.

He followed the trail past the barn and into the field that encircled the pond. It was a quiet, restful place he'd already visited many times, and Shirley had told him about the wildflowers that grew here in the spring and how tall the grass could grow. There would be no people traffic here. Shirley wouldn't be running over it with the riding mower or tilling it to plant beans. Only the passing seasons would touch it.

He looked up toward the house. "You see that? I can see down here from my study. I can watch the seasons go by like we used to do, and thank God that we shared so many. And every time the wildflowers come up . . . well, I guess they'll be yours, won't they?"

He uncapped the urn and released the ashes to the breeze. They drifted like mist over the field, spreading, thinning, reaching far away. He stood and watched until the last trace had come to rest.

In a five-second ceremony, Eloise took her hobo hat from her head and hung it on a coat hook next to the front door. Perfect. Symbolic. She now had a place to hang her hat.

The apartment was unfurnished but as cute as she could ask for and—*right on!*—within walking distance of McCaffee's. Sarah Middleton's husband, Roy, built it over their garage, his mother stayed there until her death, it housed Sarah's art projects and Roy's junk until Roy's death two years ago, and then, to generate extra income, it became a clean apartment again and Sarah needed a tenant. Mia knew Sarah, connected Sarah with Eloise, and right about that time Eloise had the money to rent the place.

It had to be a God thing.

There was no table to eat from, no chair to sit on, and only an air mattress and some blankets to sleep on. There was no television or radio, but they could surely wait; she had to get a telephone first thing, with a number she could give out for people to call, *with* an answering machine. She had two cardboard boxes for her foldable clothes, but there was a closet and the thrift store provided hangers for Eloise's growing wardrobe, mostly this-and-that, mix-and-match items she used for costumes. Eloise arranged her shirts and blouses by color, her costumes by venue, and her shoes—a pair of tennis shoes, a pair of sandals, a pair of cloddy boots, and one pair of black loafers—in a neat row.

Friday, November 5, at McCaffee's. Full house, great crowd, lots of coffee, sandwiches, and pastries moving.

Eloise dug out a deck of cards and approached a young lady seated at a table. "Hi there! What's your name?"

"Pamela," said the young lady. She looked like a professional. Probably sold real estate or annuities. She had her husband and two teenagers with her.

"Want to hold these for me?" Eloise placed the deck of cards in her hand facedown, gently closed Pamela's fingers against the sides of the deck, then circled around behind her so everyone could see. "Hold 'em still now. Here we go."

Standing behind Pamela and looking over her shoulder, Eloise pointed with one finger at the deck. "Now help me out. Let the cards go where they want to go." She slowly pulled with her finger, as if an invisible thread ran from her finger to the top card. The card tilted upward toward the rear of the deck and then, once vertical, tucked itself between the back edge of the deck and the heel of Pamela's hand, sticking up like a wall.

"Just hold it there with your pinkie," Eloise said, helping her out a little.

Great move. Everybody loved it and every eye was watching.

Eloise pulled with her finger again, and the next card tilted up toward the left and tucked itself against the left side. Eloise pulled invisibly, the third card lifted toward the right, and this time she waved her hand between her finger and the card. No wires, no strings. Three little walls now.

Last card. Eloise pulled, the card lifted toward the front and tucked itself against the front edge of the deck. Now the cards formed a little box open at the top. Eloise planted her hand over the top. "So, what do we do now? Got any magic words?"

Pamela's eyes rolled toward the ceiling as she searched for one. "Ummmmm . . ."

"That's good, that's good! Everybody say, 'Ummmmm . . .'"

The whole crowd said a dumb-sounding "Ummmmm . . ."

Eloise lifted her hand away.

Pamela looked into the box and did a wide-eyed double take. "No. Way!" She reached into the box and withdrew her driver's license. The real thing, with her picture on it.

Pamela dug out her wallet and was stunned all over again to find that the little slot for her license was empty. She held up her wallet for everyone to see.

"Well, let's see if we can put it back," said Eloise.

Pamela dropped her driver's license back into the box made from cards, Eloise covered it with her hand and told everybody, "We have to do this whole thing in reverse, right? Everybody say 'Mmm-mmuh . . .'"

Everybody, including Pamela, said "Ummmmm" backward between laughs.

Eloise lifted her hand away . . . and there was a silver dollar. Aha! Eloise's eyes shot over at Larry, a middle-aged man who'd already won two silver dollars from her in a coin toss routine. She craftily twitched her eyebrows.

Larry beckoned. "Bring it on."

"What about my license?" Pamela asked.

"Is it in your wallet?" said Eloise.

While Eloise crossed the room to go eye-to-eye with Larry, Pamela opened her wallet again and there, intact and in its rightful place, was her driver's license.

Eloise was ready before the applause died down. She had Larry flip the coin and slap it onto the back of his other hand. She appealed to the crowd, "Okay, *you* call it this time!"

"Heads!" called half the crowd.

"Tails!" called the other half.

She rolled her eyes. "They want it both ways!"

She nodded to Larry, who uncovered the coin on his hand—it was now *two* silver dollars, one tails and one heads.

The house went nuts. Larry was about to give the dollars up, but Eloise wagged her head sadly. "They said heads and tails. These are tails and heads. Nuts!"

As Eloise overplayed some frustration, Larry dropped the two new silver dollars into an empty coffee cup. Now he had four.

She searched her pockets. "Burt? Anybody seen Burt?"

She looked at Larry and his group, then at the coffee cup on the table in front of them. They looked in the coffee cup.

There was Burt smiling up at them. Larry tilted the cup and let Burt roll into his hand while . . .

. . . Eloise found four silver dollars in her coat pocket and dropped them from hand to hand while everybody marveled and applauded.

"Say . . ." Big pitiful look. "Can I have Burt back?"

Larry was into it, goaded by his friends. "What about my four dollars?"

Eloise deadpanned to the crowd. The whole joke was working. "I'll make it five."

"What?"

"Give me Burt, I'll give you five dollars."

Larry tossed Burt to her. She caught the tennis ball, clapped her hands around it, then opened her hands.

Burt was gone. In her hands was a five-dollar bill. She held it up as the crowd roared and she looked at Larry. "Got change for a five?"

Larry followed her look to the coffee cup and then broke up with amazement and poured out the contents:

Five silver dollars.

They made the trade. Larry came away five dollars richer, and the folks were having the time of their lives.

"Now, what about Burt?" Eloise looked around, dug in her pockets. "Burt? Burt?"

Mark, a college student sitting in plain sight of everyone, noticed his computer case jiggling. Eloise was quick to notice it too and pointed, directing everyone's attention. "Burt!"

Mark reached down, unzipped the case, and out hopped Burt, bouncing back to Eloise, who caught him and held him up for her big finish. That was all, folks. As the whole house rose to their feet, applauding, she doffed her hat, swept it before her in a big bow, tossed Burt into her hat, and put it back on her head.

Megan and Myron passed around the tip cans, and the dollars and coins piled in. Eloise went around the tables greeting, shaking hands, thanking the folks for coming.

"Hi. What's your name?"

"Sandra Connelly. This is my husband, Ted."

"Wonderful to meet you! Hi. What's your name?"

"Mike."

"Julie."

"Christopher."

Eloise shook their hands. "Wonderful to meet you!"

"Fantastic show! Incredible!"

"Hi. What's your name?"

The man handed her a business card that read "J. Arnold Harrington, Theatrical Management," and bore a Las Vegas address, an e-mail address, and phone numbers. "I'm Arnie Harrington. Will you be performing here tomorrow night?"

A hint of thrill brightened her face. "I sure will."

"Okay. I'm crunched for time right now, but maybe we can talk tomorrow. Could we do that?"

And here came that thrill again, right to the surface. She broke into a grin. "Okay! That'd be great!"

She had to move on, shaking hands, saying hello, glancing back as he smiled at her. Megan and Myron were still moving around the room accumulating tips, mostly in bills.

Arnie watched Eloise Kramer moving through the crowd and shook his head, whistling in wonder. "Dane has to see this."

chapter

16

Corporal James Dose was serving well in Afghanistan and was a little disappointed to learn that his tour of duty overseas had been cut short for minor medical reasons. Before he knew it he was Stateside, finishing out his army hitch at Fort Lewis, Washington, not far from his family in Tacoma. Given all this, it was time to get the family together for dinner and announce his engagement to Jennifer Long, a gal he'd been courting since high school. They gathered at the Quay, their favorite steak house on the shore of Puget Sound, and James had the ring in his pocket.

The dinner would end abruptly. He would never get a chance to toast the occasion.

Dane took one look at the poster in McCaffee's front window and stopped dead in his tracks.

Arnie was clearly disgruntled to have to look back. "What?"

Dane's eyes moved across the girl's face. The Gypsy had become a clownish hobo, but those eyes and that smile were unmistakable. "I've met this girl."

Arnie looked in through the window and could see the place filling up. More folks were coming from up and down the street even now. "Can we talk about it inside?"

Eloise Kramer. How could it possibly be?

"Dane! We've got to get in there if we want a table."

He turned from the poster and followed Arnie through the door into McCaffee's, a quaint cubbyhole of clamor now filling with a hodgepodge of people, all ages, urban to organic, having thirty different conversations as they crowded the tables and lined up at the order counter. Posters of Scarlett and Rhett, Bergman and Bogey, Cagney, DiCaprio, Buddy Holly, and Elvis decorated the sand- and rust-painted walls; ceiling fans spun lazily over their heads; drink, dessert, and sandwich menus shouted in loud, colored chalk from a blackboard behind the counter; coffee machines ground, tamped, spewed brew, and spit steam; servers were scurrying, and everywhere, in every direction, were cups of coffee, cups of coffee, cups of coffee.

Arnie found a table near the front window and tossed his hat on the table to stake a claim on it. Dane removed his coat and draped it over his chair, then stood a moment to size up the room. The open floor where the magician would be doing her act was several tables distant. He and Arnie would be watching over and through bodies and heads. And the noise in this place! If Eloise Kramer could sell her stuff in here, her whole approach to performance had to have changed drastically.

Arnie draped his coat over his chair and sat. He patted the table. "C'mon, sit down, sit down."

Dane sat in his chair, elbows on the table, hands clasped under his nose, still looking around the place.

Arnie leaned in, trying to be heard above the ruckus. "You wanted a fresh start, right? That's what you told me. You're thinking about producing, promoting new talent, maybe putting a show together yourself."

"And so?"

"So that's what we're doing tonight. You're out of that house for a change. You're circulating, you're living, you're scoping out new possibilities. Are you listening?"

"Arnie, she's a street magician. She was busking out on the sidewalk illegally, freezing her buns off and fumbling. . . . I had to show her the right way to do a Bentley count."

He looked at Dane crookedly. "Are you sure you have the right girl?"

There were things Dane could say: "Well, if I do, things have really changed."

And there were thoughts he wouldn't share with anybody: *She's just a young girl minding her own business, it's not her fault, I don't even know her, I've been off my medication for more than a month now so hopefully she won't bother me, and I have to remember—remember!—that I'm an emotional train wreck.*

Eloise Kramer? Where'd she get that name?

Arnie was talking. Dane caught the tail end: "... I like what I saw and I'm not saying she's the best thing since sliced bread. I'm just saying you might find her interesting. She might spark some ideas, that's all."

Dane found himself nodding in agreement and made it a point to relax. Why not enjoy the evening, have some fun? He scanned the big chalkboard. "So let's get some coffee."

Seven o'clock. The lights blinked and the restaurant clamor quieted to murmured phrases, the distinguishable tinkling of spoons, the occasional creak of a wooden chair. Dane and Arnie craned like everyone else, watching that center floor, scanning around the room, wondering where the magician would make her entrance. In the lull, the girl named Megan made one final dash across the floor to bring someone their order just as the guy named Myron, having served a table, was heading back. They passed each other in the center of the floor, Megan obscuring Myron from view on one side, Myron obscuring Megan from view on the other, for an instant. When they continued on, reopening a gap between them, music started, jazzy and rhythmic, and . . .

There was the Hobett, spinning into place, then moving to the music, worn old hat on her head, hands in the pockets of her oversize, trampish coat, and a teasing, mischievous look on her face. She danced lithely into a bow to half of the house, then the other half, sweeping her hat in front of her.

It was a great opening, something Dane wasn't expecting. He shot a quick glance at Arnie, who raised an eyebrow back at him.

The magician produced a bright yellow tennis ball from her empty hand, got it bouncing, and jazz-danced with it in a dazzling display of technical polish and energy, legs, arms, and coattails flying as the ball, seemingly with a mind and energy of its own, bounced, veered, rolled, and rebounded along with her. Every eye in the place was glued on her, incredulous.

Invisible thread, Dane thought, though how she managed to avoid tangles and breakage with all that movement was uncanny. She must have perfected a way to attach and reattach, or maybe she had a spring-loaded reel under her coat. Or maybe there was more than one ball and she was vanishing one while producing another to direct the bouncing. A gyro? A system of magnets? This routine had to have taken months to perfect.

This couldn't be the Gypsy.

The dance number ended as she caught the tennis ball in her hat, plopped the hat back on her head, and froze in a closing ta-da! position, all in one smooth move.

Dane broke into applause along with everyone else. He could feel Arnie looking at him, rubbing it in with his silence.

She went into flourishes with silver dollars and cards, producing, vanishing, transferring, yakking it up with the audience, and making instant friends with her charm. When she did the Rainbow Bridge with the cards, Dane held his breath with everyone else. He'd seen that kind of energy produced with cards, but never that degree of control.

Then Megan, working behind the counter, held up a coffee cup.

"Oh, what's that?" the magician asked Megan.

Megan replied, "Venti triple-shot Caffè Americano."

Hobett stared blankly. "Huh?"

"Coffee."

"Oh, whose is it?" A man in the corner raised his hand.

"Oh, far out!"

Far out?

"Hi, you've been here before, haven't you? What's your name?"

"Clarence."

"Boy, you like drinks with long names, dontcha? Tell you what, lemme send it to ya. Just stand right there." She pointed toward the end of the counter. The folks were snickering already. She grinned mischievously. "I wouldn't do *that*!"

Clarence weaved through the tables and stood at one end of the counter. Eloise Kramer stood at the other end and set the twenty-ounce cup on the counter. She extended her palms toward it, waving a bit, a magician's gesture. "Okay, now everybody tell it to move. Say 'Mooove!'"

The whole crowd called out *"Mooove!"* They sounded like a herd of cows.

The cup began to slide along the counter, slowly at first.

"Say 'Mooove!'"

"Mooove!"

"Oh-oh."

Too fast. That cup was sure to fly right off the end of the counter. Clarence ducked aside.

"Stop!" the magician pleaded.

It lurched to a halt right in front of Clarence.

Magnet under the counter, Dane thought. *Megan or Myron or some other stooge was making that cup move from below. Now we'll see how she palms the magnet under the cup.*

The magician was moving along the counter but didn't get to the cup before Clarence picked it up and one big unified gasp filled the room.

The cup came up empty in his hand. The twenty ounces of triple-shot Caffè Americano remained on the counter, the hot brown liquid suspended in the shape of the cup.

"Oops, sorry!"

Bowing in apology, looking sheepish, playing it for astounded laughs, the girl took the empty cup from Clarence's hand and carefully aligned it around the coffee again. She lifted the cup from the counter intact, the coffee contained inside, and handed it to Clarence as the house went nuts. Fantastic illusion, and Dane was so captivated by the stand-alone coffee he forgot to watch for her palming the magnet.

Clarence hardly smiled at all as he walked back to his table. Kind of a rough-looking character anyway. His face was deep-featured and pockmarked, as if he'd just taken a nap on a bed of pea gravel.

Then she started spinning quarters and perching them on spectators' fingertips, and Arnie leaned in and said only, "Heh?" and Dane had to lean back and say, "I haven't a clue."

And with that admission, she had him. The skeptic in Dane had fallen away and now he was watching her with different eyes, almost laughing at himself. Forty years in the business, working with the best, designing and performing hundreds of illusions, and here he was, of all people, caught up in the magic.

And for another surprise, even though the illusions were uncanny, the thing he liked most was this magician's performance. She *was* the magic, playfully immersed in everything that happened. When she kept losing the toss of the coin he could read the mischief in her face. When she produced the driver's license in the box made of cards, the enchantment in her eyes drew his attention away from the cards and her right hand—had she flashed a sleight or botched a pass he wouldn't have noticed and he wouldn't have cared. Her eyes were playful, then teasing, then full of wonder like a child holding a butterfly. . . .

And then it struck him. That was it: wonder. This young girl was as fascinated and awestruck by her magic as her audience, and her wonder was infectious, so infectious that . . .

Well. She *was* a magician. She'd gotten around his guard, slipped by his critical eye, and taken hold of his heart. He not only appreciated her skill, he also was rooting for her, longing for her to do well. *Come on, kid, pull it off, don't blow it. Win the crowd! Love what you're doing and they'll love you. Don't lose the wonder.*

His stomach tightened. *Don't lose the wonder.* Mandy always said that. "Hey, great illusion, but where's the wonder?" "Don't scare them, make them wonder." "Hey kids, I bet you've never seen anything like this before!" "Wow, it feels like something God would have done."

Mandy's love of wonder was a treasure sequestered in his heart and memory until at this moment, in this girl, he could see, feel, live it again.

And oh, how he missed it.

His eyes grew wet, his vision blurred. *Oh, brother,* he hadn't planned on this. He blinked and wiped his eyes. *Be professional, Dane!* He cleared his mind, put on his best objective face, tried to kid himself and everybody else.

And then she looked at him.

. . . keep a clear mind . . . objective . . .

And the moment halted right there.

"Oh, dear God . . ."

Where was that guard he thought he dropped? She got around it the first time and now there was no guard at all to protect him. He couldn't look away even as he fled to safe thoughts: *She's just making eye contact, working the crowd, she doesn't really know me.*

But the showbiz went out of her eyes for that tiny instant and it was *her* looking, the girl who *used* to be the Gypsy. . . .

And then she smiled a smile he didn't just recognize but knew from somewhere else, before this place.

She has no idea, he reminded himself. *It's not her fault. She's just a sweet kid doing her act, making a living. It's my problem, I'll work it out.*

He thought he should smile back but his emotions were so mixed up he couldn't get a smile together.

Too late. The showbiz returned to her eyes and she stumbled back on track, looking at others. "Well, so now . . . did I give you your five?"

Dane wilted a little and let go a breath. He felt he'd just been released from a choke hold.

Eloise was stumbling inside and trying not to show it.

It's the guy! That man I met on the street! He's here with that Mr. Harrington, so he must be a pro. Well, sure he is. The stuff he showed me, how he knew everything . . . just like Daddy.

Just like Daddy.

She could just look at everybody else, but she couldn't *just look* at him without getting stuck there, pulled through a window to . . . somewhere she'd been.

Focus, girl, focus! What's next?

He's not smiling and I know he can smile. He doesn't like my act.

Oh, bummer, where am I? I changed the five for the silvers. Oh! I still have to get Burt back.

She patted her pockets, looking perplexed. "Burt? Where are you, buddy?"

She'd planted Burt's double in Winifred the college prof's handbag. She reached with the part of her that nobody, not even she, could see, and found him in the bag with Winifred's cell phone, makeup, car keys, checkbook, grocery list, and a paperback edition of *The Grapes of Wrath*. She tugged, he jumped, the bag wiggled, everybody freaked, and she got Burt back with a nice flourish and a great ta-da!

She had 'em back! Great applause. Final bow . . .

But he still wasn't smiling! He was staring!

Oh, man. Encore? What? Her mind was an empty box, and she was groping around in it. They were applauding, but it wouldn't last forever.

Now or never, kid!

Well, what can I do that's going to impress this guy?

One more thing. Maybe.

Ohhhh, doom. Certain doom and destruction. Don't do it.

She looked in his direction—*oh, let's try not to be so obvious! What's he staring at? What, I've got a horn growing out of my head?*

The applause died, and she was still standing there. They were waiting, ready for magical dessert. A little girl stood on her chair, eyes hungry, hands ready to clap again should Eloise do *anything*.

Uhhh . . . well . . .

Without a word, she stepped to the center of the floor, *feeling* her way into her final stunt. All this stuff was so much a matter of *feeling*, working her way deep into her crazy world, stepping off little cliffs and learning new rules every day. She'd been working on this stunt in her apartment. Sometimes she could get it to work, and sometimes she couldn't. Whatever she'd tried there, she'd have to repeat here in front of all these people.

Which could be a big mistake. Maybe.

The tension in the place could have powered the lights. She slipped out of her shoes and set them aside. People were leaning forward. A child spoke, and her mother shushed her. Eloise stood with her feet together, arms outstretched. She met the eyes of the people seated all around her, and then looked one more time at the guy.

He was not just watching her. He was *really* watching, and his gaze came through that window to somewhere she'd been.

And Daddy was there.

Oh, dear Lord, don't let me flop.

She closed her eyes to shut everything out. With hands she didn't have and with senses outside herself, she groped for what she'd come to know as folds and ripples in space, and it came easily this time. She could feel them like veins of thickness in water, moving and shifting like the Northern Lights, here, then there, close, far, thin, wide, sharp, shallow, but always within reach. With hands that were not here in the room, she grabbed hold. She was connected, in sync. She should be okay.

She opened her eyes. She'd made it. Everybody was still watching, sitting in the same room, and she was still in the center of the floor, with one key difference: she was also somewhere else. That was as near as she could explain it.

Come on, girl. Do well. Don't look at me, look at them. Focus.

Arnie whispered, "Is she gonna do a levitation?"

Dane could see it coming, but how could she do a levitation with people on all sides? He and Arnie rose to their feet as one, watching her feet, sizing up her pant legs. She'd be doing this without shoes. How?

The room was silent. The serving staff became a tableau behind the counter, Myron with a pitcher in his hand but not pouring, Megan with a towel in her hands but not drying, the owner and his wife transfixed as if watching a moon launch at T minus five seconds.

The magician stood still, waiting, eyes full of wonder as if watching something no one else could see. Her hands were extended as if reaching for something, trying to grab hold.

She's building the tension, Dane thought. *She's driving us all nuts.*

A lady at a front-row table gasped, and on cue everyone leaned forward, craned, stared at the girl's feet. The heels were lifting from the floor millimeter by millimeter, smoothly, with no visible muscle strain or quiver. A full inch. Two inches.

Dane was impressed by how impressed he was. This girl got a gasp just for lifting her heels off the floor. *Come on, girl, pay it off. Finish well.*

Now every eye was on those toes, which was a good clue for Dane to look elsewhere. He searched the ceiling and walls for an apparatus, perhaps a glint of a thread or cable. Nothing.

He returned his attention to the girl's feet.

Another gasp.

"Whoa!"

"Is she off the floor?"

Folks in front were bending way down, marveling at the gap appearing between her feet and the hardwood. Some were leaning right and left, trying to see wires.

She was off the floor by two or three inches, still rising, and seemed as astonished as anyone, her eyes wide, her whole face sparkling like that of a child just learning to ride a bike. She squealed with nervousness, with delight—a sound Dane could have recognized across a huge room full of partying people.

Ten inches. A foot. Two feet. She bent her knees, pulled her feet up, and hovered there, laughing and hooting along with the crowd, as amazed as they were. About three feet above the floor she began to rotate, eyes passing over the crowd as they cheered and she waved at them. It was becoming a real party.

"She didn't do this yesterday," said Arnie, eyes locked on her.

"Maybe she's never done it," said Dane.

I can't believe this! I'm doing it! I'm really doing it! I'm crazy! "Hi, down there!"

She waved and hollered at them and they waved and hollered back. As easily as climbing a step she rose higher, then kicked her feet and did a somersault. The audience wasn't having half the fun she was. Such an incredible sensation, like moving through some kind of *stuff* that held her up while she, and herself, and lots of other Eloises pressed and pushed and bore her weight from . . . well, from somewhere *outside. Toe-Tall-Lee Freaky!*

Was somebody smoking in here? She could smell something burning.

From somewhere came the crash of shattering dishes and she heard people screaming. It stole her attention. She looked and nearly lost hold, wobbling in midair like a beginner on skates, dropping several inches until she grabbed hold again. *Concentrate! Stay with it!*

Corporal James Dose was standing, raising a glass of wine for a toast when his shoulder exploded, spattering blood on the restaurant table, his father, his mother, and his new fiancée. He lurched forward and fell across the table, scattering dishes, splattering food, smashing the centerpiece. The restaurant erupted in screams and panic. Patrons dropped to the floor and cowered under chairs and tables. Heads spun, waiters scrambled, the hostess got on the phone as she crouched behind her desk. *Where is the shooter?* everyone wondered. *Where is the shooter?*

17

M iss Eloise Kramer, may I present Mr. Dane Collins."
"Hello." She managed to get that much out as they shook
hands and settled into their chairs. Her hands were visibly shaking
and she knew her face was flushed. She'd come in for a soft landing,
but inside she was still flying, her mind like a picture book in a strong
wind, and now she was face-to-face with . . . well, she couldn't explain it, but he was more than just the man sitting at the table across
from her. She couldn't help but stare at him, which had to be okay
because he was sure staring at her.

Well, Dane, you'd better say something. "That was quite a performance."
"Whoa, thank you, thank you!" She looked at her hand. "Whoo!
I'm still shaking!"
From across the room the impression, the illusion, the . . . okay,
the delusion . . . was somewhat deniable. He could attribute it to the
lighting in the room, the distance, perhaps his age, his eyes, the ten-
dency of young girls to sound alike when excited, all the details his
mind could have altered to match the template in his memory. But
close up, right across the table, the sound of her voice, the laughter in
her eyes, the funny expressions . . .
There must have been too long a silence. Arnie piped up, "I
was . . . um . . . I was here yesterday, as you know, and I saw your performance then, and I thought—no, I knew—that Mr. Collins would

be interested in meeting you." Now Arnie looked at him, a clear and forceful cue.

The hobo makeup and outfit gave him room to imagine this girl as the one he first saw at the Spokane fair with long, blond tresses floating in the breeze, the quintessential surfer girl/farmer's daughter/flower child. He could see this girl dressed in that girl's blouse and jeans and, oh, yes, the ankle bracelet with two silver doves worn over her white crew sock. It looked a little goofy on that day, but he loved it about her and forty years later she was wearing it again . . . on the day he lost her.

Arnie was staring at him.

"Umm . . ." He had to clear his throat. "That's an interesting name, uh, Eloise Kramer."

Her eyebrows perked up and her eyes widened into that sweet, innocent look he'd enjoyed every time he saw it. "Really?"

"The, umm, the . . . well, you have a very unique approach."

Weird feeling. Like she'd hit a nice grounder into left field, had rounded first, and this guy, this Dane Collins, was second base. Safe! That's what she'd be if she could only get there. "Thanks for all that great advice."

"Huh? Oh! Yeah, sure thing. It was pretty cold out there."

"Yeah. Sure was. And thanks again for the hat and sweater."

"It was a . . . it was a good meeting we had."

What was it about this guy that was so . . . stable, like a rock in a river? She wanted to come right out and ask him, *Do you know Arthur Whitacre? Have you ever been to the Wooly Acres Ranch? Are you really sitting there or are you just another delusion from a past I never had, or did I really have it? Just what is the connection here?*

The only question she could think of built up inside her and she blurted out, "Who are you, anyway?"

Wild. He didn't seem to know.

"I'm . . ." *Was?* "I'm in . . . I was in . . . show business. I was a professional magician and producer."

Arnie piped up again. "He's on hiatus from the stage now, but thinking he'd like to do some producing, maybe some managing, you know, develop new talent."

Her eyes brightened at that. "Oh! And here you are, talking to me."

"That's right," said Arnie, who looked at Dane again.

Here I am, talking to you.

Dane wanted to talk to her, talk *with* her, stay right there and talk about magic, performance, the heart of it all. They could go on to talk about life with its turns, twists, ups, and downs and laugh at how events could turn in such unbelievable ways. Her eyes would sparkle the way he'd grown to love, her smile would shatter his fears and self-doubts, her voice . . . well, he'd be able to hear it again. He'd sit here all night just for that.

Oh, brother. He broke his gaze and let his eyes sink to the table, his brow resting on his interlaced fingers. *Dane, you are one sick individual.*

He looked up. She was hanging on the edge, hungry for his next utterance. "But . . . I'm sorry."

She looked at him blankly. So did Arnie.

"I . . . I think you have a real talent and you'll go a long way, but I . . . I just can't participate in your career. Keep going, kid, you're going to do great." He rose, grabbed his coat.

Oh, the tragedy in her eyes! The letdown! He couldn't look at her.

Arnie was aghast. He was showing it with everything he had.

"We have to go," Dane told him, and didn't wait for an answer. He just headed for the door.

Arnie wanted to talk, of course, but Dane just kept walking, getting some city blocks between them and that girl.

"I absolutely cannot believe what I just saw back there! That, that was the most astounding talent, the best fertile soil for development, the best business opportunity you could have asked for. Dane, stop and talk to me!"

They were almost to the car. He felt safe enough, so he stopped. "Eloise Kramer."

Arnie just stared at him. "What?"

"Eloise was Mandy's middle name, remember? She was named after her mother, Eloise, and Kramer was her mother's maiden name.

She's named herself after her mother, or Mandy's mother, or, or something!"

Arnie's jaw dropped, his hands raised. He was at a total loss. "Are you nuts?"

Dane started walking again. "Yeah, yeah, I think I am." He stopped walking and went nose-to-nose with his manager. "You didn't see that back there?"

"See what?"

He looked at Arnie just long enough to know he was going to get nowhere and kept walking. "No, I suppose not."

Arnie stayed right on his heels, then alongside, pushing himself, almost loping to keep up. "Hey, come on, cut me some slack here."

Dane halted and got in Arnie's face again. "You saw it! You saw who she looks like."

Arnie must have understood. He grimaced as he looked away, searching the dark night for a glimmer of sanity in this nutty world.

"Yeah, deny it."

Dane tried to keep walking, but Arnie headed him off. "All right, all right. I saw . . . I saw a kind of resemblance, sure. But is that the girl's fault? Is it?"

"Who's blaming *her*?"

Arnie looked up and down the street for his next thought. He found it. "All right, listen, you've suffered a great loss. I understand, I respect that, I feel for you. But I'm not responsible for who you think the girl looks like or how you feel about it—and let me tell you something, neither is she! No matter how you try to justify it, that was rude back there! It was thoughtless and it was mean and that poor girl did *not* deserve one bit of it. What does she know about your grief? Why make her suffer for it? She worked hard, she put it all on the line, she totally wowed that audience, and you just threw her on the floor! It was a bad move! *Bad* move! And let me tell you something else, Mr. Big Shot with a screw loose, *somebody's* gonna sign that girl and it could've been you! Heck, *I'll* sign her!"

Dane turned aside and let a little reason sink in. "This has not been easy."

"Yeah, you're telling me. I can't take you anywhere."

"Maybe you *should* sign her."

"Maybe I will." Arnie took a moment to fidget, look up and down the street again, cool his jets. "But I'm not blind. You're the one she wanted to see. You have the connection, whatever it is, I don't know. I think she'd rather work with you. And think about it. She's up here, you're up here, I'm heading back to Vegas tomorrow. I don't want to pull her out of her neighborhood before she's ready, and you're the only one who's gonna know when she's ready."

"So now it's all on me."

"You bet it is. It's all yours, baby. You made the mess, you clean it up."

"Well, did you get her number or anything?"

"That was gonna be part of the meeting you walked out of."

Dane could only whistle out a sigh and rub his fingers through his hair.

"Dane, this girl, backed up by everything you are and everything you know, I guarantee she'll go places. She could do a solo act, you could put together a whole new show featuring the two of you, kind of a brand-new Dane and Man——I just walked off a cliff, didn't I?"

"Even as we speak."

"Sorry."

Dane mellowed and gave Arnie a nearly imperceptible smile. "You do try, Arnie, you do try."

Arnie only shook his head. "One of us has to."

Dane slapped a hand on his shoulder. "Guess I just need some time."

"Yeah, but don't take forever."

McCaffee's was a quiet place with no customers there, the doors locked, most of the lights out, the ceiling fans motionless. Roger and Abby were turning out lights, putting chairs up on the tables, re-stocking the coffee urns, replenishing the towels in the restrooms . . .

. . . and waiting for her.

She remained on the same chair at the same table, her hat at her elbow, Mr. Harrington's business card in her fingers, trying not to feel lonely and wondering why she did.

"Yerrrr OUT!" she muttered.

Yep. Rounded first, headed for second, second got up, and walked out. Tagged. Third out. Game over.

She had such a great night. She did so well. The most amazing things happened, things that astounded even her. The crowd loved it. Roger and Abby loved it and told her so.

So why did he leave?

She came so close to something, as if she were in a big maze and for one second she saw a glimmer of light from the opening, but now she couldn't find it no matter how hard she looked.

Or . . . as if she were trying to pluck her keys from the very edge of a sidewalk grate and they slipped off the tips of her fingernails and fell the rest of the way down. She provided the sound, "Ker-sploosh!"

Or . . . as if she knew the answer to a question on a quiz show, had known it all her life, but it just wouldn't come to her when she really needed it and then the buzzer sounded and the host said, *I'm sorry, your time is up.*

Or . . . as if she were trying to remember where she saw a pair of pruners so she could go get them. She could remember them sitting on top of a can but she couldn't remember, for the life of her, where the can was, or what kind of can it was, or how long ago she saw it, if she did, or whether she just dreamed it.

The frustration! "Aaarrrggh!"

Roger wanted to go home. He touched her on the shoulder. "Why don't you just go find the guy? The least he should do is give you a chance."

She'd written DANE COLLINS on the back of Mr. Harrington's business card. She looked at it again for the umpteenth time and considered out loud, "I need a car."

In his bedroom, Dane stared at Dr. Kessler's business card lying on the nightstand. His hand came one inch from picking up the telephone and dialing, but then he came up with a good excuse: it was too late in the evening and he'd only get an answering machine.

So, leave a message.

Naw . . .

He flopped on the bed, trying to be honest with himself. He had to get on with the grieving. He had to let her go. He couldn't go on painting her face on every young girl he encountered.

Oh, come on, it's just that one girl.

So what? It was still . . . warped, that's what it was. Was this where dirty old men came from?

I'll call in the morning.

The Division of Motor Vehicles examiner behind the counter was nice enough. She handed Eloise the list of requirements to get an Idaho driver's license, all of which Eloise could not meet, and then smiled and said she was sorry, Eloise would have to come back when she could provide . . .

Proof of Idaho residency
Proof of age and identity
Acceptable legal-presence documents
Social Security number
Blah-blah-blah

So Eloise, printed government info in hand, backtracked along the line of folks who'd been waiting behind her, all of whom existed as real people in this world and probably would get what they came for.

Sometimes she just wanted to scream.

"Eloise?"

Now, that was new: somebody out in the middle of everywhere calling her name. She paused just short of the front door and looked.

It was Pamela the professional lady, still looking professional! No problem remembering her. Eloise had transferred her driver's license from her handbag into the box made from cards, and then back to her handbag, one of her first big triumphs at McCaffee's. *Hmph.* Her driver's license. How was that for irony?

Pamela strode right up, all confidence. "You look like you've had to deal with the bureaucracy!"

Well, now. What to say? How much to say? "I was trying to get my driver's license so I can drive a car. So I can even buy a car."

"You don't have a driver's license?"

"Umm, I don't have a lot of things. I was—" *What's the going lie these days?*

But Pamela held up a hand to stop her. "No, you don't have to tell me. Suffice it to say you don't have the necessary documents." Pamela prodded her toward the door and said in a lowered voice, "It's lucky I saw you. Let's talk outside."

Pamela gave Eloise a lift to an inviting, neatly landscaped little house one block off Sherman Avenue. A sign hung on the front porch: SEAMUS A. DOWNEY, ATTORNEY AT LAW. She led Eloise through the front door and into a reception area that used to be the living room. "Have a seat. I'll let Mr. Downey know you're here."

Besides Pamela's reception corner, the room had a couch, a recliner, two plastic stackable chairs, a coffee table with old magazines, and a struggling ficus in a ceramic pot. A Hispanic lady with two squirming toddlers occupied the couch. The recliner looked inviting, but taking that chair would be like taking the bigger half of a shared candy bar. She sat in one of the plastic stackables while Pamela went behind her desk.

"Is this going to cost very much?" Eloise asked.

Pamela only smiled. "I don't think that'll be a problem." She picked up her telephone and had a quick, quiet exchange with "Mr. Downey" regarding a "Miss Eloise Kramer," who was there to see him. Eloise figured the Big Guy had to be behind the door that used to lead to a den or bedroom. She could hear voices talking in there. "Mr. Downey is with a client, but he'll be finished real soon."

Eloise settled in and smiled at the Hispanic lady. "Hi."

The Hispanic lady only half smiled back and wouldn't meet her eyes after that. The kids were getting tired of their toys—a Barbie rip-off and a GI Joe without an arm—and looking for trouble.

Mr. Downey's door opened and a steely-eyed, Middle Eastern guy stepped out, a manila envelope in his hand and a guarded smile on his face. Behind him, Eloise guessed, was Mr. Downey, in a gray suit coat and blue shirt with no tie. He was so young he surprised her. Dark, wavy hair, quite good-looking. He shook hands with the Middle Eastern guy and the man got out of there in a hurry, stashing the manila envelope under his jacket.

Mr. Downey looked at Eloise and smiled disarmingly. "Eloise?"

Eloise almost rose from her chair, but directed an indicating finger toward the Hispanic lady.

"She's waiting for her husband," said Pamela. "You can go first."

The chair in front of Mr. Downey's desk was far more comfortable.

"So," said Mr. Downey, slipping behind his desk like a cool dude slipping into a sports car, "Pam tells me you're quite the magician."

Nice opening. "I'm glad she thinks so."

"And she tells me you can't get a driver's license."

Okay, she was up to the edge of another cliff. He looked legit enough. He had a nice car parked outside, and Pamela's car smelled new and had one of those talking GPS things in it. He had degrees hanging on the wall and a tennis racket propped in the corner. No family pictures. She took one step. "No."

He smiled and nodded as if he understood everything already. "Well, I'm a bit of a magician myself. I make problems like yours disappear." He smiled and raised his eyebrows at her.

She didn't get it. "How's that exactly?"

He leaned back in his chair and touched his fingertips together like the old spider doing push-ups on a mirror. "I do estate planning mostly, but on the side I do pro bono work with documents because I see a real need there. This country is one huge bureaucracy, and decent people like yourself can't make a living or live a normal life without the right paperwork. You want to make a decent, honest living, don't you?"

It sure would be nice if this guy was legit. "I sure do."

"And you'd like to be able to buy and drive a car?"

"Right on."

"So. Why can't you get a driver's license?"

She hesitated.

"Let me guess. You can't establish your identity. You don't have an acceptable ID, you don't have a Social Security number, you can't find your birth certificate, you can't even prove you're a citizen who belongs in this country."

She shied a bit but finally admitted, "That's about it."

"So how do you manage to make a living?"

"I'm an independent contractor, but—"

"But one of these days the tax man's going to come calling and he's going to ask why you haven't filed."

She nodded. "Render unto Caesar, you know?"

"I would if I were you." He took a pen from his shirt pocket and started scribbling on a legal pad. "Okay. The first thing you need is a birth certificate. It looks to me like you were born, am I right?"

Well, that much was certain. "Uh-huh."

"So that's not so hard to figure out. It's just that some people need a piece of paper or they don't believe it. What's your full name?"

"Uh . . . Eloise Kramer."

"Do you have a middle name?"

"Uh . . . Elizabeth."

He recited it as he wrote it down. "Parents' names?"

Wow. Some of this she hadn't figured out yet. "Uh . . . Arthur and Eloise. Kramer." Close enough to the truth.

"Where were you born?"

"I . . . I don't remember the name of the hospital . . ." Actually, the hospital where she was born wasn't there anymore.

"Kootenai Medical Center, I imagine."

"Uh, *Spokane County* Medical Center." In a way, Eloise was born there.

"Date of birth?"

"January fifteenth, 1991."

"That makes you nineteen. That might be a little young, but we'll see."

"There . . . there might be a problem."

"Yeah? What's that?"

"If you check into all this I might not be in the system."

"Oh, don't worry, you will be." He winked at her.

This little cliff was growing. Her conscience was making her insides ache. "Well, I'm trying to say—"

"You don't have to."

"Are you—you're not, you know, are you . . . is all this legit? I mean, we're not doing something wrong, are we?"

He was unruffled. "That's a fair question and here's the honest truth: our government is one big inefficient mess, full of red tape, redundancy, and contradiction. Call one office, they'll tell you one thing, call another office with the same question and you'll get a completely different answer. I've made it my job to comb through the maze and learn where to get the right answers from the right people in the right order so we can get what we need while still using the system, and in an acceptable amount of time.

"It might be a revelation to you, but our government doesn't care if you're here illegally. That's just paper, politics, and PR. All they care about is whether you're their kind of people, and me, I don't care at all. I just want you to be able to make a living and contribute to this country because I think it's a great country.

"So yes, I'm a little slippery. I have to be clever and a little deceptive, but I make the machine work for you, and incidentally, it's pro bono. That means I do it for free because it makes me feel good."

Then he gave her a moment to think about it.

She sighed. She even got a little teary-eyed. It was funny how right and wrong could get so messed up for a person who was crazy, especially when doing the "right" thing would mean starving or landing in jail or the nuthouse. She sure wished she knew what God was thinking because she didn't have a clue.

"Want to keep going?" he asked.

Her insides still ached a little, but she nodded.

"Okay then. You're going to need some other documents besides your birth certificate. Social Security card for one, that's a biggie. And photo ID: U.S. passport and . . . we might try for a military ID." He tapped a button on his phone. "Pam? Let's do a photo shoot, passport and military."

Click! Click! She stood in front of a blue background looking as groomed as she and Pamela could make her.

Click! Click! She stood in front of a white background wearing a camouflage shirt and with her hair pinned back.

"That'll do it," said Pam.

chapter

18

Corporal James Dose was a good soldier, so even though getting shot through the shoulder in a restaurant in Bremerton, Washington, had to be the most unlikely of events, he didn't ask a lot of questions.

He marveled at how a team of paramedics just happened to be dining in the restaurant at the time of the shooting and had all their emergency medical gear in their cars parked right outside, but he just said thanks, not, *What are you guys doing here?*

He felt rather important when a tight-lipped trio of army brass met him the moment he was wheeled into the hospital and, in terse, secretive phrases, advised him it was a matter of national security and therefore he couldn't discuss it with anyone, so he just said *Understood*, and not, *Who in the heck shot me?*

He was miffed that his family, particularly his fiancée, was barred from seeing him even when he was out of danger until a colonel let him know, off the record and under wraps, that he might have been shot by a terrorist cell group connected with the Taliban in Afghanistan, now operating in the vicinity of the naval shipyards and trying to send a message. Obviously such information couldn't get out, as it would hamper containment efforts, risk lives, and, who could say for sure, even endanger his loved ones. He made no objections after that.

He even got out of bed in the middle of the night so army medics could load him into an ambulance and whisk him away for a secret debriefing in an undisclosed location. He didn't ask if they would be bringing him back to the hospital in Bremerton or his company at Fort Lewis afterward, and they didn't tell him.

They didn't tell his family either.

And they never brought him back.

The team that conducted the crime scene investigation at the Quay were tight-lipped but pleasantly efficient. They were so thorough in gathering up anything bloodied, spilled, or broken that, after they left, one could never guess there'd been a shooting. As for the bullet that everyone thought had passed through James Dose—the exit wound was quite dramatic, to say the least—there was no bullet hole in the walls or woodwork, none in the furniture, simply no sign of a bullet anywhere. The official word from the hospital cleared that up: the bullet was lodged in the shoulder of the victim and was successfully removed in surgery. The victim would recover.

"Congratulations," said Seamus Downey, sliding a manila envelope across his desk. "You now exist."

Wow. In just three days! Eloise opened the envelope with a touch of awe. Inside, she found what amounted to her personhood: a certified birth certificate, a Social Security card, a U.S. passport with her photo, and a U.S. military photo ID card, all for Eloise Elizabeth Kramer, born in Spokane, Washington, January 15, 1991. Each came encased in a plastic slipcover, and each was so real, so pristine, she felt irreverent touching them.

"But don't forget now"—Seamus gave her a lecturing look— "you're not a ghost anymore, the government knows you're here. They'll expect you to obey the laws and pay your taxes. Better read up on self-employment taxes, quarterly filing, and prepayments, all that. I can recommend an accountant if you like."

She still had trouble believing all this. "You mean, the government has this Social Security number for me? I'm in the system?"

"Yep."

"So I can work anywhere I want now."

"Anywhere they'll hire you. And you have an official passport so you can travel outside the country should you get the hankering."

"How did you do it?"

"I didn't. The government did. Eloise, they can give you a real runaround, but deep in their hearts they want you to be a person. Otherwise they couldn't tax you."

"Wow."

"But the next thing you're going to need to get a driver's license is proof of Idaho residency. You're renting, right?"

"Right."

"Get your rental agreement, your utility bills, your home address, anything to verify that you're really living in Idaho, and you should be all set to go—if you can pass the driver's test."

"Oh, I can do that."

"All right then. Oh, and I wouldn't flash that military ID around too much, only if needed. The army computers think you're still serving, but if anybody asked, the army couldn't actually find you."

"Oh. Okay."

"Now, one more item. Are you hungry?"

She didn't quite hear his question. She was just beginning to fathom what he'd done for her. If Dr. Angela or Dr. Lorenzo or Bernadette Nolan ever asked her again who she was, she could tell them and they could check it out and she'd really be Eloise Kramer, born in a real place in 1991. Now she could win for a change. The days of fear and helplessness were over. Really.

She broke down. Seamus came around his desk to stand beside her, a comforting hand on her shoulder. Pamela knelt beside her, arms around her, and offered her a tissue. They were just so kind, such good friends, just what she needed. "Thank you, thank you, thank you."

"Oh, you're most certainly welcome," said Seamus. He then asked Pamela, "What time does Angelo's open?"

"Five, every night but Monday."

Seamus leaned close to Eloise, his voice gentle and comforting, and wow, even his breath was clean. "Do you like Italian?"

She blew her nose. "Sure."

"Pam and I would like to take you to dinner to celebrate."

Her smile would be the first of many, she was certain. "I would love that."

November 22, Monday, Dane awoke to find the yard outside sugared with an inch of snow. The snow came right when Shirley predicted.

She was quite the weather watcher and had much to say about how the coming winter would compare to the last one: more snow this time around, starting about mid-November, and she was right.

By the time he settled at his drafting table up in the loft, he could look out the east windows and see the snow shrinking into patches on the meadow. The roof of the barn was clear and steaming in the sun while snow remained within the barn's long, November shadow. Wisps of morning fog drifted over the surface of the pond.

Looking out the south windows, he could see the driveway winding down to the gate on Robin Hill Road, and beyond them, the valley, the deep greens now giving way to yellows, browns, and patches of white.

So the seasons were changing, the morning was beautiful, and it was about time he got to work on something, anything.

Perched in his chair, No. 2 pencil in hand, he stared at a rough drawing he and Mandy had brainstormed: an escape trick using a tight metal cocoon hanging from a one-hundred-foot boom. It was a spin on metamorphosis, being trapped as one thing, escaping as something or someone else. Intriguing idea, but so far the whole thing was easy and boring. It needed more tension, which meant more danger, which would mean more safety design, which would mean more money. Funny how it always came to that.

So, safety bolts on both sides, a backup clevis . . . secondary cable, but now we're blocking the hatch and how do we hide it . . .

After maybe two minutes of his thoughts and pencil lines meandering around a vast white void, he glanced at the erasable calendar on the wall above his desk and noticed he'd walked out on Eloise Kramer a week ago yesterday. *Well?* he asked himself, *any regrets? Should you have gone back, looked her up again? You told Arnie you'd give it some thought. Did you?*

So this was Robin Hill Road. Gorgeous! Driving a Volkswagen Beetle through this valley with its farms, forests, barns, and pastures brought back feelings Eloise had sorely missed. Call her crazy, but she—or Mandy—grew up in a place like this and once drove a car like this. The classic whir of the engine behind her took her back to when she was, well, the *other* nineteen, and as the little car topped each rise and rounded each gentle turn, another beautiful sight made the feelings go wild inside her. *Oh, dear Jesus, please let me come home to a place like this someday.*

She eyed the mailboxes she passed, watching the numbers count upward, looking for 1250 Robin Hill Road.

1090 . . . 1180 . . . 1200 . . .

She came over a rise, and her foot came off the gas pedal. The Beetle eased to a crawl.

On her right was a white paddock fence and a gravel-lined ditch between the fence and the road shoulder. The pasture was yellowed and patches of snow trampled the grass, but she knew this place. Didn't she?

She pressed the pedal lightly. Up ahead were a mailbox and a heavy wooden gate.

She let out a yelp, her fingers over her mouth.

It was *the* gate, *the* fence, *the* driveway, *the* three aspens, and atop the hill at the end of the long driveway, *the* house, in glorious, magnificent daylight.

On the mailbox: 1250.

Actually, Dane had thought about Eloise Kramer enough to decide not to think about her. Life was much simpler with his eyes forward, planning projects, designing, imagineering. Most every day he thought about not thinking about her. He was thinking about not thinking about her even as the phone rang, the rings coming in pairs. It was the gate.

For no reason that he knew, Dane glanced at one of Mandy's pictures—she was doing a curtain call in flowing, sequined white, with diamonds in her golden hair—before swiveling his chair toward the south-facing windows.

There was a blue Volkswagen Bug down at the gate.

The phone rang again. He had an extension beside his drafting table. He picked it up.

"Hello?"

"Hello, Mr. Collins?"

The voice was unmistakable. *Oh, God, no.*

"Hello?" she asked again.

"Yes . . ."

She sounded breathless. "This is, this is just so unbelievable! I can't believe I found this place, I can't believe I found you!"

Oh, I just so much do not need this. "I can't believe it either."

"It's amazing! It's a God thing, you know? I don't know if you believe in God, but that's what it is!"

"Did God show you where I live?"

"Umm . . . it was, I got your name, you know, I wrote it down on the back of that business card and then I got your phone number, and then I met a nice lineman from the phone company. He was fixing some wires and he had a map in his truck."

This *was* unbelievable. "Why?"

"Umm . . ."

"Don't say 'umm,' just answer the question."

"Umm—I . . . oh, this is going to sound so crazy. I think we're supposed to meet or something, I don't know why, but, I don't know, I just have this really big *feeling.*"

A feeling. Right. It's all about feelings now. "Young lady, feelings can get you into trouble. Be careful with feelings."

"Yeah, yeah, I know. I guess I just need the time to explain it."

"I told you I wasn't interested."

"But you are! I know you are!"

He opened his mouth but only an agitated breath came out. What could he say without lying? "Are . . . aren't you being just a little forward here?"

"It's got to be important. I got a driver's license and then I got a car and then I found out where you lived so I could talk to you about it."

Well, actually, really, considering all the ramifications and what constituted wise business, he could be honest saying . . . "I'm not interested."

He could hear the click of a door latch and the groan of hinges, and through the window he could see her getting out of the car and standing beside it. What was she . . . ? He grabbed some binoculars from his desk.

There she was, in blue, untucked shirt and blue jeans, juggling four tennis balls . . . in slow motion, and looking toward the house with a big, showbiz smile on her face. "Can we talk?"

He watched her juggle, the balls floating in a high, graceful arc from one hand to the other. She made it look effortless and didn't even have to watch the balls but looked toward the window with that teasing smile. How did she do that, standing outside? Did she have some kind of device in the VW? If so, she'd gone to a lot of trouble to impress him.

He set down the binoculars. Feelings. Nothing more than feelings. What to do?

He could have refused a million-dollar check because he didn't like the color of the ink; he could have been drowning and refused to grab a rope tossed to him because the rope was nylon instead of hemp; he could have jumped out of a plane without a parachute because the chute didn't match his socks. But no, he did worse: "Go away!"

"Just a few minutes?"

"I said, 'Go away!'"

He hung up.

And then he watched her sadly catch the balls, one after the other, toss them in the backseat of her Bug, get in, start up the engine, and drive off.

Feelings. Oh, they were so very powerful! His insides hurt to the point of nausea.

He looked at the drawing on his drafting table and sighed. Just when he was starting to think about other things and get back to some projects.

Well, here was another day shot.

chapter

19

She drove back the way she came, kicking herself for getting all wound up and full of hope like a believer in fairy tales until she put her foot deep in poop and lost her shoe.

She felt sick. Stupid. Juvenile. She should have known better.

She heard a hiss-hiss-hiss from her right front tire and then it started flopping and shaking the whole car.

She pulled over, moaning, whining, pounding the steering wheel, and trying to think of words that weren't too dirty, the little car growling and wobbling to a halt on the gravel shoulder. She pushed her door open and struggled from the car as if she were tangled up in it. Getting out was very uphill because the car was leaning forlornly toward the right.

She opened the trunk—in front of the car, she always loved that—and pulled out the spare and the jack.

She jacked up the car to take the weight off the wheel but keep the tire touching the ground so it wouldn't spin when she twisted off the lug nuts. The spare lay on the ground beside her, ready to go. Good enough. It wouldn't be the first time she'd changed a tire. Things could have been worse. It could have been raining.

A big SUV came by, slowed down, then pulled over just ahead of her.

She wilted a little. Not that she didn't appreciate the help, but right now she wasn't in the mood. "Oh, got a flat tire, huh?" she mimicked to herself. "Yeah, sure is flat, all right. Hey, but it's only flat on one side! You live around here?"

A nice-looking guy got out the passenger side. Young and studly. Olive complexion, black, wavy hair. "Hello," he said. "Looks like you have a problem."

"Oh, guess it happens."

"Can I give you a hand?"

Well . . . "Okay. Sure. I appreciate it."

The man extended his hand. "Lemuel."

She shook it. "Eloise."

He squatted by the lame tire. "Oh, you need to jack it up more."

So she had to tell him, "You need to get the lug nuts off while the tire's touching or the tire will spin."

He went for the jack handle. She decided to let him find out for himself. *Klinka klinka klinka*, he pumped the jack up farther and the wheel came off the ground.

The first lug nut he went for, the tire spun.

She would have had the spare on by now.

Lemuel pointed. "What kind of lugs are these?"

Eloise squatted down beside him. "What do you mean?"

Lemuel had a friend, the driver of the truck. She heard him get out and walk along the street side of the Bug to circle around the end.

"They metric?"

"That's right."

"Right- or left-hand threads?"

"Rightsy-tightsy, lefty-loosie."

He broke into a grin. "I like that." He tried turning the wrench again. The tire spun again.

"You gonna lower the tire?"

"Well, I guess I'd better."

The friend came alongside them. Quiet, wasn't he?

Lemuel lowered the tire so it touched the ground. The first nut twisted off easily. He had the concept now. She looked up at the friend.

The man was blond and must have had terrible pimples growing up.

"Hey! You're, um . . ."

He crouched down beside her and smiled.

"Clarence! You were at—"

She didn't see what was in his right hand. She felt only a bolt of lightning enter her neck and shoot out her fingers and toes and she couldn't stop trembling, as if her whole body was a funny bone that got whacked. He met her eyes. Misdirection, and she fell for it.

She teetered and slumped to her side on the ground and couldn't help it, couldn't do a thing about it. They were on her, taking hold of her and she couldn't kick, couldn't hit. She could scream—Lemuel, or whatever his name was, clamped his hand over her mouth.

A hornet stung her neck, hurting and hurting more! She twisted her head in time to see Clarence withdrawing a needle. She screamed into Lemuel's hand.

Dane's pencil sketched and scribbled, expanding the drawing, trying out ideas. *Seal the cocoon with rigged bolts? A little obvious, but how else would we—*

His mind switched so suddenly it jarred him. Mandy. He could think of only Mandy.

Mandy . . . what? What about her?

His eyes went to the photos and posters. She was smiling in her pictures, looking great, but he felt troubled when he looked at her, as if, behind those great looks, she wasn't doing great; behind that beaming smile, she wasn't happy but afraid.

I'm losing it.

He looked out the windows, at the floor, the ceiling, anywhere but those images. What was this, some kind of seizure? Was he having a flashback? A drug reaction?

He gripped the edges of the table and tried breathing, just breathing.

Dr. Kessler? Maybe you should call . . .

I can handle this.

What was that? He held still and listened. Somebody was in the house. Shirley? But Shirley wasn't working today, and she never came in without announcing herself.

Maybe he didn't hear anything. Maybe he *felt* it.

* * *

They were strong, holding her down and patiently, ruthlessly waiting for her strength, her fear, her mind to slip into chemical-induced surrender. Only her mind was still free, her terror keeping her alert for so very few, extra, precious moments. She concentrated even as she whimpered in fear, reaching, reaching for the other arms, the other hands, the other Eloises that could still grab, kick, hit, run.

She couldn't see the lug wrench with her own eyes, but somehow, through time and tea-stained, wavering space she knew where it was, propped against the spare tire, glinting in the sun. She could feel the cold steel in a hand she didn't have. With anger, with animal viciousness, she yanked the wrench aloft and toward *him*. Maybe she was only dreaming . . .

CLANG! She didn't see the wrench hit the back of Lemuel's head but she heard it and some distant, separate part of herself felt the shock ring through the metal. His grip loosened. He teetered, his eyes rolling, going blank. She kicked her legs loose—all six or eight of them, she couldn't count—while someone somewhere named Eloise took the wrench to Clarence. He saw it coming at him like an angry insect and held up his arms, trying to block the blows, trying to grab it, but she was in a different realm of time, could move faster, and fully intended to work through those arms to reach his head and body. The steel rang and she could feel the shock of the blows, but her grip never tired.

One man was stunned, the other was fighting off a wild lug wrench. Eloise was doped and fading, but free. She wriggled, crawled, then dug in with her feet and bolted away, staggering, weaving, disconnected from her feet, barely understanding what her eyes may have been telling her.

But somewhere in her mind she could see the gate, the white fence, the three aspens, the big house on the heavenly hill . . .

"Hello?" he called. There was no answer save for the ring of his voice off the vaulted ceiling.

He looked over the rail into the house below, listening again for a stirring, a creak, a rustle, whatever may have clued him in that he was not alone. He looked out the south windows, searching the front acreage, the driveway, the distant gate. No, not out there.

She came to mind. Eloise Kramer! Every time he saw her, every time she showed up in his life . . .

He caught something in his peripheral vision, looked toward the east windows—gasped with a start, then froze.

There was a woman standing by the windows, looking out, her back toward him. Her hair was golden blond with a sheen of silver, teased, layered, and draping her shoulders. She wore a blue bathrobe that reached nearly to her feet and had a cup of coffee in her hand.

After forty years, he knew who she was. He didn't move, didn't make a sound, was afraid to breathe lest anything scare the vision away. *Please. Just let me look at you, just for a moment. Please.*

She turned, every feature of her face more alive, real, and lovely than he ever could have remembered, and he almost said her name. She was looking straight at him, but she looked puzzled, alarmed.

He didn't say it but thought it, his face and body carrying the question *What is it?*

She immediately looked out the window again with intent and alarm, enough to make him approach.

What is it? he thought, and then he whispered it, "What is it?"

He could have touched her. He could smell the scent of her hair. She was looking out over the meadow. He followed her gaze.

What in the world was this? At very first glimpse he took it to be some kid traipsing across his land, but his next impression was the right one: it was Eloise Kramer, just coming around the pond and up the meadow, staggering, falling, crawling, walking again, looking seriously injured and crazy with fear.

And—who was that guy rounding the pond?

He looked at the woman.

She was gone.

But she'd reached him. He thundered down the stairs, bounded through the living room, grabbed a sword off the mantel—it was a stage prop that wasn't sharp and would probably break, but it was all he could think to grab—and burst out the back door.

She was so small, so far away. It would take so long to reach her. The man coming after her was closing fast, running like an athlete, definitely not sixty. Nagging little thoughts squeaked in Dane's brain: *You don't know what you're doing. That guy could kill you.*

The girl may have seen Dane coming. She staggered one step in his direction, then another, then crumpled, half disappearing in the yellow grass. From there she tried to crawl, reaching and pulling with one feeble arm and then the other.

Dane stopped listening to little thoughts and charged, wielding the sword, animal rage sending strength to his legs and a war cry from his throat, a maniacal, high-pitched scream.

The other guy kept coming, but Dane didn't slow down. He passed the barn—it was only a blurred flash of a shadow on his right—and galloped down the narrow trail into the meadow, sword waving above his head, teeth bared, a crazy, screaming barbarian.

It didn't seem to be working. The other guy was still coming at him, and the way things looked, he and Dane would reach the fallen girl at the same time.

Well then, there'd be a fight even though Dane didn't know anything about fighting. He'd just have to bite the guy's ear off first chance he got.

But then the guy stopped, just came to a halt about thirty yards away and stood there, sizing Dane up through impenetrable sunglasses.

Dane reached the girl and positioned himself between her and the stranger, holding that sword out with murder and mayhem in his eyes and not the slightest idea of what threatening thing he ought to say.

The girl was still trying to crawl away, her hands too weak now to grip anything, her arms only swimming over the top of the ground, flattening the snow-wearied grass. Her speech was so slurred she could have been talking in her sleep, "I'm Eloise . . . I'm . . . driver's license . . ."

Only now did Dane notice how hard he was breathing, how tired and sore he was. If that guy wanted a fight . . . well, maybe the girl could still get away.

But the man only looked at him with a tilt to his head, the trace of a smile on his lips. What, he was amused? He thought this was funny?

He looked familiar. Blond hair. Steely expression. That guy from the other night? Hard to tell from this distance. But he didn't look well, even for him. His face might have been a little puffy in places, and Dane thought he might have a streak of red by his right ear.

The man looked down for a moment as if thinking things over, then wagged his head with resignation, gave both hands a little flip as if to say, "Well, so much for this," and turned. Putting his hands in his pockets, he walked away. He didn't run, he just walked.

Dane stole quick, precautionary glances at the girl. She'd fallen silent, her eyes closed, and after two final twitches of her hands, she was motionless. He knelt and checked her pulse. Still strong. She was breathing.

His eyes remained on the stranger, his stage sword ready to bounce harmlessly off flesh. The sinister stranger never checked behind him. He just walked across the meadow, climbed through the fence, crossed to the road, and disappeared over a rise.

What had he gotten himself into?

Eloise Kramer couldn't tell him. She lay on the wet grass, her hair smeared across her face, unconscious—right where he'd scattered the ashes, he realized.

But he didn't dwell on that. He knew only what he had to do next, and after that . . .

He stooped and gathered her up. She stirred a little, then clung to him like a frightened child, her arms around his neck.

"Dad . . . dy," she said, and she may have been crying.

He carried her into the house.

chapter

20

She was a svelte, young-bodied girl and should have been easy to carry, but she went totally limp and offered no more help—no arms around his neck to support some of her weight, no curling against him as he supported her behind her back and under her knees. No, she just hung over his arms like a big sack of dog food, arms dangling like empty sleeves from a laundry basket and her head—oh, her head! It was like trying to balance a bowling ball against his shoulder with no free hand to hold it there. He feared for her neck and had to stop and lurch rearward several times to get it back in place. By the time he reached the side door his arms and back were sending him warnings.

Then he discovered he had no way to grab and turn the door-knob. Somehow—and it did not go smoothly—he got her flopped over his left shoulder so he could open the door with his right hand and get inside, trying not to bang her dangling arms and head against the door frame or the walls.

He made it through the kitchen, his wet soles squeaking on the tile floor, then into the living room, where he gingerly let her unfold from his shoulder and flop on the couch, cradling her head lest she hurt her neck. He put a pillow under her head. One leg still hung off the side of the couch. He lifted the leg as if it were crystal and set it neatly next to the other. Her clothes were wet from lying in the grass. Her shoes were smudging the couch. Little running shoes. Size six, probably. *Cute.*

Was she breathing okay? He placed his fingers under her nose and felt little puffs of warm air. *Okay. Alive. Breathing.*

Pulse? He felt her neck. Yeah, her heart was pumping away, not too rushed.

He backed away, eyes scanning the girl for anything amiss. Her right arm was jammed between her side and the back of the couch. He lunged forward, lifted the arm out, and placed it on top of her.

He backed away again. Well. She *looked* comfortable. Now what?

Shirley. Right. He should call her. There should be a woman here and not just him. What about an aid car? But what would he tell them?

Just get Shirley on the phone!

He crossed the room to the phone, sidestepping and peering sideways to keep his eyes on the girl. "Hi, Shirley. This is Dane. Uh, could you come right over, right now? Well, I've got a girl on the couch and she's unconscious and . . . Well, I don't know. She was running from a—well, you're an EMT, aren't you? Do you have your tool kit, all that EMT stuff with you? Yeah, yeah, bring it. I'll tell you when you get here. Yeah, okay, I'll call 'em."

Call the aid car, she said. He tapped out 911.

"Nine-one-one. What is your emergency?" The lady's voice was calm. She could have been working for an insurance brokerage.

Dane knelt by the couch, peering at the restful face. He felt as if he were doing a scene from *Sleeping Beauty.* "Uh, I have a young lady here asleep on the couch and, uh, I wanted to be sure she's okay."

"A young lady, sir?"

"Uh, yeah, right."

"Are you calling from the McBride residence?"

"No, this is Dane Collins."

"You're not calling from the McBride residence at twelve-fifty Robin Hill Road?"

"Oh! Yeah, yeah, yeah I am. I forgot. I just bought the place."

"So this is twelve-fifty Robin Hill Road, Hayden, Idaho."

"Yes, yes, it is."

"And what's your emergency?"

"I just brought a girl into the house and she's unconscious."

"Is she breathing normally?"

He listened, leaning close. "She's snoring a little."

It wasn't a loud, rude snore, just one of those cute little ones that Mandy used to do when her head was tilted a certain way and her mouth dropped open.

"So she's breathing normally?"

He raised her head slightly and adjusted the pillow. The snoring stopped and she breathed in sleepy little sighs. "I would say she's breathing just fine."

"How old is she?"

Young. So very young. "Umm . . . I don't know. Early twenties, I guess."

"Is she injured?"

"I don't know. She might be."

"And what's your name, sir?"

I wonder if she has Mandy's teeth? "Dane Collins. Uh, Daniel."

"Duane Collins Daniel?"

He peered into her slightly open mouth. "No, no, Dane. I mean, well, Daniel, just Daniel."

"Why don't you just say your first and last name for me."

Well. He could only see the sides of a few molars. Maybe they looked like Mandy's teeth, but was that because he wanted them to? They were nice teeth, but teeth are teeth, even nice teeth—

"Sir?"

"Huh? I'm sorry, what did you ask me?"

"I need you to say your name."

"Okay, right. Daniel Collins. Dane is a nickname."

"Okay, got it."

"Are you going to send somebody?"

"They're already en route, sir. Now, you don't know of any injuries?"

None that he could see. Of course, she was wearing a coat. *Oh, brother. Shirley, where are you?*

"Did she hit her head? Is she bleeding anywhere?"

He swept his eyes over her small shoes, her slender jeans, her blue shirt tail hanging out, her hooded jacket, and then her neck up to behind her ear where the brown hair had fallen aside. "There's a . . . a little scratch or something on her neck, just a little bit of blood." What about her hair right there? Were those blond roots?

There was a knock, and the side door opened. Dane spun away from the girl on the couch. "Hey! Shirley!"

Shirley strode on her short legs into the living room, lugging her big orange EMT kit.

"Okay," Dane said into the phone, "we have an EMT here."

"Oh, the crew is there already?"

"No, my neighbor is an EMT. I called her."

"Oh, very good. Well, the aid crew should be arriving any minute."

Dane told Shirley, "The aid car's on its way."

Shirley was already checking Eloise's breathing and pulse. "Better open the gate."

Dane said good-bye to the dispatcher and entered the gate open code into the phone.

Shirley struggled trying to remove Eloise's coat. "Give me a hand here."

He helped her get the coat off. That didn't go so smoothly either, but he felt better with Shirley doing it and him helping. Eloise's shirt was damp with sweat. Shirley rolled up the left sleeve and wrapped a blood pressure cuff around the arm. "Better bring us one of those blankets in the upstairs hall closet. Bring the purple one."

By the time he returned with the blanket the aid car had arrived, lights flashing, and two paramedics came to the front door. One was a big-bellied, balding everybody's neighbor, and the other could have been a high school basketball coach, young, tall, and buzz cut. Shirley knew both of them. The big-bellied guy was named Ron, the young guy Steve. Steve got out an oxygen bottle while Ron shined a penlight into Eloise's eyes.

"Is she on any drugs?" Ron asked.

The phone rang. "I don't know," Dane said, then picked up the phone. "Hello?"

"Dane? Dane Collins?" It was a woman. He didn't recognize the voice.

"Did she hit her head?" Ron asked. "Do you know?"

To the phone, "Uh, yes," and to Ron, "I don't know."

The woman said, "Dane, this is Dr. Kessler, from Las Vegas."

She could have punched him in the jaw. His mind went into little blips and flashes that didn't connect to anything. "Uh. Dr. Kessler?"

"Do you remember me?"

Ron asked, "What's her name?"

Dane covered the phone and answered, "Eloise." He uncovered the phone. "Yeah, sure, I remember you."

"And how are you doing?"

"Uh . . ." He looked toward the couch.

Ron was gently shaking Eloise by the shoulders. "Eloise? Wake up. Eloise? You hear me? Wake up."

Dane lowered his voice, he wasn't sure why. "I'm, I'm not sure this is a good time right now."

"Sounds like you have someone there with you," Kessler said.

He was watching Eloise. They'd put an oxygen mask on her. "She's . . ."

Eloise made a little whimper, beginning to stir. Ron signaled for Shirley to step in. "It's all right," said Shirley. "You're all right."

"Who was that?" asked Kessler.

"That was . . ." Why'd she need to know? "Uh, Dr. Kessler, could we start over? Hello, how are you doing, and why are you calling me?"

Eloise's eyes half opened and she jolted, still dopey. Her little yelp was muted inside the oxygen mask. She blinked at Shirley and the paramedics like a dazed, cornered animal.

Kessler was saying something. ". . . to find out how you were doing. You remember the conversation we had?"

Oh, yeah. He remembered it. "Sure." His eyes were on Eloise. She didn't seem to be focusing yet, but being hemmed in by paramedics was troubling her.

"I was wondering if you were having any problems such as those we talked about."

He didn't want to tell her how much Eloise Kramer looked like Mandy, very much when she was knocked out—she even snored like Mandy—and almost perfectly when she was awake, a fact that was overwhelming him this very moment. "Such as?"

Kessler wasn't having an easy time of this either. He could imagine her consulting her invisible notes again and shifting in her chair. "Umm . . . we would call it a delusional disorder, in this case, your thinking you see Mandy."

"How about some for instances?"

He could tell she didn't want to humor him. "Well, for instance, you might think you actually see her, or you could even see someone else and think she looks just like Mandy."

Eloise's eyes focused—on him. *Oh, good grief.*

He looked away from her and spoke into the phone, "What exactly makes you think I would see something like that?"

"Dane?"

"Dane?" said Shirley.

"What?" he asked Kessler as he looked in Shirley's direction.

Kessler said, "You have someone there with you now, don't you?"

Shirley, Ron, and Steve were watching Eloise look at Dane. Eloise was staring as if trying to make sure who he was. Dane gave her a weak little wave and smiled. He couldn't see her smile through the oxygen mask, but her eyes smiled with relief and she sank back against her pillow.

Kessler asked, "Who does she look like?"

Dane studied Eloise's face. "She looks . . . What the heck kind of question is that?"

"Does she look like Mandy? Be honest."

"I don't think this is a good time—"

"This is a very good time. It gives you a chance to see exactly what I warned you about."

They were taking off the oxygen mask—he'd lived with that image, but this time she was young and alive, not burned and dying. She and the medics were talking.

"Dane? Can you hear me?"

"I need to get off the phone."

"What's her name?"

Okay. Kessler had crossed the line. "That is none of your business."

"Dane, she isn't Mandy. You have to realize that." She didn't sound as if *she* believed it. "She doesn't even look like Mandy. You just think she does. Did you hear me?"

Gal, either you're crazy or . . . I think it's you. "I'll call you later."

He hung up.

"No! No hospital!" Eloise said with a moan, still under the heavy influence of whatever it was.

"We just need to be sure you're okay, just get you checked over," said Ron.

That upset her more. "Oh, no you don't!" she muttered, her eyes barely open, her neck like a rag doll. "I know who why yam! I'm Meloise Kramer and I've live here all my life and you cann take me to da hosp'al!" She groped about blindly, trying to find something. "Where my wallet?"

Dane stepped up while Shirley handed Eloise her coat. "She's Eloise Kramer. She works at McCaffee's, that little coffee shop in Coeur d'Alene."

"Has she taken any drugs?" Ron asked.

Eloise dug out her wallet and flashed her driver's license at them. "I'm Meloise Kramer. Says so ride 'ere."

Ron checked her license and told Steve, "She's nineteen."

Steve gave a nod of acknowledgment.

Dane asked Ron and Steve, "Is she all right?"

Ron answered, "Her vitals are fine, but she's doped to the gills on something."

"Booze?"

Ron shook his head. "Some kind of sedative. That could be a needle mark on her neck. Did *you* give her anything?"

Well now, how was that for a blunt question? Dane could feel himself bristling, but he held himself in check. "No. I wouldn't know what to give her. She was like this when I found her."

"Found her where?"

"Outside in my pasture."

"How'd she get there?"

"She ran. Some guy—"

"No!" said Eloise, waving dazedly in Dane's face. "Doan! Doan lettem take me."

Don't let them take me. The look in her eyes broke him open, her fear knifed through him as if it were his own, as if she could have cried those words the last time but no one listened; as if he should have cried out for her but didn't because Dr. Kessler and her white coats knew so much better, controlled everything, pronounced her dead, and wheeled her through a door that closed between them forever.

He'd never known the man he was right here and now, never felt this kind of anguish. He suspected that seeing her face and hearing the echoes of Kessler's voice could be making him irrational, but in this moment he wasn't about to trust a doctor or a hospital. He leaned, lifted her chin with a fingertip, and met her eyes. "Eloise, you do not have to go to the hospital if you don't want to." He looked at Ron and Steve. "Isn't that right?"

They were hesitant to say it, but they both did. "That's right." Then Ron added, "But this could be a matter for the police."

"No!" Eloise was even more vehement about that. "No police! Doan call 'em, I doan want 'em!"

"Easy, girl, easy," said Shirley.

Dane asked Shirley, "Can you stick around a little while?"

She nodded with a half shrug.

He told Ron and Steve, "Thanks, guys. Really appreciate it. Looks like we'll need to talk to her for a while. Is she out of danger?"

"As near as we can tell," said Ron.

"Okay. Thanks, we'll keep an eye on her. Shirley'll be right here."

They weren't happy about it. They gave in, but didn't leave before pulling Shirley into a private discussion outside the door. Dane could imagine the subject matter. "Eloise?"

She turned her head just enough to see him.

"You are nineteen, aren't you?"

"Uh-huh."

Ron was sneaking sideways glances at Dane through the door's window. Well. This would all have to resolve in its own good time.

Shirley came back inside. Dane pulled a chair closer for her, then another for himself. Eloise tried to sit up, but her eyes rolled and she rested on her pillow again. She groped and touched Dane's hand. "Thank you."

Shirley arranged the blanket under her chin. "You warm enough?" Eloise nodded.

Dane asked, "I suppose you've met Shirley?"

Eloise looked at Shirley and nodded.

"Shirley works for me. She takes care of the place."

Eloise seemed glad to know that. "'Ello."

"Hello, Eloise," said Shirley, patting her hand.

"Cute girl, isn't she?" Dane asked.

Shirley gave Eloise a smile. "Oh, yes."

"You like her shoes?"

Shirley looked quizzical, but checked out one shoe poking out from under the blanket. "They're okay. Nice."

Dane craned to look. "What kind of shoes are they, anyway?"

Shirley leaned. "I don't know. Running shoes."

"Silver and gray? Nice color choice."

"Uh-huh."

"And what do you think of her hair? Cut kind of like yours."

Shirley examined Eloise's simple, short hairstyle, definitely not looking its best at the moment. "Well, kind of. Her hair's straighter and there's no frosting."

"Brown, and yours is . . ."

"Brown with blond highlights." She put her hand to her hair, playfully showing it off. So far she seemed to think he was just making calming conversation. Good enough.

He asked Eloise, "Who cut your hair?"

"Rhea," she answered. "A girl frien'."

"Nice color." He told Shirley, "It sets off her brown eyes."

Shirley gave him a look. "Her eyes are blue."

Dane took a second look and feigned enlightenment. "Oohhhh . . . excuse me."

"So," said Shirley, "are we gonna talk about what happened?"

Eloise tried to sit up and slurred, "I havuh go to the bathroom."

Dane helped Shirley get her up, and Shirley took her around the corner and down the hall.

Got to make sure, got to make sure. Dane made a quick circuit around the living room. He found a vase of dried flowers knocked over but not broken. A stack of magazines on the end table had slid off onto the floor. The celestial globe he kept against the window next to his telescope had hopped off its stand. So he did hear real noises down here. He replaced everything with little time to wonder about it before Shirley returned with a towel and started wiping down the couch.

"Dane? Her clothes are wet. I could put them in the dryer and maybe she could wear . . ." She let her face ask the question as her eyes looked upstairs.

He knew what she meant. Mandy's things, tucked and folded away in drawers, hanging in the closet, safe on shelves. Inviolable. Sacred. "Sorry. No." He felt guilty but couldn't bend.

"What about a bathrobe? Do you have a bathrobe?"

Fair enough. He bounded up the stairs to the bedroom to get it, tossed it over the railing, and Shirley took it down the hall. He hurried back down to wait.

When Shirley and Eloise returned, the young girl wobbled, hanging on Shirley's arm with one hand and clutching his robe about her with the other. It hung from her like it was melting, and the hem almost touched the floor. She shuffled to the couch and sank into it, checking up and down herself for any breach of modesty. Her eyes had progressed from dopey to early morning drowsy and she didn't seem too happy about having to wear that robe. "So here we go again," she muttered.

Shirley started packing up her gear. "Okay, guess I've got an elk to cut up."

Dane wasn't ready for this. "You're going?"

Shirley cocked an eyebrow Eloise's direction and answered, "I understand you have a meeting."

"But . . ."

"She's all right for now. If she keels over, call me." She extended a hand, and Eloise gave it a shake. "Nice to make your acquaintance, Eloise."

"So nice to meet you," said the girl.

"Her clothes'll dry pretty quick." Shirley grabbed her coat and kit, then paused in the kitchen door to ask Eloise, "You're sure now?"

"I'll be fine," said Eloise, her head still a little too heavy for her neck.

"Okay." Shirley headed through the kitchen for the side door and called out, "I told her you're a gentleman so there's nothing to be afraid of."

And out the door she went.

So they'd had a little talk, the two of them. He looked at Eloise. "A meeting?"

Her eyes implored him through the drugs. "It'd be nice."

Well, this was a nice little checkmate, so perfect she had to have planned it. It was awkward. It was even scary.

But he had questions of his own. "All right."

chapter

21

Dane noticed his body language: he was towering over her and he wanted answers so badly his expression probably seemed unpleasant. He made himself relax, slid his chair back a few feet, and sat down.

And then they stared at each other. Her eyes fell away a few times, perhaps to deal with a thought, perhaps because she was still half asleep, but they always returned and met his gaze again. He was trying to read her; she was probably trying to read him.

"So what did you tell her?" he asked, nodding in the direction of Shirley's exit.

"That I came out here to see you, but then I had a problem with some drugs."

"What drugs?"

"I don't know. I made it up."

"You made it up? You lied."

"Well, I didn't know what to say."

"So what did happen?"

She laughed an apology. "It sure could have gone better."

"Tell me what happened."

He could see she was thinking, coming up with something, her eyes shifting to the left as she worked on it. "I guess I don't remember most of it."

"Do you remember ingesting or injecting any drugs?"

"You sound like a doctor."

"I'm not. Do you?"

"I'm not sure."

"Are you a drug user?"

"No. I don't do drugs."

"Do you remember running across my field?"

"Really? I mean, I did?"

"That's where I found you. You fell down in my field."

Those little tidbits helped her. "Oh! I think I hit my head! I was fixing a flat tire just a little ways up the road and I bumped my head with the lug wrench. I guess I wandered back here trying to get some help and finally conked out in your field." She looked at him with a dull, spacey rapture. "And you rescued me, right?"

"I guess you could say that."

"That is just so cool!"

"So who was that guy chasing you?"

Oh. Now she looked caught. "What guy?"

He cocked his head at her and raised an eyebrow.

She dug a little deeper. "You mean . . . who did you see?"

"I saw a man chasing you. Who was he?"

"Chasing me?"

"You were running from him."

"I was?"

He held his forefinger and thumb a tiny gap apart. "You're that far from getting thrown out of here, wet clothes or not."

She searched through her brain another moment but gave up. "I don't know—I mean, what did he look like?"

"Blond. Young, agile. Rough face. He looked like he'd been in a fight."

"And he was chasing me?"

He leaned into this one. "Who was he?"

She shied back and replied, "Clarence."

"Clarence. From the other night at McCaffee's?"

She brightened and leaned toward him, managing a horse's nod. "Yes! Remember him? He was my volunteer for the coffee mug trick."

"His face is memorable."

"He's been there a couple times. He was there for my very first performance!"

"So?"

Now she didn't know where to go. "So . . . what?"

"Why was he chasing you?"

"Um . . . are you sure he was chasing me?"

"You ran into my pasture, he was running after you, you were passing out, his face had blood on it and some really nice bruises, and he didn't turn around until I threatened him."

Her eyes got that wide, spacey look again, like she was looking at Superman . . . or Prince Charming. It made him cringe. "You threatened him?"

He held up a hand. "I'm lucky he bought it. I was waving that sword over there."

She marveled at the sight of his stage sword, now resting on the floor against the wall. "You rescued me with a sword?"

"It's a prop for a magic act."

She brightened. "You used to stab your pretty assistant with it while she was curled up in a box!"

"My wife."

"Far out. I always wondered how that trick worked. Is it a depth perception thing?"

Trying to change the subject? Nice try. "You say I rescued you. Did Clarence mean you harm?"

She looked away, rubbed her fingers, scratched her ear.

"Did he mean you harm?"

She had nowhere else to go. She nodded, then spoke as if confessing. "I got a flat tire and I pulled over and got out to fix it, and then these two guys—Clarence and another guy, named Lemuel— drove up and acted like they were going to help me, and when I wasn't looking they gave me some kind of a super-zap like they were electrocuting me or something, and then they gave me a shot"—she pointed to the mark on her neck—"right here, and the next thing I knew I was waking up here on the couch."

Well, it all fit. "They tasered you?"

"What's that?"

"Taser. It's an electric shock device that immobilizes the victim."

"Oh! Whoa, yeah, I hope to shout!"

"So what about the other guy, this, uh . . . ?"

"Lemuel."

"Yeah. What'd he look like?"

"He was cool-looking, Hispanic or Arab or Greek or something. But you might've seen him with Clarence the other night at McCaffee's. They were both there."

"But you don't know them?"

"No."

"But they jumped you, tasered you, gave you a shot to knock you out, chased you into my pasture. I take it you struggled."

"I don't remember anything after the shot."

"Clarence looked like you'd landed a few."

She enjoyed the thought of that. "Maybe I did."

"But you don't want to call the police."

That got a reaction. "Ohhh, no! Let's not, I don't wanna . . . No, no police!"

"Why not?"

"I don't like them. They do stuff to you."

"What stuff?"

"Anything they want, and they don't even ask if it's okay. Them and motherly doctors and cute, redhead 'designated examiners.'"

He braced himself. "So there's more to this."

"I don't know."

He rose. "Your clothes ought to be dry by now."

She reached out to him. "No, no, okay! Okay!"

He stopped, standing over her. "You are the one who called this meeting we're supposedly having, and I take it it's to discuss your career. Your career! You expect me to work with you in trust and confidence when all you do is lie to me? This is absurd!"

She wilted, gathering the robe around her.

He settled in his chair again and waited, just waited, hoping a good, steady glare would do the job.

Finally she muttered, barely audible, "They were from the hospital." Still he said nothing. She tried to look at him but couldn't. "I was in the hospital and I got away."

"What hospital?"

"Spokane County Medical Center."

"And why were you there?"

She had to gather some courage to finally let it out. "I was in Behavioral Health. I guess I'm sort of crazy."

"Oh, now *you're* crazy." He waved off any follow-up to that. "How crazy is 'sort of crazy'?"

Now she met his eyes. "Not real crazy. Just a little crazy, and not all the time, just sometimes."

"Enough to be in the hospital."

"Uh-uh. No way. I've never hurt anybody. I have a job, I have an apartment, I have my very own driver's license . . ."

"But you've been on the lam all this time?"

"Almost two months."

"So what kind of crazy are you?" She looked puzzled. "Are you . . . paranoid, or split personality, or manic-depressive, or what?"

She looked away, but then, with a new resolve, she faced him and answered, "I'm delusional. I think I'm somebody else."

He was silent, and not because he chose to be. Did she really say what he heard?

"But I've learned to live with it and I'm doing fine and I just want to be left alone. If they find me they'll lock me up and drug me and I may as well die because my life will be over. There's no moving forward in that place. All you do is sit and get moldy." She was much different when she was honest. She was strong, able to face him. *Good.*

"And since you asked and I'm telling, I'll just let you know that I'm badly in need of some friends right now. I don't need pills and shrinks. I just need a chance—if you're interested."

A soul at the mercy of other wills. He could see it so clearly. It chilled him to realize he could feel it within himself. "Who?"

His one-word question puzzled her.

"Who do you think you are?"

She wagged her head. "That would be going back. I'm Eloise Kramer, and that's all."

It was self-serving, he knew, but he asked, "May I ask when you were born?"

She had to think a moment. "Umm, January fifteenth, 1991."

Mandy's birthday except for the year. He tried and failed to hide how that caught his attention. "January fifteenth?"

She nodded and reemphasized, "1991."

"Where?"

She made a face as if she didn't get the point of the question. "Spokane."

"Are your parents still around?"

"No. They've both passed away."

Something told him he was being silly. Maybe he was. "What were their names?"

"Arthur and Eloise. I was named after my mother."

That hit him in the stomach, and he knew it showed. "Arthur and Eloise?" He would have touched her had it been appropriate, just to be sure she was there. He shook his head ever so slightly before he realized it and stopped.

She saw his reaction, and her eyes filled with . . . it looked like hope. "Did you know them? Arthur and Eloise . . . Kramer?"

"I . . ." He actually chuckled at himself. "No," he said. "I'm sure I never met them."

She sank back.

The robe she was wearing. It was his blue robe, the one she—the woman he saw upstairs, the vision, the hallucination, whatever she was—was wearing.

She was looking at him, getting concerned.

"Just thinking," he said.

As he watched, a smile formed, widened, and filled her entire face with a glow he remembered. "Bet you've never done an interview like this one."

He laughed, and what a relief. He put his hands over his face, rubbed his eyes. "Oh, no, I sure haven't."

She laughed, too—and she *did* have Mandy's teeth.

He talked in order to wrestle every thought and word back onto the rails of reality. "But since we're being honest, you need to know I'm not in a good place right now—and I'm becoming more and more aware of it."

The words still stuck in his mouth, difficult to force out. "I've just lost my wife . . ." *Well, Dane? Are you going to tell her what an emotional wreck you are? That you can't trust your feelings, or even your perceptions? That you have trouble looking at her and seeing only Eloise Kramer, born in Spokane in 1991?*

He spoke the next safe thought he could find. "My wife and I were professional magicians; we were a team. We designed and wrote our own show. We could read each other, anticipate every move, every gag. We did shows in the States, in Europe, in Japan, Australia,

New Zealand. We were together for forty years. *Forty* years. And for us, *that* was the magic. That was what it was all about.

"But now she's gone. She's really gone, and I'm having to deal with that." Looking at the girl's quiet attentiveness, he realized afresh that she was only nineteen. He could try to explain how it felt, but she still wouldn't know, not really. "It's been an unbearable surprise, like our life was an epic movie and right in the middle the film broke and I'm thinking 'Now what?' and . . . and I don't know, and what really drives me crazy is, I'll *never* know. I'll never know how the story could have turned out."

He jerked his head in the direction of the barn. "Our unfinished story's out there in the barn: all our shows, all our inventions and memories, all the skill we put into it, all the years and dreams and concepts, they're all out there, boxed up in crates under tarps, and I'm running on memories. What's coming up, I don't know. How the rest of my life is going to turn out, I don't know.

"So anyway, whoever you are, or whoever you think you are, I'm not the mentor you're looking for. You need a guide who isn't lost. You need someone whose head isn't . . . well, 'scrambled' isn't a bad word.

"I have no doubt you'll do well—uh, the hobo thing, if you ask me that's like the Gypsy thing, you keep slipping into characters who aren't you, I don't know why unless it's part of your being crazy—but *you*"—he sighted down his finger as he wiggled it at her—"you have it in your*self* to be truly delightful and I really mean that. You just have to find out who you are, and once you do, you'll be unstoppable. You don't need me."

He thought it was a pretty good speech, hopefully enough to establish truth so the mirage would go away. He was honest with her, and most important, honest with himself despite himself. It felt like dragging a sharp rake sideways through his guts, but it was honest.

Without a moment to contemplate she said, "You can't stop now."

Oh, right. He chuckled. *Youth.* How little she knew! "Young lady, things can look a lot different from this end of your life."

This time she digested his words for a moment, her head tilted, her eyes narrowed.

"Once you've paid your dues, you'll—"

"Excuse me?" Was she bristling at him? " 'Young lady'? 'Paid my dues'? For your information, I've lost *everyone* I've loved! I've got a whole life behind me that may not have happened. I don't know who I am now, and—*aww*!" With a burst of anger she clapped her hands to the sides of her head—punishing herself? Giving herself a make-believe shock treatment? "You've got *me* doing it! No. No, no, *no*!" She shot to her feet, fumbling with the robe, pacing in her bare feet. "I'm *not* going there." She pointed right in his face. "And you can't make me! Nobody can, not anymore!"

He knew what she was going to say next. He just knew it.

And she said it. She found a *slightly* kinder voice somewhere and she said it. "Mr. Collins, I respect your pain and your grief, but you can't just sit around feeling sorry for yourself, it'll give you a case of leadbutt, just sinking into the bottom of your chair in this big, empty house making nothing happen and going nowhere, whining about the good old days like some, some *old man*."

If this was a delusion, it was stunningly accurate. He never liked it when Mandy got like this, and yet—

"Sure, grieve, but . . . May I sit down?"

He gestured to the couch and she perched on its edge.

"You think your wife would want that, after all that traveling and magic and adventure, you just chucking the whole thing and turning into an old raisin? I know what she'd say: buy some testosterone, get a motorcycle, do whatever it takes to get living again, but don't waste the years God still has for you. You believe in God?"

"Yes."

"Well, so do I, and I think you should give Him some credit. He *might* know what He's doing." Then, as if realizing her mouth had run off without her, she rolled her eyes heavenward in amazement and horror at herself. The deer-in-the-headlights look that fell over her face was so comical it amazed him. "Oh-oh. Big oops."

And yet, when Mandy got like this, she was always right. As long as he had ever known her, and in some of the darkest times, even through tears, Mandy could find this jarring, "Get real" way to be right.

Eloise didn't just have Mandy's teeth.

She cringed, ashamed, and withdrew into her robe like a tortoise into its shell. "Guess I'm waking up now."

All he could do was sit there, trying for the life of him to fathom what just happened.

She got up from the couch. "Like you said, my clothes must be dry."

He wanted to laugh, and she made him feel that way. She was almost to the hall. "Could you let me think about it?"

She stopped. "Think about what?"

"The . . . whatever it was you wanted?"

She studied him, raised one eyebrow slightly, tilted her head, and then . . . there was that smile again.

chapter

22

Mortimer was driving the SUV. Stone sat in the passenger seat, bandage in front of his right ear, bruises darkening. They were heading for Vegas, driving straight through.

"We heard back from Kessler," said the voice on the speakerphone. "She was ready to wring our necks—and I'm ready to wring yours. The subject is in the house, all right, no doubt talking with Collins, so instead of preventing any contact you've done exactly the opposite."

Stone winced, in enough pain already. Mortimer tried to counter, "Sir, no one briefed us on what we were dealing with."

"There was no need because you weren't to have any physical contact with her."

"But how else could we prevent them from contacting each other? She was at his gate."

"And he turned her away."

"Yeah, this time."

"Watch your tone!"

"Sorry."

"If you two had checked in before acting on your own you would have saved yourselves a beating. Orientation to the Machine is intuitive, and she's figured things out. You weren't up against her, you were up against tens, possibly hundreds of her, as many as she needed."

Stone and Mortimer exchanged rueful glances.

"So tell me about the tire." The tone of the voice was derisive. "Tell me no one's going to find that bullet hole."

"We have the tire," Stone answered.

"You don't think she's going to miss it?"

"In any case, it won't tell them anything," said Mortimer.

"Fingerprints on the tire iron?"

"Wiped clean," said Mortimer. He didn't mention Stone's blood on the tire iron being the initial reason they wiped it down.

"And what about the Hansons?"

"They'll be back after they finish their week in Mexico. The house is back the way it was, like we were never there."

"So what do we do now?" asked Stone.

"You guys better get out of the loop," said the voice. "We'll find something else for you to do—something less important."

Thanksgiving Day. Twenty-eight degrees, four inches of snow on the ground, and light snow falling. The trees were white and drooping. The pastures lay under an undisturbed mantle, and the usual flitting, breezy, lowing sounds of the valley were muffled to a wintry quiet that made Dane stop and listen.

He got a fire going in the fireplace, put on some classical guitar music, and set the dining room table with a white cloth, formal silverware, and place setting, and a dinner wrought by his own hand: a small turkey that would provide plenty of sandwiches afterward; dressing, gravy on mashed potatoes, French-style green beans, a lavish salad he chopped, tore, diced, sliced, and anointed with his own homemade vinaigrette; two thick slabs of cranberry sauce, two wheat and sesame dinner rolls (they came from a bag), sparkling cranberry apple cider, and a glass of Pinot Noir. He would follow all that up with a dessert of pumpkin pie (store-bought) and fresh coffee he roasted and ground himself.

Mandy always served up Thanksgiving dinner at three in the afternoon, and he took his seat at the table right on time, spreading the cloth napkin across his lap. With Christmas card scenery outside the windows and a cheerful fire burning, he bowed his head and gave thanks.

The meal was so good it was emotional. He was tasting again, enjoying again, savoring the work of God and his own hands. What a concept. It wasn't testosterone or a motorcycle, but it was working. He took it slow, imagining how a meal like this would taste in heaven, especially with Mandy sitting in that other chair. Twice he raised his glass to her picture on the wall: "Here's to you, babe."

Eloise was right. Mandy would have wanted it this way.

"Cadillac, purple, zebra," Eloise said. "See? I still remember."

Seamus smiled but still needed more explanation.

"Mr. Collins and I only found the spare tire. The flat tire was gone. Clarence and Lemuel or somebody else took it, I don't know, but Mr. Collins was looking at me like I had a bad memory, so I just told him the three words Bernadette gave me."

"Cadillac, zebra . . ."

"Purple."

"Purple. Right. Was he impressed?"

"I think he believed me after that."

"So then what happened?"

"He helped me put the spare on and then he followed me in his truck all the way to my apartment." His silence and raised eyebrow made her add, "And then he saw me to my door and left and drove home."

"But you showed him where you live."

Well. He was Seamus. He was bred to look after her. "Well . . ."

"I'm just teasing you a little. For your own good."

"He's not that much of a stranger."

"But how much do you know about him?"

He meant well, didn't he? She didn't want to get defensive. "He saved me from 'Clarence' and 'Lemuel.' When I was out on the street he gave me his hat and his sweater and he took the time to coach me with a card trick. He's been a professional magician for more than forty years."

"*And* he's a widower," Seamus reminded her, "and he told you himself how he was going through some emotional issues."

"Which was very honest of him, don't you think?"

"Fair enough. But I'd be careful. As long as it's business, fine, but I'd stay away from any personal conversations until you know him better."

She sighed, if only to breathe out some tension. "Actually, I'd say he reminds me of my father, if anything."

"So he's a father figure."

"Sure. Is that so bad?"

"No. No, that's all right. But you've told him everything you've told me?"

"Pretty much."

"Well, I wouldn't tell him any more. He does deserve our gratitude, absolutely, but we need to keep your life private and you safe and secure."

"But that's just the thing. Am I? I'm not so sure yet."

"I've been looking into it."

She locked eyes with him, awaiting more, but he smiled like somebody hiding a secret and spread his arms toward the table. "Let's eat before it gets cold."

Eloise took her place at one end of the table, blown away by the care Seamus had taken with every detail: the fine china, the silverware—a soup spoon *and* a dinner spoon, a salad fork *and* a dinner fork, a butter knife *and* a dinner knife!—the autumn leaves and colors centerpiece, the lit candles, the napkins—no, the *serviettes*—in silver napkin rings. His dining room was like the rest of his quaint bungalow near the lake: warm, embracing, with dark wood beams and leaded windows, a setting fit for a Jane Austen novel. She'd dressed in the best blouse and slacks she owned; she should have been wearing an empire-waisted dress.

"Lovely," she said. "Lovely, lovely!"

Seamus smiled at her over the centerpiece. He looked great. The candlelight shimmered in his eyes, and the warm glow from the wall sconces highlighted his hair. "I think I'll return thanks." They bowed together and he prayed, "Dear God, for all we have received and for all we will be mindful to share, we give you thanks. Amen."

The meal was like a fireworks display for the mouth, just one *oooh* and *aahhh* after another except she had to hum the sounds to be polite. The whole mood changed for the better, even as she brought up the same old business. "Anyway . . . what can I do? What if Mr. Collins doesn't want to hassle with somebody who might be a mental case? What if Roger and Abby find out?"

He took some time to chew a bite, leaving her in suspense, then said, "I spoke with the hospital."

She almost dropped her fork and peered at him over the center-piece. "You didn't! Can you even do that?"

He loved to draw things out. He stabbed another bite of turkey.

"Don't you dare!"

He laughed and set his fork down. "I don't worry that much about 'can' or 'cannot.' There's always a way once you find the right people, preferably the ones who are nervous. They tried to tell me that all patient records were strictly confidential and that they had nothing more to say, but when I told them I was your attorney and confronted them with what I knew, we fell right into a discussion about what they couldn't talk about and what they hoped I and my client wouldn't talk about either, and from there, lo and behold, they brought up how they might make amends for any pain they may have caused you in exchange for your not pressing matters any further."

Her mouth was hanging open. Luckily she'd swallowed just before that. "You were going to sue them?"

He smiled and shook his head. "It never came up. They wanted this whole thing kept quiet, and all I had to do was wait, just look at them until they were ready to talk about a settlement." Now he made her wait, maybe to show how it felt. It felt terrible. She was about to break the silence when he wiggled a pointed finger. "Take a peek under your plate."

She scrunched down and lifted the edge.

"Here's a little piece of my magic," he said.

There was an envelope tucked under there. She pulled it out. It had her name on it, Eloise Kramer, written in Seamus's hand.

"Go ahead, take a look."

She used her butter knife to slit the envelope open, feeling like a volunteer in a magic act. Her reaction was the kind every magician hopes for: wide-eyed astonishment.

The envelope contained a cashier's check for fifty thousand dollars.

The Friday after Thanksgiving, while Christmas shoppers were going nuts at the malls, Dane drove to a Starbucks in Liberty Lake, halfway between Spokane and Coeur d'Alene, to meet a lady for coffee. He spotted her the moment he stepped through the front door. She was the one sitting at a small, round table in the corner, a bulging computer bag at her feet, a twenty-ounce coffee cup on the table between her hands, and red waves and curls covering her shoulders like lush vines in autumn. She met his eyes as he approached.

"Bernadette Nolan?" he asked.

She extended her hand and he greeted her.

They'd reached a unique agreement. She told him over the phone that she could not tell him anything because of confidentiality laws; she couldn't even let him know whether he had found the right person. Nevertheless, once he described a particular individual they both might know—he did not name her—as an up-and-coming magician who could do card tricks and recall the words "Cadillac," "purple," and "zebra," she agreed to visit with him. It seemed they both realized between the lines that even though she could not talk about the individual, he could, and given that, she was interested.

He ordered a venti café mocha, nonfat but with whipped cream— his way of splitting the difference—joined her at the table, and they began circling each other verbally. Who was he, who was she, what did he do for a living, what did she do, how long?

"Just how did you happen to call me?" she asked.

"Half shoe leather, half luck," he replied. "I called the hospital and got nowhere; I called the Behavioral Health Unit and still got nowhere . . ."

"Confidentiality runs through the entire system."

"So I discovered—and I admire that. I appreciate it. But I still had some key words: 'Spokane County Medical Center,' 'designated examiner,' and 'cute redhead'—her words, not mine. And"—he indicated her hair—"I see you fit all three." He reached into his shirt pocket. "Since I'm not under a confidentiality law I guess I can show this to you."

"And of course I can't comment on it."

"Of course. But I suppose you can let me know if there's any point in us talking."

He unfolded a photo of Eloise Kramer as the Hobett, something he clipped from a poster Roger Calhoun gave him. She looked at it carefully.

"The makeup and the costume don't help," Dane admitted.

"No, they do obscure the likeness, if that's what you're trying to show me. And what's your interest in this?"

"Management. Coaching. Producing. I've found a real talent here but I need to know who and what I'm dealing with."

"So it appears she's working."

"Pretty steady. She has a regular gig at a coffee shop in Coeur d'Alene and then she's booking private functions: you know, birthday parties, church youth groups, conferences. She has a trade show coming up."

She was visibly pleased. "I am very, very glad to hear it. Really." Beyond that, all she could do was slide the photo back across the table.

He returned the photo to his pocket. "So why don't we talk about something outside the bounds of confidentiality?"

"Such as?"

"Such as the system you work in. The hospital, the laws, how patients are handled . . ."

"Okay."

"How would a patient wind up in the Behavioral Health Unit in the first place?"

She looked down and traced little patterns on the table with her fingers. "A variety of ways. Some know they have a problem and admit themselves. A family might admit a loved one. The courts may do so." Now she remained casual, her hands absentmindedly busy but her eyes meeting his. "Sometimes a person will appear to be in a state of mind where they could be a danger to themselves or to others, and if they're, let's say, homeless or wandering about and can't identify themselves, the police can bring them in on a police hold and they can be held for twenty-four to seventy-two hours while they're evaluated. The designated examiners are appointed by the state to examine the person and determine whether there is imminent risk, in which case the examiners—usually two—would recommend further evaluation. If the attending psychiatrist concurs, the matter would go to a judge who can extend the hold, release the individual, or have the individual sent to a state hospital."

She took a sip from her coffee. The pause seemed to signal the turning of a page. "If, on the other hand, the DEs find the patient is no danger to herself or others and recommend release or outpatient treatment, and the attending psychiatrist concurs . . ." She smiled. "It's not against the law to be crazy. Anyone can be crazy and still mix with the rest of society as long as they don't pose a danger." She leaned toward him slightly. "They can have jobs, they can get training, they can pursue careers." She held her eyes on him to make her point, then settled back and had another sip of coffee.

"What if the patient escapes?"

She gave a knowing half chuckle, as if they'd shared an inside joke. "Oooooooh boy."

Dane just waited. This was good.

She thought about that one, looking at her coffee, looking at him, looking out the window. Finally she drew an audible breath and said, "As far as anyone knows, no patient has ever escaped from the Behavioral Health Unit. Given the security measures, it would be next to impossible." Then she let her eyes drop off sideways as she added, "And if it did happen, especially after the seventy-two hours had elapsed, it would be such an embarrassment to the unit and to the hospital that"—she thought another moment—"that they could decide to go with the recommendations of the designated examiners and chief psychiatrist, record the patient as officially released, and close the file."

Not exactly the answer Dane was expecting. " 'Officially released'?"

"As a matter of record. She would have been released from the hospital anyway, so her leaving on her own at a time of her choosing would be a mere technicality that could be cleared up in the paperwork."

"So . . . in that case the hospital would not be looking for the individual?"

"Looking . . . ?"

"They wouldn't send people out to find and apprehend the person, sedate them, and bring them back?"

Her face fell. "Oh, dear." He could read the incredulity, even dismay, in her face. "No. That's not . . . the hospital would not do that. If anything, they would contact the police, and that's only if the original hold was still in force."

"They wouldn't send two men in an SUV with a taser and a hypodermic—"

She winced. Her fingers went to her forehead. "Ohhh, Mandy . . ."

For Dane, all forward motion stopped. His next thought went on hold. Did she say . . . ? "Excuse me?"

She recovered and told him, "I hope you realize that some people live in a different world than ours."

He steeled himself, drew on any stagecraft he could muster to look normal, and said, "Mandy can be that way."

She signaled him with a slight raise of her hand. "Could we forget I used her name?"

chapter

23

It was the classic bottle-and-glass routine. The Hobett started out with a glass and a wine bottle on a table and two tubes to slip over them. "Tube one goes over the glass, tube number two goes over the bottle." When she lifted the tubes away, "The bottle has become a glass and the glass has become a bottle." She replaced the tubes, lifted them away again, and the bottle and glass had traded places again. "So you see, you just—oops!" A second bottle appeared from a tube that should have been empty, and from there the trick was on the Hobett as more bottles appeared from the tubes until eight bottles cluttered the table. She played it all for laughs and got plenty, mugging and intentionally fumbling, the unwitting foil through the whole routine.

Her twist on the routine was when she lined up the eight bottles, blew across their openings to produce a musical scale, and then made them sing "Row, Row, Row Your Boat" simply by waving her fingers at them. As the bottles ended the song in four-part harmony, she slipped a tube over each one and made it vanish until the last bottle, singing the highest note, disappeared into the tube and went silent. She held up the tube, looked at the audience through it, then put her arm through it, showing it to be empty. Great finish.

Dane was one of four folks sharing a table just one row back, and he wouldn't have gotten that seat without a reservation. Every table in McCaffee's was full, and there were folks sitting in chairs anywhere the chairs would fit. Whatever the room's maximum legal occupancy, they had to have reached it.

Roger Calhoun must have been doing well enough to spare a little change. Eloise now had a small stage and backdrop to work from,
some spotlights, and some additional recorded background music,
something between Sinatra saloon and hip elevator.

If he were her coach and mentor, Dane could have addressed
a few weaknesses in the performance, mainly in the timing of her
reactions—just a shade too soon, as if she knew what was going
to happen—and in her body placement—sometimes she held the
bottles and other objects too high, blocking her face; sometimes she
played things too open, where a slight turn of her body would withhold a reveal and increase the surprise. These were small details,
easy to fix. Overall, her pacing was just about right and she was
connecting with the audience, making eye contact, pulling them in.
The wonder, the delight in every little event were still there. She
was a natural.

Just like Mandy.

Oh, yes. He always came back to that. Much as he tried to watch
only her performance, he couldn't help but watch *her*. Much as he
tried to see Eloise, with every turn of her head, every tease in her
eyes, every playful smile, he was seeing memories. He tried again and
again to blame it on grief, denial, delusion, fantasy, even coincidence,
but such explanations were tiresome and easily trumped by what
he'd heard today: her name coming from the lips of a total stranger.
Unless he imagined that as well, the supposed "delusion" now existed
outside his mind, in the real world, which only restirred the aggravating madness of it all.

And what in the world could he tell her? As much as he wanted
to share his meeting with Bernadette Nolan and alleviate her fears,
the good news came with questions, and the answers could make
things worse.

Well, he would step carefully, but he had to go there.

She was winding up her show, starting the levitation. Some of
the folks had seen it before and were shooting sideways glances at
the friends they'd brought: *This is it. This is what I told you about.*
Dane was interested in how she would sell it. Was the wonder still
there? Was it still an adventure for her as much as for the audience?

Her feet came off the floor, and the crowd leaned into the act,
marveling, questioning, astounded.

Hmm. Now Dane leaned in. She was trying a different tack, one he wouldn't have advised: Fear. Dark forces. The unknown. She was acting tentative, extending her hands into space as if something might bite them, her eyes darting about as if seeing something sinister. She was playing it well and giving people the willies.

Still, Dane winced to himself. This wasn't consistent with the rest of her act, her wonder-eyed, playful persona. The fun was gone, and he was disappointed. He made a mental note. The goofy Hobett tampering with the dark side? That would have worked better with the Gypsy.

She'd also trimmed down the routine. No rotations, no gleeful somersaults. She rose a few feet, held herself there in the precarious grip of whatever power supposedly had her, then settled to the floor at the peak of the crowd's interest. She got her enthusiastic big finish. To Dane's thinking, the response would have been even better if she'd not "tapped into the unknown" and come back sweating, trembling, and looking faint even as she greeted members of the audience. Some folks asked if she was all right, and her acting was so good they couldn't be sure from her assurances that she was. As the folks sharing Dane's table rose to go, a lady said, "Creepy!"

Well, that said it all. Dane would talk to Eloise about it as soon as the crowd thinned down. They would talk about many things. He scanned the menu.

"Hello. Would you happen to be Dane Collins?"

A handsome young man who dressed well and cared about his hair stood by Dane's table, extending his hand. Dane took it. "That's right."

"Seamus Downey, Miss Kramer's attorney. May I sit down?"

Dane didn't mean to delay an answer. It simply took him a moment to process the words "Miss Kramer's attorney." "Uh. Sure. Have a seat."

Downey chose the chair directly opposite Dane and planted himself there, spine, shoulders, and chin exuding confidence, authority, maybe even ownership of the table.

"Miss Kramer's attorney," Dane repeated. "No kidding. I didn't know she had an attorney."

Downey put on a smile he learned from another attorney, a banker, or a job interviewer. "Well, we're good friends mostly, but the longer our relationship the more I've accepted the role of legal counsel, watching out for her interests."

Your relationship? "How long have you known her?"

He smiled that smile again. "Long enough. We've had some great times together."

"I see."

"But I understand you've approached Miss Kramer regarding a professional relationship?"

And now that's your business? "Actually, she approached me last Monday and we had a lengthy chat. I assume she's told you all about it."

"Oh, yes."

"Well, I am considering working with her."

"Oh, then it's very timely that we met." Downey looked around the room. Eloise was just finishing up with some admirers. "Eloise?"

She said good-bye and came to the table. She looked more than tired; she looked troubled. Seamus stood—which reminded Dane to do the same—and gave her a peck on the cheek. "Wonderful performance!" They sat, Dane and Seamus facing each other, Eloise on one side. Her head drooped. She removed her hat and rubbed her eyes.

"Dear, your makeup," said Seamus, pulling a napkin from the table dispenser.

"Oh," she said, using the napkin to dab her face. The napkin quivered in her hand.

"I've just been making Mr. Collins's acquaintance. We were about to discuss his possible future relationship with you."

"Oh," she said. "Oh, right." The eyeliner left smeared shadows under her eyes, and her whiskers were streaked. Her hair was matted with sweat. She had yet to smile.

"You okay?" Dane asked.

"Yeah," she said, and managed a smile. "Pretty tired."

Downey said to her, "I think Mr. Collins would be interested to know how we've resolved some of your issues."

"Oh, yeah, right." She looked at Dane and said, "This is Seamus."

"Your attorney," said Dane.

By her inquiring glance at Downey it seemed she was still learning that idea. "Uh, yeah. And he's, he's really incredible. He talked to the hospital and got everything straightened out."

Now, this was unexpected news. "Everything? Really?"

"First of all," said Downey, "again, thank you for intervening and taking care of Eloise after that whole incident. It's just unbelievable what happened. It was horrendous."

Dane looked at one, then the other, unsure whom to address as he said, "You're welcome."

"But you'll be glad to know that I've met with the hospital and they've agreed to a settlement."

Yep, unexpected news. Once again, Dane had to draw on some stagecraft to keep from broadcasting his confusion and surprise all over the room. "They have?"

Downey nodded.

"Spokane County . . . ?"

"Spokane County Medical Center." Downey smiled at Eloise. "Eloise will be starting up an investment portfolio, I imagine."

She smiled back at him.

"Uh, wait a minute," said Dane. He lowered his voice to ask, "You talked about the two guys in the SUV?"

Downey looked to Eloise. When she nodded, he replied, "After all you've done for Eloise you have a right to know. I can't say the hospital was at fault—that's part of the agreement—but I can tell you that they have compensated Eloise for any damages and that they will cease and desist from this particular method of rounding up wandering patients. No more thugs in SUVs or any other form—ever!"

Dane held himself back. Any questioning of Downey's story would suggest Dane had his own version and now that version was bleeding value like a bad stock in a bear market. "No kidding."

"As for any personal, private information about Eloise, that is expunged. Cleared. The hospital has no further interest in her and will respect her privacy."

"Okay. That's great."

"So since this may have been a matter of concern to you, we wanted to clear this up *and* . . ."

And?

"In light of any professional interest you may have in Miss Kramer, we need to be clear that the rules of privacy apply to that relationship as well. She has already shared some things with you not realizing that they were a private matter and that she had no obligation to divulge any of it to a prospective employer, manager, instructor, whoever. So, to be fair to her, we would ask you to bar any of that information from your considerations. Wipe it from the record, let her start clean, and judge her on her own present-day merits. Are you following me so far?"

Was that a door Dane heard closing? "I think I understand what you're saying."

"And you must not encroach on her privacy at any time in the future. Any conversation you have with her must pertain to the business at hand, to her training, your management agreement, and so forth. Nothing personal. You follow?"

Dane rested back in his chair and eyed Seamus Downey, Miss Kramer's attorney, taking all the time he needed to decide if he was offended or not. *Mmm, yeah.* He supposed he was.

"May I ask Miss Kramer a question?"

"If it's nothing personal."

He asked her, "Did you really hire this guy?"

Downey answered, "That's privileged."

"He's my friend," was all she said.

All right, all right, it made sense—on the face of it. She was young, Downey was young, they'd found each other, they were beginning a relationship. What could be more normal and to be expected than that? And an attorney! Could be a good catch—*if* Downey was a good man. Right now Dane wasn't so sure. *Slimy* came to mind. *Slippery. Scheming.* It was even tempting to draw out the s's. *Pardon the impressions of an old raisin, kid, but he's not right for you.*

Old raisin? Right. Another s word came to mind: sixty, his age in a few weeks. It was a good thing to keep in mind. Acting and thinking that age would keep him from being stupid enough to feel . . . well, the way he was feeling.

"Okay then" Dane rose, grabbed his coat and Louis L'Amour hat. "Miss Kramer, should it still matter, I agree to your request. I will be happy to coach and manage you *and*"—he shot a direct look at Mr. Downey—"I also agree not to ask you any more personal questions or violate your privacy." He looked directly at her. "I'd like you to work for me in exchange for my services for, oh, let's say a two-month probationary period. Once we get your career started and you achieve enough success to pay me a commission, then we can talk about that. Agreeable so far?"

She nodded, with respect.

"We'll be happy to discuss any offer," said Downey. "Of course, she may decide she already has sufficient management."

"You?" Dane found that amusing and didn't hide it. He told Eloise, "If you're still interested I'll be available at my ranch nine o'clock Monday morning. Bring a lunch and a change of clothes because you're going to get dirty"—a glance at Downey—"and don't bring him."

He put on his hat, pinched the brim in her direction, and left.

Monday morning.

There was one last picture of Mandy to put away: the studio portrait from 1990 that hung in the dining room. It was one of Dane's favorites because Mandy was posing outdoors with a serene, green landscape behind her, a reminder of where she grew up. She hadn't lived on a ranch since they were married, but in her heart she never left it. Dane lifted the picture from its hook and carried it in front of him, her face close to his, as he went up the stairs.

Dane, he told himself, this *is Mandy. This is the one who locked arms and souls with you and stayed at your side as long as she possibly could. This is the one who made* you *the center of her life, who gave* you *her smile every morning. You* . . .

Not some hotshot, on-his-last-pimple kid who thinks he's a lawyer.

It was ten minutes to nine. He quickened his step up to the landing and hurried down the hall.

The real thing, that's what she was, and she stuck by you for forty years. She was no nineteen-year-old. She was well seasoned, life-proven. A complete package.

He went to a room at the end of the hall, a section of attic space that had been nicely finished to create a storeroom, hobby room, sewing room, whatever. Inside, all the pictures of Mandy throughout her life, all the framed news articles, reviews, and magazine covers, everything that had to do with Dane and Mandy leaned against the walls several layers deep. He gently set the dining room picture alongside the one of him and Mandy receiving Magicians of the Year at the Magic Castle in 1998, then stood, surrounded by all the printed and photographed proclamations that there ever was a real Mandy who loved him. He'd even hidden their wedding picture.

All right. As far as he knew, Eloise had never been anywhere in the house or looked in any direction where she could have seen these things. Now, if she showed up, she would be whoever she was with no input from him or his memorabilia, no information she could borrow to build on. She wouldn't know of any resemblance or be burdened by it. She wouldn't even know Mandy's name.

Was he being rational? By now, that was becoming a very cloudy issue.

He made his way downstairs in time to hear Shirley knocking on the kitchen door.

"Knock knock?" she called.

"Come in."

She had the mail and set it on the counter. "Good morning, Mr. C."

"Good morning."

"I'm going to shut down the pond skimmers today and I'm making a dump run if you have anything you want to throw out."

"What'd we do with those patio tables that were out on the deck?"

"I put 'em in the barn."

"We may need to move them into the dining room."

Her eyebrows went up slightly. "Okay."

"I want to set up the dining room like a restaurant, set up some tables to walk around and turn in different directions and talk to people sitting there, you know what I mean?"

She went into the dining room to get the concept. "A restaurant?"

"Not for real. Just for training purposes."

"Oh." Her eyes were lingering on the walls and shelves with empty spaces they didn't have before.

"And I'm thinking about that barn. We could use all that floor space if we got it cleaned out, got all that straw out of there, all the junk and the animal stuff. And all that old magic stuff could stand to be gone through and stored more safely."

She nodded, taking just enough steps to give her a view of the living room, then turning back again. "That'll give me plenty to do this winter."

"I might have some help for you."

Her eyes narrowed. "Eloise?"

"What do you think?"

She wasn't overjoyed. She took one more look around the dining room and then, wincing a bit, ventured to ask, "You realize she has a drug problem?"

"I'd like to know anything you can tell me."

"Well, you saw her for yourself, the condition she was in, and when we were alone in the bathroom she told me she had a little problem with drugs that day."

He considered that and nodded. "I guess that's what you'd call it."

"And you're sure you want to hire her?"

"She's very talented. I'd like to help her with her career if I can, and in exchange she can work on the place—if you're agreeable."

Shirley was trying to act agreeable but looked constipated. "With me?"

"You're in charge. You can set her to work on that barn for starters, and it's okay if you give her the dirty work. I want to see how much grit she has."

"And what if she's just a flake?"

"It won't take long to find out. And I want you to tell me either way."

She just wagged her head, dark thoughts behind her eyes. "You're the boss."

The phone rang a double ring.

Dane checked the wall clock. It was nine o'clock, on the button.

They went to the front window.

"Oh, Lord," said Shirley.

It was the blue Volkswagen.

chapter

24

"K now how to handle a pitchfork?" Shirley asked.

"Sure," said Eloise.

"How about a rake?"

"Yes, ma'am."

"Well, we'll see." Shirley handed her both, along with a wide aluminum dustpan. "Okay, start with that corner stall. Pitch all the straw out into the middle area here and then rake the stall clean. Go through all the stalls on this side and then do the other side, and then we'll come through here with the trailer and pick up all the straw and haul it out to the compost pile. Once we get all the straw and manure out of here we'll start dealing with the junk."

And have it all done before noon? Eloise didn't want to sound lazy so she didn't ask, but she wondered.

They were standing in the barn, a huge block of cold, very old air with four walls and a roof built around it. The main floor was a gym-size expanse of trampled straw and manure dust, and along each side were five stalls that used to hold horses and cows but now held junk that had to have been here as long as the air: big tires with no wheels, big wheels with no tires; engine blocks and a transmission with the gearshift sticking out of it; a ringer washer—what's a barn without an old ringer washer?; a three-bladed plow; a big, circular saw blade that scared Eloise just standing still; an old, delaminating desk and a gray couch that used to be blue, peppered with mouse droppings; a mound of old carpet in a corner—at some point, she would have to lift that stuff up and she just knew a zillion mice were going to scurry out. Even though winter was coming on, some diehard flies were still buzzing around.

The only thing new in here was a mountainous island of crates, trunks, cases, and containers resting on pallets and shrouded in tarps in the center of the floor. That had to be Mr. Collins's "unfinished movie," all the "years and dreams and concepts" he talked about. It was sad to think that all that stuff might end up like the engine blocks, the tires, the plow, and the mousy couch: left behind, forgotten, with no one ever coming back for them.

"You work here until noon, then you clean yourself up and have lunch with Mr. Collins," said Shirley. "I'll be back to check your work, so don't disappoint me."

"Yes, ma'am."

Shirley turned to leave, then turned back with another thought. "Where are you from?"

"Umm . . . Coeur d'Alene, I guess. Or maybe Hayden."

Shirley made a little face, and Eloise couldn't blame her. "Well, which is it?"

Eloise smiled at herself. "Guess it depends on when I was there."

"I thought you were from Las Vegas."

Las Vegas? "No, I've never even been there."

Shirley thought that over. "Huh. But you're some kind of magician?"

"I hope so."

"Well, work your magic here. We'll see how you do."

She went out through the big door at the far end and closed it after her.

Sigh. That was a downer. Shirley was so nice the first time they met. Today she seemed perturbed for no reason Eloise could figure out and treated her as if she'd never used a pitchfork or even a rake before, as if she'd never even *worked* before. What brought that on?

Well, all Eloise could do was her best.

Eloise sized up the first stall, laid a plan as to where to start and how to keep from going over the same area twice, then got into it, raking the stuff into piles, stabbing big slabs with the fork, and flinging it out the stall door.

Nothing new about this. The pitchfork felt natural in her hands, as if she really had used one before, and the smell of the straw, the old barn, even the dust were exactly as she remembered them from the life she was afraid to think about. The questions Mr. Collins asked her when she first arrived played through her mind: *Ever worked on a ranch? Know anything about horses? Can you drive a tractor? Ever done any plumbing or carpentry?* She felt just this side of being a liar and may have looked like one answering yes every time, but it was the truth and that was just so weird. If she'd never grown up on a ranch and learned all this stuff, how did she know it now?

Her only answer was to dig in and keep pitching toward the stall door. It was a lot easier to pitch and rake hay and horse poop than figure out how she could have acquired skills she could not have acquired in a life she could not have had. The work, right there in her hands, she could understand. She could do that, and hopefully do it well enough to please Mr. Collins.

Dear Lord—she flung another forkload of straw out the stall door—*I only ask one thing of You: don't let me mess up.*

She finished the first stall, then the second, then the third. She was sweating now, feeling a little crusty with the dust, and hoping she was doing all right. She thought she was. She stretched her back, gently stretched the work curl out of her fingers, and got going on the fourth stall.

Oh-oh. Shirley was working in the next stall, pitching hay and raking. This was no time to slow down. Eloise put the tines to the ground and pushed all the harder, moving straw toward the door and then heaving it onto a mounting pile just outside. She was getting tired. Her arms were aching.

Fling! A sizable wad of straw came flying out of the next stall. Shirley was putting her back into it, looking good. No doubt she expected the same from Eloise, so Eloise kept at it, grunting with the effort, moving, moving, moving that straw.

The floor was finally clear. Eloise used the rake to pull the last straggling bits into the dustpan, then emptied the dustpan on top of the heap outside. Shirley must have finished as well. Things were quiet over there.

Very quiet. Eloise paused to listen and watch. No sound, no motion.

No pile outside the stall either. What did Shirley do, haul it off already? Eloise's heart sank a touch. How could she ever keep up with that?

"Shirley?"

No answer.

"I've got these all done. Did you want to take a look?"

No answer.

Eloise approached the stall, neck craning.

No Shirley. All the straw and debris still lay on the floor of the stall as if she'd never been there.

"Shirley?"

Eloise looked, listened, and called again, but Shirley wasn't in the barn. She closed her eyes in a long, earnest blink and opened them: same barn, same stalls, all quiet and normal, the scent of hay and manure still hanging in the air. She was still in the same place. Nothing had changed.

After a quiet, watchful moment she was able to sigh and tell herself, *Well, this isn't the first time. Take it in stride. Live with it.*

But why today, of all days? What if things got really heavy like the other night, and she couldn't tell the difference between real and weird right in front of Shirley or Mr. Collins?

She went into the next stall and got to work. It was all she could do, the best she could do. She dug in, pitched the hay out the door, raked some more, pitched some more—

Until she heard someone in the previous stall, pitching and raking. *Oh, please.* She wilted, rolling her eyes. *Well, okay, live with it, but no messing around this time!* Pitchfork still in hand, she dashed over and looked in the stall.

It was all cleaned out, just the way she'd left it, and no one was there.

Don't think about it, she told herself. *Just keep your mind and your eyes in the real world and don't go anywhere else, especially today.*

As she showered, she tried to experience nothing but the hot water drenching her head and streaming off her nose and chin. As she stood in front of the bathroom mirror she tapped the side of her face to see if her reflection would do the same. Still there? Still Eloise? So far.

Okay. This is real.

What if he asks me how I do what I do? What if he expects me to levitate and I start seeing . . . he's going to think . . . oh, bummer. I can't go there.

She put out a hand and touched the wall next to the mirror. *You're in the bathroom in the shop building. You have fifteen minutes to get down to the house and have lunch with Mr. Collins. It's down that gravel path, the same one you came up with Shirley. Stay with it now.*

Dane had prepared a small lunch for himself. He'd set the breakfast nook table for two, just functional, not fancy. He was heating up some chocolate syrup to make a café mocha, not for himself but for Eloise, and for no other reason than to see if she liked them. Mandy always did.

As he punched in the settings for a double shot—that's how Mandy liked her mochas—he reassured himself once again that he was being rational. Yes, there were emotions involved, but he was aware of them, they were on hold, and he would deal with them with no denial. Yes, the very notion that she could be . . . that she was somehow . . . well, it was madness, self-delusion, a trick of emotions, hormones, and/or painkillers, *but* he was approaching this whole thing logically, at minimal risk. In his orientation interview with her that morning he'd slipped in perfectly acceptable, nonpersonal questions for an employer to ask and gotten a string of yeses: Yes, she'd worked on a ranch, had worked with horses, could drive a tractor, had done some plumbing and some carpentry, and this was information that would not have been publicly available—just like her beverage of choice. This café mocha would be another question, a tiny, risk-free inquiry. If she didn't care for mocha he could always drink it.

Oh! There she was, freshened up, in a clean change of clothes, hair shampoo-soft, looking timid, as if she were a troubled student and he was the vice principal. His first impulse was to smile and try to set her at ease. "Well, hello. How'd your morning go?"

She returned his smile, but it wasn't her real one. "I think it went fine. I got four and a half stalls done."

"Would you like a double-shot café mocha—decaf?"

Now the smile was half real and the eyes widened with surprise. "Wow! That's my favorite! Thanks."

Bam! Another yes.

The look on his face made her look herself over. "What?"

He got over whatever it was and laughed at himself. "Oh, nothing, I'm just . . . amazed. Boy, did I guess lucky! Have a seat." He nodded toward the breakfast nook. She gravitated to the far chair facing the kitchen and checked by pointing at it. "Yep."

The table was set with plates, silverware, and paper napkins. She pulled her chair back and placed her sack lunch next to her plate.

He brought her mocha as she sat down. "It's dirty work, isn't it?"

"I don't mind."

He had half a sandwich prepared for himself—a nice-looking stack of wheat bread, tomatoes, pickles, and what appeared to be prime rib, along with a cup of nonfat strawberry yogurt and a cup of coffee. He took the chair across from her. "Well, right, you've worked on a ranch before."

Well . . . in a way. "Uh-huh."

"Was that your home?"

"Uh . . ." *Come on, Eloise, answer the question. How?* "Um . . . most of my life. I think."

"So you raised horses. Any cattle?"

Her answer was a totally dumb-sounding "Uh-huh," and it sounded so guilty a cop would have arrested her.

"So I guess your dad was a rancher."

The answer stuck in her throat.

"Oh, would that be too personal?"

"Um . . . it could get that way."

"I understand."

She groped in her lunch sack and found some celery sticks with peanut butter. She bit off half of one just to stuff her mouth. He took a bite from his sandwich and there was sweet, safe silence.

Not for long.

"I knew some folks who raised llamas," he said.

*   *   *

It wasn't even a question, but it stopped a stick of celery halfway to her mouth, and the look on her face made him check himself for a drool or a spill.

"We raised"—she had to clear her throat—"we raised some llamas. Isn't that a trip?"

Now he had to mind what his face might be doing. Oh, yes, it was a trip, all right—and the vernacular had not gotten by him. "You—you really did?"

"And my dad was an architect. We did ranching because we loved it."

"So that's where you learned to drive a tractor and do carpentry and all that?"

"My mom died when I was thirteen, so it was just Daddy and me to run the place. But Mom used to do all that stuff, and Daddy told me, 'When you get married and have a family of your own, you'll need to know all this stuff too so you can take care of them.'"

He went for it. "And I'll bet you raised doves."

All right, now, that was just plain creepy. Was it happening again? Her insides hurt the way they used to when her folks would catch her doing something wrong; her fingers were quivering as she groped for her lunch sack and peered inside. "Did you . . . ? What did you say?"

He was studying her. She felt very looked at. "I said, 'I'll bet you raised doves.'"

"Is, is this a magician thing you're doing?"

"A magician thing?"

She pulled out her apple and cheese slices and didn't take her eyes off them. "You know, uh, mentalism? Reading my mind? You're really good. You've got me shaking." She took a big bite. It was easier than talking.

It was time to back off. "Oh, oh, no, no. It's just luck, just probability. You grew up on a ranch, I just started guessing the animals on it. And the doves"—she never really answered that one, did she?—"well, doves are a staple for most magicians, you were a magician in your youth, on a ranch, so I thought you may have had some doves. I think we'll be working with doves at some point, so I asked."

She looked relieved but kept on chewing.

"So . . . you had doves?"

She looked as if she hated to admit it, but finally she nodded, one cheek still full.

Well, that was enough load for either of them to bear for now and still maintain the agenda that brought them together—oh, yes, there *was* that, wasn't there? He took a bite from his sandwich and gave them both a break to depressurize. She took several more bites; apparently she was going to extend the silence as long as she could.

Now he cleared his throat. "Anyway, getting around to my little opening sermon . . ." She was chewing and receptive. The pressure was off for now—soon to return, he feared. "I've seen you perform at McCaffee's twice, and there was that time on the street . . ."

She winced a little and said, "Right."

"So I've seen you as a Gypsy, I've seen you as a Hobett, I've seen you as . . . well, let's call her the Enigmatic Damsel in Distress . . . and I've seen you as a Secretive Attorney's Client hiding behind, oh, let's call it the Downey Doctrine: 'Teach me and coach me and help me to be somebody but don't ask me who I am.' But that issue right there is the one I keep coming back to. Through all of this, I find myself constantly having to face the same fundamental question: who are you?"

She'd run out of apple slices so she had no excuse for her silence. Even so, not a *speakable* word came to her. She thought, *I'd love to know*, but dared not tell him. She could only stare at him, tilt her head, and stare some more. One of her minds, one of her brains, one of her selves might know, but by now they were all so mixed up, like scrambled eggs.

And maybe that was his point.

Oh, thank the Lord, he's going to keep talking. "You have to be sure about that for two big reasons. Number one: because knowing who you are, and liking who you are, are going to read right through to your audience. If you're hiding from them, they may not be able to pin down what it is they feel about you, but they won't be able to connect, and if that's the case, you'll never rise above that sea of magicians out there who all bought the same trunkful of tricks from the same catalog. Maybe you've noticed how a great trick in a bad magician's hands can be a same old thing, klutzy and boring, while a mundane trick in a great magician's hands can be a thoroughly entertaining experience. That should tell you something: the magic is in the magician."

He stopped and looked away, and the silence was awkward. He looked to her again, tried to speak but had to look down, stroking his face. "Anyway . . ." She got teary-eyed watching him. He drew a deep breath and tried again. "Anyway . . . getting to my point . . . you're a natural. You can connect and charm and enchant better than some of the best performers out there. But I still get the sense you're working a little too hard to get through and it's because you're hiding. All the characters you've tried—the Gypsy, the Hobett, the Client—they're not you. I know that sounds pretty obvious, but any performer who knows herself and isn't afraid to show it can wear any outfit and be any character and still come through. I'm sensing that you're afraid to do that, that these other faces are there so you don't have to be. If we can, I'd like to see if you can drop that barrier and touch your audience directly. You have the nature within you, the wonder, the joy of the experience. We need to turn those things loose so they flow right through without a bulletproof shield in the way. Am I making sense here?"

Now, *she* was trying not to cry. He'd not only described her work; he'd also described her life. Her fingers went over her mouth, an unconscious gesture, as if she could bar her real self from bursting out and saying . . . well, such things simply could not be said.

Dane had been piecing together this little speech for quite some time, gathering it like fallen apples from every moment he'd spent with her up until now. He knew it was right for her as a performer, which justified delivering it. That it was right for her as a person he hadn't wanted to address, but now her silent gaze, her glistening eyes told him he'd addressed it anyway. His own emotional investment aside, maybe it was still for the best.

He pushed ahead. "The second reason you need to know who you are is the nature of this business. Mark my words: if you ever achieve the level of success I think you're capable of, you're going to find yourself in a world that wants to repackage you and make you something you aren't; they have to sell you, so they'll put a face and a name on you that will be bigger and more glamorous than you really are. They'll dress you up, stand you up, light you up, and print you up with the specific aim of squeezing every last possible dime out of you, and if you do not know who you are, you'll make the same fatal mistake so many others have made: you'll believe *them*. You'll buy what they're selling, thinking it's you, and oh, the euphoria, the cloud-nine high you feel!

"But it's all a lie, and lies don't last. When the commodity they have made you has outlasted its marketability—when the stores start returning all the T-shirts and school folders and posters and lunch boxes and coloring books that have your face on them—when nobody wants to buy 'Eloise Kramer' anymore, they'll pitch her into the nearest Dumpster, they'll recycle all the paper and cardboard, and they'll make room for the next big star, and then who will *you* be?

"Ask those who have gone before you, the ones who thought the business, the crowds, the applause defined them. It's no picnic betting your soul on a personality, an image that is other than you, because when you lose the bet, you end up sitting alone in your room and there's nobody there."

She was wiping her eyes with her napkin. He could plainly see he'd stirred up all kinds of little ghosts inside her. Once again, it was time to back off.

"It's okay," he said. "Now, I do remember what you said about thinking you're somebody else, and I wonder if, at least as long as you're around here, you might not trouble yourself about that? You are somebody. Just be that. That's how I'm going to play it. During all your training, I'm going to assume that you are not the Gypsy or the Hobett or the Attorney's Client, or any other face that comes along, but yourself, however you may emerge over the days and weeks. And if you need permission, if you need someone to tell you it's okay to be who you are, I'll do that for you. Can you look at me, please?"

Her blue eyes returned from a moment of reflection and he saw in them a longing she'd never shared before, a hunger so deep it seemed a life's store of wisdom and answers might never satisfy it. "When you are here on this ranch, when you are working, when you are learning from me, you may be yourself. It's all right. It's perfectly safe. Do you understand?"

She broke into sobs, her voice quaking. "I don't know who she is."

Pay dirt. He got a little excited and pointed. "That. That right there, whoever's crying right now, whoever's feeling, whoever just said that, that's you. Let's work with her."

chapter

25

Daddy used to say one of the big rewards in life was looking back at a job well done, and you had to have done it to know. Cleaning out a stall in a barn was not glamorous, definitely not cushy, but in Eloise's frame of mind on a snowy Tuesday morning, the work had a good old feeling to it, stirring something deep inside that left her better than she would have been.

Being solitary was part of it, by herself in a place by itself, raking, lifting, and pitching, her thoughts free to relay through her mind and no sound in that barn-tainted air but the rustle of the straw and the soft chime of the pitchfork tines.

The memories were part of it, memories this place brought back from not so long ago. They were Mandy's, but Eloise had permission, so she let them return and drank them in: the quiet nicker of the horses, the steam on their breath, and the thumping of their hooves; the continuous, brown-eyed stare of the llamas; the cooing and head bobbing of the doves; the smell of tractor exhaust and diesel and the black smear of grease on her gloves.

Permission, yes, permission was part of it. Wow. Never mind whether Mr. Collins had the power or right to change the rules, he just did it, and ever since yesterday's session warm little fires began to glow inside her, thawing things out, waking things up. What had she thought that night when he first came to see her perform, that he was some kind of window to somewhere she'd been? Though she hadn't a clue whatever gave her such a notion, her first day under his tutelage made her all the more a believer.

Mr. Collins started with conventional stuff right there in the breakfast nook, going through palmings, flourishes, loads, and steals, just talking, teasing, loosening up over coffee until he had an idea what she could do and she had time to get comfortable. He never said that was his plan, but it probably was, and it worked. After an hour of gentle guidance and good laughs, she was sure he wouldn't bite her and she wouldn't have to die of embarrassment.

When she was ready, they moved into the makeshift restaurant in his dining room, three tables with tablecloths and dishes set out as if someone were sitting there eating or having coffee. He took a seat at one table and became her audience.

Before she could start she had to know—and she was afraid to ask, "Do I . . . do we need to talk about how I do the tricks?"

To her surprise, he didn't care to know. Apart from proper technical execution, he said, the "how" didn't matter. What mattered was the "magic," what her audience experienced. If all they brought away from her performance were question marks, she'd shortchanged them. It was never to be a case of "I can do something you can't" but rather "I'm glad to be with you so we can have a grand time together."

"It's not about you or your ego, it's about them," he told her. "To categorize it, you're after three things: rapt attention, laughter, and astonishment, and all three of these have one big thing in common: they're human. They're about unique moments and feelings. They create memories, and that's what good showmanship is all about."

And that was his guiding principle as she did her show and he commented.

"I love the wonder in your eyes," he said. "Never lose that. You might do the same trick a thousand times, but if you never lose the wonder, you'll always pull them into the experience and they'll feel it with you."

"Oops, watch your body position; you just lost this table over here. There! Play in that arc right there! Now we can all see you."

She faltered the first few minutes, but he cured that by giving her attention, laughter, and astonishment, as if he'd never seen her act before. Maybe he was role-playing for teaching purposes, but she bought it and drank in everything he told her.

"Hold the cards up about chest height so I can see them over all these heads in front of me. That's beautiful. See? Now I can enjoy your facial expressions at the same time."

"Give those silver dollars names, at least in your mind. That's what makes Burt so effective—he's a living thing, like a pet, like a goofy sidekick. When he has a name and a mind, people feel for him so they love to see him win—which is a mark of your genius, by the way. So complete the story: the dollars are mischievous so they get lost, but then they still love you so they come back. Keep it subtle, but humanize them; give them feelings."

They worked so carefully and talked about so many things it took them close to three hours to work through the first ten minutes of her act.

But what a finish! "Eloise, you can do this. You have the instinct for it, the magic inside you. You've made me real proud."

You've made me real proud. Words from Daddy, Mandy's fondest memory, and hers today. She finished the last stall on that side of the barn, then skipped and pranced to the other side, throwing in a stag leap that wasn't very good but was okay, she was wearing work clothes and dancing on straw. She sang music for the move "Raindrops keep fallin' on my head . . ." But not so much that her eyes would get red because crying wasn't for her today, and she had no complaints. She had belief in herself and memories she didn't have to worry about.

She started the first stall, raking and pitching, raking and pitching, and it must have been her mood, because songs kept coming to her. "Do, do, do, lookin' out my back door!"

Nearly finished with stall one. "She's just a hawwwwwng keetonk woman!" Daddy would have frowned on that one, so she found another, "I'll Be There," by the Jackson 5—come to think of it, little Michael may have become a solo act; she'd heard his name mentioned here and there.

And whatever happened to Elvis? Boy, he'd be really old by now. "Well, since ma babay lef' me! I foun' a noo plaze to dwell . . ." The pitchfork made a great mike stand and she still knew the moves.

Oops. She wasn't getting work done. Back to it.

Ed Sullivan. She could do a great impression of him—she didn't bother moving like him because he hardly moved at all and she'd get no work done. "Right heeyer, on our really big shoo! The Bee-uls! Less hear it, less hear it!"

Flip Wilson. "The devil made me buy this dress! I said, 'Devil, cut it owwwt!'"

Dean Martin. "Everybody . . . loves somebody . . . sometime. . . ."

Laugh-In. "Sock it to me, sock it to me, sock it to me!"

Scrape. Swish. Clunk.

Right when she was having fun. She stopped to listen, stifling her breath. Somebody was in the next stall, raking and pitching straw, same as yesterday.

Come on, now, I didn't ask for this. I was having a good time here.

But now the sound stopped.

Her heart was racing. She didn't want to know, but then again she did. She went to the stall door and peered out into the barn.

There was a pile of straw outside the next stall that hadn't been there before, and now she heard a quiet, almost sneaky kind of padding in the straw next door.

"Hello?"

Just like yesterday, no one answered.

"Is anybody there? Please?"

No answer.

"Pretty please, with peanut butter on top?"

Okay. Time to look.

She held her pitchfork in front of her, tines raised as if she'd ever impale anybody, hands clasping the handle tightly but trembling anyway. The fact that she was scared made her angry, which gave her the gumption to step out of her own stall and look in the other. "Just talk to me." Her voice was high and quivery. "I won't hurt you. And if you're not there, then you don't have to say anything because you're not there and it's all my problem, okay?"

Somebody'd been working in the stall. Half of it was cleaned out, the straw and debris in a heap just outside the stall door. She stopped short of going in. Somebody could be waiting just around the corner of the doorway and jump her if she stuck a toe in there. Better to stay outside and listen, just listen and see if anything moved. She kept the pitchfork straight out in front of her, standing motionless until she felt silly. At last she decided, *Well, okay, I looked. If I stop here I won't hurt anybody, including me, and that's the big deal in all this, not to hurt myself or anybody else. After that, I just need to not act weird.*

And standing out here pointing a pitchfork at an empty stall was weird. What if Shirley came in?

She calmed herself, put on Normal, and went back to her own stall to finish it up. "Let's go surfin' now, everybody's learnin' how, come on a safari with meeee!" The songs didn't come quite as easily this time, but they came.

When she'd finished the first stall, she took a peek toward the second.

The heap of straw that used to be in front of the stall's door wasn't there anymore. The stall wasn't cleaned out either, not half of it, not any of it.

Hoo, boy. Second verse, same as the first.

Live with it. Roll with it. Get to work. If this was as bad as it got . . .

But she'd seen it worse than this, and that was what scared her. That whole levitation thing the other night she probably brought on herself, but some of the other stuff, including this, she never asked for, it just came along and happened to her, and what was she supposed to do, act like it didn't?

Just don't hurt anybody. Don't hurt anybody and they won't lock you up.

She got to work, unable, unwilling to sing anymore. She just pitched the hay out the door . . .

"The devil made me buy this dress! I said, 'Devil, cut it owwwt!'" It was a voice that sounded just like her trying to sound like Flip Wilson.

"Everybody . . . loves somebody . . . sometime. . . ." It was coming from the first stall, her voice being silly and singing like Dean Martin.

"Sock it to me, sock it to me, sock it to me!" She'd heard recordings of her voice, but this was downright, flat-out real. Or wasn't it? Was it live, or was it Memorex?

Eloise yanked in her pitchfork and it scraped on the ground. The hay swished aside. She flipped the tines upward and the other end hit the ground with a clunk.

The girl in the last stall went silent and still. She was listening, Eloise could just feel it. The straw crunched and squeaked ever so quietly under the girl's feet as she went to her stall door.

What in the heck am I gonna do? Who is that over there really?

"Hello?" came the voice. It was *her. She. Herself.*

Get out of sight, that's what you do, because if you see yourself stand-

ing in this stall you're gonna freak out and you might get stabbed by yourself with a pitchfork and that would be way too freaky, that would be the ultimate implosion of your brain into itself and what are you going to tell Shirley when you've stabbed yourself with your own pitchfork, I did it but it wasn't me? Eloise padded carefully, as silently as she could, to the corner of the stall adjacent to the door, the only place she could hide from anyone looking in. "Hello?"

Oh, God help me, she's going to come over here, isn't she?

"Is anybody there? Please?"

What if I did answer?

"Pretty please, with peanut butter on top?"

Here she came. Eloise could hear her stepping through the straw. "Just talk to me." Her voice was high and quivery. "I won't hurt you. And if you're not there, then you don't have to say anything because you're not there and it's all my problem, okay?"

She stopped outside the stall, and Eloise remembered—how totally nuts was this?—that when she was the girl out there she was too afraid to come in and look. *Okay, so don't look. I don't want to see you either.*

She didn't come in, but she stood there and stood there forever. *Get back to work, uh, me.*

Finally! The girl who sounded just like her gave it up and headed back to her own stall.

Eloise had to look. She didn't want to, but she had to. She tiptoed to the stall door, leaned, and stuck one eye and her nose outside.

It was her. She. Herself, in the same clothes with the same pitchfork just slipping out of sight into the other stall. Vivid. Real. Eloise could have touched her.

Would her other self have felt it?

Her other self started singing again, her voice weak and looking for a key, "Let's go surfin' now, everybody's learnin' how, come on a safari with meeee!"

And then the singing stopped and there was a heap of straw and manure outside that stall and no movement inside. Eloise stepped over and looked, finding what she expected: the stall cleaned out, just the way she left it, and no one there.

* * *

Her encounter with herself made it all the more awkward—close to miserable, actually—when Mr. Collins suggested doing the card box routine with Shirley as the volunteer. "You need a live, self-aware, emotional person to work with on this one."

But Shirley? Her supervisor? Maybe Mr. Collins wanted Eloise to work under stress by working with a fussy volunteer. Wonderful. All Eloise had to do was keep her brain in this universe while poking around in another to do the trick—without having another Eloise show up—and put on a great performance with both Shirley and Mr. Collins watching her every move.

Well, as Daddy would have told her, she could either get back into her hospital scrubs or take this dadgum bull by the horns and wrestle it down.

Shirley came in right after lunch, took off her winter coat, hat, boots, and gloves, and sat at the third table in Mr. Collins's restaurant. Eloise launched into the routine, putting the deck of cards in Shirley's hand while Shirley just sat there playing along because her boss asked her to.

What was that Scripture about a prophet being without honor in his own country?

Well, those winning moments do eventually come around. When the cards stood up one after the other and formed a box at Eloise's finger-wiggling command, Shirley's stoic face finally broke into a smile, as if she were holding a baby chick.

When Eloise produced the key to the tractor from the box, she had Shirley right in the astonishment zone. "That was clever!"

"Excellent," said Mr. Collins. "I like you working from both sides, that breaks it up visually, but let's motivate the moves a little more. Can you manipulate the cards with your other hand as well?"

Eloise could, and did, and Shirley sat there just being the center of focus for Eloise to move around.

"And let's try a different gesture each time you make one stand up so you aren't repeating yourself."

Oh, right. Eloise hadn't thought of that—among many other things.

"Okay, now, slow down. When each card stands up, give that moment your emotional attention, and your audience will follow you. They need to feel what you're doing, not just see it."

Emotional attention? Well, she found it with God's help and worked it in.

When Shirley got back into her winter coat, hat, boots, and gloves, she cocked her eyebrows at Eloise, nodded to herself, and said, "Huh!"

And then she left.

"That should help," Dane said.

His student looked relieved. "I'm not sure she likes me."

"Shirley's a good gal. I think she's just looking out for me."

"Well, she likes how I clean up the stalls."

"She likes your magic, too, and so do I. Just give her time. So . . . oh, right! Before we wrap up I wanted to talk about your levitation."

"Oh, I can't do that here." Instant reaction, as if he'd proposed doing a root canal.

"Oh, well, sure, I figured as much. That's incredible rigging. It's got me stumped, so give yourself a pat on the back for that."

"As a matter of fact . . . I don't think I ever want to do it again."

She really was afraid, as if he'd cornered her. "Hey, it's all right. It's your illusion, your show. Did you need any kind of help with it?"

She shook her head and he could see a barrier going up. "No."

"Okay. End of subject. No problem. You look tired."

It was nearly the same "tired" she displayed after she did the levitation the other night. "I am."

"And stressed."

She managed to laugh some of it away. "I am."

"Well, the stress was planned, as you may have gathered. But you did well, so let's call it a day. Go home, flop on the couch, and be happy with yourself."

She managed a weak smile as she reached for her coat. "Thank you."

"Nice earrings, by the way."

That brought a better smile, close to her classic, as her hand went unconsciously to her ear. "Why, thank you!"

Hmm. Had she ever worn those before? He couldn't recall.

chapter

26

She bought another pair of earrings, real silver this time, dangling just below her haircut with tiny diamonds sparkling. They weren't cheap but they weren't beyond her budget either, they came with a matching necklace, and hey, they were only the second pair of earrings she'd owned since September 17. The reason she bought them was simple enough: she was being a girl because, after all, that's what she was. She'd lost the thought somewhere along the way with her mind so full, but it was finding its way back to her—and making things a little scary.

Being a girl wasn't hard when she was with Seamus or Mr. Collins. They were friends. They knew her situation—well, *parts* of it. But driving to McCaffee's on Friday night for her seven-o'clock show, walking by those posters announcing a whiskered, red-nosed Hobett, and coming through that door looking like a girl was the strangest feeling, like that dream about being naked in public, like every person in the place was staring at her. Mr. Collins was right. She didn't know she was hiding until now, when she really felt like she wasn't and wished she was.

Roger was busy behind the counter, but she held his attention the moment he saw her. "Oh, what's this?"

All she could say was, "I thought I'd try being myself tonight."

He looked her over and nodded agreeably, but then he scowled a little. "Are we gonna have to reprint the posters?"

Abby just beamed. "I like it."

Megan looked at her and immediately looked at herself. Myron looked at her and whistled. Eloise turned red and Megan gave him a shoulder slap.

It wasn't that big a deal, just dress slacks and a white blouse, a lacy vest, good shoes she could still dance in, some accessories, a little more jewelry, girl makeup instead of hobo, and since she wouldn't be wearing a goofy hat, she had Rhea give her hair a little wave, a little frosting.

Maybe if the Hobett hadn't looked so terrible . . . *Guy*, she felt stared at!

Dane arrived at about six-forty and this time he got a chair at a table right in front—and right next to Seamus Downey.

"It appears you've had quite an influence," said Downey, but it didn't sound like a compliment.

Dane took it as a compliment anyway as he followed Downey's gaze to a sight that surprised and then pleased him: Eloise Kramer mingling and chatting it up with the customers prior to her show— and looking as good as he'd ever seen her.

She figured the only way to be among friends was to make a few be-fore the show started. It turned out that Eloise was naturally chatty, much more than the Hobett or the Gypsy, another little thing she'd forgotten about herself. She got to know John and Kathy from Sand-point, Marge and Winnie from the Gateway Senior Center, Jim and Cindy from Kellogg, and several others, and the only comment she got that could have been referring to the change from Hobett to Girl was from Sheri the mom, "Well, you're very pretty!"

Okay. Cool. But as seven o'clock approached and Eloise stole be-hind the curtain into the pantry she wondered, did "pretty" amount to "funny"? Without the Hobett's bumbling ways this was going to be a whole new shtick and she hadn't been there yet.

Well, bring it on. It was better than going back.

Dane noticed the house wasn't as full tonight, probably due to the snow. Winter was going to slow things down, which meant a kind of catch-22 for his client: she'd have to find more gigs elsewhere, but there probably wouldn't be as many available. They'd better line up some Christmas parties, maybe a New Year's party at a safe venue, hopefully something for Valentine's Day, any birthday parties she could fit in, and she'd better get a Web page started and know how to budget. They'd have much to talk about. Oh, and he'd definitely have to compliment her on her good looks tonight. That frosting in her hair fit so well. It was easier to imagine her as a blonde.

So he'd had quite an influence. Nice feeling.

Anyway, back to business. He watched the folks still coming in, hoping for a good crowd. One man had found a single chair in the corner by the window and sat there all by himself with a computer in his lap. Not odd for this place, but odd for this hour. It would be interesting to see if Eloise could draw his attention away from whatever he was working on.

Eloise tucked Burt into the pocket of her vest. He made a pretty obvious bulge, but wouldn't be there long. She stretched a little. She'd reworked a few of her dance steps to accommodate her new outfit.

She could hear all the voices, the clinking of spoons, the hissing of the steamer, the cacophony of her audience waiting, twenty-plus different conversations going at the same time and none of them understandable, like a henhouse at slow speed. She loved that sound. She stopped every other thing just to listen.

It's all about them, Mandy. Those are . . .

She broke inside. She wasn't expecting it.

Those are your friends. . . .

Tears came to her eyes. *Mandy?* And thinking the name again brought a fresh wave of tears, a trembling lip, a quake in her diaphragm. She broke down, right there, without choice or warning and only minutes before she had to go on.

Desperate, she pulled the emotion in, breathed deep, tried to settle, wiped her eyes. She had a mirror hanging from a nail and her makeup bag resting next to the Kenyan coffee beans. She checked herself, tissued off the smears, touched everything up.

She just wanted to be *her.*

She put the tissue to her eyes again, trying to hold back the flood, but she couldn't keep herself from thinking it, from officially posting it on the bulletin board in her brain, *I just want to be her, that's all.*

She was still trying to steady up, still sniffing a little when she peered through the curtain. It was five minutes to seven. Myron and Megan were getting ready to do the crisscross magical appearance with her. She could see the crowd all visiting, smiling, expecting—her friends.

Breathe. Settle down. Think of your first moves.

Something was burning.

Was there smoke in the room? Everything looked kind of brownish, like she was looking into the room through a glass of tea.

She blinked, looked at the ceiling, the floor, scanned from wall to wall trying to break the spell that had come over her eyes.

From somewhere under the floor came a low rumble. The voices in the shop began to echo, as if falling back into a long hallway.

She forced her eyes shut as hard as she could. She clamped her hands over her ears.

When she opened her eyes, *somewhere else* was swirling through the coffee shop, a building within the building: strange halls and doors, other voices and sounds.

"Ready, Eloise?" It was Megan's voice coming from somewhere, broken up into pieces. Eloise looked right at her and looked right through her.

Go with it. Live with it. Act normal. Don't let anyone know.

She heard her own voice somewhere else in the room saying, "Sure, let's go."

The recorded music started, her jazzy opener, off-speed, fast, slow, the tone heaving up and down, the lines repeating and overlapping. Myron was already across the room, ready to cross back, just waiting for Megan and Eloise . . . and waiting for Megan and Eloise.

"You ready?" came Megan's voice.

"You ready?" came Megan's voice.

Eloise stared through the curtain and through other walls and other rooms to see her audience. Ghostly shapes like people passed through the coffee shop and through the tables. The posters of Rhett and Scarlett, Bogey and Bacall drifted over small rooms with beds, obscured then revealed an old lady in a wheelchair, a couple coming through the wall carrying flowers. Corners, walls, streaks of light spun past as if on a carousel.

And mixed into it all, far away though right in front of her, was herself—not an image of herself, but herself—floating in midair, arms extended, legs gathered up, as her audience sat in astonishment.

"You okay?" came Megan's voice.

The music was playing, Myron was waiting, she still smelled smoke, she could feel herself floating above the floor, arms extended, legs gathered up—and somewhere far away she felt terrified.

She blinked, gawked, looked about, tried not to lose sight of the coffee shop, but it had vanished around one of many corners and all she could see was a long hallway submerged in tea and she was floating between floor and ceiling, helpless, carried along on a slow current like a leaf in a river. The ghostly shapes like people became doctors, nurses, aides in scrubs and uniforms, and then the place became places, and places within places, a swirling soup of hospital rooms, doctors, a gurney, wall posters, offices, doctors, IV unit, exam room, nurse, wheelchair, smell of smoke, operating room—huge lights, blurred, streaked—curtains, doors, beds, more doctors, visitors, a lab with microscopes, an old man in bed, nurses, orderlies, hallway tilting and reeling, an elevator—it sucked her in, spit her out, there was a huge door locked up tight with red letters on it, a blinking keypad. She drifted toward it with no will of her own, no choice, no chance, no time . . .

She was inside, in the dark, surrounded by electric hums, fluid gushing through pipes, air rushing through ventilators, and far away, muttering voices. Red and green numbers flashed from consoles. Little green, red, yellow, and blue lights glowed out of the dark like stars on a clear night. She could smell something burning, like singed hair.

An orange glow drew her and she saw two faces in flickering light.

Lemuel and Clarence?

Floating like a ghost, she circled them, afraid they would see her, wanting to see them, wanting to be sure. It was them, all right, small figures in an expansive, windowless chamber, faces illumined by the light of a fire. Lemuel was holding a plastic garbage bag open and Clarence was pulling out . . . they were hairy, with pink faces, big ears, dead, half-closed eyes. Monkeys. Little monkeys, at least a dozen, easily more. Clarence was wearing rubber gloves and throwing the monkeys into a furnace like they were cordwood. Each one landed on the one before it, smoked, sizzled, blistered, then flashed into flames, the belly swelling, then bursting with steaming entrails.

She'd never been so afraid. She screamed . . .

Someone else screamed, there was a group shout and gasp as something like concrete smacked her in the side of the face, on her shoulder, her hands, her side. It hurt.

She was shaking, sick inside, whimpering. She wanted to run.

People were talking, murmuring, rustling. Chairs were squawking on a floor. She was waking from a dream, tuning in to . . .

Hands touching her, gently turning her. She saw Mr. Collins's face, then Seamus's face, both blurry, full of concern, a ceiling fan and its afterimages fluttering above them. Now Roger and Abby leaned and looked at her, reaching like a distressed mom and dad. "Easy now," said Mr. Collins. "Give yourself time."

She realized she was looking up and they were looking down. The concrete that had hit her was the tiled floor, and *she'd* hit *it*.

"Is she all right?" someone said.

She jolted, looked about. Was she safe? Was it a dream?

"Oh, her nose is bleeding," said someone else.

The floor still felt like it was moving.

"That had to hurt."

"Incredible!"

"Look, you can see there aren't any wires or anything."

"Maybe they all broke."

"How *did* she do it?"

"Is this part of the act?"

Megan and Myron were busy with a broom and towels, cleaning up spilled drinks and some broken dishes on the floor. A lady was saying ". . . don't know, it just went sailing off the table."

Cheryl from Pinehurst gave Mr. Collins a paper napkin, and he put it to Eloise's nose. Eloise could feel the texture of the paper and the warm blood soaking into it, both real enough. She held the napkin in place, and with some helping hands managed to raise her head, then her body, and sit up.

The good folks broke into whoops and applause, as if she were a fallen quarterback.

It was over? She knew it was. She remembered these faces, remembered being here, remembered where she planted Burt and who got the spinning quarters and who kept winning the coin toss and the name of the lady—Tracy—who did the card box trick with her and Chuck the miner who got the magic coffee cup. Burt hid in Cindy from Kellogg's handbag. She'd been here. She'd done her whole act.

The levitation was the only thing that was still a little foggy, as if she hadn't really been *here* when she performed it.

She met the gaze of all those eyes full of wonder, astonishment, and concern. The show. She hadn't closed it. Forcing a smile—it hurt—and still holding the red-blotched napkin to her nose, she asked, "Did I do it?"

"Oh, yeah," they all said, clapping, looking at each other, looking back at her.

She got her feet under her, and Mr. Collins, Seamus, and Roger helped her stand. Abby was already behind the counter, getting some ice.

"Ladies and gentlemen, Eloise Kramer!" Seamus announced, and the folks gave her a fresh wave of applause.

"Some kind of act," said Bruce, a senior at NIC, and his girlfriend, Julie, shook her head.

"Well, that's live entertainment," said Mr. Collins. "Thanks a lot, everybody!"

Eloise waved with her free hand and called a muffled "Thank you!" while Mr. Collins and Seamus helped her hobble behind the counter and into the pantry. There were a few little claps here and there, but mostly the folks had to chatter. Word of this would be everywhere.

Roger brought in a chair and they all helped her into it, fussing, dabbing, acting medical.

Roger passed his hand over her eyes. "Pupils are good."

Seamus lifted her right hand. "Any pain here?"

"Sure," she answered.

"Can you move it?" asked Mr. Collins.

She waved at them.

"She's just shaking!" said Abby as she brought in a Ziploc bag filled with ice and helped Eloise press it to her face.

"That was quite a spill you took," said Roger.

"Did you lose control?" asked Seamus. "Is that what happened?"

She drew a breath to answer, but first realized there was no answer she could be sure of, and then realized there was no answer she could tell them. She let the breath quiver out of her without a word and repositioned the ice pack. *Don't let them know. Go with it, live with it, act normal somehow. Be Eloise.* But she hurt so much, inside and out, and she was so scared.

"She never tells us anything," said Roger. "Magicians!"

"Well, whatever you did, don't do it again," said Abby.

Abby was right. She was shaking and she couldn't stop. "I killed the show . . ." she said, looking for Mr. Collins. "Did I kill the show?"

But Mr. Collins had bolted through the curtain as if chasing somebody.

Dane had no idea who that guy was. Maybe Eloise knew and never told him because it was one more little secret of hers, but Dane didn't want him getting away without their meeting each other and discussing what he'd been doing on that computer all through Eloise's performance.

Dane had paid the fellow little mind at first, wanting to watch Eloise and see how she might do being herself, or nearly herself, for the first time. She was off balance at first, caught between two styles, but interacting with the folks gradually brought out the class and sass, that endearing feminine side he'd always known was there and she just had to discover. The more she found her stride the more naturally she could charm, enchant, tease, and play the twinkle-eyed foil of her ornery coins, cards, and tennis balls. The folks loved it.

Which let Dane relax and relive a special joy as he watched her and the reactions of the crowd—and also renewed his interest in Mr. Computer. The man's eyes seldom lifted from the glowing screen before him. As a matter of fact, it was during the most dramatic moments of Eloise's act, when the illusions were at their height, that he leaned toward the screen, swiped his fingers over the touch pad, tapped the keys.

This was no disinterested computer user just getting some work done over a cup of coffee.

He was in his forties, to guess it. He was small in stature with thin, graying hair, wire-rimmed, professorial glasses, very focused demeanor. He was interested in only two things: what Eloise was doing and what his computer was apparently telling him about it.

It was while Eloise was in a prime moment, engaging everyone's attention—which was just about constantly; he'd have to commend her on that—that Dane slipped toward the back of the room and from there, ever so casual, ever so passive, he drifted sideways to where he could see the reflection of the computer screen in the window.

The image was angled and reversed, but he could recognize numbers in columns, bar graphs that twitched up and down, undulating lines, and wispy blue waves that seemed to move whenever Eloise moved and rest whenever she stood still.

Now Dane was craning to find the visitor but could go nowhere as well-meaning fans stood in his path to ask him how Eloise was.

Eloise withdrew the napkin to check the bleeding of her nose. It hadn't stopped yet and the napkin was scary to look at. Abby brought a fresh tissue and a few extras. "Rest your head back," she said. Eloise complied. The pain was starting to register. Her head was throbbing and her whole right side ached.

"Maybe we should get her to an emergency room," said Roger.

How many times would she have to say it? "No. Don't even think about that, please."

"What if you've broken something?"

"I haven't broken anything."

Seamus asked Roger and Abby, "Could you give us a moment?"

Roger and Abby weren't so comfortable with his request, but they stepped through the curtain.

Seamus leaned close and spoke quietly, "Was all this Collins's idea?"

What kind of a question was that? "What?"

"The levitation with all the risk involved."

Was he being . . . ? He sounded so childish. "Absolutely not!"

"He didn't pressure you into it?"

This was just the kind of conversation she needed while staring at the ceiling with a bloody napkin at her nose and an ice pack against her face. She could feel some swelling. "No. I wasn't even going to do it."

"Then why did you?"

"That guy back in the corner."

"Who was he?"

"I don't know."

"Do the levitation! Do the levitation!" the man had called out, which got everybody else calling for it, and all along Dane could tell Eloise didn't want to, that she was actually afraid to go there, that her dark and mysterious approach to the illusion was no act at all.

But many had heard about it, some had brought friends they'd told about it, they would have been disappointed, so Mr. Computer got the illusion and plenty of numbers and undulating patterns to watch and now Dane was kicking himself. He should have warned Eloise, given her more complete coaching: yes, of course the show is for the audience, it's about them, but not to the point of endangering yourself. Whatever it is you're doing up there, the risk has to be strictly illusory. You never take chances!

Dane's first priority had been to corner that guy immediately after the show, but Eloise's nasty fall preempted that. Now she was safe and stable—and the man's table was empty. Dane weaved and jostled through the crowd to the front door and pushed through to the sidewalk, looking up and down the street.

Of course, the man was gone.

"Aren't you acting a little . . . young?" Eloise wanted to know.

Seamus was trying to keep his voice down, but a temper was showing. "You just about killed yourself out there."

She brought her head forward and checked the bloodied napkin. "I'm abundantly aware of that."

"And this"—he indicated her appearance—"was this another idea of his, this . . . what is this, your new look?"

"Seamus, you helped pay for it. And I like it. I like being myself." It dawned on her and she stared at him. "Don't tell me you're jealous."

He rolled his eyes. "Have you noticed any pictures of his wife around the house?"

"No."

"Does he ever talk about her?"

"Seamus, aren't you the one who laid down all the rules about he and I not getting into personal matters?"

He came in close, finger pointed. "This could get personal if—"

"If what?"

"If—pardon me—if he happens to be a lonely old widower who enjoys the company of a pretty young girl."

"Woman."

That stopped him short. "Now, I find that interesting."

"Seamus. I'm going to tell you this one last time, and I'd like it to be a matter of record between us: if anything, Dane Collins is like a father figure to me. That's my own view of it, I haven't given him any indication that I feel that way, but I'm not ashamed of it." She kept looking him in the eye. She surprised herself.

"So noted." He looked away as if reading labels on the coffee bags, then deflated a little as he let out a sigh. "By way of explanation, I guess I've gotten a little attached to you."

She applied a fresh napkin to her nose. "Well, I'm flattered."

Which was all she wanted to say about that.

chapter

27

It snowed on Monday morning, so Eloise left for the ranch early. The little Bug made it to the gate and up the long driveway with time to spare—time to tap on the door—"Come in!"—go into the kitchen without taking off her coat and ask just to know for sure, "Is everything okay?"

Mr. Collins was just finishing his oat flakes and toast, and looked at her over his last sip of coffee. "I would say so, especially now," he said. "How are you?"

"I just . . ." Groping for words again. One of these days, she deeply hoped, she'd be able to tell him everything.

"Your face looks like you lost a fight," he said. "How's the rest of you?"

"Sore." She'd spent Saturday and Sunday trying to find a comfortable way to lie down while waiting for the ibuprofen to kick in. "I had to cancel the rest of the weekend."

"I figured as much. Have a seat. Want some coffee?"

"Oh, no, thanks. Shirley wants to check me out on the tractor so I can plow the driveway. I just wanted to make sure . . . you know . . ."

"This'll be on company time." He gestured at the chair across the table from him, and she plopped into it with her coat still on. "You're still troubled over Friday night."

"Way troubled. It was a disaster."

He put up his hand. "No, no, now don't say that. The ending could have used a little work"—he winked at her—"but overall you pushed on through and made the best of it. I couldn't have asked for more under the circumstances."

A sack of bricks lifted from her shoulders and she let herself smile. "I'm so glad to hear that."

He smiled back. "I'd just like to know, what were the circumstances?"

"What do you mean?"

He set down his coffee cup with a firm motion that sent the same message she could read in his eyes. Daddy used to do the same thing. "You know better than that."

Her eyes dropped. It would be quite a list if she told him all about the tea-stained soup of hallucinations that messed up her show and got her hurt, the miserable night she spent in her apartment going over and over what happened and wondering if she'd gotten mixed up in the occult or a permanent drug trip or was being tormented by aliens or was just plain nuts and bound for worse and never better. That would be just the thing to tell him when all she could conclude during the last two miserable days was that she wanted to be here in this safe, real place more than anywhere else in the world.

She met his eyes. How much of the man she imagined—well, yeah, *dreamed*—him to be was he really?

He was waiting.

She could try a small step—as if a small step off a cliff wouldn't hurt as much as a big one. *Well . . . Geronimo!* "It's . . . I guess it's my mental difficulties."

"Don't be afraid. Just tell me."

"I was having flashbacks of the hospital."

He crinkled his brow. "The hospital . . ."

Had he forgotten? "Yeah, the hospital, you know, where they thought I was crazy and had me locked up and then sent those guys after me."

He cleared up and nodded. "Right. *That* hospital."

"It was like being in McCaffee's and the hospital at the same time, stumbling around trying to figure out where I was and I couldn't control it. I could see the hallways and the doctors and . . . and a really weird room."

He was about to take a bite from his toast but set it down.

"It was dark, and there were lights and control panels like the inside of a spaceship, real sci-fi-looking. And then there was this big, empty room like a basement and two guys . . ." This was going to sound so weird! "And they were burning dead monkeys."

He raised an eyebrow and his face was one big *Huh?*

"I know it sounds crazy. That's because it is."

"Describe it to me."

Why? "Well, they had a black plastic bag full of dead monkeys and they were throwing them into a big furnace to burn them up." And she didn't want to go any further.

He seemed to be envisioning it. "Well. Those were quite the circumstances."

"So I think . . . I think I need a breather—not from magic altogether, just from the weird stuff. I think it would be great—if I could, I mean—just to work here, just do whatever you need to have done and rest my brain, and then you could help me learn things that are, you know, from this planet, stuff I can get my hands on and work with and be . . . be here and not way out there." Was he sold yet? "I'd work for free and you wouldn't even have to train me."

He tried that on for a second, then gave his hands a little toss. "Well. Okay. So what do the Calhouns say? How soon do they want you back?"

"As soon as I heal, I guess."

"And you need to rest your brain."

"I sure do."

"Well, we could just make you an apprentice. I want to finish cleaning out the barn so we can move stuff out of the shop. Then we can make room in there for a working stage and develop a stand-up show featuring you. If you can show up every day—what would you like, a four- or a five-day week?"

She was trying to keep her emotions steady as she worked up an answer. "Umm . . . five, if we can work around my magic gigs."

"Got a few?"

"Some birthday parties. I can show you my calendar."

"We'll work around your gigs. Always. You need to be out there."

"Right, right."

"Five days a week, and working around your magic gigs, which includes McCaffee's when you're ready?"

She was getting wide-eyed, nodding as her heart raced.

"I'll get you on the payroll as an employee. You'll earn an hourly wage while we put a show together and see if we can make it fly—uh, when your brain's ready. Sound good so far?"

It sounded so good she was afraid it might not happen. "I want to work. I want to work and get my mind together, get my life together, get in charge of things . . ."

"Instead of things being in charge of you."

Who *was* this guy? "Absolutely."

"I'm all for that. All right. Why don't you help me clean up the dishes here and then we'll go unearth some history."

The crates, trunks, and travel cases, all the imagined, designed, and painstakingly built props and illusions that brought thrill and sparkle to the Dane and Mandy stage for forty years, now rested in a great, squarish heap in the middle of the barn. To the farthest reaches of Dane's knowledge, the stage lights blackened and the final curtain fell on Dane and Mandy when the last corner of the tarp was tucked in and the last knot in the rope was tied. He never imagined he would return, never thought he would look back, could not have dreamed that he would be standing before this monument with young Eloise. What an image: the finish and the start in the same moment gazing up at the span of time between them.

"Wow," she said.

Yes. Wow. "Let's see if we can get this rope undone." He worked on one side, she worked on the other. The knots could be stubborn. He worked one loose. "How you doing?"

"I think I got it," came her voice.

The rope went slack. He pulled it over to his side and let it fall. "Okay, come around and let's ease this tarp off."

They gently, even reverently, drew the tarp over and down, letting it gather in crackling folds at their feet, and then he gave her time to take it all in: the ruggedly built travel cases with steel edges and corners, the plywood crates nicked and scraped from years of touring, the solid wood trunks with their metal latches and hinges.

And stenciled on the side of every one of them were the words DANE AND MANDY, LAS VEGAS, NEVADA, USA.

Her eyes rested on the words. He remained silent, pretending to look things over and tuck away the tarp as he watched.

She lingered, her mouth open, then faintly smiling in amazement as she tilted, then wagged her head. "Her name was Mandy?"

"That's right."

She gazed at the name as if gazing into a face and then, reaching as a child reaches for her parent, she placed her hands flat upon either side of the name and framed it. "Whoa!"

"Forty years."

"That is just so cool." She studied the name as if reading it for the first time. "You know, I really like her."

He was thinking of Mandy and looking at Eloise as he said, "So did I."

She withdrew her hands and her eyes searched out every appearance of that name on every container, her eyes arcing over the stack as if she were in awe of a rainbow.

This would be enough. He could feel his soul, his insides warning him to move on. "I guess we'd better . . ."

She snapped out of it. "Oh, absolutely, yes. Didn't mean to . . . It's personal, I understand."

"No problem." He had to do a little acting, had to push them onward. "Now what I want to do is re-create a stage such as you would find in a small to medium venue, something with more geography. I'd like to build it in the shop and use some of this stuff to create a setting, just give you some things to work around, handle, bump into, use if it fits your style. Going from close-up to stage means everything has to be bigger, wider. Here's a Zigzag. You know what that is?"

"The optical illusion. The lady stands in the box and then it looks like you remove the middle part of her."

"Right. I . . . I don't see you doing this as part of your act, but working with some larger props might be a good exercise to help you think in bigger, wider concepts."

"I'd love the experience."

"Here's a sub trunk—uh, substitution trunk."

"Metamorphosis!"

"Okay, you've seen this one."

"The magician's assistant gets tied inside a bag and locked inside the trunk. The magician raises a shroud around the trunk and then bammo! The magician trades places with her, just like that."

"It uses a lot of basic principles: timing, misdirection, creating an expectation, and then defying it—and just plain physical ability. We could try that out to hone the basics. It's easy in principle, not so easy to perform convincingly. Once again . . ."

"The magic is in the magician."

"You get an A." Now he had to laugh. "And this one . . . this is our old levitation. It's a dinosaur. There are so many better designs out there now—which I guess you're aware of."

"I guess."

"Mandy and I worked it into a gag routine and put a whole new life into it. That's another lesson right there: even an old trick that everybody's seen before can be fresh if you give it a little twist—which brings us to another little idea of mine. Considering how good you are with tennis balls and quarters, this might be just the thing."

Just the thing? This was more than "just the thing," this was a God thing, a reunion, an awakening of an old happiness she remembered but hadn't thought was hers. She muffled a squeal behind her hand, laughed through her tears, and gave Mr. Collins a hug.

Four little pairs of dark eyes looked warily at her through the wire cage; four heads bobbed as the snowy white birds ruffled and sidestepped on their perch, checking her out. Newbies, she could tell. Everything was unfamiliar to them.

"I remember you told me you raised doves," said Mr. Collins. "Well, I just got these in and they're going to need taming and training. I thought you might be interested."

She leaned close to the cage and the timid faces just inside the wire. She cooed at them, spoke gently, and they watched her, not afraid but not so sure either. They were four little angels, a visitation from that beloved dream—the return, in their own way, of her first loss.

"Two girls, two boys," she said. Just like Mandy's prizewinners.

"They'll need names," said Mr. Collins.

"Names . . ." Looking into those attentive little eyes, she didn't care if Mandy Whitacre's life was delusional, it was still hers. She reached into the memory, grabbed this one small corner of it, and hauled it into this room, where it could be real. She studied each dove and got to know its markings, the shape of its head, the curve of its beak, and then announced its name. "This little fella, his name is Bonkers. And this little girl, she's Lily. And you—yeah, cutie, I'm talking to you!—you're Maybelle, aren't you? And that means *you* must be Carson. Glad to meet you." She added only in her thoughts, *again*, then looked away to dab her eyes.

She heard, then saw Mr. Collins sink into an old plastic patio chair, his hand over his mouth as if he'd seen the Red Sea part down the middle. He looked as if *he* would cry.

"Mr. Collins?"

He smiled away the emotion and wagged his head at a thought he didn't share. "Call me Dane," he said.

chapter

28

Eloise dubbed them the Gleesome Threesome—herself, Shirley, and Dane—a crew bent on a goal and getting a good old feeling getting there. Lifting, rolling, dragging, and hand-trucking tires, wheels, a ringer-washer, a couch, an old desk, and other rusted, mouse-chewed, bent, and seized-up junk out of the barn and carting it all to the dump was dusty, dirty, and difficult, but it was a pleasant kind of misery. Daddy always said hard work was good for the soul, and each evening, as Eloise zonked out on her bed, her soul felt better.

Working alongside Dane—and being able to call him that—sure added a shiny side to it. Handing to, getting from, struggling, lifting, hauling, cracking jokes, and having laughs with that man were healing, as if a big, lost chunk of her life was finding its way back. Sitting on a stool beside him at his drafting table, studying his drawings of the stage he had in mind, and making out a materials list for the lumber store was a sweet flashback. She'd done the very same thing with Daddy when they built the aviary for her doves, the raised bed garden behind the house, the coop for the chickens. That day, not only did her soul feel better, she also went home feeling special, and that night she fell asleep with little movies of her second daddy playing through her head.

Wednesday morning they moved the tiller, box scraper, tank sprayer, brush hog, and backhoe out of the shop and into the barn, which cleared floor space in the shop for a stage. By midmorning, the materials arrived. Eloise wore Dane's nail apron and wielded his hammer, Dane did the cutting and layout, Shirley ran the power nailer and drill, and by quitting time on Thursday the Gleesome Threesome had completed a rough, unpainted stage, fourteen by fourteen, in portable sections bolted together. No lights, no curtain or backdrop, just a big frame and plywood box about three feet high with steps at either end.

"That'll do for the immediate future," Dane said, snapping a picture. He'd snapped a lot of pictures during the process. Eloise was always smiling for the camera. "We'll dress it up as we go along, but tomorrow we have to get you up there and start filling out a show."

The thought made her tingle. She climbed the steps and pranced onto the stage, imagining the shop as a theater, Dane, Shirley, and the Kubota tractor as her audience. She did a pirouette into a ta-da pose, arms outstretched.

"How's it feel?" Dane asked, looking up at her.

She said, "Real good," but that didn't come near the feeling. She wasn't just on this stage; she was also on this stage in this shop on this ranch with that man sitting down there in front of her, watching and caring about her. She added, "Like where I belong," and that was more like it.

Joy bubbled up and burst out in a squeal as she did another spin, flinging out her hand as if materializing something.

A microphone flew from her hand across the stage. There was a gasp from the audience of at least five hundred—especially from the sound crew. The mike slowed, then stopped in midair. Eloise flashed a bedazzled look at the audience, stared at the mike as if she hadn't a clue how it did that, and then, as if getting an idea, struck a dancing pose and drew it back toward herself with a beckoning wave of her hand. It floated toward her then, obeying her fluid gestures, halted just beyond her reach, tumbled end over end, then spun laterally like a bottle. Eloise was loving it and so was the audience.

She was dressed in her best, a silk blouse and gold cravat, black slacks, black vest with gold embroidery, hair done perfect and shining in the lights. Her audience was dressed in jeans, sweatpants, sweatshirts, snow boots, camouflage pants and shirts, beer logo T-shirts, and billed caps. It was the annual Community Christmas Show at the Wallace High School auditorium in Wallace, Idaho.

The gig came up suddenly. A barbershop quartet had to bow out, leaving an open twenty-minute slot between the combined Kellogg and Wallace High School concert bands and the Christmas Carol Collection Community Choir. Someone telephoned Roger Calhoun, who telephoned Eloise, and Dane thought it was a great idea, a perfect way to test new material on a big stage.

With a fluid, pulling gesture, she made the mike float past her and sang a note into it as it went by. It kept on singing the note as it circled behind and around her like a moon around a planet. When it came back around, she let it pass behind her hand, and as it did, it split into two microphones, exact duplicates. The first continued orbiting while Eloise sang a second note into the second mike, which set it in motion, and now two mikes were orbiting about her head singing a continuous chord in her voice. Mike One came around and passed behind her hand again. Presto, Mike Three! Eloise sang a third note, Mike Three carried it into orbit. A fourth mike joined the others and they sang a four-note chord that became the opening bars of "Let Me Call You Sweetheart," a bow to the barbershop quartet that couldn't make it. The folks got it right away. They laughed, she milked it.

Dane and Eloise had six days to put a twenty-minute show together, six days of eye-to-eye, mind-to-mind brainstorming, discussing and arguing, trying this and then that to see how it looked, working out the dance moves, the props, the appearance of everything for a bigger crowd and bigger stage. They worked all day, talked and debriefed through lunch and dinner, kept at it until nine each night, when she drove home to sleep. It was intense, grueling, focused.

She loved it. She never felt so alive.

The microphones held the last chord of the song as they orbited faster, approaching blurring speed. Abruptly, Eloise put out her hand, caught Mike One as it came around, did a graceful spin, flung her hand outward . . .

The mike became a dove that flew out over the audience in a wide arc.

Eloise caught Mike Two, did a spin, flung out her hand . . .

Another dove flashed into view and followed the first in a wide circle over the heads of the audience.

Another catch, another fling, another dove. Three doves fluttered along the same trajectory like white-feathered boomerangs. Another spin, another fling . . .

The fourth dove set out to fly the big circle just as the first was finishing.

Ooooh! Ahhhh! Laughter. Astonishment. Applause.

Dove One flew in close to Eloise, but she waved it on. It circled the room again, the others followed, and then they came home, one, two on Eloise's right hand, one, two on her left. She brought her hands together in front of her, bowed with the birds to receive the applause, then straightened, threw her hands upward . . .

The doves became a flurry of snowflakes sparkling in the lights, settling ever so slowly to the stage floor.

Backstage, Dane gently put Carson the dove back in his cage. "Good work, little buddy!"

Then he watched her work the crowd with wonder in her eyes, her childlike expression reaching the back row and saying, *Wow! Did you see that? How did I do that?*

So alive. So free.

On the left side of the auditorium, sitting on the very top row of the bleachers toward the back, a man in his thirties, wearing a crisp, new Cabela's camouflage jacket and a billed cap, was honestly enjoying the show while he watched the screen of his laptop computer. In a small window in the corner of the screen was a video stream of Eloise's performance, captured through the tiny camera mounted atop the screen and time-coded. On the main screen, locked into the same time code, columns of numbers rolled faster than the eye could follow, wave patterns rose and fell, blue shapes like time-lapse clouds formed and dissolved against the vertical and horizontal axes of a graph, and all in concert with every stunt and illusion produced by the girl onstage.

The data were streaming in faster than he could study and analyze in real time, but it was easy to see the trends and appraise the situation. The readings from the coffeehouse were confirmatory and alarming.

These readings were worse.

The lights in the living room dimmed except for the multicolored lights on the Christmas tree and the glow from the fireplace. "And can you turn off that lamp?"

Dane reached over and switched off the table lamp, then settled back on the couch.

"Ta-daaa!"

Eloise made her grand entrance into the living room, face glowing and eyes sparkling in the light of six candles atop a fancy chocolate cake. She didn't just walk into the room, she made a procession of it, bearing the tea tray out in front of her as if conveying the crown jewels into the presence of the king. "Merry Christmas to you, and happy birthday to you . . ." When she came to his name in the song she sang it for several counts, grinning at the privilege, then set the tray with the cake, two plates, and two forks on the coffee table. She sat on the love seat opposite, elbows on her knees, chin propped on her knuckles, eyes giddy. "Make a wish!"

All he could do was gaze at her while the candles burned. *Make a wish?*

His birthday was on the sixteenth, but Christmas on Saturday was the ideal opportunity to celebrate both, and Eloise leaped at it. She prepared a dinner, Chicken Kiev, and baked the cake in his kitchen, accepting help from him only with questions that began with "Where do you keep the . . . ?" and "Do you have any more of . . . ?" She set the table in the dining room with his best silverware and dishes and brought some candles for the centerpiece in case he didn't have any, which he didn't. Dinner was at six o'clock, and at her request, he wore a jacket and tie. She made all the meal preparations wearing her jeans, blouse, and running shoes, but then, with a magical flair, she vanished into the guest bedroom and reappeared for dinner in a dress. It was black, cute, and tasteful, conforming to her waist and draping from her hips to a teasing hem above her knees. The diamond earrings twinkled just below her haircut, and the diamond necklace adorned her neck. She sat with her ankles crossed, and around her right ankle was another surprise: a silver anklet.

The candles kept burning, and her eyes softened from giddy to serene. She eased back, folded her hands in her lap, and said nothing more about the wish. She just returned his gaze, then playfully shrugged a shoulder, her smile closing the distance between them, her hair a sunrise in the glow of the fireplace.

What he thought, he couldn't share: he was sitting across from a perky, take-on-the-world, blue-eyed kid, but in the eyes of this girl were the depth, the spirit of a woman—the woman he would make his own and share his life with for the next forty years—forty years ago.

Oh, he could make a *lot* of wishes.

"What?" she finally asked.

All he could tell her was as much truth as his best wisdom would allow. "Ellie, I am compelled to say that you look absolutely lovely tonight, and you have made my Christmas a manifold and uncontainable blessing. Thank you so very much."

And without a wish, he blew out the candles.

Eloise stared at the candle wicks as they smoked and smoldered down to a cold, black nothing. There was a dead space. No words.

Oh, and she wasn't smiling. She put her smile back on and gave a little clap. "Yay!" Then she stepped to the wall and eased the lights up about half.

Was he happy? Was he having a good time? She hurried back to her seat and met his eyes, looking for . . . well, just the look he had a moment ago. It was sort of there, but now . . . well, the candles weren't lighting up his face anymore, the lights were half on, the wishing was over.

The cake was a little crooked, but it came out great otherwise; all he had to do was taste it. The Chicken Kiev could have been a little more crumbed and maybe a little lighter on the pepper, but he loved it, he really talked about it, he ate a bunch of it.

She just had to know, "Are you having a good time?"

"Very much. You've no idea."

She cut a slice of cake for him—he wanted only a little one—and one for herself, just a little smaller. "So, how does it feel being sixty? Is it . . . I mean, I can't imagine being that old . . ." Her hand went over her mouth, and she laughed at the gaffe.

But so did he. "Don't worry, you'll get your chance, Lord willing. I kind of like it. I get a big kick out of asking people where they were when they first heard Kennedy was shot. Used to be you could ask anybody and they'd know."

She took a bite of cake instead of telling him: seventh-grade music appreciation class with Mr. McFaden. "I guess you've lived through a lot of history."

"So will you. Someday you'll be the only one who remembers where you were when you heard about 9/11."

"I . . . I suppose you remember the Beatles."

Big, oh-yes nod. "Grew my hair out long, bought all their records, got a lot of flak in church about it. I can remember standing in line outside the Paramount Theater in Seattle waiting to see *A Hard Day's Night.*"

She went with Joanie at the Wilma in Coeur d'Alene. She screamed because Joanie did.

"I lived through Vietnam and Watergate. I remember Mandy and me sitting in a motel room in Elko, Nevada, watching the Watergate hearings on a black-and-white TV." He laughed. "Oh, wow, that old Sam Ervin! You should have seen him. What a character!"

Missed that one, too.

"I remember Neil Armstrong first setting foot on the moon: 'That's one small step for man, one giant leap for mankind.'"

With Walter Cronkite on CBS. Daddy and she had made popcorn. Right?

She was such a liar . . . She had been there, but she was pretending she hadn't because, come on, how would it sound to say, guess what, I remember that stuff, too?

"You okay?"

"Huh? Oh, yeah, great. I'm just checking out this cake. How is it?"

"It's great. It's perfect."

*   *   *

That was one stabilizing influence: the birthday cake.

Sixty. The Big Six, the Big Oh. The numbers embedded in the top of the cake were curly, festive, oversize, loud, obvious, made of sugar, but, in Dane's thinking, cast in concrete: inflexible, unflinching, altogether true, the only thing in the room right now that smacked of reality. They poked and prodded him with it, waking him up with every glimpse.

"Sorry it was a little lopsided."

"Ellie, it was beautiful. The whole evening's been beautiful. Thank you so much."

"I like being called Ellie." Oh, that was dumb! "Eloise is . . . it's kind of formal between friends."

"So is Mr. Collins."

Maybe she shouldn't have worn this dress. Maybe it was saying too much. Her anklet was showing.

"What are you thinking?" he asked.

"Umm . . . I'm thinking . . . this is all about that day in October, out on the sidewalk in Coeur d'Alene. The Gypsy meets the big guy in the cowboy hat and her life changes, maybe forever."

"I've thought of that day often."

You *have?* "It was a God thing. Don't you think it was a God thing?"

Six and zero.

"I think . . . I think it sure seemed like it. Of course, when you trust God with your life, most everything is a God thing, so, sure. It was a God thing."

Oh, she really loved that answer. "And then, how we met again at McCaffee's!"

And how you became an inescapable, inseparable part of my life; how you ruled my thoughts; how I didn't want to see you again because I wanted to so badly. "Well, we're both magicians. It was bound to happen."

* * *

True. But where was the magic in an answer like that? "Anyway, I just wanted to say thanks. For everything."

"Thank *you*."

He took his last bite of cake.

She shoved her last bite around the plate with her fork.

The fireplace cast a warm glow on the whole room, and the only sound was the lilting, jazzy ballad coming from the entertainment system.

"Did your wife ever dance?"

He didn't seem to mind the question; he even smiled faintly and far away at the memory. "A lot like you. Graceful, elegant, very natural. She was born to dance."

"Did you ever dance with her?"

Wow. She could see him watching the memory, and it must have been a great one. "Boy, did I. She didn't want to dance onstage by herself and look like a typical magician's female assistant—you know, just adding pizzazz, filler, misdirection—so we danced together to set up the illusions. It was very classy, a lot of fun."

"What style?"

That made him laugh. "Whatever Mandy was into at that particular second. Actually, we based everything on West Coast Swing because it was showy, it was fun to watch, and it gave Mandy so much freedom to improvise. I guess you'd call it West Coast Swing for a Family Show."

"Can you show me?"

"Show you . . . ?"

"I've never danced with anybody, not like that."

"Have you ever done any swing dancing?"

She stood and offered him her hand. "Show me."

And she couldn't believe it: he stood up, took her hand, and led her to the warmly lit floor space in front of the fire.

* * *

Speaking of God things, maybe this was another one. It was one of the wishes he didn't think he could wish and didn't wish and now here it came true anyway. So to speak. *Teaching* her to dance was a safe and practical way to have his wish but not really, and in any case it would serve her professional interests and widen her creativity.

She was facing him, still holding his hand, filling his vision and his mind, pushing aside the thoughts he was *trying* to have. "Well, getting really basic here, it's slotted."

"Uh-huh." She seemed to know what he meant. She was scoping out the floor.

"So we could run the slot this way, parallel to the fireplace."

"Okay." She repositioned herself so they stood facing each other, parallel to the fireplace.

"The show and the dancing shifted all over the stage so we were constantly moving the slot around, but we always knew where it was. So, uh . . ." Now he had to touch her. He slipped his right hand under her left arm and cupped her shoulder blade. "We start with a swing closed position." She placed her left hand on his right biceps. "Yeah, yeah, that's it. Now your right hand rests in my left hand, my palm up, yours down—our hands are lower, down here, swing position. Good! Tone in the body, tone in the arms, good frame, good connection."

She smiled up at him and he could see admiration. "Hey," he said, "don't be too impressed. Mandy was the real teacher." She laughed. It eased him a bit. "So first we move in the slot, six count, I start with my left, you start with your right, I step back . . ."

Step forward, step forward, tap, two steps backward and a triple step . . .

Spinning into open position, connection, and counterbalance . . .

Before long they were moving with the music and she was following his lead, stepping, styling, syncopating in the slot. His lead was subtle, experienced, on time every time so she knew just what to do on which count and where she would arrive after each variation.

And that's what turned on the ideas. They began to fire like sparks in her mind and body, which brought her joy, which brought her more ideas, and she could imagine how it must have felt to be Mandy Collins dancing onstage with her man. Safe. Free to create, take a chance, tease a little, feel the joy, then snap right back into the shelter of his arms, his touch, her creativity always secure.

Imagining the feeling became the feeling. She squealed with delight and did a spin on her way out of the slot, and right out of the spin, there was his hand to take hers and draw her back. Safe. Home. She was lost in the dance, moving, alive.

All the moves came back and he fell into the routine with no need for thought or plan, leading Ellie as he'd led Mandy for thousands of shows, connecting, protecting, and turning her loose to light up like a sparkler. He was onstage again, and Mandy was there in Ellie's eyes, in her rapture, her playful tease, her every fluid step. Ellie *was* Mandy. She . . .

He drew her in, she slid past, and an idea sprang from the last one, starting on the *and* before the *one* count.

But he dropped his hand from hers. She went into a spin but it fell behind the count; a triple step died beneath her; what may have been her next idea turned to blowing sand; she sank to the earth, heels and toes on the floor.

He looked at the fire, the cake on the coffee table, even at the ceiling, but not at her. "Anyway," he said, "that's how we did it."

Her heart was falling out of orbit. She forced a smile, a little laugh. "That was great. I've never had so much fun." She even squeezed his arm, her cheek touching his biceps.

But he wasn't there.

"Guess it's time we tackled those dishes," he said.

chapter

29

She kissed him on the cheek as she went out the door, stepping carefully on the icy walkway to her Bug. She wore her hooded parka over her dress, her winter boots over her pantyhose. It made a great picture, sort of like Big Bird in black, just goofy enough to end the evening on the right note. They had a great time.

Dane carried his notebook computer into the living room. The lights were still low, the fire was down to glowing embers, the tree was the same cheerful clarion of joy. He sank into the couch, flipped the computer open, and waited for words to come.

Tremendous Christmas, spent in the company of . . .

His fingers hung over the keys, drummed in space, then went to the delete key and held it down. He folded his arms, stared at the tree, watched the glowing embers in the fireplace, and finally tapped:

I suppose I should have found a church by now and some friends closer to my own age.

Better talk to Arnie, get him up here, let him see the show, and get her working.

Maybe on a cruise line far, far away.

He closed the computer and went to bed.
He couldn't sleep.

* * *

She would have kissed him. She really would have. If he'd turned his head just a little bit she would have gone for it, honest to God.

Ohhh, and that would have been so terrible. That would have ruined everything. He would have banned her from the ranch and never let her anywhere near him ever again.

She rolled over, fluffed her pillow for the umpteenth time, and buried half her face in it, not sleeping, not sleeping.

What time was it? Almost midnight.

She would think about tomorrow. Yes, tomorrow. What were they doing tomorrow? Blocking out the second half of the show. They had almost an hour's worth, the best of the Wallace show, the McCaffee's show, and anything else that plays big. Those doves were really getting the hang of it. She'd have to warm them up in the morning, refresh them on release and return. She'd have to make sure they had enough greens . . .

Ohhh, the way he looked at her. Did she really see what she thought she saw—

No, no way, that was ridiculous. It was all in her head. He was an old man, a Daddy. Sixty. The big Six Zero.

She would think about curtains. Right. Curtains for the stage. Well, it was best not to need them, to find other transitions. She never knew where she'd have to perform.

But wow. His wife's name was *Mandy*! Now, what kind of God thing was that?

"Mandy—I mean, *Eloise*, it's nothing!"

But that had to be cool being his wife, dancing with him in every show, going home with him every night. Kissing him . . . being in his arms . . .

A thrill coursed through her and made her wriggle.

Oh, Lord, I'm terrible, I'm terrible!

She smelled something burning.

And I think it's love . . .

Oh, cut it out!

Something *was* burning.

She sat up and sniffed. The room was dark but didn't seem

smoky. She saw no haze in the amber streetlight coming through the windows.

But the windows were wavering like heat waves, shifting sideways.

Oh! She felt something that startled her, then made her wriggle again. Her right hand was resting in his hand—not here, not now, but somewhere and soon. She could feel the warmth of his palm, his embrace upon the small of her back. Another thrill coursed through her, feelings like colors, a trembling, and she reached as she sat in the bed, knowing she'd find his shoulder. She closed her eyes . . .

And saw herself, far away, circling, floating through the dimensions, the layers, the walls, windows, lights and sounds of several worlds passing by each other right in her apartment. She was gliding and turning like a princess, every sequin of a beautiful blue gown flinging jewels of light about the room.

Sitting on the bed, she could feel the floor under her, the air moving through her hair, the flight of her soul as music bore her aloft. She lifted the sheets aside . . .

Her feet alighted on the apartment floor and she danced through the dream, touching notes and rests with heel, with toe. She opened her eyes. All around her, the apartment was a carousel of colors, sounds, times, and places.

And she was the dancer wearing the gown, the center of a galaxy, dancing through dimensions, floating above worlds, embraced by strength, safety, and . . .

She was wandering carefree, lost in wonder, heart flooding with . . .

A song played inside her, a song that had waited for this time, this now, a song of . . .

Everywhere rushed inward, becoming here and now within her, drawn from afar by . . .

She knew herself, knit into one by . . .

The floor pressed evenly, steadily against her feet. She came to rest while multirealities swirled around her, and let herself think the word.

Love.

At home within her, gathered from her scattered worlds and now her very own, so new and still so known. She closed her eyes to seal it in, folded her arms about herself to hold it close like warmth inside a blanket.

This was God's gentle, loving doing, speaking to her through the mystery, showing her a glimpse of a faraway light she had long and secretly hoped for . . .

There was a man in her bed.

She jolted with a yelp, which made him jolt and then start to curse, "Holy . . ." He clamped his fingers over his mouth, dumbstruck, staring, looking her up and down.

She covered herself with her arms, though she was modestly dressed—in thrift store pj's.

He was young, probably in his thirties, not too bad-looking with curly black hair, a Tom Hanks kind of face. Now she could see that he wasn't in her bed, but in a metal-framed single bed against a strange wall in a room she'd never seen before. She'd seen those blankets and sheets before—in the hospital.

"Who . . . don't be afraid," he said as if addressing a timid spirit.

Well now, just who was the ghost here? She could see him, but she could also see her own bed in her own room in the same place, all mixed together like a double image, and he was looking a little transparent himself. She didn't move, afraid the whole jackstraw pile of dimensions would blow and flutter away, including this man, before she found out who he was.

"Can you see me?" the man asked, propping himself on his elbow.

She nodded.

"My God," he said. "Oh, my God!" He sat up slowly, as if trying not to frighten her. "Who are you?"

Around her, worlds still moved, crisscrossed, swirled. Even her visitor, his bed, and as much of his room as she could see, were rippling, fading, reappearing.

The only thing not moving was she—and she felt that way, inside and out. She knew the answer to his question, the only answer, and she spoke it clearly for anyone in any world to hear her. "I am Mandy Eloise Whitacre."

That seemed to horrify him even more. He couldn't even manage another "Oh, my God!" He was about to say something . . .

His image got wavy, began to fade behind a tea-stained shadow. "No, wait!" he said, hand extended. "Wait! Don't go away. I won't hurt you!"

He was gone.

She was staring at her own bed, standing nowhere else but in her little apartment. The alarm clock said half past midnight. She looked down. Thrift store pj's, bare feet, plain wooden floor in the amber streetlight coming through the windows.

Who was he? Was he even real? Was *anything* real?

With no answers, *ever*, she could only tuck such questions away to wait for their time. She would remember his face. For now, she was swept up in everything else that had just happened, and what remained.

"Mandy," she said. The dancer was Mandy. She was the dancer. She enfolded herself with her arms. The warmth had not left her. "Mandy Eloise Whitacre."

There had been a development. Dr. Jerome Parmenter could see it in the face of Loren Moss, his project manager. Moss was wan and shaken as he closed the door to Parmenter's office and sank into the chair facing the older gentleman's desk.

"What's happened?"

Moss had been manning the lab while the rest of the staff was away for the holidays. Now fear lingered in his eyes. "I saw her."

The news was not a surprise, but it was not welcome. "Where?"

"In the staff room, not more than ten feet from me."

Parmenter turned to the computer console adjacent to his desk. "Did you note the time?"

"December 26, 12:22 A.M."

Parmenter scrolled through the readings and found a spike in activity at precisely that time. "A 23-degree fluctuation in the Kiley, 19 in Baker . . ." Unbelievable! "*42* in Delta! Initiating at 12:22:04, resolving 12:23:36."

"That was it. It felt like a small earth tremor, and it woke me up. She knocked some books from the table, and my water bottle went rolling." Moss leaned forward. "She had at least 50 percent opacity, and I'm guessing I had the same opacity to her. We could see and hear each other. I asked her who she was, and she responded. She gave me her full name, Mandy Eloise Whitacre."

"Did you tell her who you were?"

"The corridors diverged before we got to that. But she was startled and disoriented. I don't think she had any idea where she was or what was happening."

"Does anyone else know about this?"

"No one."

Parmenter immediately scrolled to the readings he'd obtained in the coffee shop. "During her levitation she deflected the Delta 29 degrees and I thought *that* was extreme."

"She only deflected 17 during the Wallace performance, but collectively there was a trend outward." Moss shook his head grimly. "She's becoming very adroit at this, to the point that her inputs have priority over ours."

Parmenter sighed, sharing the frustration. "We set, she resets, we reset, she resets again. She's getting so we can't keep up with her."

"And she doesn't even know she's doing it. This latest event was clearly involuntary, which confirms for me that many of the events we've observed were also involuntary, triggered by emotions, her subconscious, maybe stress . . ."

"Maybe even . . . her spirit?"

Moss paused to weigh that. "If there is such a thing, it would correspond to what we're observing, yes."

"To a substantial degree, I would say. It's a niggling question we try to avoid, but we're not dealing with a lab rat here, or even a monkey. I believe there are aspects of Mandy Eloise Whitacre that our science can never touch or control."

Moss considered that. "And that would provide an explanation for her behavior and these events."

"Yeah, well, DuFresne and the others are never going to buy it, but here's my take on it: we've stolen her away and she's trying to find her way back. We can alter and revert every atom of her being, but at a certain level beyond our reach, she knows who she is and where she belongs."

Moss sighed, visibly burdened. "So we've crossed the line."

"Oh, we did that a long time ago."

Moss looked away. "And not with impunity."

Parmenter felt a visceral response: fear for his friend. If Mandy Whitacre's corridor passed through the staff room only ten feet from him and only a few yards from the Machine . . .

"Loren, are you all right?"

Moss only looked at him, the answer in his eyes.

"Oh, no . . ."

"I remember everything."

Parmenter's hands went to his face.

"I remember volunteering and everything that happened before that: the first experiments on the lab animals, the installation of the additional mass, working with you on the Kiley/Baker protocol. All of it. A whole year."

"We'll have Kessler examine you."

"The cancer's back. I can feel it. It was a pronounced and sudden change, quite noticeable."

The worst had occurred. Neither man could speak for a moment.

Moss offered, "The deflection of her corridor encroached on mine and overwhelmed it. Similar to what happened to the soldier, Dose."

Parmenter looked at the computer. All the data that once promised discovery now confirmed failure. It was like reading a postmortem report.

"We saw this coming," said Moss.

The elder scientist agreed. He just couldn't bring himself to say it, not yet.

But Moss had had time to think about it—and now had nothing to lose. "The early models all predicted inexorable return to equilibrium, and sure enough, all the inanimates, and then the rats, and then the monkeys retraced. We could push the deflection debt ahead of us, but . . ."

Parmenter nodded ever so slowly, scrolling through the data on his screen. "But you can only stretch the universe so far. Looking through the lens of dead rats and monkeys—"

"*And* a retraced soldier *and* a retraced scientist," Moss reminded him.

"These figures all make sense."

"And all proverbial hell is going to break loose with Mandy Eloise Whitacre *the* pivotal factor."

Parmenter hated being so cornered. "And DuFresne and Carlson in sole possession of the ears and pockets of the military."

"I don't suppose a moral argument will work?"

"Coming from us?" That made Parmenter chuckle in bitterness. "We've already explained our way around the data, disposed of the rats, incinerated the monkeys, held back what we were really thinking—that we were exploiting and jeopardizing human lives." The moral question had always been clouded by bitter divisions over secrecy, propriety, national security, and the omnipresent god of funding, but now it was as clear as the data on the screen—and the dying scientist sitting across from him. "It's going to be a terrible note to end on, wouldn't you say?"

Moss sighed and rubbed his eyes. "You could say that."

chapter

30

That evening, Eloise knocked on Sally and Micah Durham's door. It had been so long, and the Durhams were so happy to see her. Yes, Rhea was still doing hair. Darci had moved back to Sioux Falls, Iowa, and was engaged. Two new girls, Shelly and Doris, were staying in the home as part of their probation. Sally and Micah were fine. Micah had a job with flexible hours, so he could help out more.

And how was Eloise? Once she got past "Fine," "Doing all right," and "Staying busy," she sat with them in the cozy living room and got down to the main purpose of her visit: "I'm ready to tell you now. I *have* to tell you. Eloise is actually my *middle* name. . . ."

The Monday after the New Year's weekend, Arnie Harrington, fresh up from Vegas, got his first look at the Collins-Kramer-Morgan Magic Theater. "I'll be jiggered!"

For a training stage built in one end of a shop building, the stage was one impressive piece of work. It had footlights fashioned from work lights, movable access stairs, backdrops that rolled into place on casters or lowered into place on cables, teaser curtains, a rack of lights Dane bought secondhand from a concert promoter, a spotlight, and one main curtain operated by a revamped garage door opener.

"The birthplace of exciting new talent and many new wonders to come, I trust," said Dane.

Wow. If Eloise Kramer's act had benefited from the same Dane Collins touch . . . "So where's our magician?"

"I think I heard her Bug coming up the driveway."

The shop door opened and she stepped in wearing a hooded parka and pulling off her gloves. "Well, hi!"

"Hi there!" said Arnie. *What a picture.* The Gypsy Hobett Coffee Shop Girl had an entirely different air about her in this place. *You'd think she grew up here.*

Dane exchanged a warm smile with her and a thumbs up.

She made a whimsical, tentative kind of face and pulled back the hood of her parka.

Dane became frozen in time.

Arnie stared unabashedly.

Her hair was blond, golden through and through. She cast them a little sideways glance as she hung up her parka and pulled off her boots, but said not a word.

"What's this?" Arnie asked.

"You did it," said Dane.

Her hand went to her hair, fingers combing, fiddling with it. "I did. I had my girlfriend put me back the way I was."

"The way you were?" Arnie asked.

"She's naturally blond," said Dane, and he loved how it looked, it was rather obvious.

"Huh." Arnie was still staring, getting a little message. "How 'bout that."

"The roots were growing out anyway, and it just came time to be myself," she explained.

Arnie nodded and forced a smile—it wasn't a very good one; he was trying to hide a gut feeling.

"Anyway," she said, offering her hand, "it's wonderful to see you again."

"Yeah," he replied as he shook her hand with a sideways glance at Dane. "I guess it's been a long time."

Arnie sat in a folding chair just ten feet from the stage, the Kubota tractor at his back. Dane manned the lights and curtains, Shirley doused the shop lights and cued the music, and Eloise Kramer, in her one and only stage costume, did her show with playful, high-energy confidence, performing for Arnie as if he were the only one there. She made eye contact, she dazzled, she teased, she mugged, and most of all, she wove the wonder through everything she did.

The cards flew from her hands, arced from one hand to the other, sailed over Arnie's head and back to her hand, vanished as if they were never there; the bottles popped and multiplied out of nowhere and sang in harmony; choreographed tennis balls bounced and teased all over the stage as she danced with them; doves materialized from her empty hands and circled the room, only to vanish into snow-flakes; her microphone had clones that sang in orbit around her.

She got a hula hoop spinning around her waist, then stood still while the hoop continued to spin on its own. As she gestured magi-cally, it rose around and then above her body until it was spinning in midair over her head. Then it became her partner and she danced with it, leaping through it, dance-dodging it, flipping and twirling it around herself like a cowboy with his lariat, and all without touching it. The hoop split into two, the two hoops circled around her like two unicycles without riders, then merged into one hoop again.

The finale went off like a fireworks display: the music crescen-doed, and Eloise took her grand ta-da pose flanked by tennis balls bouncing, hula hoops spinning, doves doing figure eights over her head, and playing cards shooting like a fountain from her hands.

The music thundered and drummed to a big finish, Dane closed the curtain on Eloise's triumphant tableau, and Arnie rose to his feet, applauding and whistling. *"In-credible!* Absolutely astounding!" Dane opened the curtain again so she could perform a graceful dancer's bow.

Shirley threw the wall switches in the back, and the shop lights came up. Arnie kept clapping and Eloise, high as a kite, sprang from the stage and leaped into Dane's arms for a congratulatory hug, and then a laughing, father/daughter hug, and then a hug between two friends. Arnie found himself calling out a few extra bravos and ex-tending his applause so the hugs wouldn't outlast it. What would he have to do next, sing some background music? Finally, when the stu-dent and her master were aware of someone else in the room, Arnie stepped forward and extended his hand. "You've definitely fulfilled my highest expectations and, uh, more besides."

They debriefed in rapid chatter, they reviewed, they fired off ideas as they came:

"Now that we have the routines just about timed out, we can get Robbie Portov to work up a music score," said Dane.

"And costuming. Better costuming," said Arnie. "Something brighter, eye-catching . . ."

"Something that follows her and accentuates her moves."

"Several changes if we can swing it."

"But with class."

"Like Mandy made famous." Arnie's eyes asked if the reference was okay.

"Well . . . exactly," said Dane. "Is Keisha Ellerman still designing?"

"And how."

Dane sighed through pursed lips. "Budget, budget. We'd better talk venues first."

"Let me take you to lunch."

"Great!"

"I guess I should change," said Eloise.

"Just Dane," said Arnie.

There was a short, awkward beat, and then she recovered. "Oh. All right."

Arnie smiled and explained, "We've come to that point, kid: Dane and I need to talk about you behind your back."

Dane patted her shoulder. "That means things are getting serious."

Arnie didn't build on that comment. He just let the sideways stretch of his mouth and the arch of his eyebrows concede.

She smiled, adjusting. "I've got some housecleaning to do."

Dane took Arnie to Rustler's Roost, a log-structured, ranch-style barbecue place with log furniture, red checkered tablecloths, and waitresses in cowboy hats. It wasn't Vegas, was definitely Idaho, and had plenty of room so they could find an isolated table and talk privately.

"They have great food," Dane assured Arnie.

"Bring it on."

They ordered, then Arnie gave Dane a look he'd seen before, a look that meant this lunch could go kind of long, Arnie had a difficult topic on his mind.

Dane thought he might be able to steer around it. "You know, I was thinking it would be a great idea to get her booked on Preston's show. Maybe she could even take up a challenge. That would get her in the public eye and give her something unique to say for herself."

"He'd take her apart," said Arnie.

"Well, not if we set it up right. Maybe we should leave out the challenge part and she can just be a guest magician."

Arnie repositioned himself on the log bench as if his rear end were getting sore already. "First let's talk about Eloise."

"I thought that's why we were here."

"I don't mean the business part. I mean the other part."

Oh, brother. We're going to go there. "You mean, umm . . ."

"I mean, I want to know if I'm seeing what I think I'm seeing."

Cornered. Arnie wasn't blind and he wasn't stupid. "She . . . she tends to be affectionate. She has no parents. I guess I'm like a father to her."

"Dane . . ." Arnie put up his hands. "Listen, if that's the case, or even if you have something more going with this girl, I'm not your parents or your pastor, I'm okay with it. I work in Vegas, I see everything."

"It's not like that."

"But do you know what it *is* like? As your friend, that's what I want to be sure about, that whatever it is, you know, you really know."

"What it's . . . what are you talking about?"

"All right." Arnie leaned toward him and made an effort to keep his voice down. "I'm thinking about you and me on the street outside that coffee shop, and you going on and on about that girl looking and sounding just like Mandy. You do remember that?"

Dane couldn't hide the fact that he did.

"And now I see this same girl"—Arnie balked, waiting for words— "the blond hair. I just—"

"It's her natural color."

Arnie waved his hands as if erasing everything and starting over. "Okay. Umm, let me just spell it out for you and then you tell me if I'm wrong, okay? Friends?"

"You're wrong."

"Hear me anyway."

He would have to. There was never any turning Arnie around. "Go ahead."

Arnie tiptoed, one word at a time. "You're a widower, you're lonely, you miss your wife, you have money and connections . . . and then, somehow, this young, good-looking, ambitious girl catches on that she resembles your wife."

Dane shook his head in dismay. "No, no, you've got it all wrong. You have no idea."

"That performance I saw today. That was Mandy. Move for move, the gags, the expressions, the hair, everything! She's done some homework, she is into the role."

"Arnie—"

"Dane. I've seen this kind of thing before, and so have you, come on."

"I coached her, remember."

Arnie rolled his eyes heavenward, seeking wisdom with a frustrated pat on the table. "All right. Let's start here—and then you can talk me out of it. I'll let you try, okay?" He took a breath and tried again. "Nobody can look and act that much like Mandy without *really* trying, and it's easy to see that she has an emotional effect on you and knows it. She's an incredible performer, but given what I'm seeing, I don't trust her, and because I don't trust her, I don't like her, and because I don't like her, I can't be her agent. All right. Let's start there. Go ahead."

Arnie took a bite from his barbecue beef sandwich and waited.

Dane tried to think of a gradual way to ease into it, but finally resigned himself to the one overarching question in his mind. "What if she *is* Mandy?"

She trailed the long central vacuum hose behind her as she moved up the stairs one riser at a time, running the brush head back and forth.

Once upstairs, she ran the hose down the hall to the upstairs vacuum outlet, just past Dane's bedroom door.

The bedroom door was open.

She looked in from the hall. *Wow.* It had its own fireplace—propane, neat and clean, with a carved mantel. Classy-looking dresser and a full-length mirror. The bed was made. Beautiful bedspread with big, fluffy shams against the headboard.

Would there be—was it snooping?—a picture of his wife anywhere? She leaned in.

Off-limits, Shirley'd told her.

The closet door was open . . .

She gasped, fingers over her mouth. *Oh, no, you're killing me.*

The gown—the blue gown from her vision on Christmas night—was hanging right there and looked exactly as she'd seen it: floor-length, a skirt that would float and billow when she spun, full, sheer sleeves, sequins that could throw diamonds of light upon the walls and ceiling, metallic embroidery about the waist and bodice. She knew that gown, every detail. She'd worn it in another world, another time. Hadn't she?

And she was dancing, wasn't she?

Ten steps in and ten steps back out again, that was all it would take. She wouldn't touch anything. She darted to the south windows and looked toward the long driveway. Shirley'd gone home to take her son Noah to the dentist. Dane and Arnie wouldn't be back for at least an hour.

I'm not being sneaky. I just . . . it isn't everybody who has visions like I do and then sees something . . . just a few seconds and I won't touch anything.

The step through the bedroom door brought a pang of conscience; the step through the closet door brought the fear of divine judgment.

But her fingers took hold of the sleeve—just to lift it outward and have a look at it—then the shoulder—yes, same material—and then the skirt of the dress, feeling, remembering, and it was all so real, more than déjà vu. She held the sleeve beneath her nose and inhaled a scent she vividly remembered. Taking the gown on its hanger, she held it against her body—just her size.

She put it back. *No, better not.*

"She grew up on a ranch, she raised llamas, horses, and doves, her father's name was Arthur, her mother's name was Eloise. She knows how to do carpentry and how to fix a leaky faucet, her favorite coffee is a nonfat mocha—"

Arnie held up his hand. "Dane, stop. Hold it a second."

"She dances like Mandy, she laughs like Mandy, she gets the same look in her eyes—"

"Dane?"

Dane stopped. He was running off at the mouth and knew it.

"Dane, Mandy is dead. Pardon me for asking, but are you aware of that?"

The answer stuck in his brain and wouldn't go through.

Arnie pressed in. "I was there with you at the hospital the day she died. When she died she was fifty-nine. This girl is nineteen."

"She'll be twenty on the fifteenth."

Arnie's voice rose despite his effort to keep it down. "What the— what difference does it make? She's still a different girl, Dane, a different girl who is" —he lowered his voice but he was shaking— "who is forty years younger. Forty years!"

Her jeans, shirt, and shoes lay in a neat pile on a chair next to the fireplace.

The black formal slid over her shoulders and hips and conformed to her body like it was made to be there. She turned in front of the full-length mirror, holding a diamond necklace against her skin to see how it looked with the dress. She'd never worn anything so lovely.

She found a pair of shoes that matched. They slid onto her feet like the glass slipper in *Cinderella*.

The feeling!

A white, sparkling gown and matching slippers fit just as well, draping from her body in such graceful lines that she had to dance like a princess, circling the room in front of the mirror as the skirt swished through the air and the jewels and sequins sparkled.

"I know it sounds crazy," Dane admitted.

Arnie's sandwich lay half eaten on the plate. A waitress had come by to check on them. Arnie quickly told her they were fine, thank you. "Crazy. That's right."

"But how else do you explain it?"

"That's what I'm warning you about."

"I got her four doves just to see what her reaction would be. She named them Lily, Maybelle, Bonkers, and Carson."

"Research, Dane. She's smarter than you think."

"Those were the names of the doves Mandy had clear back at the Spokane fair. There's no way she could have known that."

"She's a magician, Dane, a very good one. She found out. Listen, there are things she does that neither of us have been able to figure out, but that's how magic works, that's the whole point."

"She has a way with doves. It's how we met."

Arnie touched Dane's hand and looked into his eyes. "Dane. Explain it to me. And listen to yourself as you answer."

"I can't explain it. I've never been able to explain it."

"*I've* explained it. Now, can you come up with something better?"

Dane's mind had never been able to land on anything that made sense. "I only know what I know." He was still amazed by the next fact even as he spoke it. "She has the same teeth, the same smile. She even smells like Mandy."

Arnie's eyes stayed on him for one more brief moment, but then a gradual change like the sun going down came over his face. He eased back on his bench at a loss, disbelief and despair clouding his face. "Dane. Have you really come to that point? Have you really gone crazy?"

A snappy pink dance outfit—his wife must have used it for the jazzier dance numbers and the contorted box illusions—slipped on as if made for her. The stagey shoes, the pants and cute waistcoat got her moving, finding a groove, and God help her, there was just something so *right* about it, as if in some way, in some nearby other world, the clothes were old friends, her music was their music, her moves their moves.

Arnie didn't finish his sandwich. He didn't finish the conversation either. "I'd better leave, right now!" he said, standing and stepping free of the bench.

Dane had never seen his friend this way before. "Arnie, it's so hard to explain—"

"Stop. Don't say another word. Don't drive any more nails into this coffin." Dane tried to say something but Arnie leaned down, finger in Dane's face. "I'm saying this to your face, all right? Remember that I told you to your face: you have lost your mind and she is going to break your heart. She is going to use you, and then she is going to discard you." He tossed some bills on the table. "And after she does, and you are the real Dane Collins again, a man with some sense and some kind of future, I'm not sure what, please give me a call. I'll help you pick up the pieces."

"Arnie!"

"Not another word!"

"Book her on Preston's show. Just that much. I'd consider it a real favor."

"And a monumental abuse of friendship!"

With that he hurried to the front of the restaurant and spoke with the hostess. Dane caught the words "cab" and "airport." It occurred to him that Arnie had left his travel case back at the ranch in the guest room, but . . . oh, well. He was Arnie Harrington. He'd never go back for it now.

31

There was still the blue gown. She told herself she wouldn't touch it, but then her hand just fell on all these other things and one thing led to another and . . .

The gown was in her vision, after all, and the embrace of love, the encounter with herself that came to her that night, were here now, in this room, in these clothes all hung according to color and occasion, in the jewels neatly arranged in little drawers, in the beautiful shoes in neat rows on two shelves.

She ached for that blue gown as she looked at the clock beside the bed. Could she try it on and put it away in five minutes, ten at the max?

Dane remembered seeing Arnie standing in the front window of Rustler's Roost watching him go. He remembered giving Arnie a pitiful little wave as he opened the door of his car, and wondering how long it would take Arnie to get a cab of any kind in northern Idaho. From that moment to closing the door of his car in his own garage, the drive up Highway 95 and all the way back to Robin Hill Road was by rote. He didn't remember it. His mind was elsewhere, everywhere.

He hadn't lost a friend, he knew that. That was precisely why Arnie had cut their visit short, to save the friendship. They'd bailed on each other before to depressurize and were always able to put it back together. Still, that didn't remove the fact that this was one bleeding, messy feeling he had, as weighty as lead, and it wasn't likely to go away until . . .

Until what? Until he denied every little treasure he'd found in the girl, every flame of hope she'd lit inside him, every undeniable fact he'd gleaned that anchored his heart to hers? Until he slapped himself awake from a dream he'd always wanted, that wonderful, wishful state of heart that came uninvited, unexpected, and brought cleansing joy to his darkened state of mind?

Such was love, he supposed. Love only made sense to a point, and beyond that, didn't answer to logic or practicality, it just went on making people complete in its own mysterious way.

And where would he be without it? That answer was easy. He'd been there already, and going back was not a happy option.

As for what lay ahead, only God knew, so maybe he didn't have to. It would all make sense someday.

As he slipped quietly in the back door, just being home made him want to see her again, even if she was dusting the shelves or running the vacuum in her same old shirt and work jeans, even if the topic was emptying the vacuum canister or rotating the garbage cans. This house—and he—needed the sound of her voice, the prodding of her plans and intentions, the promise of her friendship.

Her VW was parked outside. She had to be in the house somewhere.

The golden-haired lady in the full-length mirror, glorious in her blue gown and shimmering jewelry, was too lovely, too regal to be she. From wherever the lady had been—and it must have been many wonderful places—she looked back into the bedroom at the cleaning girl and whispered what seemed impossible: "Mandy Whitacre."

And the cleaning girl whispered back, "I want to be you."

She clutched a fold of the dress and gracefully lifted it, striking a pose as the belle of the ball, and circled in place, a hint of a waltz, her feet barely lifting from the floor. From somewhere in her memory, the strains of Offenbach's "Belle Nuit, o Nuit d'Amour" began to play and she began to sing the melody, stepping lightly, eyes closed, dreaming . . .

There was a man in the doorway.

She jolted and yelped as with an electrical shock, hands trembling before her face, insides so stressed she felt sick. "Ohh . . ." she said, and thought, *I'm dead. Totally dead. Oh, God, I've ruined my life, I've ruined everything.*

The sight stunned him speechless, motionless. She was trembling, a cornered animal, trying to cover herself with her arms as if to hide—and the most beautiful woman he'd ever laid eyes on, just as she'd always been. Memories of Mandy in that dress came flooding back—the shows they did, the dance numbers, the illusions, the curtain calls. He'd kept it just for those memories, and now . . .

She was back, standing right before him.

She was falling apart, as if she'd been assembled with nuts and bolts and every nut was coming loose, every bolt was falling out, and every piece of her—her mind, her heart, her hopes, her ability to put one doggoned sentence together—was clunking to the floor. Her hands, though they tried, could never conceal her, never hide her. They finally went to her face, closing her in and covering her shame. In the dark behind them, she managed a broken, high-pitched lament, "I'm sorry. I'm sorry." Her hands slipped down, uncovering her eyes—he was still there, still looking at her. She said again, "I'm sorry."

He didn't say a word and hardly moved except to sink into a chair near the door, never taking his eyes off her. He didn't look angry. He looked . . . lost . . . broken.

His lingering gaze made her look at herself, touch the lovely material, gently grasp and animate a fold of the skirt. "It's just so pretty . . ."

Then, meeting his eyes again, she read it, sensed it: he was *looking* at her, in no unkind or improper way, but in a way, she just now realized, she would have wanted—did want, as if the mirror were telling the truth, as if she really were the beautiful lady, as if she really could be . . .

With a wag of his head and wonder in his eyes he said, "Mandy."

* * *

He could have hit her in the forehead with a beanbag. Her head jerked up, her eyes widened, and she gasped. What was this, another yes to another question?

"I was going to tell you," she said, her voice trembling.

He felt for her. She was scared and in trouble. He smiled, and that helped. She quit trembling, drew some breaths to steady herself, and then smiled ever so sheepishly, her fingers over her mouth, a nervous giggle bubbling out. With decorum and honesty he looked her up and down, cocked an eyebrow, and sent her an approving nod. Those also helped. She let go a breath in what had to be relief, her smile broadening but still apologetic. Lifting a fold of the dress with each hand, she rotated once around, letting the dress rustle and billow in ladylike, ballroom fashion. She completed the turn with a repentant shrug, eyes anxious and asking.

And how else could he tell her?

He rose from the chair and came to her, eyes gentle and voice safely academic. "As you can imagine, this dress is best suited for a waltz."

Her left hand went to his shoulder by itself as his hand rested gently against her back. Her right hand took his left, and immediately, spirit-deep, she felt safe. The fear was gone.

"What was that tune you were humming?" he asked.

She sang it to him, and the steps just came, one-two-three, one-two-three, in a safe little box. He knew the tune as well, and sang it with her note for note as he widened the pattern into an idyllic carousel about the room. The steps flowed without a thought as she followed his lead, the walls, windows, and furniture of the room passing like scenery behind him.

When this room became many *rooms*, when her other worlds arose in this time and place with their shifting depths, bending dimensions, and blurring colors, his touch became her fortress, his shoulder a bulwark. From within his arms she could watch without fear where she was, where else she was, where she'd been, and where she'd be. Over his shoulder, for a fleeting shred of time, she saw her apartment—the windows, the kitchenette, her bed, and *her* watching them dance. *Full circle*, she thought. *The other side of the mirror. Hi, Eloise! It's me, Mandy! You were right! I'm dancing in the dress, with* him!

* * *

Completeness. The other half of every emotion. All he'd lost so tangibly present, as if the past few months had never happened.

He might have drawn her in with an unconscious lead of his hand, she might have chosen it herself, but as the music faded from their voices and the waltz stilled from their awareness, her arm went around his neck, she rested her face against his shoulder, and he welcomed the firm closeness of her body against his, the curves of her waist and hips, the cashmere-soft warmth coming through her dress.

Not reliving, but *still* living; not like then, but like always.

She could have stayed here forever, real and timeless, no matter when or where or which world it was. The dance had fallen behind them, slipping into one of her forgotten pasts. While worlds and times swirled around them, she and Dane became the sun, the unmoving center of it all. She clung to him as to life, caressed his back and with a slight bow of her head kissed his hand, then kissed it again. He kissed her on the cheek.

And this time she only had to turn *her* head.

It was meant to be. It had to be. It *was* and he surrendered to it, incredulous and thrilled, remembering then, living now, lost in the taste of her lips and the scent of her hair, tracing the delicate shape of her neck, her ears, her face.

So this was what it was like. She had dreamed, but now she was there, embraced by love, carried by yearning, unable, unwilling to contain the feeling and finding a whole other side of herself who'd been here before, who knew, who pressed against him, gave herself to him. Oh, to be the one who shared her life, her love, her very being with this man . . .

* * *

She was just as when he first met her, newly blossomed, flawless and pure, delighting in life and love as her greatest adventure—

He stopped.

She opened her eyes, met his, then dropped her head, her hands still draped over his shoulders.

He took her hands from his shoulders, gave one a kiss, and let them go. He walked into the hall, escaping with deadening reluctance into the real world.

She came to rest against the closet doorpost, arms covering her because the wonderful blue gown made her feel naked.

She was framed in the doorway, her head down, her body wilted. With arms still covering her, she tried to form words but could only shake her head.

He gathered himself and said, "I've made a terrible mistake. I'm very, very sorry."

She looked at him. The joy and wonder had died from her eyes. "I, I never meant to—"

"I know. You're very young, and not at all to be blamed. The fault for all of this is mine. To put it simply, I'm very much in love, more than I realized, but not with you. I'm in love with my wife, and I guess I always will be."

"And . . ." She dabbed some wetness from her nose. "I know I could never replace her."

With a sad smile he replied, "That's right."

There was a silence as each waited, but there was nothing more to say.

"I guess I should leave."

He nodded, making sure his face was kind. "For your sake, and for the whole wonderful life you still have ahead of you, yes, you should leave. You should leave right away and never come back."

He turned, then paused. "You can report your hours to Shirley and she'll send you your check. I'll see to it that Arnie has your contact information. I'll be downstairs. Be sure to put everything away where you found it."

He left her in his bedroom, wiping her eyes and leaning like a dying lily.

Downstairs, he lit a fire in the fireplace and sat on the couch to watch the flames. He heard her footsteps when she came down the stairs. She stood for a moment in the other end of the living room, but he couldn't turn to say good-bye. He just watched the flames while she went out the door, started up her Bug, and drove down the long driveway.

He was still sitting there after the fire had died to embers and the embers to ashes.

chapter

32

Black television screen. Fade up.

Illuminated by a single, hard light source to the left of screen, white hair backlit to create a corona around his head, the bearded, sagelike face of Preston Gabriel turned toward the camera. In a low, rumbling voice reminiscent of Orson Welles, he spoke.

"Psychokinesis, the claimed power to affect matter by mind alone. Spoon bending, moving small objects, causing items to fall over or fly through the air solely by the power of the mind. Is it real, or is it illusion? Tonight we find the answers on . . . *Gabriel's Magic*!"

Spooky, haunting music played. Blue and fiery red images collaged across the screen: Preston Gabriel, dressed in his signature black and looking much like a wizard himself, materializing a flute, then turning it into four doves in his bare hands, levitating a girl from a table, making money appear in a volunteer's hand, vanishing a girl from a chair, lying on broken glass while a truck runs over him, producing a girl from an empty cabinet with a puff of smoke, stabbing a selected card with a knife from a cascade of falling cards in midair. Amazing moments, looks of astonishment, teasers of things to come bombarded the eyes as the music rose to a crescendo and a title burst from a tiny pixel to huge letters that filled the screen: *Gabriel's Magic*.

The show's intro cut to live cameras and a studio stage—a touch of stage smoke bringing out the bluish pin spots as the theme music played and an announcer said, "From Television World in Hollywood, ladies and gentlemen, this is Preston Gabriel."

The studio audience cheered and applauded as the Man strode boldly into the floodlights, white mane shining, face pleasant, eyes steely. "Good evening. The art of magic is built upon a covenant between the performer and his audience: he will attempt to fool them, and they will let themselves be fooled in the full knowledge that the magician is only an actor pretending to be a magician, performing the impossible, but through trickery and illusion. Our 'actors' tonight: the amazing magical duo from Montreal, Canada, Torey and Abigail." Applause. "And an astounding newcomer all the way from Coeur d'Alene, Idaho—I'm sure you've heard of it." Laughter. "The young, the beautiful, the talented Eloise Kramer."

Mandy Whitacre, she thought, but didn't say as the applause rang from the television in the green room. Mandy sat on a soft sofa, all made up, dressed up, and up against the full impact of this being her first time ever on television.

Arnie, sitting in a chair far from her, looked up from his laptop computer with an expression that said, *You asked for it, kid.*

She smiled at him the way she always did, wishing him well, hoping for friendship, and getting used to the idea that it was never going to happen. He was there to look after her, and he was doing a great job. He'd handled the whole booking, every detail from her flight to her hotel room, meals, schedule, the works, but he'd been honest with her, he was doing it for Dane, and their relationship was strictly professional.

In other words, they could never be friends.

So stick around, Arnie, I want to be alone. She and her favor-paying agent hardly spoke to each other.

She looked over at—was it Dwight or Dwayne, she couldn't quite remember, her brain was so occupied with the performance coming up. He was a young man decked out in a flowery martial arts outfit, and he didn't smile much, if at all. He was watching the screen, eyes narrow and lips grim. She figured he was getting psyched up.

Preston Gabriel went on with his opener. "And then we have tonight's million-dollar challenger, a man who claims not to be a pretender but to have a genuine ability to move and manipulate objects by the power of his mind. If he can demonstrate this power to the satisfaction of our judges and this master pretender"—pointing to himself—"he could be eligible for our prize of one million dollars, offered to anyone who can prove psychic powers under controlled conditions: Mr. Dwight Hoskins." Applause.

Dwight. Now she remembered.

"But first a little skulduggery. Sir, may I borrow a handkerchief?"

Linda, the producer, wearing a wireless headset and carrying a clipboard with every minute of the show planned out, stepped into the room. "Dwight? Torey and Abigail will be on for ten minutes, and then we'll go to a break and then you're on."

He nodded.

Linda looked down at Mandy. "And Eloise, after Dwight's had his spot we'll go to a break and then you're on."

"Okay." Like waiting for your turn with the dentist.

"Do you need anything?"

She already had a bottle of water in her hand, half empty. Her mouth was still dry. "Uh, no."

Linda took a second look at her. "We'd better have Amber touch up your forehead. Why don't you come with me."

"The person you are calling . . . 'Dr. Margo Kessler' . . . is unavailable. Please leave a message after the beep. When you are finished you may simply hang up or press One for other options."

Dane heard the same old beep but left no message. He'd already left two. Dr. Kessler had become a phantom, just like the girl who'd driven her Bug down his driveway and evaporated from his life.

Actually, he felt relieved. What was the point in calling her other than the fact that he said he would? She'd already stated her position, that he was crazy. Besides a pill, there wouldn't be much she could add to that.

He smirked and put the phone down. *There. I called.*

It was surreal sitting all alone before a cold, dead fireplace in a big, empty house with a .357 Magnum in his hand. He'd theorized that actually buying the gun would help him think things through, get him past *What if I . . .* and down to *I really can.* It worked. A little. The weight of the steel, the feel of the grip, the smell of the oil, the rattle of the bullets in the box were real, not hypothetical. He was able to hold the barrel to his head, say "Bang," and conceive more clearly what would follow. That was how he decided that down in the meadow— Mandy's Meadow—would be a better place than in the living room. He would stay preserved in the winter cold until Shirley, the cops, or the neighbors found him, and there'd be no messy cleanup.

Yep. Surreal.

Amber the makeup girl carefully dabbed Mandy's forehead with more foundation and powder. "You feeling nervous?"

Mandy was captivated by the pretty girl in the big mirror, but not out of vanity. She'd seen this girl in another mirror . . . and she was still wishing. She nodded at Amber's question.

"Oh," said Amber, giving her a looking over, "it's showbiz, like any other gig. Forget the cameras. Just go out there and wow that audience."

With everything Dane taught you, she thought, *but all by yourself, cut loose and lonely. Small, but smile. A screwup, but you show 'em. Spread your wings and fly. God's still with you even if he isn't.*

God?

"Hey, why the face?"

She put on the professional social interaction smile she'd been practicing. "Sorry. Just thinking."

It's not fair.

Applause came from the television on the wall. Preston Gabriel was back from a commercial break and introducing . . .

"Dwight Hoskins."

Hoskins strode onto the stage looking like a flower vase. He shook Gabriel's hand. Gabriel asked some questions and Hoskins talked about psychic powers: everyone has them, they just need to be developed, he developed his abilities through kung fu and learning the laws of nature from an old Chinese master . . .

Lord, if I only knew how to feel.

. . . learning to recognize his inner self, his outer self, and achieving a level of consciousness matching the absence of mind to the motions of the body . . .

Your grace is enough. I'd love to feel that.

Hoskins placed a pencil on a low table so that it teetered on the edge in precarious balance.

And Arnie—oooo, Arnie! I can't explain it to him—maybe because You've never explained it to me!

Hoskins crouched, waved his hands about in cool, martial arts gesticulations, the pencil moved, the audience applauded.

So he can make a pencil move. Wow. Got a show to go with that?

Next came the phone book lying open on the same table, sideways in relation to Hoskins. Hoskins did his little martial arts dance again, slicing the air with his hands and striking poses, then came in close and made a few pages flip, apparently by themselves.

The audience was impressed, or maybe just being nice.

"It's an old trick," said Amber. "Preston's going to nail him."

Gabriel was talking about controlled conditions being a requirement for the challenge and bringing out a canister.

"A million dollars," said Mandy.

"It started out as ten thousand thirty years ago and it's grown from there, probably because nobody's ever won it."

"Nobody?"

"Nope. Nobody's ever produced a psychic phenomenon that Preston hasn't been able to expose."

Gabriel was spreading Styrofoam packing pellets all around the phone book. "It's widely known among magicians that objects can be made to move by a surreptitious puff of breath. Just to be sure that isn't the case here, I'd like you to try again, this time with these Styrofoam pellets surrounding the phone book."

Hoskins stared, and his face was readable even on television: he was trapped like a fly in a spider's web and trying not to look like it. "The pellets might absorb the psychic energy, I don't know."

"What if we placed a mask over your mouth and nose. Would that be fair?"

This guy was melting on his feet. "I don't know. I need to concentrate."

"One last offer: suppose we turned the phone book ninety degrees so that the pages are upright in relation to you and would have to be turned sideways as one would normally turn pages? In that position, it seems to me that only psychic power would be able to move them."

Amber wiggled a finger at the screen. "He's gone."

Hoskins tried it with the Styrofoam pellets around the phone book, but his energy had left him. Too much interference, he said.

"So it appears you have not met the million-dollar challenge, but I thank you for trying," said Gabriel. To the audience, "Please bid a kind adieu to Mr. Dwight Hoskins." They applauded him off the stage. "Next up, the lovely Eloise Kramer. Don't go away."

Linda, the producer, came for Mandy. "All set?"

"All set," Amber answered, swiveling Mandy's chair around. Mandy got to her feet, her legs a little weak. In the hall behind Linda, Dwight Hoskins passed by as if looking for the nearest exit.

The .357 Magnum remained on the lamp table near the fireplace. Dane sat in the breakfast nook, winter scenery glorious outside the windows, and tapped on his computer,

> Suicide Note, First Draft
> By now you have found me
> (delete, delete, delete)
> If you haven't found me yet, look down in Mandy's
> Meadow.

Would they even know which meadow was Mandy's Meadow?

> (delete, delete, delete)
> I've thought long and hard about this and
> After giving my life due consideration
> You may be wondering why I
> (shift up arrow, select, delete)

Mandy's Meadow. From where he sat he could see the meadow cloaked in a winter mantle, crisscrossed by the hoofprints of deer and elk, the lope and rest patterns of white rabbits. Shirley had talked about the wildflowers that would bloom in that meadow come springtime, the yellow fawn lilies, mountain bluebells, purple shooting stars.

The computer screen was waiting, having only four words: Suicide Note, First Draft.

He extended his hands over the keyboard—they were still in pretty good shape, no arthritis to speak of, good tendons, clear skin. Most of his body was that way. His legs were good enough to climb the stairs two, sometimes three at a time. He was watching his cholesterol, and his blood pressure was normal. His prostate . . . well, he couldn't pee over a fence, but there was no cancer and he could pee well enough.

Was he getting—what did she call it—"leadbutt"? He checked and didn't see himself sinking too deeply into his chair. He hadn't started whining about the good old days yet—but he had started thinking about them.

You think your wife would want that . . . you just chucking the whole thing and turning into an old raisin? I know what she'd say: buy some testosterone, get a motorcycle, do whatever it takes to get living again, but don't waste the years God still has for you. You believe in God? Well, give Him some credit. He might know what He's doing.

Dane's hands fell into his lap. He felt chastised.

He might know what He's doing.

Well . . . He just might.

Delete, delete, delete.

Dane tapped on the keys,

Since when did God choose only painless lessons for His children?

He closed the file without saving it, then strode back to the lamp table by the fireplace, wrapped the gun in its plastic wrapper, and tucked it away in its original box. He still had the receipt.

He thought he might like a cup of coffee, maybe with some of those little bake sale chocolate cookies he bought from Noah Morgan.

Arnie remained in the greenroom as Preston Gabriel announced from the television screen, "Ladies and gentlemen, Miss Eloise

Kramer." Her recorded music began, and he saw two hula hoops roll out into the stage lights, one from the left, one from the right. They rolled in a circle in opposite directions and then, as they crossed each other from the camera's viewpoint, poof, as quick as a blink, there was Eloise spinning to a graceful ta-da pose in the center. The audience gasped, and Arnie had to concede, *Just wait, you ain't seen nothing yet*. Her act was astonishing, total fun, total entertainment. She would go far, no question—but without him. Someday her shady morals would catch up to her. She'd pick the wrong man, cross the wrong woman, get the wrong kind of attention. He was thankful that it wouldn't be his job to cover her back or explain a scandal to the news hounds.

He opened his e-mail account and typed a quick e-mail to Dane:

> FYI: Booked Kramer on Preston's show. Taping today,
> January 17. Have since withdrawn as her agent. She has
> secured other management. Take care. Arnie.

No, her performance was not up to her standards. She danced in, around, and through the hula hoops as they danced with her; she set her doves flying in tight formations the cameras could follow and materialized bottles that floated around her singing counterpoint to the music; she did it all with a big smile on her face and boundless energy that played well on television, but it felt slow to her, mechanical, and she was trying too hard. The life wasn't there, the playfulness and wonder that always popped up and surprised her to the delight of her audience. She was pretending, working against a lingering, leeching knot of sorrow she couldn't shake.

She pushed through, draining herself, then struck her closing pose, standing in one hula hoop while framing herself with the other, the doves perched atop it. The crowd rose to their feet, as did Preston Gabriel behind his Johnny Carson desk at the side of the stage.

Stagehands gathered up the hoops, doves, and bottles, and she took a bow. She was so relieved she wanted to cry, but she laughed, smiled, and bowed again. Sweat dripped to the floor. So much for her makeup.

"Eloise Kramer, ladies and gentlemen!" bellowed Preston Gabriel. As planned, she crossed the stage, shook Gabriel's hand, and took her place in the chair next to his desk for a short interview. She was still panting for breath.

"Marvelous!" said Preston Gabriel, taking his seat. "Truly refreshing!"

"Thank you."

He was smiling at her, but with a piercing gaze that made her want to cringe. "From Coeur d'Alene, Idaho."

"Yes, sir, born and raised."

"And just barely out of your teens—or are you?"

"I turned twenty last Saturday. Two days ago." There was some applause, about the only celebration her birthday got. She rehearsed on that day, alone.

"Remarkable." Gabriel leaned on his elbow, fingers supporting his face, still looking at her as if he were trying to figure something out. "And you studied with a close friend of mine, the great, the one and only Dane Collins."

If that was supposed to be a surprise to catch her off guard, it was. Some folks recognized the name, went "Oooh!," and applauded again, which gave her time to recover, nod, and say a bit weakly, "Uh-huh." *Great, witty answer. Arnie told you, didn't he? Please, no more questions about that.*

"You must have been quite a handful"—the glint in his eye telegraphed he'd used a pun—"with a remarkable trademark, bringing objects to life and making them your co-performers."

Did he just suggest . . . ? She was insulted whether he meant it that way or not. How was her smile? Was she having fun? She noticed a dead space in the conversation. It was her turn. "Uh . . . it's . . . it's like being a kid. When you're a kid all your toys are alive."

Gabriel nodded. "Did you see our last guest?"

Now, come on, it would be mean to talk about him. "The kung fu guy?"

"I'd say you did a lot better than he did."

Some folks clapped, but at the kung fu guy's expense. It felt mean. "Well . . ." She shrugged it off.

Gabriel stood a pencil up on end on his desk. "How about this pencil?"

There was a hush. She looked at the pencil, then at him. This couldn't be happening. "How about it?"

"Can you make it move?"

No magician would do this to a fellow magician. What was he thinking? *Smile, play along!* "Sure—if I brought my own pencil." She mugged to the audience and they chuckled.

"So you don't really have the power to make this one move."

The audience was hanging on what she would say. It was palpable. And what could she say? Saying "no" would break the spell, the whole covenant that made magic what it was, that made her performance what it was. He had to know that.

She smiled and made a funny little show of thinking about it. Preston Gabriel gave her precious airtime to do so, his eyes locked on her. Maybe he was building the suspense . . .

Or maybe he was trying to shrink her, make her wither like the kung fu guy. Arnie and he must have had a little talk between old buddies before the show. A tremble of anger went through her. *Yeah, I can make it move. I can stick it in your ear.*

She tried to put on Playful and Teasing. "Which way would you like it to move?" It didn't quite work. Her tone came across as challenging. The audience went "Ooooohhh . . ."

This guy had gall that soured her stomach. "How about making it levitate?"

In the greenroom, Arnie had come out of his chair and crossed to the television. *Preston, what are you doing? Forget what we talked about, this is showbiz. I wouldn't even fry her on television!*

Smile! "How high?"

"Oh, let's say—"

The pencil shot to a foot above the desk and hung there. The audience was all over it: it was part of the act, planned as a surprise, *Wow, great, we love it!*

And Mandy wasn't about to disappoint them. She locked eyes—most pleasantly—with Preston Gabriel, friend of Arnie Harrington.

She remembered how she and Dane spent his birthday, how she wished they could have spent hers.

She made the pencil spin a cartwheel. "What else?"

Gabriel eyed the pencil, fascinated.

Fascinated wasn't good enough. The folks deserved a real finisher, and Gabriel deserved . . . well, she'd be careful.

The pencil shot around the stage like a frantic bird, circled back, dropped, and touched eraser down on the top of the desk. As if the pencil were doing the lifting, the whole desk rose a foot from the floor and rotated, colliding with the old man's legs and making his chair spin—she enjoyed that part, but threw up her hands for the audience, Don't look at me, I can't control it! While the desk continued lazily rotating in midair, Camera Two lifted from the floor and rose above the frantic attempts of the camera operator to hold it down. It floated above Preston Gabriel, and a lovely crane shot appeared in the monitors: Preston Gabriel, stoic demeanor cracking, about to duck aside in case the camera fell. *Oh, no you don't.* Mandy scurried over, put her arm around the snooty, thoughtless old geezer, and looked up, waving, her smile big with sarcasm.

The audience was rumbling, applauding, gasping.

Mandy let the camera and desk down gently, then gave Preston Gabriel a kiss on top of his head. The audience went nuts. They rose to their feet. She pranced forward and bowed, threw them a kiss, and scampered offstage.

They were still applauding as she brushed past Linda the producer—"Hey, that was incredible!"—and slammed through the soundstage door.

Preston Gabriel's voice came from monitors in the control room—"The incredible Eloise Kramer!"—as she rushed down the hall to the ladies' room.

The closing theme music and Preston Gabriel's sign-off came from the ceiling speakers in the restroom as Mandy pressed her face into a corner and let herself cry, really cry.

33

"First and foremost," said Preston Gabriel, removing his hat and coat, "you're not crazy."

Arnie said nothing. He just hung his coat in Dane's front closet.

"We need a table," said Preston.

Dane, face-to-face with his oldest and best friend and his agent who thought he was crazy, was at a loss other than to say, "I'm taking orders for coffee."

They gravitated to the breakfast nook, that well-lit corner of the house with a great view and close to the coffee. Dane brewed lattes for Arnie and himself, a cup of black for Preston. He put some of Noah Morgan's cookies on a plate, but by then the nook table hardly had the space. Preston had spread out snapshots, eight-by-tens, trade articles, and promotional photos featuring Mandy, most dating back to the earliest years of Dane and Mandy's career. One was a snapshot from a magic convention in Miami in 1974: Preston and Dane, in long, '70s hair and sideburns, had first met, and now they posed on either side of the long-tressed flower girl, Dane's beautiful bride and performing partner of two years.

Arnie, still somber, provided recent photos from Eloise Kramer's promotional packet and laid them alongside the others. Dane brought his computer and opened a folder of digital photos, the "Gleesome Threesome" building the stage in the shop building. Among these he found his favorites, close-ups of Eloise.

Arnie scanned them all from a standing position with no comment and a predisposed detachment.

Preston bent over the table, slid photos around, examined close-ups of Mandy and Eloise under a magnifier.

Dane mostly waited. He'd already anguished through this exercise so many times in so many ways he no longer trusted his own eyes. He looked at Arnie, the skeptic.

Arnie reminded them, "Of course we can all agree that she looks like Mandy. I've never argued that point."

"Dane," said Preston, "may I see that close-up of Eloise, the one where she's holding up the hammer?"

Dane brought it up on the computer screen.

"Can you zoom in on the mouth?"

Dane zoomed in until her smile nearly spanned the screen.

Preston pointed to the screen. "Just for one of many examples, note the flaw, the little dip on the left side of that tooth." Then he pointed to the magnifier he held over an old promo photo of Mandy Collins. "Take a look."

Dane deferred to Arnie, but Arnie let him go first. He looked through the magnifier and found exactly what he expected. Both girls had the same flaw on the same tooth. "That freckle, too, on her upper lip."

"Mmm-hmm. And the tiny mole under the left eye, and the asymmetry of the smile, the way it stretches just a little more to the right."

Arnie huffed in exasperation. "Do you guys know where you're going with this, where you'd *have* to go?"

Preston told him, "We welcome your arguments, Arnie. This is so bizarre we need some checks and balances."

"Well, how about, Mandy is dead?" he said. "I know it's a small detail, but I feel I should bring it up."

"But can we agree on one redeeming fact, that except for different hairstyles and color, these two girls are physically identical in every way?"

"I told you, I've never argued that point."

"But it means that Dane isn't crazy. Any sane person would have the same conflicts."

Arnie thought for a moment. "I'll accept that this gal could fool anybody. Dane, if I'd been you . . . yeah, she could have fooled me."

Yes, of course it was a relief, but it had been so long, so torturous that the relief could only trickle in, displacing despair and supposed madness one drop of comfort at a time. "All right, so we agree on that." Preston pulled a chair over and sat down. The others did the same and they faced each other across the table, all the photos spread out between them. Dane sipped his latte. It was cold. Preston drew a DVD from his leather satchel and handed it to him. "This will bring you up to speed."

Dane slid the DVD into his computer and they watched Eloise's performance, the on-edge interview with Preston, the mayhem that followed. As the closing credits began and Dane clicked the stop button, he was smiling like a proud father.

"Whom did you see?" asked Preston.

Dane felt safe. "I saw Mandy."

Arnie let out a quiet whoosh and stroked his brow.

With an acknowledging glance at Arnie, Preston said, "That was my experience as well."

"Careful," said Arnie.

"Keep an eye on us."

Arnie nodded.

"I first met Mandy Collins when she was in her early twenties . . ." Preston looked at Dane. "She would have been . . . twenty-three?"

Dane did some quick figuring. "1974. Yeah."

"Dane, my heart goes out to you. Except for the shorter hair I could have sworn I was meeting the young Mandy Collins all over again. You should have said something."

"And what would you have done?" Dane asked.

Preston nodded, conceding, "Not having met her, I would have tried to talk you out of it. I would have thought you were mentally disturbed." Preston cocked an eyebrow. "But that's why you wanted her on my show, isn't it?"

Dane nodded. "You had to see her for yourself."

Arnie countered, "And I thought you'd be clever enough to see through her."

"The resemblance was astounding," said Preston, "but not the only factor. There were also her abilities."

"I told you she was good," said Arnie.

Preston looked at one and then the other. "You've both seen her perform. How did you think she was doing it?"

Arnie answered, "Wires, magnets, gyros. Rigging small enough to carry on her person."

Dane admitted, "I tried to figure it out, but then . . . I thought I was meeting my wife all over again. I thought I was going crazy. I let it go, I just threw it in with everything else."

Preston slid some of the photos around, looking them over again as he spoke. "I tested the resemblance further. I baited her to see how she carried herself, how she related to me after I needled her, how she handled anger. Turned out, once again, she was Mandy to a tee. From there, I went out on a limb."

Arnie wagged his head. "And I couldn't believe you'd do a thing like that."

"In retrospect, neither can I. What I did just isn't done." Preston wagged his head as he recalled it. "We are deceivers, but we're honest about being dishonest, and no magician exposes the dishonesty of another. It would spoil everything. The audience would be disappointed." He smiled. "But Mandy Collins never, ever disappointed an audience."

What Dane suddenly understood, he also had trouble believing. "You forced her to move that pencil."

Preston was amused by the twist of it. "And I was as lucky as any man could ever be. I bet on her being dishonest about being *honest*. I bet on her really being able to do it."

Arnie was stung for a moment. "Whoa, whoa, hold on. What are you saying?"

"You asked if we knew where we were going with this. Well, for a moment, let's go *here*: It would not have been enough for her to rig the pencil or my desk or the camera, as impossible as that would have been anyway. She would have had to rig the whole room. My desk is at least two hundred pounds, that camera weighed well over three hundred, and yes, I did question the TV crew and the set builders, all close friends and associates. They were as amazed as I was."

"You're not saying you owe her a million dollars?"

Preston feigned offense. "Oh, perish the thought. She never made a challenge, and the offer is for anyone proving *psychic* ability."

"Then how do you explain it?"

Preston clapped his hands together, then rubbed them lightly. "All right. We are *here*, so let's do some exploring." He turned to Dane. "Pardon the question. Did you see Mandy die?"

The question hit like an arrow. Off guard, unprepared, Dane tried to grasp the question and why Preston would even ask it.

Preston asked again, "Did you see her die?"

Dane fended him off. He couldn't bear to revisit that room. "Of course I did."

"How do you know she was dead?"

She wasn't? No, he couldn't carry that hope again. He turned up his hands, let them drop. "She had to be." Preston was still waiting. "The heart monitor went flatline. She was gone." He drew some breaths to keep emotion down.

"Then what happened?"

"Preston . . ." Arnie cautioned.

"They wheeled her out of the room," Dane answered. "That was it."

"Who?"

"What do you mean?"

"Who wheeled her out of the room? Who was there?"

"A doctor and a nurse." Something connected, something so far from credible . . .

Preston pressed his gaze.

Dane could see Kessler standing over his dying wife and the nurse continually fingering the wires from the monitor. He could remember a strange hastiness in getting Mandy out of the room. Why the hurry if she was dead? "Dr. Kessler. Margo Kessler."

"Did you see Mandy cremated?"

Dr. Kessler was wrong, wasn't she? There was never an effect from the medication, Dane was never crazy, never hallucinating. She was wrong, all along—or lying.

"Dane? Did you see Mandy cremated?"

"Of course."

"In a cremation casket?"

"Yes."

"Was she in it?"

Wasn't this grasping at straws? He wished it wasn't.

"Do you have direct, personal knowledge of Mandy's body being in that casket? Did you see it yourself?"

The question was unfair. "I didn't pry the casket open and look, no."

"Preston, come on," said Arnie. "Give the man some space."

Preston pulled a photograph from his satchel and placed it on the table in front of Dane. "Have you ever seen this man?"

Dane was afraid to hope. He'd been through so much, and this . . . what could it accomplish other than to stab him with fresh pain he'd taken months to get over? He cared little for Preston's photograph . . .

. . . of a man he'd seen before. A man in his forties. Thin, graying hair, wire-rimmed, professorial glasses, a somewhat stern, focused expression.

He plucked the photograph from the table. "Who is he?"

Preston was intently reading his face. "So you *have* seen him before?"

"Who is he?"

Now Preston was the one shaken. "His name is Jerome Parmenter, former professor of physics at Stanford. I say 'former' because he seems to have disappeared."

chapter

34

D ane was trying to breathe. His hand was shaking.

"You need some water?"

Dane nodded. Arnie hurried to bring a glass.

Dane's heart was racing. Anger, hope, relief, anxiety, all boiled inside him at once. "He was there at McCaffee's . . ." He told Dane and Arnie the whole story of the man he'd seen in McCaffee's, sitting in a corner with a computer while Mandy—Eloise—tried to levitate and came crashing to the floor.

Preston was as agitated as he ever got, which wasn't very, but on him it was impressive. "Unbelievable! The odds! I was shooting in the dark, following a hunch! Unbelievable!" He grabbed at the photos on the table. "Let's make some room here!"

They put away the photographs. Dane set aside his computer. The table was clear.

"The odds!" Preston was still recovering. "But I shouldn't be surprised. Sooner or later the pieces had to fall together." He reached again into his satchel and produced a small stack of lengthy articles in fine print from professional journals and scientific publications, some featuring the same photograph. "No, this is not from my pleasure reading list. My staff is always investigating new ideas and technologies that could be useful for new tricks and illusions—and psychic hoaxes, either one—and they sniffed out Parmenter. Here's a man with cutting-edge interests: interdimensional crossovers, electromagnetic pulse, scalar waves, time travel. He's a regular Tesla, or Einstein.

"This article deals with his work on interdimensional displacement, ID, the whole idea that an object can be shifted from one dimension to another, moved an inch or a mile, and returned to its original dimension so that it seems to have been instantly transported from one place to another."

"Beam me up, Scotty?" said Arnie.

"It would be that impressive if it really worked and a stage magician could get hold of it. Imagine the illusions—but they wouldn't be illusions, would they? They'd be the real thing."

Dane couldn't believe it yet, but a building tension was gnawing at his insides. "Her entrance on your show . . . she used to do that sort of thing at McCaffee's, just appear out of nowhere."

"Okay," said Arnie, "we're doing sci-fi now, everybody keep that in mind. We're not going to get carried away here."

"I'm afraid there's more." Preston leafed through the stack and found an article from *Scientific American*. "Timelines. How it could be possible for an object—maybe a person?—to occupy multiple timelines at once and thereby exist as a multiplicity."

"Multiplicity. Of course," said Arnie. He was kidding.

"Take comfort, I'm not that far ahead," Preston assured them. "Here's what I gathered from the article: Dane, here you are, sitting in this chair at . . . two thirty-five in the afternoon. On our timeline, in our time dimension, you're the only Dane there is. The Dane who was sitting here five minutes ago doesn't exist anymore. He was the two-*thirty* Dane. You're the two *thirty-five* Dane."

"But he's the same guy," Arnie countered.

"Except for the *time*; that's the point of the article. You'll never see both Danes—the Dane in the present and the Dane from the past—sitting in the chair at the same time *unless* you can place the two-thirty Dane on a separate timeline, then pull that timeline up to a point contemporaneous with the timeline of the two thirty-five Dane. Then you'd have two Danes existing at once in the same place because they would be in the same place at different times. It would be the same event happening twice at the same time."

Dane and Arnie stared at him blankly.

"I don't totally get it either," he admitted. "The article uses the example of a railroad car passing through a railroad crossing." He pointed out the illustration on the second page. "Here we are, the observers, sitting in our car waiting for the train to go by, and right in front of us, at this instant in our time, is the railroad car. Consider that an event, the railroad car passing directly in front of us. But two seconds ago it wasn't in front of us, it was about a car length down the track to our left. Imagine that as another event that happened in the past. Now imagine if you could isolate that past event, that car at that place in that instant of time, move the event to a parallel track, analogous to a second timeline, and then shift that track forward so that both events are now occurring side by side at the crossing. You would have what would look like two identical but separate cars going through the crossing at the same time, but what you're seeing are two different events on two different timelines. The same car twice at the same time."

Dane thought it over. "Two railroad cars? Out of one?"

"Bizarre, isn't it?"

"Two Danes sitting in the same chair."

"Yes."

"What would that look like?"

"I don't know. You might see them both, you might not. Only Parmenter would know."

Another connection, a lightbulb coming on. "Carson!" Dane said. Preston and Arnie waited. "Carson, the dove. The four doves out of one. She did a routine with four doves but she only brought one. . . . I figured she secretly loaded the other three."

"Maybe she did," said Arnie, not sounding very sure about it.

"Or she"—Dane reviewed, piecing it together—"she generated three more Carsons in three other time dimensions and made them look like four at once in ours."

"Four events that could have been microseconds apart made to happen in the same place at the same time," Preston suggested.

Arnie sang the theme music from *The Twilight Zone*.

"So!" Preston leaned forward in his chair, intense like a storyteller. "Imagine this with me. Here's . . . Eloise . . . sitting in her chair and I'm telling her to levitate a pencil over which she, the girl in the chair, has no control. Somehow, through some connection with this Parmenter and whatever he's come up with, she generates a second Eloise on a second timeline, unseen by us, who picks up the pencil, rotates it, and makes it fly around the room."

Dane ventured, "An Eloise who was there five minutes before?"

"Or a microsecond. Or a *nanosecond*. And on her own timeline so that she is writing her own unique history, free to act in her own way, make her own choices, carry out her own actions, but still remain in essence the original Eloise. Mind-boggling—and pure speculation, of course."

"So this second Eloise can fly?" Arnie asked.

"*If* any of this really works, I'm guessing—*guessing*, mind you—that she can interpose herself between our time and space and hers anywhere she wants. If she could position her time and space four, six, however many feet above ours and penetrate our time and space from there, she would appear to us to be suspended in midair, flying, or at least the pencil she's holding would appear so."

"So how does she levitate?" asked Arnie.

Preston could only throw up his hands.

Dane's mind was racing along with his heart. "So Eloise Kramer is some kind of timeline duplicate, the Mandy Whitacre who existed forty years ago."

"But would she have any idea?" Preston mused.

Arnie winced. "All right, time to call a halt here. Gentlemen, you took a wrong turn. Reality's the *other* way."

"I was hoping I could speak with her after the show, but she'd left abruptly."

"And I can't imagine why, with you being so nice to her."

Preston gave Arnie an impatient look. "Well, she didn't exactly go crying to *you*."

"I wasn't her manager anymore."

"And not her friend either."

Arnie took the blow but didn't bend. "No. I wasn't. She has that attorney to manage her now. She caught a flight back to Spokane, back to him and his big plans. Let him deal with her." Then he told Preston, "And she *was* crying, by the way."

Oh, the feeling. Dane sighed, resting his forehead on his fingertips. "And I told her to leave, to get out of my life and never come back."

For a moment, words fled away. Arnie crossed his arms and looked out the window. Preston drew a deep breath and sighed it out long and slowly. Dane just remembered the last time he saw her; she was wearing that beautiful blue gown. She was wilting, dying against the doorpost, and he was walking away.

At last Preston asked Dane, "Well, did she ever say anything to you, anything that would reflect on, uh . . ."

"She said she was a little crazy, that she'd been in a mental ward . . . that she thought she was someone else."

Preston's hands covered his nose and mouth as his eyes widened. "Who?"

"She didn't want to tell me, so we never talked about it." Then he gathered strength and added, "But I did find out from a person connected with the hospital that when she was in the hospital she called herself Mandy."

Preston reeled a little at the news. "Oh, Dane. Ohhh, Dane. And this was before she met you?"

"That's right."

"She was calling herself Mandy before she even met you?"

Dane could feel Arnie's stern, cautionary look and just wagged his head. "It's hard to be sure."

"You need to talk to her about this." Then Preston thought again and his face fell. "But that wouldn't be easy, would it?"

"That's why I never went there."

"What?" asked Arnie.

Now Dane was feeling impatient. "You're the one who thought *she* was hustling *me*. What if I, the older guy, were to suggest to her, a cute, sexy twenty-year-old, that I married her forty years ago, so she's my wife, or is about to be, or was?"

Arnie wilted a little. "I see your point."

"Especially since we don't *really* know what we're talking about," said Preston.

"Ah!" said Arnie, "now there's wisdom!"

"But Parmenter knows," said Dane.

"If we can find him," said Preston. "I tried to track him down. I wanted to be the first magician in line to be his friend and collaborator . . . and it didn't happen. Last I heard from my sources, he'd left Stanford. He said he was pursuing a privately funded project and had relocated"—pause for effect—"to Las Vegas."

Another uncanny connection. Dane sank back in his chair.

"Oh," Arnie mused. "A privately funded project in Las Vegas! I've seen those, the guy shooting dice, downing some drinks, a couple of younger women along . . ." He snapped his fingers. "Hey, *younger women!*" Dane sent him a corrective glare. "Think I'll get some more coffee. Where are those cookies?"

"There *is* money there," Preston countered, "and people who know how to make it and invest it to make more."

"We have to find him," said Dane. He felt ready to die trying.

"And maybe we've picked up his trail again as of today. Or, you could say, as of September 17, 2010, at that intersection in Las Vegas. I'd say that's your starting point. Dane, my friend, it's time to ask questions."

Doris Branson, a lady in her fifties, managed the Orpheus Hotel Casino just off the Las Vegas Strip, was good to her friends, honest and shrewd in business, twice divorced, and—it seemed everyone knew it but she—prone to drinking.

Among friends such as hers in a town such as this, it was hard to make a case against alcohol abuse, but she got a strong hint about it when she bent her car around a palm tree in someone's front yard. She paid a one-thousand-dollar fine, agreed to perform forty hours of community service in lieu of jail, lost her privilege to drive for ninety days, and had to devote a great deal of time and money to getting insured again after her insurance company dropped her.

Even so, her friends marveled and kept telling her how lucky she was. From the looks of the car and the blood on the dashboard, she should have been seriously injured, but she woke up in the hospital with no greater complaint than a hangover and no recollection of the accident. The doctors also reminded her—until she was tired of hearing it—how lucky she was. They kept her for one day of observation and then sent her home.

Lucky? As of today she still had fourteen hours remaining on her community service commitment and twelve days to get her driver's license reinstated *if* she completed a substance abuse class and could prove she had insurance. With luck like she'd had, she wasn't about to place any bets, not even in her own casino.

That's where she was headed today, by elevator from the administration offices on the third floor to the casino on the main floor. It was routine, just verifying some numbers with the floor manager.

She would never have that meeting.

The Prospector's Lounge at the Orpheus Hotel boasted twenty-five tables and ten booths and could seat a hundred, not a big venue for Las Vegas but impressive, even intimidating, to a girl raised on a ranch in Idaho who drove to Vegas in a tired VW. It was quite a leap from McCaffee's, too, trimmed out in scrollwork and filigree, with a red carpet that was soft under the feet, red velvet curtains and brass fixtures, a totally clean, reach-everywhere sound system, a real stage with a powered curtain that disappeared into the ceiling, racks and racks of stage lights, a rear entrance direct from the dressing rooms—real dressing rooms!—and a three-person stage crew who knew everything there was to know about the place and were there to meet her every need.

And all she was doing was auditioning.

She gave it her best, as she always did, and maybe it was the total strangeness, the fantastical bigness, the mind-blowing color, light, and show-offishness of this city that provided the rush to get her through it. For sixty minutes she let the routines carry her along, let the pasts and futures and other places pitch and roll around her as she reached, moved, animated, levitated, and commanded her props, birds, and her own body from inside and outside herself, inside and outside of here and now. It was the same old madness that had dogged her for months but it got her work, and right now work was all there was.

Her closing tableau with hoops, birds, bottles, and cards was as good as some of the fountains she saw around town—did anybody else in Nevada have water?—and right on cue, the big automatic curtain dropped and the stage became a box.

She relaxed, deflated with relief, and stood quietly, letting her other worlds play out around her. Scenes from the ranch happened through: the shop with the tractor and the home-built stage passed over her; she could stand on the path outside the barn and look up the hill toward the house—the lights were on in the kitchen but she couldn't see anyone; just a thought of the snowy meadow made it sweep past her like an ebbing ocean wave up to her knees. Hospital hallways—they always showed up for some reason—flashed across her vision in fast motion and then vanished, as they always did. An earlier version of herself, so solid and real they could have collided, danced around her doing stunts with the hula hoops, then broke into pieces and faded away. Suddenly, rudely, the casino just outside the lounge doors surrounded her, slot machines jingling, warbling, ding-a-linging. She braced herself, startled, as she, or part of her, or another one of her, raced past a row of elevators.

Doris Branson rode the elevator alone, mildly bored by the quiet until the door slid open and the pleasant sound of money and more money being raked in sang in her ears. It was like walking into a factory with hundreds of machines running except that the machines didn't produce anything, they just transferred it. It was a business doing pleasure with these people.

Oops! She nearly collided with a pretty girl in a blue costume and holding a hula hoop. Great. A cabaret girl who hadn't learned the rules: no costumed performers on the casino floor. She ought to know that!

"Miss! You don't belong out here!"

The girl looked astounded that Doris would even address her, which only raised Doris's temper another notch. "Don't look at me like that!"

Where was Vahidi? She grabbed her cell phone from her pocket . . .

Well, now she felt silly and couldn't remember the number. The phone was blurry and the floor was moving—

The phone dropped to the floor as Doris uttered a truncated scream, lurched and twisted with arms flailing, then toppled to the floor, an arm and a leg broken and blood trickling from her nose and mouth.

A lady vacationer screamed. Security personnel came running. Before she passed out, Doris dizzily searched for the girl in blue. "Not onna casino floor . . ."

But the girl was gone.

* * *

Did that lady really see me? Was I really there?

The girl in blue sank to one knee, her hand on the floor, and worked to keep her balance until there was only the stage and it wasn't moving. She thought she heard a distant scream from the fading casino floor—somebody must have hit a jackpot—but after that, the only sound was her own windedness.

It was alarmingly quiet on the other side of the curtain. There was no applause at all, just a muffled conversation between two voices. With a mere whisper of a thought she reduced her twelve doves down to the original four—Carson, Maybelle, Lily, and Bonkers—received their cage from a stage guy, and tucked them safely away. She set the hula hoops aside, left the bottles, silks, and cards in a heap, and peeked through the curtain.

The place was empty except for Seamus and the hotel's entertainment director, Mr. Vahidi, sitting at a center table just a few rows back from the stage.

"Don't come into the lounge area, miss," said Vahidi. "You're underage."

"She knows," said Seamus. He had his planner open on the table in front of him.

Were they working a deal? She sat at the edge of the stage, trying to see their faces. The stage lights blinded her.

They were muttering, talking about dates, weeks available, dollar amounts. She heard Vahidi say "one-fifty," then Seamus said "three hundred," then Vahidi asked, "What's she gonna wear?"

She looked at her blue pants outfit with gold embroidery. It was her newest and best, reminiscent of a certain blue gown. "This."

Vahidi looked her over and told Seamus, "For three hundred you should get her into something striking."

Seamus began explaining her choices in costume, how she didn't normally present herself "that way."

"Hey, this is Vegas," said Vahidi. "She's competing with some big shows out there, and she's got what it takes. You kidding me?"

"We'll discuss it," said Seamus.

Come on, Seamus, do what you do best: look out for me.

The stage lights shut down and the house lights came up a little. Now she had a better view of Vahidi, a man who must have been raised on cheeseburgers and Crisco, with a face like a road map and a very expensive watch. Besides the wrinkles and folds on his face he had two scars he must have gotten from a street disagreement in his youth.

"So how's she bill herself?" Vahidi asked.

"Eloise Kramer," said Seamus. "Or the Amazing Eloise—"

"Mandy," she said.

Seamus paused. Vahidi waited.

"What?" said Seamus. "I thought we were—"

"Mandy Whitacre."

Seamus leaned toward Vahidi, "We can let you know."

"It's Mandy," she said. "M-A-N-D-Y."

Seamus gave her a corrective glare, which she bounced right back at him. He said to Vahidi, "Eloise Kramer is her legal name; Mandy Whitacre is a stage name. She'd like to use the stage name." He threw her an inquiry with his eyes, *Okay?* and she threw him back an answer, *Guess it'll do for now.*

Vahidi shrugged and wrote it down. "Does she do escapes?"

"Sure she does," said Seamus.

Escapes? "Sure I do," she said.

"We need something big to set up out front. Not just chains and handcuffs," said Vahidi. "Everybody does that. We need something outrageous to get her in the papers, get her known by the tourist and visitors bureaus, get her in those, those whaddayacallits, the what-to-do loops they play in the hotel rooms. She's got a great show, but people aren't going to know if they don't come in and see it."

Oh. She had a great show. That was nice to know.

"We'll come up with something," said Seamus.

"End of this week? We have to premiere it the same day as she premieres, make a big splash."

"We'll get right on it."

"All right, all right," said Vahidi, scribbling with his pen. "We're looking at three weeks starting next Saturday, two shows a night, six days a week, three hundred dollars a show. Sound good to you?"

It did sound good. Seamus was nodding at her. "Sounds good," she said.

"Sounds good," he told Vahidi.

Vahidi stood as he told Seamus, "We'll work out the details and get you a contract." He and Seamus shook hands.

Mandy sat there watching her life being managed, her flesh being peddled. So human warmth wasn't part of the business down here. Well, okay. She'd live with that. She'd make the best of it. She'd show them.

"And don't go out on the casino floor either," Vahidi reminded her. "You're underage."

chapter

35

Doris Branson was tucked away in a private room at Clark County Medical Center, stabilized and sedated.

Dr. Margo Kessler, medical director, stood by her bed going over her chart. "Bruising over her face with swelling . . ." From the air bag, she thought but didn't say. "A 3.5 linear laceration of the right shoulder overlying the deltoid, running transverse to the axis of her arm and extending down to the muscle fascia." From a loose object in the vehicle. "Right knee is diffusely edematous, but without evidence of joint space effusion. There is deep ecchymosis in the suprapatellar region." Just like last time. Interesting that the patient's clothing had no tears even though the shoulder was lacerated.

She looked at the patient's face, the expression marred by the bruising and troubled by the dispute over what really happened. The paramedics said she'd fallen down some stairs, but they got that from witnesses on the scene. The patient herself, seemingly intoxicated and erratic, insisted otherwise. For now, Kessler simply noted, "Obtunded mental status secondary to presumed concussion."

She looked at the crew standing by. "All right, let's do a CBC and chem panel, and . . ." *Now, this should be interesting*: "Let's get a urinalysis for blood ethanol and drug screen." She checked the IV. "What's she getting?"

A nurse answered, "IVD5 normal saline with 20mEq of KCl, 100 MLs per hour."

"That'll do for now. Let's line up a CT scan of the head."

"The family is waiting to see her," a nurse told her.

Kessler nodded approval and got out of the room before her facade faltered. A safe distance down the hall she slipped into an alcove, punched a number on her cell phone, and fidgeted until her party picked up. "This is Kessler. Yes, the patient is Doris Branson, the injuries are exactly the same, and"—she nearly raised her voice—"I will need an explanation." She listened, huffed a flustered breath. "I'll see you in my office in five minutes." She caught an elevator to the main floor.

When she reached her office, immediately adjacent to the emergency room, Dr. Martin DuFresne was there waiting for her, expression calm as always, something Kessler found aggravating—that, and DuFresne's ghostly way of appearing for updates, briefings, and consultations, then disappearing into the bowels of the medical center, never to be seen. As usual, he wore scrubs and a white coat with the CCMC logo on it, something else that aggravated her. As far as she knew, he had no affiliation with the hospital, only that secretive bunch of ghouls in the basement—as if she were not one of them, especially now.

She closed the door and the blinds, then stood facing him down. "Well?"

He spread his hands and perked his eyebrows as if he were asking her the same question.

"Were you listening? I'm sure you're fully aware by now, Doris Branson just came through the ER—again."

"I would say she's had another accident—"

"Don't insult me. I could show you the chart from her automobile accident three months ago and it would be identical to the chart she has now, the same injuries in the same places, apparently by the same causes. So history has repeated itself and I'm sure you know what I mean even as I don't."

He paused, the same mild look on his face.

"Don't stand there thinking of a clever answer. Just tell me what went wrong down there."

He gave her half a smile and conceded, "We don't know. Not yet." She threw her head back and sighed out despair. "But the Machine is down so the only medical options are conventional. I can assure you, we're working on it."

"You said that about Mandy Collins." She sank into the chair behind her desk, closed her eyes, and breathed, clinging to control.

He leaned over her desk. "As I began to suggest, she had a second accident. She was drinking again, she got disoriented and took the stairs instead of the elevator, she fell down the stairs and then stumbled as far as the casino, where she collapsed and her people found her."

"*Your* people, you mean, covering your backs every moment, but I predict her UA is going to come up zero; no blood alcohol." He gazed at her as if he could communicate with eyes alone. Maybe he could. She got his drift and rolled her gaze away in disgust. "So you just assume I'll rewrite the lab report."

He gave her one, diminutive nod. "And bear in mind, she was never told what her injuries were the first time. She thought she didn't have any, so for her, history has not repeated itself."

"Yes," she said, slightly reassured. "Yes, that's an important point."

"And you've sedated her, so that will help to fog her recollections. No one actually saw her until she fell and drew attention. By the time she wakes up she will have slept off her intoxication and . . . you're the doctor. You can tell her what happened. Your explanation is the only explanation."

She thought it over. *It could work. Maybe.* "What about Mandy Collins?"

"She's the reason the Machine's malfunctioning. But we know where the problem's originating, so it's only a matter of time—pardon the pun. Don't worry, you won't be seeing her again."

The thought. The horrendous, unspeakable thought. She blinked it away.

"Let us know how things go with Ms. Branson." And with that, the ghostly DuFresne slipped quietly out her door and out of her sight.

The intercom on her desk came to life. "The salesman from Baylor Pharmaceuticals is here."

She cursed, something she rarely did.

"He had a two-o'clock appointment?"

She grabbed a bottle of water from a minirefrigerator. "Yeah, send him in." She uncapped the bottle and gulped half of it down. Pharmaceutical salesmen. If it weren't for the free lunches . . .

A tap on the door.

"Come in." She touched up her hair even as the door swung open.

"Hi," the man said. "I'm Willard Chatwell from Baylor Pharmaceuticals. Not really."

He sat down in a chair opposite her desk, a briefcase in his lap, and smiled at her, just smiled at her without a word.

If there was a God or gods, they had to have come up with this. Her insides felt pummeled, her face hot. *Payday. The time of judgment*.

The man was Dane Collins.

Wow! He'd never seen a white-coated professional, a knowledge-is-power doctor looking so fallible. Her hand was trembling. All she could do was gawk at him.

So all he did was smile and let her gawk. The torturous silence was delicious.

"You're not . . ." Phlegm made her voice rattle. She cleared her throat. "You're Mr. Collins."

"That's right," he answered, clicking open the briefcase.

"Isn't this a little underhanded?"

"You wouldn't answer or return my calls, not since you called that one time to tell me that I was seeing things."

Without another word, he produced the promotional photographs of blond Eloise Kramer and the early photos of Mandy Collins and laid them side by side on Kessler's desk.

The photographs spoke very well for themselves, and Kessler was definitely getting the message. She studied one, then another, her hand going to her face, her head shaking.

"This one"—Dane pointed it out—"calls herself Eloise Kramer. We happened to meet in Coeur d'Alene, Idaho, where Mandy grew up. I took her in, trained her, got to know her. It turns out she spent some time in a mental ward because she thought she was someone else. Someone else named Mandy."

She finally looked up at him. "What . . . I suppose you have a point to make."

"Eloise Kramer was the maiden name of my wife's mother, and Eloise was my wife's middle name. Eloise is a magician just as Mandy was; she grew up on a ranch near Hayden, Idaho, just as Mandy did;

she talks, acts, laughs like Mandy; she even has the same teeth as Mandy."

Oh, now the doctor was recovering her strength. The know-it-all face was coming back. "And your point?" Her voice was still weak.

"These are photographs taken by people other than myself who are witnesses to their authenticity. These images are not hallucinations, not delusions, not the side effects of medication. I want to hear you say I'm not crazy and that I truly saw what I saw."

"Well . . ." She drew a breath and her voice was stronger. "I can't deny that the girl bears a remarkable resemblance to your wife when she was that age."

"Which is something you seemed to anticipate in your warnings to me about my medication, am I right?"

She was struggling, a terrible liar. "I assure you, what we have here is a stunning coincidence."

"You did tell me that I might see Mandy again, or think I saw her, correct? Well, I did, only she was real, as these photographs prove."

"I am amazed," she managed to say.

"But I suggest that you warned me about it because you knew it would happen."

She wagged her head. "I didn't know it would happen."

What did he expect her to say? "No, of course you didn't. But given the evidence, would you say I'm crazy if I think I saw a girl who exactly resembled my wife?" She fumbled at the question so he asked again, "Am I crazy?"

She indicated the photos. "Given this, I would have to say no, you're not crazy. You're the victim of an incredible coincidence I can't possibly explain, but you're not crazy. Is that all?"

Her shocked, blown-to-pieces reaction to the photos had already told him volumes. "Good. We're clear on that." He began gathering up the photos. "I know this was only a ten-minute appointment, so to get right to the point—*the* point—I believe there's a reason for what appears to be a stunning coincidence, and now I believe more than ever that you know what that reason is. I'll be staying in town for a while." He gave her a slip of paper bearing his cell number and the phone number and address of Preston's Las Vegas home, now at his complete disposal. "I'd like you to think things over, and if there's anything you need to tell me, you can get in touch anytime.

Also"—he produced Jerome Parmenter's picture and bio from his briefcase—"I'm looking for this man and what he knows. If you know him, if you ever run into him, let him know I want to see him." He left a photo of Eloise and a photo of Mandy on her desk. "I'll leave you these. Of course there are duplicates."

He snapped the briefcase shut and went to the door. "Give it some thought, will you?"

She said nothing more. She only looked down at the two photos as he closed the door behind him.

"Now, that's cute, that's really cute!"

Keisha Ellerman, veteran costume designer, was a grandmotherly type, warm and immediately likable, always ready with pins, chalk, and a measuring tape draped about her neck. She was so delighted, even awestruck with how Mandy's new outfit looked one would think she hadn't made it herself. "And you are so perfect for it!"

Mandy turned this way, then that, striking little poses and looking herself over in the full-length mirror in her dressing room. The costume was cute—a pink top with puffy sleeves and matching capris that hugged her hips, both lavishly embroidered and trimmed out in silver. The bare midriff took a momentary decision to like—not that it didn't come across as teasing, playful, and fun, and not that she'd never dressed in short summer tops before, but just because, well, because she felt she was dressing this way for Mr. Vahidi and her navel was not her own. Something about that man took the fun out of everything.

But the reflection in the mirror captured and held her just as it had back in Idaho, as if the mirror were a window into a real world where that girl who was she, but in some mysterious way, not she, lived, dreamed, loved, and danced. Even the style and workmanship of this costume looked the same as the dresses and gowns she'd worn that day, as if the same person had made them all.

"I just have to ask you," said Keisha, studying her from across the room. "Have you ever heard of Mandy Collins? She and her husband used to have a magic act, Dane and Mandy?"

Mandy's heart thumped so hard she could feel it. Her next breath came with conscious effort. Were she and this nice lady living in the mirror's reflection, or were they here in this room right now and had Keisha really said that? She couldn't be sure. So much of her heart and memory still lay in that other time when she almost *was* the girl in the mirror, when she danced a waltz through a special world . . .

When she couldn't find her voice to say good-bye.

She put on her professional, social interaction smile—or at least half of it. "I, I sure have."

Keisha shook her head, looking at Mandy and marveling. "You look so much like Mandy Collins you could be her daughter, I swear!"

Her gasp came so slowly it could have been a drawn breath. Keisha's words played and replayed through her mind as she stared, transfixed, first at Keisha, then at her own reflection.

I look so much like . . . I could be her daughter?

No one had ever told her that. Maybe Dane had tried in certain ways but she didn't catch it. Now the girl in the mirror became more than a longing; she became a revelation.

He called me Mandy. He must have meant that *Mandy, his* Mandy, *the one I look like.*

Not me.

She turned to Keisha and tried to answer. "Is that . . . really?"

"I did her costumes. I was Dane and Mandy's designer for years."

Mandy felt her jaw drop open. She turned away from Keisha and toward the girl she longed to be. So her costume had a family, all beautiful; she'd met them, worn them; she could see the resemblance, feel the kinship.

So this was what Mandy Collins looked like?

A knock on the door drew her back from the mirror, back into the room. "Come in."

It was Seamus. "All set. Hey!"

She turned so he could admire her, and he did, and she might have appreciated his gaze up and down her frame, she wasn't sure.

"Well . . . that should make Mr. Vahidi happy."

Whatever smile she'd managed fell away.

"Be careful you don't get it dirty." He prodded her toward the door. "Great work, Keisha! Magnificent! We'll do another one, something in the same style to complement this one, maybe in blue. Bring us by some ideas, some swatches, all right?"

Mandy gave Keisha an adoring hug and the sweet lady kissed her on the cheek. "Good luck, dear."

Seamus draped her in an overcoat and they walked through the lobby of the Orpheus, past the jangling gambling machines—an adult could accompany a minor across the floor of the casino provided they kept moving—and out a side door.

"So how's the room at Priscilla's?" he asked.

I look like her. That's why.

But Seamus had asked her a question about her lodging. Right, the room at the bed and breakfast. Priscilla was a sister of Seamus's cousin's friend—or something like that—who ran the place. With kind words and some dealing, Seamus had secured a room there for Mandy, something she could rent by the week.

"It's very nice. I even have my own bathroom."

"My invitation is still open, of course."

She knew he was going there. "I appreciate the offer but I haven't changed my mind."

"If you saw my place, you might decide you like it."

She yanked her own leash but her feelings slipped through. "Could we wait till I'm through risking my life to talk about this?"

He backed off.

Out in the parking lot, a gaudily decorated stage was set up, the silver bunting shimmering in the light breeze, and in the middle of the stage was a big, green, ugly-as-an-alley Dumpster. Canned music, obnoxious stuff, was playing over a portable PA system, and behind the stage was a banner: MANDY WHITACRE, A DIFFERENT KIND OF MAGIC. The stage and Dumpster had drawn a crowd of maybe fifty. A clown was busily making balloon animals for the kids—all four of them—and a keno runner, not to miss an opportunity, was taking tickets for the next game. Mandy and Seamus ducked behind a barrier and hurried to the rear of the stage, where she shed the overcoat and took her place just behind the Dumpster on a small platform charged with a thousand pounds of compressed air.

Andy the stage manager checked his watch. "Two o'clock straight up. Ready?"

Focus, girl. They need you now, all your emotions, your whole mind, your best.

The music changed to a fanfare. She crouched, just as they'd rehearsed. Things worked pretty well the last several times they tried it; here was hoping. She steeled her muscles; her hands clenched involuntarily.

"One, two, three . . ."

Ba-boom! Smoke exploded around the Dumpster, the people jumped and shrieked, and like a pink Peter Pan, Mandy shot up from behind the Dumpster and landed like a feather on the lid, striking a pose. That got an excited round of cheers and applause. Good start.

With a wide, exaggerated wave and a pull on thin air, she beckoned a wireless microphone to come to her and it did, circling around her, then plopping into her hand. The crowd stirred at that one. They were with her.

She noticed the folks were wearing jackets, hats, even some gloves. The sun was out, which helped, but a sign across the street said the temperature was fifty-seven degrees. Not bad, really, for the pit of winter.

But she couldn't wait to get into the stunt and into some coveralls.

"Helloooo, everybody, and welcome to the Orpheus, where anything can happen and dreams can come true!" Vahidi must have written that opener. It was her job to say it. "I'm Mandy Whitacre, opening tonight in the Prospector's Lounge, bringing you a Different Kind of Magic." She flung her hand out, and Lily the dove appeared. One more fling and Carson followed Lily as they circled over the crowd. While the doves did a circle, and then, to everyone's astonishment, a series of vertical loops, a police siren sounded and a Las Vegas Police Department squad car pulled out from behind some landscaping.

"Oh-oh. Aerobatic birds without a license!" she quipped. She extended her arms and the doves came to rest, one on each arm.

Oh, the folks loved that!

Andy brought the doves' cage and they tucked themselves back home as an officer stepped onto the stage, handcuffs in hand.

"Officer Steve Dykstra of the LVPD!" she announced.

They applauded, though a few booed. The Las Vegas cops were great sports. She put her hands behind her and he handcuffed her. Then he did the same to her ankles. "Don't worry," she said, "you'll get 'em back—I hope."

She hopped into a large canvas bag that lay open on the stage, then Andy and crew member Carl pulled the bag up around her and cinched the top closed.

The Orpheus liked doing things big. They'd hired a crane just to hook that bag and hoist it into the Dumpster. It was noisy, it was big and noticeable, it was great show business.

And she was blind to the world, trying to keep her body moving, kicking a little so they'd know she was still in the bag as it dangled on the end of the cable. They'd worked this through. *Come on, don't let me swing too much* . . .

She felt Andy and Carl's hands steadying her as the crane lowered her into the Dumpster. *Eeesh*. The Dumpster was empty but it still smelled like garbage inside. She touched down and settled to a sitting position against the Dumpster wall, Andy unhooked the cable, and then SLAM, the lid closed and she was in the dark.

Now for the trick, and quickly, before the garbage truck arrived. She drew a breath, relaxed, and thought of the ranch, the white rail fence and the three aspens, the long driveway. She reached outside herself . . . and nothing happened.

He never loved me. He was in love with his wife. He said so.

She winced, concentrated. *Reach out . . . if not the ranch, then—no, not the hospital. Don't go there.*

My invitation is still open. Was she supposed to feel flattered? Seamus was such a child! At least Dane Collins showed a little honor, a little respect!

But he told me to go away and never come back. He's in love with her, and I just look like her.

She could feel the wad of cloth in the bottom of the bag, a pair of coveralls she was supposed to slip into after she got free of the cuffs. Other magicians would have picked the locks by now; they would have been free of the bag, they would have been wearing the coveralls and using some trick to get out of there—a double, a secret panel, a mirror system, a false bottom.

But she had no trick. She was still stuck in this world, this present where the handcuffs were cold, tight, and unyielding.

She reached in her thoughts, her will, but the ranch would not clarify in her mind; she wasn't welcome there.

She wriggled against the cuffs, but that was pointless.

I never told him my real name. At least that would have been honest.

Oh, no. She could hear the garbage truck roaring around the corner of the hotel. *Concentrate!*

On what?

The crowd was stirring—and growing—as a garbage truck rumbled up to a ramp on one side of the stage and lurched to a halt, brakes hissing. Climbing out of the cab like it was just another day, another Dumpster, the driver and his partner walked up the ramp onto the stage and rolled the Dumpster down the ramp toward the truck, the huge casters grating and shrieking, the lid on top rattling.

The floor of the Dumpster was jittering and banging under her backside, and the sound of the lid clapped her on the ears. This was a new experience. She was supposed to be out of the Dumpster by now.

The driver went to the levers on the side of the truck and operated the boom. Down came the forks like an elephant's tusks, ready to pluck the Dumpster into the air. The crowd was stirring, getting playfully nervous. *She's not in the Dumpster anymore, is she? It's all a big act. Isn't it?*

The handcuffs hurt, as real and secure as cold steel could be. The cloth of the bag was scratching her face; she was starting to sweat.

Rumble . . . scrape . . . clank! The garbage guys rolled the Dumpster forward, pushing the slots on the Dumpster over the forks on the boom.

Oh, dear God, now or never. What if there's no soft garbage in that truck for me to land on?

*   *   *

With a powerful roar from the truck and a surge of hydraulics, the Dumpster arced into the air over the cab of the truck, over the container in back, and tilted completely upside down.

The crowd screamed, laughed, waited to see . . .

The lid wouldn't fall open. The driver jerked the levers, jerking the boom, shaking the Dumpster like a salt shaker, which made the crowd groan and gasp, feeling the pain for the poor soul inside.

chapter

36

*F*inally!

Just before the shaking, Mandy reached for the last place on earth she wanted to go: the hospital. It sprang into her reality and she let herself fall into it, slipping out of the bag and handcuffs, out of the Dumpster, and into a wavering, tilting, tea-stained reality she'd come to loathe, the same hallways, doctors, nurses, signs and labels, medicinal smells, beds, gurneys, wheelchairs, that same, ominous door with the red letters on it. Why did she have to keep coming back here?

Her feet touched down on the linoleum—it felt like a soft rubber mat under her feet—but she didn't step into this world. She had to get back to the hotel, the garbage truck, the show. She reached, groped, *thought* for another fold of reality, another curtain she could pull back.

She found an opening, slipped through it . . .

She was . . . where? It looked like the inside of a house under construction. It was empty, with no fixtures, just bare walls and the smell of fresh paint. It was almost solid; she could see the ghost of another world through the walls.

No, still wrong, still lost.

"Whoa! Who are you?"

The voice scared her. She almost lost hold of the in-between and fell into this place, but she recovered and held back. She couldn't get stuck here.

Keep reaching . . . get back to the hotel . . .

It was a painter, a friendly sort of guy all in white coveralls with a painter's cap on his head and a roller in his hand. He was circling her warily, keeping some distance, looking right at her, nearly solid.

"Who are *you?*" she asked.

"The name's Ernie. Ernie Myers," he said. He stared intensely, studying her from different angles. "Are you really there? You look like some kind of Tinkerbell or something."

He reached with his finger to touch her but she shied back. "No, better not touch me!"

"But how do you do that?"

"I need to get back to the Orpheus Hotel!"

"The Orpheus Hotel! Little girl, you are *lost!*"

She tried to look beyond him, to see that world, the stage, and the garbage truck. She thought she could hear the truck rumbling . . . somewhere.

"You sure you're really there?" he said, and this time he did manage to poke her.

As if he'd been electrocuted he jolted, screamed, twisted, his arms enfolding his pain.

She didn't see what became of him. The moment he touched her she spun away as if caught in a whirlwind and fell out of there, through space, through blurring lights and sounds. She heard the truck and locked on it.

She was floating above the crowd, still watching the Dumpster hanging upside down above the truck as the driver jerked the levers and shook it.

She'd lost no time!

Somehow—she still didn't know how; thinking it was the same as doing it—she zipped through the Dumpster, grabbed the coveralls into the in-between and got into them, then aligned herself with the ground so she could step out onto it. She yanked a billed cap from a pocket of the coveralls and put it on. Ready? There wasn't a moment to spare.

The driver of the garbage truck gave the levers a wiggle, the Dumpster made one final lurch, and the lid dropped open. The bag, limp and empty, and the two pairs of handcuffs dropped into the truck's container.

That was the moment of misdirection, when all eyes were on

the Dumpster. Mandy stepped into the real, solid, present world just behind the driver and touched his shoulder; he ducked under the truck, out of sight. Mandy hopped up on the truck's running board, let out a whoop to get the crowd's attention, then took off her cap and waved it at everyone.

The effect worked. She'd vanished from the Dumpster and appeared in the place of the driver.

Great stunt. The crowd loved it.

She ran onto the stage, reached with an unseen hand, and brought the microphone to her. "Thank you!" she said to the crowd, and then toward the heavens. "Thank you!"

For that one fleeting moment onstage, the sorrow lay buried under the moment and the show business. She knew it would be back, but right here, right now, she relished her own little victory, the very pleasant fact that once she was captive, but now she was free. "I am Mandy Whitacre!"

The first time Ernie Myers fell off a ladder and his crewmen brought him into the emergency room with a cracked rib and broken clavicle, Dr. Margo Kessler and her secretive associates were able to send him home the next day with no broken bones and no memory of the accident.

The second time there would be no way to fix his injuries but the conventional way and he was sure to remember everything that happened to him. This inconvenient complication originated in the bowels of the off-limits basement, but it fell to Dr. Kessler, the benign face aboveground, to clear it up. She was steaming, feeling put upon and jeopardized, but she put on the best demeanor she could muster to wring information out of him.

"Silly ladder," he said, the pain keeping him still as he lay in his hospital bed. "The legs are crooked, so the thing rocks. I should have learned from the first time, right?"

Me, too, she thought. "So no dizziness beforehand? No vision problems, anything like that?"

"No, ma'am."

"No hallucinations?"

"Hallu——what are you talking about?"

"The guys who brought you in—"

"Jim and Don. My crewmen."

"Yes. They said that right before the accident they heard you talking to somebody who looked like a . . . Tinkerbell?"

He winced and wagged his head. "That was my *roller*. I got names for everything. The roller was getting kinda flighty, leaving gaps, so I was talking to the roller."

"Talking to your roller."

"Yeah. I talk to things, talk to myself."

"So, who was lost and looking for the Orpheus Hotel?"

Now Ernie got a little mad. "What? Those guys don't have any work to do, they're just sitting around listening to the boss talk to his roller. What's up with that?"

She smiled pleasantly, trying to keep him at ease. "I'm just covering all the bases here. I have to make sure there's no head trauma. You hit your head the last time, remember?"

"Not really."

She chuckled and nodded. "That's right, you wouldn't remember that." She wrote something down on the chart—made a scribble, actually; she was buying time. "Ernie . . ." First-name basis. She pulled a chair close to the bed and sat down, closer to eye level, more personal. "You don't have to be afraid to tell the truth. I'm the doctor, I'm here to make sure you're okay."

He seemed to be listening.

"Sometimes when people have had a head injury, they see things, they might see people who aren't really there. It's nothing to be ashamed of or embarrassed about but you see, if you fell and hurt yourself due to a prior head injury, I need to know about it."

She raised her eyebrows slightly, suggesting she was waiting for his response.

He looked at her for a long moment and she looked back, hoping, expecting . . .

"I fell off a ladder!" was all he had to say.

Sunday morning, Dane went through the doors of Christian Faith Center, embraced old friends, worshipped, then remained in his pew afterward, joined by friends and Pastor Chuck. Dane told them he was still working through his loss, wondering what to do, trying to resolve lingering issues, and could they pray with him? They nodded and prayed accordingly, even though he meant more than they thought they understood. He just had to hope the Lord would appreciate the spirit of their loving generalities while he silently footnoted the specifics:

That he would not be crazy, that somehow everything would come to rest on a rational explanation he could take home. Preston had a great-sounding theory, but it was so much like everything else he'd been through, simply outlandish, that it could not quell his doubts and fears even as he pursued it.

That he would not do anything really stupid.

That the Lord would help him get over Eloise—he thought it best not to call her Mandy. Whatever this fixation with a twenty-year-old was, it had to be affecting his thinking. It could be the single reason he was back in town, and that was dangerous. However it turned out, whatever he found out, it was to resolve his own issues and get peace of mind, not . . . well, he didn't even want to think about it.

But he did pray that God would take care of the girl, keeping her strong and pure, and not let anyone in this town—and that included the likes of that Seamus character—soil her or lead her astray.

Dear Lord, just help her find out who she is and where she belongs.

The prayer huddle took place in the second pew from the front, Dane and Mandy's favorite spot for the whole fifteen years they attended the church, and where Dane sat for the worship service that day.

She'd dressed up for church, sat near the back, remained just a few minutes to pray a prayer not too different from his. She slipped quietly out, lost in the mix, saying hello to the friendly people, feeling so much better until some heads turned and she heard a lady say, "Doesn't she look like . . . ?"

She walked quickly, turning her face away. She didn't want to hear it.

A few miles down the freeway she finally corralled her emotions and got things at least half sorted out; she was glad she went to church and glad she heard the lady say that. It was a God thing, the good and the sad. God was just being honest and making her face things . . . *ooohh, pun!*

Yeah, yeah, she'd been a fool, a teenybopper with just the face and hormones to fall into a fine kettle of fish, right along with Dane. Well, thank God, she could see that now, and there was no need to blame Dane or beat herself up about it. God still loved and forgave her. It was time to grow up and move on.

So, to be grown up about it, silly mistakes aside, she learned a ton from Dane Collins and she should just be thankful for the productive days they had together. Maybe she'd write him a letter—in a few years—and thank him for that part of it.

To be grown up about it, that simple hour and a half spent with other believers in the embrace of God's presence was real and familiar, like finding land after being adrift. The sweet God things she'd grown up with were still there, unchanged and rock solid under her feet, so there was still a big part of her world she could depend on.

As for the rest of her world, the part that was always smack-dab in front of her, brought her work, and helped her survive, but was so totally out to lunch she had to be nuts, that was another kettle of fish altogether. Any sane person would think it weird and scary, but she was getting used to it so it was becoming less weird, and *that* was scary. Stepping through a veil into another place she'd never been before, making things move by touching them even though she wasn't, meeting and talking to people she could see through, and seeing herself ahead of herself, all of these were becoming as real as making a sandwich, crossing the street, leaning against a wall. She'd heard that crazy people couldn't tell the difference between delusion and reality, and she was getting awfully close to that now.

And she sure didn't want to end up in the hospital again.

So could she tell the difference?

Her little blue Bug had to be real, and the pavement rushing under it at sixty-five miles per hour more than just her imagination. That her hands were on the steering wheel, keeping the machine from veering off and flipping over the guardrail, was a fact she'd better not have doubts about.

Oh, great. Was that her exit? *Nuts!* See, there was another real thing: she wasn't paying attention so the real exit in the real world went right by her and she missed it. She wouldn't have made that up and caught herself off guard like that. She drove on to the next exit and took that one, hanging a left at the bottom to duck under the freeway, where she could hang another left back onto the freeway . . .

There was no on-ramp here.

Guy!

She kept going straight, lost. She'd have to pull over, look at her map, get her bearings . . .

She'd been here before.

That mall over there . . . that Kinko's. She was seeing them again . . . for the first time. Wasn't she?

Turn right at the Kinko's.

She turned right. She didn't know why except that it seemed the thing to do. Just like déjà vu, you kind of know which way you're going to go and what you're going to see before it happens.

Oh, what was this now? The hospital district. She got nervous. She'd just been thinking about hospitals and it wasn't pleasant, never was.

Here came a blue sign: HOSPITAL. She'd seen that sign before.

Well, of course she had. There were plenty of signs in plenty of places she'd been that said HOSPITAL. Just like that big red sign that said EMERGENCY VEHICLES ONLY and that little blue one that said AD-MITTING and that one that said VISITOR PARKING.

It was the big blue logo on the side of the building that made her slow down, then make a right into the visitor parking lot. Before she even parked in a slot she stopped the car, flung the door open, and leaned out to see it better.

It was a stylish, modern logo in big blue letters against the cream-colored building: CCMC. Beneath the logo was the name of the place: CLARK COUNTY MEDICAL CENTER.

Another car pulled in behind her. She scurried, found a parking slot, killed the engine.

She couldn't climb out of the Bug fast enough, but once she did, she remained beside it, staring at the building, then the parking areas around it, then the streets, the trees, the multistory parking garage. It was more than déjà vu. It was memory. She'd been here.

"God, is this real?"

As real as the pavement under her feet. As real as the curb she stepped up on, the grass she ran her fingers through, the palm tree she touched. Nothing moved, nothing wavered, nothing shifted into and out of her world. The smells, the feel, the sound and sight, all remained right where they were, exactly the way they were.

Why did she remember this place?

Her eyes came to rest on two young men by the front door under the big breezeway, parking valets in blue shirts. The heavier one on the right; she'd seen him before. She even knew his name: Kerry.

What if he knew her? What if . . . she didn't know what if, she only knew she had to get inside that building and check it out.

She crossed the parking lot, went under the breezeway and right up to Kerry.

"Hi," she said.

He smiled, entirely pleasant, maybe even a little stricken by her looks. "Hi." His name badge bore his name: Kerry Mathinson.

She gave him time to recognize her.

He only looked puzzled at the silence. "Can I help you?"

"I'm Mandy Whitacre."

"Oh. Well, it's great to meet you. This is Mark, I'm Kerry."

They shook hands and it was all very cordial, just like strangers meeting.

Okay, she ventured the question, "So you've never seen me before?"

Kerry checked with Mark, who shrugged. "Afraid not. Believe me, I would have remembered—uh, no offense."

"None taken. Thanks."

She went through the doors, they eased shut automatically behind her, and she was enveloped by the sights—daylight through huge windows, marble and mosaic floor, high ceiling—and the sounds—air noise, talking voices nearly lost in the vast space, the clunks, clacks, and taps of shoes on the marble—and the smells—floor cleaner, wood stain, disinfectant—of the hospital lobby. Her steps faltered and slowed until she came to a dead stop right in the middle of the big logo on the floor. She was dumbstruck. Frightened.

Was she back in the madness, in the unreal? She braced herself, tapped her feet to be sure the floor was under her, and took in every detail: the sofa seats along the windows, the big logo she was standing on, the wooden pillars and paneling, the reception desk directly in front of her, the hanging fluorescent light fixtures, the plaques and portraits on the walls.

She was not in a strange, new place. She'd been here countless times before, seen it from many angles at many speeds and distances. It was the biggest, most insistent, most pervasive feature of her madness, always appearing and vying for attention among the other worlds, wavering like a tea-stained mirage, superimposed over clashing layers of light, sound, movement, depth. But now it was clear, in full color, rock solid. No wavering, no shifting, here to stay, right in front of her, daring her to believe her eyes.

She felt weak and consciously strengthened her knees so she wouldn't crumble. Clark County Medical Center, Las Vegas, Nevada. *This* was the hospital of her madness, not the one in Spokane. She always thought, assumed, just figured she was having flashbacks, visions of that other place, but—

"May I help you?" The pretty receptionist behind the counter was looking at her as if there was cause for concern.

Mandy stared back. She knew this lady's name without looking at her name tag. She'd passed by her countless times.

The lady asked, "Are you all right? Should I call for someone?"

"Nancy," Mandy squeaked, her throat dry and constricted. "You're Nancy Wright."

The lady cocked her head and studied her. "Yeah . . . Who are you?"

"I'm Mandy Whit——"

Her own name caught in her throat. She lurched, body tense and eyes wide as a ghostly vision popped out of nowhere in front of her and became as solid and real as any person.

It was another Mandy, herself, in the same dress, same hair, same everything, happening a few yards apart from her and . . . it had to be later, she didn't know how much. The other Mandy was rattled, gasping for breath, crouching like a cat who'd just fought off a pack of wolves, and when she spotted Mandy she froze as if caught in the middle of a terrible act.

Mandy had never come face-to-face with herself and had no idea what to do. She could have asked what in the world just happened but there were people around, and she couldn't be sure her other self would hear her anyway. Clearly, the other Mandy saw her; she looked ashamed and embarrassed. She straightened, composed, and neatened herself, then told Mandy with a wry chuckle, "Oh, boy, are you in for a ride!"

The other Mandy looked down at the floor and at a couch in a nearby sitting area, then strode up to Mandy and got in her face. "Don't let 'em do this to you, you hear me?" Then she brushed past Mandy, started for the door, warped, wavered, and vanished.

"Mandy?" Nancy was still watching her and now seemed even more concerned. "Is there anything I can do for you? You okay?"

Mandy tried not to gawk at everything, but everything, down to the texture of the wallpaper and the shape of the light sconces, was spellbinding. She stepped up to the counter. "Um . . . I'm here to visit someone." It didn't matter who, it was true.

"Name?"

"Mandy Whitacre."

Nancy smiled. "I mean the name of the person you're visiting."

Oh, brother. "Uh . . ." For some reason the name seemed to fit in this place. She took a chance. "Ernie. Ernie Myers."

Nancy checked the computer. "He's in room two-oh-two." *He is? Really?* "Just go down this hallway to the end, turn right, you'll see the elevators. Go up to the second floor and someone at the nurses' station will help you out."

Mandy headed for the hallway she already knew.

"Oh, Mandy . . ."

She stopped.

"There's a gift shop on the left once you get down there in case you want to bring him anything."

Oh, yeah, the gift shop with those goofy stuffed dogs that doubled as carry bags in the front window. "Thanks."

She headed down the hallway, past doors and office windows she'd seen before—DIAGNOSTIC IMAGING; OCCUPATIONAL MEDICINE; PAIN MANAGEMENT CENTER—and signs she'd seen before: SHUTTLE PICKUP/DROP-OFF; PHOTO ID REQUIRED FOR ENTRY; PLEASE DO NOT LEAVE YOUR CHILDREN UNATTENDED.

She was familiar with the ceiling lights, the doors on either side, the hand railing that went along the walls, the same intersections with other hallways with more signs: NUTRITION; SLEEP DISORDERS CENTER; FAMILY CARE. She expected to see them and she did. The déjà vu just kept going.

A doctor in blue scrubs, a big guy with blond, curly hair, walked by and she gawked at him. He was right out of her visions: Dr. Kurt Mason, orthopedic surgeon. He met her eyes, nodded hello, kept going. She couldn't take her eyes off him. He was the one always looking at X-rays, talking about simples, compounds, linears, transverses, obliques, and then rods and screws. He looked back once. She caught herself staring, averted her eyes, and kept going down the hall.

Being in the real world was weirder than being in the *other* one.

She knew the next intersection the moment she approached it. She knew the hallway to the right led to the EMERGENCY ROOM and INTENSIVE CARE UNIT, and the big double doors marked NO ADMITTANCE, AUTHORIZED PERSONNEL ONLY were where she expected them, just three doors down that hall. She walked toward the doors, hoping to peek through the windows.

"Offices on the left," she said to herself as she peered through the glass, and there they were. "One for Dr. Markham"—there it was—"and the other one for Dr. Kessler"—right again.

There was a row of curtained rooms along the left side of the room. Funny, she couldn't see inside those curtains from here in the real world, but in her visions she'd seen how each space had a bed with beeping, feeding, monitoring hospital gear crammed all around it.

A team of doctors and nurses in blue scrubs and shower caps hurried across the room with a patient on a gurney. She recognized a young surgeon with wire-rim glasses. "Bailey . . . Baylor . . . yeah, Baylor. He eats a lot of yogurt in the cafeteria." She saw a nurse and smiled. "Rosalie. Always laughing."

Oh-oh. Some personnel—Steve the trauma guy, Rachel the assistant, Julie the nurse—were coming toward the door. She spun on her heels and doubled back to the intersection.

Safely around a corner, she stopped to catch her breath—her runaway mind, actually. She simply could not get over it: it was *this* hospital she'd been seeing in her visions, every hall, curtain, door, nook, and cranny of it.

Steve, Rachel, and Julie came around the corner. She tried to relax, look normal, and not gawk at them as they passed.

Whoever, whatever all her other selves, hands, arms, minds were, they must have been here, they might be here right now; whenever she was working her magic, this was one of the most frequent places they . . . what? Came from? Lived? Journeyed to?

And why? She'd never been here before, never lived in Las Vegas. The question shouted louder than every other thought: *Why?*

Ohhh, that brought her to Ernie—which was just another totally weird coincidence, by the way. If he was the painter she saw, and he was really here and they had really seen each other . . .

Well now, that was a thought: she'd seen all kinds of places, things, and people in her visions, but only two people who were able to see *her*: that Tom Hanks–looking guy—hey, he was in a hospital, or that's what it looked like—and the painter Ernie Myers.

So was the painter Ernie Myers the guy in 202? Man, comparing notes with him in the real world could tell her something; it just had to. Her stomach was tight and she wanted to run but she had to find out, like it or not, scared or not.

She whisked by the gift shop—yep, the goofy stuffed dogs were still there—and went to the elevators. The second floor was just the way she remembered it, though she'd never been there—how was that for weird? She didn't need to ask the nurse at the nurses' station where 202 was; she already knew how the rooms were numbered and where they were.

She got there and put on the brakes just outside the door. What if it really was *the* Ernie Myers and he recognized her? She remembered him touching her, then screaming as if he'd gotten hurt. Did *she* put him here?

She swallowed her fear. This would be quite a connection, wouldn't it, between her other world and this one?

She swallowed her fear again. How could he be mad at her? It wasn't her fault.

She went in quietly, ducking around the privacy screen and calling in a polite tone, "Hello? Mr. Myers?"

"Hello?" he answered, and she might have recognized the voice. Sounds were different between the two worlds.

"Hello?"

"Yeah, who's there?"

She ventured farther into the room and could see the foot of his bed protruding around the corner. "Uh, it's just me, Mandy, coming to say hello . . . I think."

"Mandy?"

She came past the corner . . .

Oh, my. It was he, the painter, shoulders in a brace, wearing . . . wow, it looked so much like the gown she had at the fair that day. By the pale, horrified look that came over his face and the way the ice rattled in the water glass he was holding, she figured he recognized her. "You!"

She gave him a shy, apologetic wave. "Hi."

"You—you're Tinkerbell, the pink girl!"

"And you're Ernie the painter, right?"

His hand went to his call button, and he pressed it like he was reporting a fire.

"I'm sorry about what happened. I hope I didn't do this."

"You *did* do this!" He almost couldn't say it, he was gasping so hard. "What are you doing here, you some kind of ghost?"

Oh, man, this was going south in a hurry. "No, no, I'm not a ghost, I'm real. Here, feel my hand—"

"Yahh!" He shied back, which made his injuries hurt, which made him yell in pain. "You get away from me! *Get away!*"

There was going to be trouble, no way around it.

"Well," she said, backing out of the room, "I just wanted to say hello. Sorry if I hurt you."

He was still hollering. *"Nurse!* Somebody, help!"

She got out of there.

Where now? Away from the nurses' station, down the other hallway, back to the elevators—

"Miss!" said a voice. "Excuse me?"

It was a nurse hurrying down the hall. Ernie was still hollering for help.

"Were you bothering that patient?" the nurse demanded.

The nurse was getting close enough to grab her. Mandy thought of smiling, denying, walking away . . .

She ran—in kitten-heel sandals. The nurse was in sneakers; she was going to win.

"Oh, no you don't! Stop! Stop right there!"

Mandy gave it her best and it was an all-out chase for several yards until the nurse turned back, probably to check on the patient. "Stop her! Where's Bill? Call security!"

Mandy clumped, clopped, hobbled, and hopped out of her sandals and took the first right, hoping to circle back to the elevators, but now the alarm was spreading; other sneakers were pitter-pattering in the halls, voices were shouting—but not too loudly. They would hem her in soon enough. Forget the elevators, they'd head her off there.

She found the stairs—right where they'd always been—and took them, bounding down two and three steps at a time, sandals in her hand, to the main floor. She opened the stairway door a crack, made sure the hallway was empty, then stepped into the hallway looking for an EXIT sign. No problem; there was one down the hall to the left. Time to say good-bye to this place. She scurried toward the sign, passed an unmarked elevator . . .

Stopped. She knew this elevator. She'd been in it, rode it down, down, she didn't know how far down. There was no button on the wall to press, just an electronic keypad with a card slot.

Somebody was making very good time coming down the stairs. Could she . . . ?

She placed her hand on the closed elevator door, closed her eyes, thought of so many visions she'd had of this elevator . . .

Bill, male nurse, along with Tyler the security guy, thought they saw someone through the window of the stairway door, but by the time they burst into the hall there was no one there.

*   *   *

Bad move, very bad move! The moment her feet left solid ground and she went in-between, something sucked her through the elevator door and she tumbled down the shaft like a particle in a vacuum hose, flailing and groping for control but finding none. At the bottom she made a dizzying, pretzel-bodied ninety-degree turn and shot into another hallway like a leaf from a downspout, afloat above the floor. She groped for the floor to stop herself; the floor rushed around her hand like water. She reached for the wall—her hand passed right through it. She was rushing down the hall in an invisible current, spinning in unseen vortices. One of her other hands, one that might be in this place, contacted the wall . . .

She landed on the floor with a bump, bruising a knee, banging a hip and an elbow, sliding to a stop on the tile. Clunk-clunk! Her sandals came to rest not far from her. She felt nauseated.

But she made it. She'd seen this hallway before. She remembered the quiet rush of the ventilation system, the hum of the lights, the cool, hard tiles under her, and the hallway's distinguishing feature, the steel double doors that spanned it just a few yards away. On the wall was a blinking keypad for admittance, and painted across the doors in bold red letters were the words AUTHORIZED PERSONNEL ONLY.

"Well, hi there!" she said.

So she and those doors were meeting in the real world at long last.

She rose wearily from the floor, straightened her dress, and slipped into her sandals. She walked to the doors, extended a tentative hand, and touched them. For the very first instant she wondered if she might try to pass through them, but recent experience killed that idea. As she'd just found out, going in-between in this place was like parachuting into a thunderstorm. Besides that . . .

Something on the other side of those doors had such power as to send terror through the steel, and she could feel it. She, or part of her, or one of her, had been inside and brought back the memory of electric hums in windowless chambers, senseless numbers blinking and sourceless voices muttering in the dark, the stench of singed hair, the red glow of fire . . . the half-open eyes of monkeys as they ignited in flames.

She backed away, scared to the point of shaking, remembering how those doors had once sucked her in. Even now, in the solid, real world below Clark County Medical Center, she could feel them pulling, drawing, tempting her. No. She could never go there again.

Did a person need a clearance card to get out of here? The elevator had no keypad or card slot, just a button. She pressed it, then wondered what she'd do if someone else rode the elevator down and they ran into each other.

The steel doors began to open!

The stairway door, behind her! She ducked through it and crouched against the wall. She heard two voices in the hall.

"Where's Kessler?" said one.

"We've paged her. But the subject took the stairs and then security lost her."

"She's probably long gone by now."

"Wouldn't that be better?"

The elevator dinged. She looked through the door window in time to see two doctors—at least they were wearing white coats—get into the elevator.

Before the big steel doors swung shut she caught a glimpse of a dark hallway bathed in hellish red light.

Well, this was quite enough for one day. She hurried up the stairs, one flight, two flights, three, four. She reached a landing with a door and went through.

Oh, wow, main floor, back in the hallways. A sign on the wall directed her toward the lobby, and she went back the way she came. A left turn at the next intersection should take her past the gift shop, then to the lobby and out of there. She reached the intersection, turned left—

And almost collided with a lady doctor, her sandals squeaking on the floor as she braked and almost toppled.

Try to bluff? "Oh, sorry, excuse me." *Smile, try to pass by—*

But her eyes went to the doctor's face as if the face had pulled them there, and just in time to see the doctor do a double take and turn pale, her professional demeanor melting away. "Oh, my *God!*" She backed toward the wall, putting a hand behind her to touch the wall and steady herself.

Mandy felt her own reaction, an ache of foreboding. "You—you're Dr. Kessler! From the ER!" It still astounded her that she knew.

Dr. Kessler's other hand went over her heart as she stared Mandy up and down, wagging her head in what looked like disbelief, maybe horror. Her jaw was trembling. She fell against the wall as if all her strength had gone out of her.

Mandy was stupefied. She was supposed to be running from trouble, but all she could do was stand there. A *doctor* afraid of *her?* "Are you all right?"

And then the disbelief in the doctor's face gave way to a profound look of pity, the most tragic face Mandy had ever seen.

"What's wrong? Do you need a . . . doctor?"

Kessler covered her face a moment, then shook her head in an unexplainable fit of remorse. She looked at Mandy as if trying to find words, but finally just waved her along. "Go on," she whispered, "go on!"

"Are you sure—"

"Get out of here!"

Mandy hurried, looked back—the doctor was still resting against the wall, head down, a hand to her forehead.

She made it to the lobby and slowed to a brisk but normal-looking walk, making a beeline for the front doors. She came by the reception desk, smiled at Nancy—

A hand grabbed her right arm. "Hold up there, girl!"

"What—"

It was Bill the male nurse and . . .

Tyler the security guy, grabbing her other arm. "Take it easy now."

Her first reaction was natural, to squirm and try to break away, but their hands were clamped on her, digging into her, and she couldn't move. It hurt. From somewhere she found the self-control and civility to ask, "Please let go of me."

"Not till we've cleared up a few things," said Tyler.

So here she was again, held against her will and painfully so by two insensitive brutes—like Johnny the cop and Dr. Angela's apes Bruce and Dave and the sneaky Samaritans Clarence and Lemuel—and once again, she was being held and manhandled in a *hospital*.

"Let go of me," she said, and it was a warning.

Of course they didn't. They started forcing her along and she knew they would take her down another long hallway to another door that would lock behind her.

Any thought of doing the right thing, any consideration of being reasonable and compliant, flickered out like a candle in a gale, and in their place flashed a burning, visceral rage. She growled, clenched her fists and eyes, reached from the depths of her rage into unseen places and times, and drew back to herself any and all parts of her that were free and could fight.

It happened fast. It was noisy and alarming. Nancy screamed and cowered behind the reception desk. Everyone else in the lobby froze, and some ducked. Mandy remembered making some kind of shrieking animal sound, and before she drew another breath she was coming at Tyler and Bill from every direction, fighting mad, ready to show them how it felt to be grabbed, dragged, manhandled, and hurt. Both came off the floor and sailed several yards before landing, Bill on the floor, Tyler slung over a couch in a sitting area. A lamp next to the couch shook, then slid, then sailed in Tyler's direction.

It stopped, in midair.

Mandy was looking at herself looking back. The Mandy she was had just come in the front door, neatly dressed, wide-eyed and curious, looking at every little thing until she saw herself.

The lamp crashed and rolled on the floor before it ever reached Tyler.

Mandy was crouching like a cat, panting, disheveled. She'd just decked two men twice her size and was ready to do worse and she would have . . . which scared her. She stared at who she was then, shocked at who she was now. How in the world did she get from *there* to *here*? Sense and civility returned—whipped and ragged, but they were there, along with a healthy dose of shame and embarrassment. "Oh, boy, are you in for a ride!"

She made sure Tyler and Bill got the message—they were obviously in pain as they looked up at her, not moving—then walked up to her earlier self. The words didn't come from memory; they burst from her as if foreordained. "Don't let 'em do this to you, you hear me?"

She could hear hurried footsteps from the hall, see Bill and Tyler stirring. She brushed past herself and headed for the door.

"Let her go!" came Kessler's voice. She looked back to see Bill and Tyler get to their feet. "Let her go," Kessler repeated, and they remained in place. Kessler met her eyes, but only to watch her leave.

* * *

Kessler did not want to talk to Ernie Myers. She dreaded what she would learn, loathed what she would have to do with it. But the others were waiting.

She leaned over Ernie. "You look like you've seen someone, Ernie."

He was ready to confess. "Yeah, yeah, I did. But it wasn't a hallucination! I saw her. She was standing right there. She tried to zap me again!"

"Who?"

"The ghost, the Tinkerbell girl." He spilled it. "Yeah, I saw her on the job. She was this ghost kind of thing, all dressed in pink and sparkles and she just came out of nowhere and when I touched her she, she zapped me, she did all this to me! And I'm not crazy, I swear to God!"

"It's okay, Ernie, it's all right. Did she have a name?"

"Uh, yeah. Mandy. She said her name was Mandy."

Of course.

Ernie brought out a section of Sunday's newspaper. "And I found her, can you believe that? I'm not crazy, I really found her. She was asking about the Orpheus Hotel, so I checked the paper. Take a look!" He folded the newspaper to the page and handed it to her, pointing at an ad featuring a sprite young magician opening at the Orpheus. "That's her! Mandy Whitacre! That's the gal I saw! Man, she must be really good. I'd just like to know why she zapped me and broke my collarbone."

Kessler straightened. No surprises here, just confirmation. "I'm sure she could have explained it all to you."

"Yeah, well, she'll explain it all right, she'll explain it to my lawyer!"

Her heart sank. No surprise there either.

chapter

38

Well, she hadn't had any visitors yet.

Mandy sat in her dressing room trying not to botch her mascara again, hoping she would never hear an authoritative knock at the door. There was a cop right there to handcuff her for that afternoon's Dumpster escape, but he didn't say or do anything that wasn't part of the act.

Her hand still shook a little.

Girl, you have got *to remember the rules: don't be a danger to yourself or others*. If Kessler hadn't stepped in and stopped those guys . . .

She whooshed a sigh. Oh, the things she was about to do to Bill and Tyler and that lobby. It was God's grace that she didn't.

But she really could have, and that was why she was shaking. Call it an answer to prayer—*hoo boy, what an answer!*—but ever since that visit to Clark County Medical Center, a realization had come together piece by piece, growing from a *hmmm?* to an *aha!* to a big-time life changer over the course of the afternoon: all the weird "delusions" she'd been having weren't delusions. They were weird and otherworldly, scary at times, mysterious, and hard to control, but one thing they were not and delusions were, was false. The Clark County Medical Center wasn't a bunch of nightmarish flashbacks but a real place she had visited, if not in body, in *fact*, countless times. She'd seen real things, been real places, met real people, learned real names. She'd talked to Ernie Myers from a supposed delusion and she'd talked to him in the real world, and in the real world he was mad at her for doing something to him from her delusion, which told her the delusion was as real as the real. She was never making any of this stuff up, she was really going there and seeing it.

Just like her visions of the ranch, the white paddock fence, the driveway, the three aspens, the house, the barn, all of it. She'd seen those things because they were really there and somehow, some way, she'd been there to see them before really being there. The Mandy she saw coming out of the hospital was the same Mandy she saw coming in—now, how that worked she hadn't a clue, but both Mandys were she, and both were real.

She beckoned to Maybelle, who sat with her friends on their perch in the corner. Maybelle fluttered, alighted on a lipstick, and brought it to her. The dove got a treat and returned to the perch.

Anyway, this changed everything. Seeing things that weren't real was crazy. Seeing things that turned out to be real wasn't. Thinking she could move things from somewhere else was crazy, but really moving them from somewhere else wasn't. Just ask Clarence, Lemuel, Preston Gabriel, Bill, and Tyler, and most every audience she'd ever had—to name a few. Until today she'd gone with it and figured it was just part of her crazy world, something she would never understand, much less discuss. Now she still didn't know what it was—a gift, maybe?—but she knew it wasn't crazy.

As for thinking—knowing—she was Mandy Whitacre, if all the other stuff was real, then maybe her being twenty years old in 2010 when she was born in 1951 was real, too. Sure it was. She just hadn't figured that part out yet.

Anyway, all the trouble aside, today's Dumpster escape went off without a hitch because slipping between dimensions, "interdimming," to pull off a vanish, escape, levitation, whatever she needed, wasn't so scary or difficult anymore. She was getting a handle on it—pretty much. Now, if the trouble would just stay away . . .

Well—she touched up her rouge—*maybe you're not crazy, so try not being dangerous. Behave yourself and be glad you aren't in jail!*

The nine-o'clock show had a great crowd, a nearly full house.

Les and Eileen, along with their friend Clive, all from Westport, Connecticut, were as entertaining as Sarah, Clive's wife, the one

Mandy levitated. Mandy allowed them to walk all around and under Sarah and even wave their hands over the top of her to feel for wires, and they were having such an amazed, flabbergasted, and hilarious time of it the routine was scoring big points and gold stars with the audience. What made the illusion even more fun was the fact that Sarah, unlike most pretty girls who get levitated, was not in a hypnotic trance but fully awake and as giddily mystified as her husband and friends were.

Nearly excellent, thought Dane, sitting near the back. Incredible timing, inventive effects and gags, great pacing, perfect misdirection and hand placement, lots of Vegas-style pizzazz, but where was the wonder? He couldn't see it in her eyes or hear it in her voice, not like before. Maybe the town was getting to her. Or . . .

He could see Seamus Downey standing in the back, watching— or patrolling. Downey seemed pleased enough, but with a strange lord-of-all look in his eyes that Dane had seen before and never liked. So this was the man in her life now? That could explain a lot.

What a feeling—or feelings: pride in the great progress she'd made, gladness at her success mixed with regret at the loss of her unique sparkle, sorrow at the chasm now between them, and a longing to be with her, at least to be friends again, to steer her a bit, maybe bring back what she'd lost since . . . The memory of that day would forever haunt him.

He'd come in the hope of speaking with her, but now that was looking like no small task, especially with Mr. Downey the Great and Powerful lurking about. He'd thought of finding someone in management and using his name to get through to her, but seeing her on that stage made her seem so unreachable and him so much a stranger, what could he say?

He could try congratulations, kudos, small talk, and then—*oh, this should be easy*—the question of who she really was, and how would he segue into that? He might comment on the stage name she'd chosen and how she'd come by that name, and whether that tied in with all the other facts about her that lined up perfectly with the girl he met some forty years ago.

And where from there? Oh, this should be a cakewalk.

* * *

The show went great considering what a day she'd had, but as soon as she closed the dressing room door, uncapped a bottle of water, and dabbed the sweat from her face, the highs of the performance ebbed away and the trouble loomed in her mind. Maybe, *maybe*, Ernie Myers would forget about her, maybe he wouldn't see her picture in the paper even though she told him she was looking for the Orpheus Hotel; maybe the hospital wouldn't be that interested in her even though she decked two of its employees.

There was a knock on the door. It didn't sound like a police bust. The voice was quiet and courteous. "Miss Whitacre?"

"Julio?"

"Yes, ma'am."

She opened the door to Julio the bellman, all by himself. He'd brought a small envelope. "Thanks, Julio." She offered him a treat-size Hershey's bar from a dish on her vanity. He snatched it up, gave her a wink, and let her be.

The envelope contained a note. She unfolded it and read, "*Saw you near the elevators the day of my accident, would like to speak to you regarding what you saw.*" It was signed by Doris Branson, the hotel manager. Branson included her phone number.

Mandy rested against the wall and let her lungs empty. Accident? What a day. First Ernie, and now her.

The good news could be, if Doris Branson saw her near the elevators while she was interdimming there, that was one more confirmation that something real was going on, a second witness. The bad news could be, if Doris Branson had an accident right after she saw Mandy, the same as happened to Ernie, that could mean that Mandy and all her interdimming had something to do with it, and what if it did? Double trouble.

Well . . .

She'd just have to call Doris and face the music, whatever it was. It probably would be painful, but what else was new? She might learn something more about her very strange world, so the pain might be worth it. To put a smile on it, maybe Doris would end up on her side and talk to Ernie, then maybe they'd all talk, then maybe . . . she didn't know.

* * *

Dane waited through the show, suffering and enjoying, and stood to applaud when Mandy struck her final pose. When the curtain came down and the lights came up, he searched through the heads and shoulders to find an usher, anyone—other than Downey—he might ask about having an audience with—

Someone tapped him on the shoulder. An unintended brush, of course; the place was swarming. There was an usher at the main door. He could ask him—

The tap came again. Probably Downey. Dane steeled himself and turned.

"Pardon me," said a middle-aged man in wire-rimmed glasses. "Am I addressing Dane Collins?"

Dane was looking at a miracle and made no effort to hide his awe. "You most certainly are."

"I'm pleased to meet you, sir, and glad I caught you." The man extended his hand. "I would use an alias, but you already have my name: Jerome Parmenter. Before you have your talk with Miss Whit-acre, may we have a word?"

chapter

39

Parmenter couldn't talk with Dane anywhere at the Orpheus, not in a hotel room, not in the casino, not in the lounge or in the restaurant. They had to find someplace safe, neutral, secure. Dane suggested the house where he was staying.

"No," said Parmenter, "everyone knows you're living there."

"What do you mean, 'everyone'? Who's 'everyone'?"

"We'll talk about that."

"So how much do you know about me?"

"Not here."

Dane thought of going to Christian Faith Center. By now it was after ten, but the church might still be open. Parmenter thought that would work. Dane called Pastor Chuck, who met him at the front door and gave him a key to lock up. Parmenter remained in the car until Dane could make sure no one would see him, and then went inside.

They settled for the Preschool Department, a large room painted in bright, primary colors with biblical murals on the walls, Scripture posters, pictures of Jesus, Moses, the disciples, the lost sheep, the boatful of fish, and finger paints of Jesus, sheep, fishing boats, and an empty tomb. They sat down on child-size chairs at a child-height table in a corner filled with plastic toys. It looked awkward, even a little silly, but Parmenter felt safe here. He visibly relaxed.

"Good. Good enough." He faced Dane, hands on his knees, his knees elevated because of the tiny chair he sat on. "Thank you for giving me this time, and most of all, thank you for choosing to talk with me before talking to Miss Whitacre. I'm sure you'll see it was the right choice."

Parmenter produced a laptop computer from his briefcase, set it on the table, and flipped it open. He reached for a child's wooden block and set it on the table as well.

Dane recognized the computer. "You were there at McCaffee's."

"Oh, you bet I was." He pulled a small device that resembled a GPS from the briefcase and set it atop the toy block. He switched the device on, then tapped at the computer keys, apparently responding to whatever information the device was sending. "And I'm going to answer all your questions if I can, but I suggest we cover things in order, and in small doses. You'll understand once we get into it."

A few more taps on the computer, and then he took the block and held it out. "Here. Hold this in your hand." Dane extended his palm, and Parmenter set the block on it. "To get through the introductions, I know who you are and where you live and what you do for a living, so there's no need for you to tell me. As for who I am, you obviously know or you wouldn't have made such a lasting impression on Dr. Kessler. I can tell you my age—I'm fifty-seven—and I could list my credentials and diplomas and bore you to death or I could get right to the important stuff. So hold the block up so you see where it is and also"—he indicated the block's former location on the table—"where it came from."

Dane felt like a volunteer in one of his stage routines, but he was not expecting a magic trick.

"Lucky for us," said Parmenter, eyeing the computer screen, "Mandy Whitacre is inactive at the moment, probably asleep in bed, so we'll be able to squeeze in and do this. Don't blink. You ready?"

Dane's eyes were open.

Parmenter tapped the enter key on the computer.

The block vanished from Dane's hand and instantly reappeared in its former location on the table.

Dane was impressed but not surprised. He'd already seen this phenomenon several times.

Parmenter looked at the block on the table, then at Dane. "Okay, you saw what happened?"

Dane nodded. "Interdimensional displacement?"

The scientist lit up. "You've been reading about me!"

"And this is how she does it."

"Fundamentally, yes. To qualify myself in your eyes, I have just shown you the core explanation for Mandy Whitacre's magic, and I'm not betraying a confidence. I invented it. Shall I break it down for you?"

"You have my undivided attention."

"To put it simply, I set the block on the table, then determined the exact spatial coordinates, exactly where it was, at"—he consulted his computer—"eleven thirty-eight P.M., January thirtieth, 2011. I then moved it to another location, your hand, at approximately eleven thirty-nine. Then the fun part: I sent it back to where it was and how it was at eleven thirty-eight. Where it was and how it was, the exact state it was in a minute earlier. It's crucial to understand that."

"And how did you do it?"

Parmenter sucked in a whistle, then sighed it out, trying to come up with an answer, Dane figured. "It's a combination of time and space travel, although the crucial difference is, the block didn't travel through time, time traveled through the block."

Dane had read the articles Preston's people had found. He vaguely understood. "The parallel railroad tracks."

"Yes, yes! And here's a practical way of looking at it: I suppose you're familiar with how to restore a computer to a prior state? Your computer gets snarled up or crashes because you've hit the wrong key at the wrong time, and the only way to fix it is to have it revert to exactly the way it was a day ago or a week ago, or whenever it was still working, before whatever went wrong went wrong."

"Right."

"Ever done that?"

"Yeah. A few times."

"Well, that's similar to what we just did with the block. It was on the table for a moment, then, in the course of time, about a minute, I put it in your hand. Now . . . the key difference here between reversion—that's what I call it, reversion—and time travel like you see in the movies, is that the block didn't travel back in time. What happened was"—he searched the ceiling for how to explain it—"this computer is linked with our Machine. I fed the Machine the data from the block, the Machine replicated a secondary timeline"—he

gave his hands an erasing wiggle, frustrated—"well, we put the block
on a parallel timeline . . ."

"The other railroad track."

"Yes! Right! Then, without shifting the block itself in relation
to our timeline, I shifted the secondary timeline it was on backward
by one minute. So even though the block is still here with us, in our
present, in our space"—he reached over and flicked the block with
his finger just to make the point—"it is actually existing in a timeline
that is one minute behind ours. The block is, and always will be, one
minute younger in relation to us. If the block were a conscious en-
tity, it would think it never left the table, but it would be wondering
where that last minute went. Very simple."

"Oh, yeah. Very simple."

"So, to recount the story that goes with this"—he put the block
back with its friends in a toy box—"I got to thinking about the practical, humanitarian use for such a discovery. Imagine someone getting
cancer or being injured, and medical science having the ability to
place them on a new timeline and revert them to a point and place in
time before they got sick or before they had the accident. They could
continue their life from that point and bypass the illness or injury."

"Bypass the illness or injury? Not just go through it all over again?"

Parmenter drew an extra breath before answering, "That's why
we put them on a secondary timeline, a whole new route through
time so they don't retrace the old one." Dane was figuring it out and
Parmenter could see it in his face. "Yes, you see where this is going."

Dane had been preparing himself, trying to imagine such a pos-
sibility while trying not to hope. Even now, he dared not speak it.

"It's not all roses, I'll tell you that now, but to continue the story,
some friends and I managed to build a small machine that could revert things and we experimented with blocks of wood like this one
and other small objects. We stepped on a toy car, then put the broken
pieces in the Machine and watched the car put itself together again.
We crushed a can and then reverted it to an uncrushed can. That was
exciting. We thought, Wow, with a big enough machine we could
take an old car and erase all the miles off it, or a wrecked car and
unwreck it. Great in theory, a little shaky in the practical application.

"But anyway, we got around to reverting rats—hope you won't
find this offensive, but we injured the rats in various ways and then

put them in the Machine, and voilà! The rats went back to the way they were before we hurt them. We went bigger and tried monkeys. Same thing.

"But"—he waved his finger in the air, signaling an important point—"we also did maze and memory tests on the lab animals, and sure enough, their brains also reverted. The rats learned a maze right before we injured them, and then we reverted them and they weren't injured anymore, but they couldn't remember their way through the maze either. The monkeys could perform tasks, but when we reverted them to a condition prior to learning the tasks, they didn't remember what they'd learned. They were younger, too, because reversion means everything reverts: any injuries, any bodily changes—haircuts, nail trimmings, weight loss or gain—and memory. So for all practical purposes, the rat, the monkey, the human subject wakes up behind the times. It's kind of a Rip Van Winkle effect: they've lost a minute, an hour, a few days, depending on how far they were reverted."

"How about forty years?"

Parmenter hesitated to answer.

Dane calmly asked again, "How about forty years? Can you revert someone forty years?"

Parmenter thought for a moment, then nodded his head with chagrin. "Now we're getting to it. Somehow we did, but we don't know how it happened, so at this point we can't repeat it and, on the downside, we don't know how to fix it."

Dane's mind was racing, only beginning to process what little he had heard to this point. A mountain of memories, events, and questions waited to be reworked into an entirely new schematic by which all the impossibilities would be possible. It was more than he could handle in days, much less minutes.

Parmenter could read all this in his face and chuckled nervously. "This is why I said we'd have to cover this in small doses."

But Dane wanted it all, as long as that might take. "Please continue."

"All right. Anyway, picking up where I left off"—Parmenter was delighted with himself—"not a bad play on words! That's what we've done with objects, with lab animals, and with . . . well, you see the similarity. They go back to a particular point and pick up where they left off."

"Yeah, right, so . . . ?"

"Right, right, to get to the bottom line, or near bottom line . . . we secured government funding, and let me tell you, that was the beginning of sorrows right there. The military people leaped at the prospects—I mean, they were frothing at the mouth. Think of being able to uninjure soldiers and send them back into battle perfectly fit and with no memory of ever being shot. You could recycle the majority of your casualties and just keep them rolling through your war over and over again and then, of course, the boys and girls could all come home as fit as when they shipped out. What a dream, a compelling dream! We couldn't turn away, we couldn't slow down, we had to achieve that—which meant we had to ignore . . . tromp on . . . certain moral issues. But isn't that the way it goes?"

Dane kept telling himself it was all important and he should hear it. But he couldn't keep his impatience from showing.

"Sorry," said Parmenter. "There's just so much . . . but getting to it: we procured government funding, which enabled us to build a full-size Machine that could revert human subjects, and our first was a soldier, a volunteer who'd been wounded in Afghanistan. It worked. More on that later, I know you're impatient to hear. . . . Anyway, we did have a few other human subjects with various injuries and"—he searched the ceiling for his thoughts, wiggled his fingers nervously—"the secrecy of the whole thing, that's what made it all so difficult. The experimental subjects couldn't know what we were doing or, of course, the word would get out, and we were advised, we all knew, that a—well, the military referred to it as a strategic asset, and a strategic asset like this would only be an asset as long as only one nation—ours, obviously—had it. There was no way on earth or in hell that we could let any other government find out we even had such a thing.

"But that's why we're in such a pickle now, why everything is so complex and tangled up. . . . I'm sorry, I know I'm going on and on."

Dane drew a breath and said, "I have all the time you do."

Parmenter looked about the room, trying to find the next point to launch from. "So, I'll say it, I'll admit it, we were hasty. Pressure from the military, pressure from the government, all sorts of hassles over funding and who was in charge and . . . and there were the moral aspects we could never agree on, still can't agree on, but that's a matter to discuss later.

"But we did have human subjects, civilian as well as military, which brings me to our mutual acquaintance, Dr. Margo Kessler. I won't say it was her exclusive territory, the whole thing has just grown so large and so unmanageable, but . . . we needed human subjects who'd been injured and could conceivably be reverted in such a way that they wouldn't know they'd been reverted. I know, it sounds so impossible, and I think we're finally accepting the fact that it is. But can you imagine, we actually had the first few sign consent forms, and then, after reversion, they had no memory of giving consent to anything or even experiencing anything and we, we just decided to leave it at that. Why tell them? Secrecy was the priority, right, and now we had human subjects who had no idea what we'd done to them. It was a gift, it was perfect.

"And Kessler was one of our . . . scouts. She saw injured people every day, she had the means to check their backgrounds, family ties, suitability, and when she found someone we could revert without a high risk of discovery, she forwarded them down to us. To put it succinctly, they came into the emergency room injured, we took them down the hall, down an elevator into our own version of an ICU, reverted them, they woke up with no injuries and no memory of an accident, and we sent them home after a day's observation, just telling them how lucky they were to escape without a scratch. And they bought it. All they knew was what we told them." He took a breath. He was getting visibly nervous. "You see where this is going. . . ."

Dane was there. It could take him days to accept and believe it, but he was there. He laid himself open for one more dose, and it wouldn't be small. "She wasn't dead."

Parmenter came right back with a disclaimer, "She would have been, in just a matter of minutes. The outcome was inevitable, as determined by Kessler and the ER staff. You were at a wake, a death watch, but"—he thought for a moment but apparently found no better way to say it, so he kept going—"we had yet to revert burn injuries, to see if destroyed tissue would actually return given the fact that such vast chemical changes had occurred, that so many atoms and molecules were lost in combustion and just weren't there anymore. It was an unresolvable question, like life itself. We found repeatedly that life couldn't be restored to anything dead—so God still has control over that and isn't about to share it. But your wife . . ."

Dane delivered a subtle look of permission to continue—please.

"Kessler had already notified us and we were so in need of a living experimental subject. . . . We actually expected her to die, that was the most likely outcome according to all our computer models, all the data we had at the time, so we didn't think we were risking that much. She would die, we'd take her to the morgue, the normal unfolding of the tragedy would remain the same, and in the meantime, we would have some data for whatever it was worth. It, it was a snap decision. We had to get her in the Machine and just, just see what might happen, whether moments before death or after death, either way, because we didn't know if the length of time before or after death might also have a bearing on it, or to what extent reversion, maybe resuscitation, might still be possible."

"So . . . you faked her death?"

He smiled grimly. "As I'm sure you know, we humans can rewrite anything, we can redefine our way through any moral conundrum. We didn't 'fake' her death, no, we anticipated it and brought it about as it would eventually occur anyway, then deferred it until we could make use of her body for scientific purposes. Well, after all, she was an organ donor, so . . . if the use of her entire body might lead us to discoveries that could save lives in the future . . ."

Dane understood. It turned his stomach, but he understood. "Beautifully done," he said with a cutting edge.

"Uh, yeah. We found a way to justify"—Parmenter actually showed a pang of conscience and seemed to be confessing as he said it—"we . . . the nurse . . . well, under Kessler's orders, under our orders . . . disconnected the wires to the heart monitor so your wife would go flatline. She would appear dead so we could get her body down to the Machine before she really was dead. We barely made it."

He paused for a break they both needed. They sat in silence, Dane looking at Parmenter, Parmenter looking at the floor.

As if it might moderate the impact, Parmenter recalled, "They replaced the tracheal tube and ventilated her, one hundred percent oxygen, all the way down the elevator, all the way into the Machine." Then he repeated, "We barely made it."

Dane had the thought, so he spoke it. "What about the ashes from the funeral home, the whole cremation?"

"A cadaver. I don't know the legal, procedural details. Somehow they pulled it off."

"But it wasn't Mandy."

"Ohhh, no. No, it wasn't."

"What happened to her?"

Parmenter actually laughed. "We're all wondering that. That was the question right after the reversion started. We had her in the Machine, her vitals were dropping right off, we started the sequence"—he sighed and searched the ceiling again— "it had to be a faulty computer model or an error in the power calculations, or . . . we still don't know. But . . . here's how it's supposed to work: we lay the subject in a hospital bed just as I laid the block on the table, right? Then we sedate them so they don't know what we're up to and transport them downstairs into the Machine. When we revert, we send them to a point on their new timeline prior to their injury and relocate them in the hospital bed so that, to them, they were in the bed, fell asleep in the bed, and then woke up in the bed a few hours, a few days later, whatever the case may be. With just a small amount of time lost, it looks normal enough. 'Wow,' we tell them, 'you were out for a while but you're all right now and very, very lucky!'

"But in Mandy's case, there was a power surge, a time surge, an overcompensation. We didn't expect her to live, but we did have a hospital bed prepared, we were planning to relocate her to that bed in case, just in case, she might survive. We dressed her in a hospital gown . . . just threw it on her as quickly as we could, it was almost an afterthought. But anyway, we'd just begun the sequence when . . . POOF! She vanished! Completely, totally, without a trace, and until recently we had no idea how far back she'd reverted, whether years or seconds or a fraction of a second. Worse yet, we had no idea where. She didn't relocate to the hospital bed, or to that room, or the hallway, or anywhere on that floor or the floor above. We—can you imagine trying to check through an entire medical center to see whether an experimental subject now of younger age and disoriented, or . . . pardon me . . . a, uh, a body in such ghastly condition might have cropped up unexpectedly? Can you imagine sitting helplessly, waiting for a report to come in of a deceased or dying individual suddenly appearing in the middle of a street or someone's yard or living room or . . ." Parmenter stopped to look at him, apparently to assess his reaction. "I can't imagine how you must feel hearing all this."

"I can help you out," Dane replied. "At this point, I feel disdain for you and not the slightest measure of pity. And that goes for Kessler, too."

The scientist received that and nodded ruefully. "Don't be too harsh with Kessler. We lured her with the humanitarian benefits, then closed the net with her very first referral. She may have sold her soul, but we were the devil." He closed his computer. "Anyway, to answer your question, yes, we can revert someone forty years, and we know that only because, by keeping tabs on you we finally found her, forty years behind our time and at the opposite end of the next state where she landed at precisely the right moment in her past that would place her at precisely the distance from the Machine that would exert precisely the amount of gravitational flux to expend the energy of the space warp needed to facilitate the time change. We still have no idea when or where that was, we're guessing Mandy knows and we're hoping she'll tell us, but you can see how far we have to go before we can, you know, just ask her. We'll need your help, if and when you decide I'm the kind of man you'd trust in the first place. But we'll get to that. We'll get to a lot of things." He checked his watch. "I've given you more than enough to process for now."

He slipped the computer back into his briefcase. "Isn't that the irony, or perhaps the poetry? We tailed you and surveilled you, figuring that wherever Mandy ended up, if she was still alive she would try to find you and so we'd find her. But now the fact is"—he snapped the briefcase shut—"she's a girl who never met you, never fell in love with you, never married you. You never lived forty years together, never had a career together, she didn't know you from Adam, and yet"—he looked at Dane, then far away into space—"she found you. It makes me think of a salmon swimming upriver. Nothing can turn it back. It's going to get there or die in the process." He rose awkwardly from the child-size chair. "I have to go."

Dane stood as well. "When do we meet again?"

"I'll let you know as soon as I know. There's no turning back now, you have to hear the rest, and if I may—before you approach Mandy.

And please, don't make any more waves around the hospital. Things are getting dicey over there and, sparing the details for now, things could get dangerous for you and for Mandy. I've come forward in confidence and I ask you for your patience. Timing is everything, if you'll pardon the pun." He smirked at himself. "That one's going to pop up often enough, isn't it."

chapter

40

Doris Branson lived in a nice, hacienda-style home with views of the Las Vegas Strip to the west and craggy, movie Western mountains to the east. Mandy didn't find the yard much to crow about: a minidesert with rocks, cacti, and its very own dry creekbed that had never seen water and never would. Oh, well, at least you didn't have to mow the sand.

Mandy introduced herself to the Hispanic lady who answered the door. She just said, "Come in" and led Mandy to a high-ceilinged great room toward the back, where Doris Branson appeared to be working at home, the coffee table and the couch she was sitting on strewn with paperwork and bookkeeping, a wireless headset stuck in her ear. "No, cut that order in half," she said seemingly to herself or some invisible person in the room. "I don't like the color, I don't like the capacity, I want to phase them out." She gave Mandy a wave to come in and sit down in a soft chair opposite the couch. "Since now, Larry, since now, and remind them that I'm still the manager for the next two weeks. Okay. Thank you."

She hung up—at least that's what Mandy assumed—and said, "So. We meet again."

Well . . . that was a matter of perspective, Mandy thought. She just said, "Hi."

"How's the show going? I've heard good things."

"I'm having a great time."

Linda—Doris pronounced the name Leen-da—brought them

coffee and they went on for a while, talking about the show—Doris hadn't seen the show yet but liked the numbers she was getting up-stairs; Vegas—Mandy was getting used to it, would always miss Idaho, and didn't fancy herself as much of a gambler; Mandy's future with the Orpheus—Vahidi was pleased, though he was never the type to say so, and might be speaking to Seamus about renewing Man-dy's run; Doris's history—she'd been in the hospitality business for twenty years, had been with the Orpheus for six, loved her job, and wanted to keep it.

"So," she said at last, "let's talk about my accident."

Mandy knew nothing about it. "What happened?"

Doris raised an eyebrow. "That's what I wanted to ask you. You were there. Did you see what happened?"

Well. "I was there? I mean, you saw me there?"

Doris got impatient. "Well, of course I did, and don't be afraid, you're not in trouble. I just need to know, did you see where I came from? Did I come down the stairs, or did I come out of the elevator, and did I look drunk to you?"

Out of the elevator, Mandy thought, but didn't say, not yet. And drunk? Not that she could tell.

Doris jumped into the dead space. "Here's my situation, just so you know: I've had a little trouble with alcohol. I'm kicking it, get-ting it under control, but I wrecked my car three months ago—didn't hurt anybody, got away without a scratch, but I was DUI so they low-ered the boom on me. I paid a fine, lost my license for three months, had hell to pay with the insurance companies and all that, and I'm still not out of the woods. Now, the hotel isn't happy about that, and they let me know that I'd better dry up or I'd lose my job. So I dried up, and that's the honest-to-God truth. I've never been drunk on the job since the car wreck. But then, a week ago, last Monday, I was working like I always do, I took the elevator downstairs, I stepped out on the casino floor—and I didn't have a drop of alcohol in me, I don't care what the hospital says—and next thing I know I'm on the floor like I got run over."

Like Ernie, Mandy thought. But Doris didn't touch her like Ernie did. They never approached each other.

"So I ended up in Clark County Medical Center and they say I was drunk, which I wasn't, and my staff upstairs can testify to that, but the big story going around is that I was drunk and took the stairs by mistake and ended up falling down the stairs, so now the hotel wants to fire me—well, they have fired me, they've given me two weeks' notice, but I'm fighting it. I wasn't drunk and I didn't take the stairs, I took the elevator. So I'm asking you, you were there, what happened? What did you see?"

Mandy wanted to be sure. "I hope you won't mind my asking, but are you sure you saw me?"

"I'm sure."

"What was I wearing?"

Doris didn't appreciate that question either. "You want to test me, fine. You were wearing a blue pantsuit with gold embroidery and a white blouse . . . and you had a hula hoop in your hand. I was about to run you off the floor. It's against casino policy for performers to be prancing around out there. Vahidi knows that. You ought to know that."

Wow. Then it really happened. Mandy, in some form or other, was really there. "I didn't see what happened to you."

"Did I come from the stairs or the elevators?"

Don't answer, experience told her. She sat there.

Doris leaned forward. "It's okay. You're not in trouble, all right? I'm not going to fire you even though I could. I just want to be clear on what happened so everybody else can be clear on what happened so we can clear this whole mess up. Now . . . it was you, wasn't it? You're the one who ran into me. Be honest."

Oh-oh. Mandy held her peace, smiled awkwardly. "You think I ran into you?"

Doris tried to wave away the awkwardness. "It's not, I'm not try-ing to assign blame here, I'm just trying to clear the innocent, you see what I'm saying?"

Yes, Mandy knew what Doris was saying, but she also knew what Doris was thinking. She could feel the ache of a moral twist, but whatever she was walking into, it was time to back out. "About what time was that?"

Doris actually rolled her eyes. "Why does it matter? I saw you, I know you saw me." Mandy waited for an answer. "Elevenish. I was squeezing in a meeting before lunch."

"I could not have run into you."

Doris raised a skeptical eyebrow. "Oh, really?"

"I was auditioning for Mr. Vahidi in the Prospector's Lounge at the time, and my manager, Seamus Downey, was there as well. They can tell you, they can tell anybody that's where I was."

"But I saw you out on the floor!"

"Did anyone else?"

Doris had to work up an answer. "Of course, lots of people!"

"Then why ask me?"

"I wanted to hear you say it."

Mandy shrugged apologetically. "I couldn't have been on the casino floor because I was in the lounge, and I wouldn't have gone out on the casino floor anyway because it's against hotel policy and it's against the law; I'm underage. Wish I could help you, but . . . sorry."

Doris was turning to stone, getting a cold, adversarial look in her eyes. "I am going to fight this, you can be sure of that. I was hoping I could keep you out of trouble."

Mandy figured it out even as she said it, and her own brazenness amazed her. "Well, I can't testify to something I couldn't possibly have been involved in, and just as you've told me, Mr. Vahidi likes my work, the Orpheus and I have a good relationship, and you've been given notice. Pardon the Vegas terminology, but I think it's worth a gamble." She rose. "Thank you so much for the coffee. Hope you get to feeling better."

For bureaucratic, security, or just plain calendar reasons, Parmenter said he would meet with Dane again the following Sunday, an agonizing stretch of time. Considering how many people he could spill something to and how many ways he could do something unwise if he stayed in Vegas, Dane decided not to trust his own fortitude and fled back to the ranch. At least there he could pace, agonize, sort out, shout out, have heated debates with the walls when he wasn't bouncing off them, and still keep everything to himself.

As it turned out, working was better than pacing, so he cleaned up the barn and shop and shoveled snow. He carried on heated debates with God and the forest while snowshoeing in the hills. He thought he might paint the stage, but he couldn't go near it. He couldn't bear to visit the closet, so he relocated most of his clothes. He managed to put some of Mandy's pictures back in their places around the house, but only those taken in the years when she was more the woman than the girl. Somehow those memories stood apart and above the ones broken.

He journaled on his computer, sometimes typing, much of the time thinking, remembering, and simply trying to understand; he never could.

The next Sunday afternoon he was back in Las Vegas and met with Parmenter in the alley behind Fong Fong's, a multigeneration Chinese restaurant with tattered curtains, worn furniture, pull-chain toilets, and food that kept the place busy and customers on a waiting list. He and the scientist sat on empty, overturned five-gallon buckets in front of the restaurant's Dumpster, speaking in secretive tones and eating lunch from little white boxes.

Dane swallowed some rice and chow mein. "I don't know how I or any man could sort out the feelings I should have. I'm in love with her, I always have been, always will be."

Parmenter nodded. "Still feeling disdain for me and what we've done?"

"You did save her life."

Parmenter took a moment to bite and chew. "All we did was defer her death. Beyond that, we can't be certain of anything."

"Is she going to be all right?"

Parmenter didn't take a bite. He just took a long moment to answer. "That's why we're talking."

Dane set his little white box aside, out of mind.

"I need you to understand the whole issue of control. When we lost Mandy, we lost control. You know how astronomers discover planets around distant stars?"

"Tell me."

"They can't see the planets, but a planet orbiting around a star exerts a gravitational pull on it that makes the star wobble. From the size and speed of the wobble, astronomers can calculate the size of the planet and the size of its orbit.

"Now, Mandy is like one of those planets. A normal reversion of a few minutes or a few hours produces minuscule shifts in time and gravity. Any gravitational influence coming back is measurable, but it doesn't affect anything. Mandy, now she's different. She was reverted forty years and several hundred miles, which put a really big bend in the universe and gave her incredible leverage in time and gravity. She's like a very large planet making its parent star wobble—in this case, the Machine. The Machine's following her, it's wobbling back and forth in time, changing its own settings and parameters, its own power levels, everything, to keep in sync with whatever she's doing. The tail's wagging the dog. We can monitor the readings and try to decipher what we're seeing, but as long as she's replicating multiple Mandys on multiple timelines, moving across different timelines and spatial dimensions, dipping into and out of this time and then another, encroaching on other timelines and generating security breaches . . . we can't control anything. The best I could do last week was a tiny demonstration with a toy block, and only because Mandy was inactive at the time."

Dane smiled and even took interest in his sweet and sour spare ribs. "So Mandy's in charge."

Parmenter took another bite to correspond with Dane's. After a measured moment, he spoke again. "And that teaches us an important lesson about omnipotence and how we don't really have it, much as we want it.

"For one thing—and this may sound unscientific, but hey, I can read the wobbles—we reverted all of Mandy's atoms and molecules, but we didn't touch her soul. She's still there, the real her, somewhere outside space and time and gravity, and if I may take a stab, I think that part of her knows who she is, it's compelling her to find out, and it won't rest until she does."

Dane was suddenly unaware of his spare ribs; he wasn't even aware he was sitting in the alley behind Fong Fong's. His heart and mind were back in the snowy woods where he had wandered for hours, in the shop and barn where he labored half-mindedly, in his kitchen nook where he sat before his computer but could find so few thoughts, so few words because he could not find understanding, that one missing key to it all. He'd come so close so many times, but denied it, barred it from his thinking as hopeful, sentimental, and foolish. Now Parmenter, the supposedly materialistic scientist, was handing it to him.

The scientist must have seen it in his face. "You've observed the same thing."

The look she gave him when he first sat in McCaffee's to watch her perform; her blue Bug at the bottom of his driveway; her being a little crazy, thinking she was someone else; the dinner she made and the dress she wore for his birthday; the young lady who just had to wear that blue gown, who danced with him; the young magician who dared to bill herself as Mandy Whitacre . . .

"It's a simple matter of observation," said Parmenter, "and I observe that you are afraid to trust your observations, so I'll tell you mine: she's in love with you too. She always has been, she always will be. I think it's safe and reasonable—it might even be helpful—to act under that assumption." He pointed a cautionary finger. "But before I lose you . . ."

Parmenter just about had. Dane forced himself back into the alley, back onto that five-gallon bucket. "I'm with you. God help me, I'm with you."

"Don't lose sight of the lesson here, and the pressing issue. Remember, we're talking about control, about power, and this whole uncontrollable mess is reminding us we can only go so far, we can only control so much, and beyond that, we're still nothing but amazed little creatures at the mercy of forces we forgot to respect.

"So to put the lesson simply, we are not God, and to put the pressing issue simply, nothing irks my colleagues more. They cannot afford for this experiment to fail." He reflected a moment. "And for too long, neither could I, which explains—it doesn't excuse, just explains—why I didn't see what was plainly observable, entirely predictable: one little choice at a time, we justified ourselves out of a conscience.

"When the scientists have unlimited power within their grasp, when the military can envision unstoppable armies, when the government realizes it can send undetectable spies anywhere as instantly as a thought, they talk less and less about what is the 'right' thing to do and more and more about the 'higher good' that justifies all the little evils. Do you understand what I'm saying?"

Now Dane's food would have to wait indefinitely. "What are they going to do?"

Parmenter closed the lid on his lunch. "I predict, I fear, that they will do whatever's necessary."

* * *

Mandy felt . . . pretty safe. Big Max, a nearly three-hundred-pound actor, was a nice guy with a wife and kids, but his shaved head and executioner's outfit made him look so sinister he even gave Mandy the creeps as he clamped the leg irons and manacles on her. Looking down at the crowd gathered around the outdoor stage, she saw dark delight in some faces, rapt anxiety in others, as if they'd come to witness a hanging—or a beheading. Well, that was the point, that was the showbiz, as Seamus explained. The whole point was tension, suspense, the dark side of things.

The music over the speakers was evil-sounding, she was dressed like a Middle Ages peasant, predominantly in black, and the big wooden trunk behind her—at last, the Dumpster was back in the alley, where it belonged!—looked like something from an evil castle, very rustic, with oversize black locks and chains. The aim was to get the folks tensed up, biting their nails, fearing the worst, and then, after just the right amount of waiting and suspense—ta-da!— escape in a big way and let the folks feel that wonderful, euphoric relief.

At least that was the plan. She felt nervous, and she let it show.

From the ground it looked great. Max the executioner put a dark hood over Mandy's head, then he and another leather-clad killer— Carl, the stage crew man—plucked her up as if she weighed nothing and set her inside the trunk. They took the chains dangling from her manacles and leg irons and locked them to the outside of the trunk for an extra measure of escapeproofing, then scrunched her down inside and slammed down the lid. The chains and locks on the trunk were noisy on purpose; Max and Carl made them clink and clatter for added effect as they bound up the trunk and padlocked it shut.

The big crane was still around—yeah, a construction crane in the Middle Ages. Just had to roll with it. Max hooked the cable to the trunk, and the crane hoisted the trunk up to sixty feet above the stage.

The routine had a timer—an hourglass big enough for people in the back to see. Max turned it over, and the sand began to run down.

Mandy had one minute to escape. ("Or what?" she'd asked Seamus. "It's a time limit," he said. "Every escape needs a time limit.")

Every neck was craned, every eye was on that trunk as it rocked and teetered on the end of the cable, giving the appearance of a desperate struggle inside. Some folks began to cheer, and the crowd picked it up: "C'mon, Mandy! Man-DEE! Man-DEE! Man-DEE!" As the sand ran down to the last grains, some started a countdown.

BOOM! Before the countdown reached zero or the last grain of sand dropped through, there was an explosion, gasps and screams from the crowd, a puff of white smoke. The trunk fell open, its ends and bottom hinged together and hanging end to end, its sides swinging like doors on either side of the hanging bottom. The chains and locks dangled, conquered and useless, and second best part of all, the leg irons and manacles hung at the end of their chains, empty.

The best part was the four doves that flew out of the disassembled trunk and spiraled upward in perfect circles, as evenly spaced from each other as the points on a compass, drawing everyone's eyes to a tiny figure perched on the very top of the building, twenty-four stories up. She was dressed in a white jumpsuit, harness, and safety helmet and was waving to everyone.

Was it really she? The folks couldn't believe it but did, and they loved it. The tiny lady turned to face the towering wall, then rappelled down the side of the building, kicking away from the wall in wide arcs and throwing in some spins, putting on a show while the doves circled about her. She dropped to within Max and Carl's reach, they guided her to a triumphant landing on the stage, and the doves landed, two on each arm.

Ta-da! "I am Mandy Whitacre!"

It wasn't until Mandy was safe in her dressing room that she got the shakes, same as she did after the rehearsals. Adrenaline rush. Nothing like dangling twenty-four stories above the ground to drive out the lethargy. Every cell in her body was reliving it.

It seemed to have driven out the worry, too. Sitting at her dressing table and calming herself with chamomile tea, she warmed to the fact that it had been nearly two weeks since her perilous visit to Clark County Medical Center, where she could have been arrested, and her face-to-face with Doris Branson, the hotel manager who could have had her fired. Nothing had come of them: no police at her door, no pink slip from upstairs. Instead, the new escape had already gotten attention in the press and was sure to gain more; despite it being the slow season, she was more than holding her own in the lounge, and Mr. Vahidi was talking with Seamus about a new contract, maybe even a move from the lounge to the big room. Not bad for a first-timer in big, glittery Vegas.

As for her mental condition or gift or alien lineage or whatever it was, she was going with it, keeping it her own little secret. It helped to look down and see herself safe on the stage while she was hanging from that rope, and she'd been a good girl since the hospital; she hadn't hurt anybody.

There was a familiar knock at the door. "Hi, Julio, come on in."

He wasn't quite himself as he handed her another envelope.

Now she wasn't quite herself. "Who's this from?"

"I don't know."

"It's not from Ms. Branson, is it?"

He smiled grimly. "Oh, I doubt that."

She turned it over and over. There was only her name on the front.

"Guess you haven't heard," he said.

"Heard what?"

"Doris Branson committed suicide on Wednesday."

Now, that took a good piece of time to sink in. *Oh, wow. So much for feeling good or peaceful.* "You're kidding."

"She was gonna be fired 'cause of being drunk on the job. Guess she ended it first."

"Wow" was all she could say.

Julio got his chocolate and left.

No wonder I haven't heard anything, she thought, and then felt evil and selfish for thinking such a thing. It wasn't her fault, was it? She hadn't come anywhere near Doris that day, hadn't touched her at all, and Doris did have a history, didn't she? Doris created her own problems and was trying to blame her, that's what really happened. There was a prior mental and emotional thing going here, had to be.

No, no, don't even go there. You didn't ask for any of this, you didn't have anything to do with it, let it go.

But now she was all the more nervous about the little envelope. She picked up her nail file and slit it open. Inside was a news clipping. Oh. Maybe it was about her new escape routine; maybe it was a favorable review. Maybe . . .

It was an obituary. Ernest James Myers had passed away in the hospital January 31, the day after their conversation in his hospital room—if you could call it a conversation. A simple, handwritten note was paper-clipped to the obit: "Just thought you should know."

No signature.

chapter

41

The seven-o'clock show was the beginning of sorrows. Mandy kept smiling, charming, dancing, and making 'em laugh, but every routine, line of banter, and dance step felt like climbing uphill wearing lead weights. Ernie and Doris were dead, and though she managed to empty her mind of fears and questions that could be verbalized—how else could she do the stunts?—she couldn't shake a sixth-sense connection with those two and that hospital and a debilitating dread that whatever got Ernie and Doris was crawling along that connection on its way to her. If ever she was in showbiz, it was that night; she was putting on the biggest act, the happiest facade she could muster.

The nine-o'clock show . . .

Of course, the dread played right into what happened. If she hadn't been afraid to begin with, she might have found another way to play through the difficulty, get a laugh, and move on. She'd put up with hecklers before—a tipsy lodge member now and then, a smart-aleck kid all too often—but these men were denizens of a place she'd never been, an intentional evil she'd never encountered. They got to her, they scared her, and it was the worst of all nights to do such a thing.

The show was rolling along well enough, into its second half. She could feel her inner clock ticking down the minutes before she could take her bow, call it a night, and go home to sort things out. She was sitting in a chair, mugging and bantering with two handsome volunteers from the audience: Buck—now, there was a studly name, real or not—who was in the process of tying her to the chair with yards and yards of rope; and Jim, who was feeding quarter-inch slingshot pellets from a little box into her mouth so she could spit at balloons set up across the stage.

The first alarm signals came from the rude, invasive manner Jim stuffed the pellets in her mouth. She made goofy noises and tried to talk with her mouth full to get some laughs, but he was having a strange kind of fun that told her, too late, that she'd called up the wrong volunteers.

Buck was cinching the ropes so tight they hurt, but she kept smiling, making a joke out of it. "Don't cut off my circulation, I still have half a show to do." He wrapped the ropes around her body and the back of the chair, then planted his foot on the back of the chair and yanked them tight, making her grunt with pain and a foreboding she made a silly face about.

Four of Jim and Buck's buddies were in the third row, loud and obnoxious, egging them on: "All right, Buck, she's yours now!" "Make her moan, Buck!" "Tighter, Buck, she wants it!"

"Okay, back off," she told Jim, and though she hoped the audience didn't catch it, she really meant it. He backed off and let her try spitting the pellets at the balloons.

Pfft! Bang! One balloon down. Cheers from the crowd. She gave them a comical face, manipulating the pellets around in her mouth in exaggerated fashion.

Oh! Buck tied one ankle to the leg of the chair and he wasn't merciful.

I gotta get through this. Keep 'em laughing.

Pfft! Bang! Second balloon down.

Ouch! Buck tied the other ankle, this time with some extra loops. Her foot was going numb.

Okay, this stunt's getting scratched. Never again, not in this town. What was Seamus thinking?

Pfft! She missed, but as Dane once told her, you have to show a little vulnerability so people can identify with you.

Vulnerability? How much rope was there, anyway? Buck wasn't wasting any of it. Now he was tying her hands behind the chair, and that hurt, too. She couldn't let the audience know. She kept smiling.

"Take her, Buck!" a goon hollered.

"How?" another joked.

"Don't worry," said Buck.

Pfft! Mandy popped the third balloon and looked around for Andy. She might need him. The lights blinded her. She couldn't see him.

One balloon left. One pellet still in her mouth. She decided to keep the pellet.

Buck finished the last knot, and Mandy was so fixed to that chair she couldn't move an arm, a leg, anything. He walked around the chair, leering at her, very proud of himself.

The goons in the third row started to whoop. "Hey, still got one balloon left!" "Forget *those* balloons!"

The show must go on. Mandy followed the script. She was supposed to have one of the volunteers time her escape. "Okay, Jim, you got a watch?"

"Oh, I *want* to watch!" he said.

Some in the audience thought that was funny, but apart from the hoots of the Filthy Four, it got only a halfhearted laugh. Folks were beginning to have doubts about this show, and Mandy could feel it.

"No, a watch!" she said, keeping it all in fun. "I need you to be the timer."

"Time you or Buck?" a goon hollered.

She wasn't ready for it, couldn't believe it was happening. Without warning, Buck pounced from behind her and locked his mouth over hers, making a long, lewd show of it. She couldn't breathe. She couldn't move. She tried to turn her head away, but he stayed right on her, even gripped her head from behind and wouldn't let her go. His buddies in the third row were on their feet, cheering. Jim threw up both arms as if seeing a touchdown, "YAHHHH!"

The crowd reaction was mixed. Most were trying to play along and be good sports, laughing, but the mood was going south.

Imprisoned. At their mercy. Icy, animal terror coursed through her. She groped at the ropes from outside herself, digging, yanking. The ropes were tight, the knots stubborn.

He put his hand on her waist, started working his way up.

She couldn't think of anything funny. She could only feel his hand exploring her. The whole room became tea-stained; there was a low rumble and the smell of smoke; other times, other Bucks, other Jims, other Mandys began to layer atop the present . . .

PING! She spit the pellet into his mouth, breaking off his front tooth.

He jerked backward, staggering,

. . . his mouth over hers, making a long, lewd show . . .

. . . jerked backward, staggering . . .

his hand to his mouth.

. . . saw the blood on his hand . . .

She could see him from behind, from the audience, from above, from anywhere she wanted. She also saw herself, bound to the chair. From a hundred directions, she grabbed for the ropes.

. . . grabbed for the ropes . . .

. . . see him from anywhere she wanted . . .

He saw the blood on his hand and cursed her, getting mad enough to be stupid.

With all the other hands she could find she dug at the knots and they finally came loose. She grabbed for the ropes.

The ropes came alive, uncoiling like snakes, and the audience let out a cheer. The heroine was beginning to rally!

. . . about to backhand her . . .

Buck stepped up and would have backhanded her—

One of her threw the rope around his ankle and yanked him backward.

. . . yanked him backward; he body-slammed . . .

He body slammed the stage, and it had to have hurt.

. . . she yanked the rope and he went sprawling . . .

. . . he went sprawling . . .

. . . she came out of the chair . . .

The audience didn't laugh. They weren't sure what to make of this.

Jim was stunned and squatted down to check on his buddy.

The stage was moving like a ship on a rough sea. Mandy's hands broke free as the rope fell away, but her body was tied fast to the chair.

She was standing midstage, addressing the audience, rubbing her sore wrists. "Wow! Guess you got a real show tonight!"

. . . her hands broke free . . .

She grabbed a pellet out of the little box beside her, spilling all the others, and popped it into her mouth.

Now Jim cursed her, rising, coming toward her.

She was working the ropes that bound her to the chair.

. . . standing in front of him . . . he was coming toward her . . .

She was in the chair, but standing there, too. The standing Mandy was no boxer, but anger and impulse made her throw a vicious punch to his face.

. . . the rope snaked behind him . . .

She didn't feel a thing, but he reeled back, stunned, nose bleeding.

She held the rope in many hands.

It snaked behind him and looped around his chest. He fought it, beat at it, tried to grab hold, but it was alive, still coiling around him, keeping him busy.

. . . Buck got to his feet . . .

. . . Pfft! Try using that tonight! . . .

The audience was getting noisy, some cheering, some questioning, everybody murmuring. The goons were on their feet, trying to decide what to do.

Buck got to his feet . . .

It used to work on the moose and deer that ate her and Daddy's flowers, only she used a slingshot to ping *them* in the ribs. She spit this pellet where it would really hurt, and it did. Buck doubled over.

"Try using *that* tonight, you son of a ———" Yes. She really said it, loudly, and she meant it. She wanted to hurt him, and she wasn't through.

Her ankles were free, and the other Mandys were frantically working, uncoiling the rope from around her, whipping and snaking it above the stage. One half tangled itself around Jim, the other half around Buck. . . .

From above, she grabbed hold of the rope.

The middle of the rope hefted upward as if in the hand of an invisible giant. Their bodies came off the stage, collided, then dropped in a heap.

. . . then dropped in a heap . . .

. . . Jim doubled over, hit in the groin . . .

She rose from the chair, rubbing her sore wrists.

. . . still bound to the chair, afraid . . .

By now, at long last, Andy, Carl, and two security guys ran onto the stage and gathered up Jim and Buck with the ropes still around them.

Mandy wasn't thinking much, just raging, wanting to hit somebody, bite somebody. She locked eyes with the four goons in the third row, her fists clenching . . .

They cleared out, heads down and arms raised to shield themselves.

She, in some form, would have gone after them, but Andy put out a gentle hand. "It's okay, it's okay, they're leaving."

He and the other men hauled Jim and Buck up the center aisle and out the back.

Dead space. Mandy stood in the spotlight, hair tousled, face crimson and slick with sweat, her lipstick smeared, half gone. From somewhere she heard rustling, murmuring . . .

Oh. There was still an audience sitting there. She rubbed her sore wrists and worked up a smile even though her voice was unsteady. "Wow! Guess you got a real show tonight!"

They were still undecided how to feel about it.

In Mandy's worlds, there were still Jims and Bucks on the stage, Mandys fighting and yanking ropes, different audiences watching different parts of what had just happened, was still happening, was going to happen.

Ladies and gentlemen, came a voice.

. . . let's have a round of applause . . .

. . . prop manager . . .

She focused on the lounge and audience that weren't rolling, shifting, and tea-stained. "Ladies and gentlemen, let's have a round of applause for Buck Johnson, our prop manager, and Jimmy Hansen, our, uh, hairdresser!"

. . . our, uh, hairdresser . . .

. . . Whoo! They had me scared . . .

Now they were astounded, feeling fooled, and so relieved—at least some of them were.

Johnson? Hansen? She hadn't a clue what their last names were. "Whoo! They had *me* scared!"

. . . had me scared!
. . . me scared!

Andy made the decision and ordered the curtain dropped. He made an announcement over the sound system that the show would close early. The people filed out of the lounge in many moods. Some were cheering for the brave girl, some thought it was the sickest stunt they'd ever seen, some felt gypped, everybody left the lounge talking about it.

The crew went to work. There was blood to mop from the stage and about a hundred quarter-inch steel pellets to sweep up.

Back in the dressing room there was yelling and screaming, mostly by Mandy, at Andy: What took him so long? How could he let them do that to her? Wasn't he watching? How dare he close her show?

Andy kept trying to calm her down: he wasn't sure how far to let it go, was wondering if she could play her way through it, didn't know they'd be that brazen, was just about to put a halt to it, was she all right?

"No, I'm not all right!" she cried, immersing her face in the sink, smearing on soap, sloshing and slobbering the water into and out of her mouth to cleanse herself. "I've been violated! I've been, I've been shamed!"

"And you wanted to keep going?"

"I told you, it's my show!"

"It's my lounge."

She smeared on more soap and washed her face again. "No, I am not all right! What kind of town is this, anyway, they let people like that run around violating people right in front of everybody!" She was crying, even yelling in the sink, her voice bubbling in the water. She soaped her hands and face again.

"This is Vegas," Andy explained. "People can forget themselves—"

"I am not all right, can't you see that? And I'm not one of your stripper, show-it-off showgirl bimbo nincompoops! I'm Mandy Whitacre, Mandy Whitacre, and I have some dignity!"

"You've already washed your face."

"Well, I haven't!"

"Listen, I should call a medic—"

"No doctors!"

"You should let them check you over."

"No, I'm not all right! Seamus should have known, he should have known this would happen. What are you doing here?"

"I'm making sure—"

"Well, try knocking!"

"I came in here with you. You could hardly walk, remember?"

"No, I am not all right! How many of you are there, anyway?"

He shied back, hands extended as if she might attack him. "I'll get a medic."

She saw herself in the mirror. "I gotta get out of this outfit. I gotta get out of here."

"Mandy, you're upset, you're beside yourself—"

"Is that supposed to be funny?"

"I'll get someone—"

"Get out of here! And you get out of here! And you, too!"

Several Andys went out the door like a succession of instant replays. Mandy slammed the door shut, went to the mirror—the door slammed shut again, then again—saw her crimson, overwashed face and water-spiked hair with soap still in it; she'd splashed water and soap down the front of her costume, and there was a scary, psychobanshee look in her eyes. If any medics came in here right now they'd inject her, take her away, and lock her up where doctors would give her pills, take away her clothes, her toothbrush, her freedom.

  . . . Get out of here! And you get out of here! . . .

She toweled her hair, changed into her street clothes, and got out of there, leaving the place in a mess.

She worked her way down the hall behind the lounge . . . and into the main casino, staying on the carpeted throughway next to the wall so the security guys wouldn't bother her. She hurried by the banks of slot machines, the roulette table, her hand on the wall to keep from getting lost in the wrong world.

  . . . the roulette table . . .

. . . changed into her street clothes . . .

She couldn't go home because she didn't dare drive not knowing which car she was driving through which intersection and in what order. She thought she could sit in the Claim Jumper restaurant for a while, just have a salad, stay put, and wait out the storm. The restaurant was just off the casino floor, a short walk.

She saw herself up ahead, hanging a left into the restaurant. Okay. It looked like it happened, or was about to happen. She followed herself.

The hostess looked right through her, talking to somebody else. Mandy reached for a menu on the counter. Her hand passed through it. Wrong time. She ventured into the restaurant to do a quick visual search and spotted herself sitting in a corner booth, looking miserable and picking at a Cobb salad. All right, the corner booth. Now all she had to do was find the hostess who was here now.

She went back to the front, and the hostess noticed her. "Good evening. Table for one?"

"How about a corner booth?"

"We have one."

When she got there, the miserable Mandy looked up and said, "I don't want to talk to you! Go away!"

"You go away!" She immediately had to tell the waitress, "Not you, I was talking to a bug."

The miserable Mandy dissolved. The booth was empty and the table was clean. Mandy sat down, ordered the Cobb salad, then anchored her hands to the tabletop to connect with the present world and wait until all the other worlds and times went away—if they ever did. The noise was terrible. Every voice, every spoken word, every jingle of a slot machine or clang of a jackpot was doubled and tripled upon itself, happening, having happened, going to happen, all at once. People walked by on their way to a table, then walked by again on their way to the same table, having the exact conversation as before. She overheard phrases from the tables around her several times before, while, and after they were spoken. Four people at one table sounded like twenty. She even heard conversations between people at tables that were empty, before the people arrived. She was sitting in the same restaurant again and again, all at the same time.

Oh, God, help me.

The waitress brought her salad, but it wasn't there yet. She came again with the same salad, but Mandy could see the table through the leaves and plate. The third time, the salad was real. The fourth time she ignored it and paid attention to the third.

But she could hardly touch it. How many times would she take the same bite, how many times would she swallow it? Maybe this was going to be one of those mythological hells, sitting in the same restaurant eating the same salad over and over again, bite by repeated bite, for all eternity, full and hungry at the same time, the plate empty, the plate full. She almost laughed, she felt like crying. From outside herself she was getting a kick out of this comedy, but inside she was the hapless foil it was happening to, and that girl was quietly, privately losing her mind over a plate of salad.

She forked a few leaves into her mouth and chewed.

Someone approached the table. It was she.

Oh, why doesn't she just leave me alone! "I don't want to talk to you! Go away!"

The other Mandy felt just the way she did, she knew. "You go away!"

Mandy joined the other Mandy in telling the waitress who wasn't there, "Not you, I was talking to a bug."

The other Mandy dissolved.

The Mandy still sitting there slid the salad aside and propped her head in her hand.

Tears came to her eyes. She let them flow down her face, but she was too exhausted to cry.

She reached in her bag for her cell phone but withdrew her hand, leaving the phone there. It was just a thought: *Call Dane.*

But that was over, didn't she remember? She would never see the ranch, hear his voice, or feel his touch again.

She picked at her salad because there was nothing else to do. If she stayed here and didn't go anywhere else or interact with anyone, she shouldn't be a danger. The medics or security or the police would find her eventually and take her where she couldn't hurt anyone. Pills would make all the fear and hurt and disappointment go away.

This bite tasted new, like she hadn't had this one before.

"Excuse me?" It was a quiet voice, just one, right here, right now. She looked up into the face of a lady she didn't know. "Are you doing all right?"

Mandy noticed it was quieter. The only people talking were the people who were really there, having conversations as they happened. The restaurant looked and felt like the only one happening. She looked again at the lady, a gal in her fifties, she guessed, still dark-haired, well built, and fully aware of it. She had a man with her, no doubt her husband. He was bald and, well, retired-looking, but he took good care of himself and looked proud to be in her company.

Mandy wiped her eyes, feeling no need to mince words. "No, I'm not doing very well at all. Thank you for asking."

The lady put her hand on Mandy's. "We saw your show tonight. Listen, kid, you were entirely in the right and we were proud of you!"

The man said, "If you hadn't decked those guys I would have."

Fresh tears came to her eyes, but Mandy didn't care. There would surely be a pill for it.

"No, no," said the lady. "Don't do that. You're an incredible performer! Just incredible! We were so proud!"

You haven't met the real me, whoever she is.

The lady was still talking. "We were surprised that more people hadn't heard about you."

"That's going to change," said the man with a smile.

"Oh, I'm sure of that," Mandy said glumly.

Now the lady sat in the booth, opposite her.

"Especially . . . well, maybe you won't appreciate this, but you . . ." The lady shook a finger at her, wagging her head. "You look so much like . . ."

"Mandy Collins. I know."

"A lot of people remember her, and you could be her daughter."

"I'm not. I'm Mandy Whitacre."

The lady smiled—in awe, it seemed—and exchanged a look with her husband. "Well, even that, that was something that caught our eye, your name, and then your face . . ."

Mandy started to say something about needing to finish her dinner and go home, it was nice to meet them, blah blah blah, but she only got as far as "Well, anyway—"

—before the lady kept going. "This is something only Terry and I would know about, our own little secret, but we used to know a Mandy Whitacre way back before you were born, and she was a magician, too, believe it or not, and that's why we came to see your show. Your name was just so familiar, it was even spelled the same, and we just had to come and see, you know, what this Mandy Whitacre was like, and then"—the lady shook her head in wonder—"this is going to sound so unbelievable, but you look just like the Mandy Whitacre we went to school with. It's just incredible."

Oh. Right. Went to school with. Okay, now it made sense. By now there were so many Mandy Whitacres out there, one of them was bound to bring along some old friends to liven up the party. Mandy could guess the answer even as she asked, "What school?"

"North Idaho Junior College in Coeur d'Alene, Idaho. Of course, it's called North Idaho College now, NIC."

Sure, of course. That's where Mandy Whitacre—at least the Mandy Whitacre she thought she was—went to college, and of course some old friends from NIC would just pop up in a restaurant in Las Vegas at this late hour and they'd run into each other. Mandy went with it. At least when the medics arrived and saw her talking to people who weren't there, they'd know they'd found the right person. Funny, though, how all the Mandys were the same age as she but these two friends were old, and there was something about the lady's voice . . . something about her husband's voice . . .

"Terry?" she asked.

"Yes," he replied, extending his hand. "Terry Lundin."

She gripped his hand and stared at him unabashedly, reconstructing his face from a memory only months old: wild, red hair like an explosion, black, horn-rimmed glasses, skinny like a road runner . . . he used to drive a Road Runner. They called him . . . "You're . . . you're Road Runner!"

He was taken aback, astounded. He looked at the lady, she looked at him, and they reacted as if they were seeing a magic show again. He said, "Yes, that's right!"

"You are so amazing!" the lady exclaimed, and now the eyes, the wide grin, the naturally gaga expression, were unmistakable. Yes, Terry Lundin was her boyfriend in the summer of 1970. They were getting serious.

And yes, it was her voice! Mandy did recognize it, and now the face . . . absolutely, positively, of course! "Joanie?"

chapter

42

The lady stared back at her. "How do you do that?" She looked at Terry. "How does she do that?"

"Mentalism, right?" said Terry, delighted.

Mandy smiled at what she was doing to herself. It was a great show, good enough to sit and watch. "Sure, what the heck. And I suppose I got it right?"

The lady nodded. "Yes. My name's Joanie. This is so weird."

"Joanie Gittel, right?"

Now Joanie shifted backward, more than astonished. "How did you know that?"

Even Terry was crinkling his brow. "She hasn't been Joanie Gittel for thirty-nine years."

Mandy had no ill will against these nice folks. How could she when she was the one who created them? It was just the whole dumb situation, just being a total loon that made her start playing around with it. She looked carefully at Joanie, as if plumbing the depths of her mind. She even waved her hand in little hypnotic circles in front of Joanie's face. "I see . . . I see . . . Coeur d'Alene High School . . . and Coeur d'Alene Junior High, and before that, Baker Elementary. Right?"

Joanie was really stunned now, and that face, boy, it was the same face she made in Mr. McFaden's class when she heard Kennedy was shot. She could only nod.

"Oh, wait! Now I see a big gray house on Howard Road—except it's green now and it's a real estate office."

Joanie pointed at her, getting a spark of an idea. "You must be from Coeur d'Alene!"

"Sure. Born in Spokane, raised in Hayden, went to school in Coeur d'Alene."

So they all laughed and said, "How about that?" and enjoyed the amazing coincidence and how small the world was.

"But," Joanie double-checked, "you're not Mandy Whitacre."

Mandy arched a wizardly eyebrow. "Are you sure?"

"Well, I mean, the one I knew."

"Well . . ." She went all mental again, closing her eyes as if seeing visions, wiggling her fingers as if picking up vibes from the great beyond. "That big gray house . . . your father had a '57 Ford in an old garage next to the place, and there was a Gravenstein apple tree in the front yard, and you used to wait at the bus stop and catch the same school bus with Mandy every morning. You and Mandy were in the same class together in fifth grade . . . the teacher's name was . . . Mr. Fleck, and, and, and . . . you and Mandy got in a fight once over who was going to marry Tom Burnside."

Joanie could hardly speak. "This is scary. You're scaring me."

"We must have a mutual friend," Terry suggested.

Mandy kept going. "Mandy gave you her brunette Barbie, with a spring outfit . . ."

Joanie shook her head. "Now, that I don't remember . . ."

"It had big flowers on it and came with a watering can and a little green shovel."

Joanie lit up. "The, the gardening outfit! You—Mandy felt sorry for me because—"

"Because your dad ran over your Barbie with the lawn mower."

Joanie fell silent, visibly shaken. Terry slid into the booth and sat beside her, his arm around her. They were all eye-to-eye.

"You went to NIJC in 1969," said Mandy. "You weren't sure, but you thought you wanted to major in business administration. And Road Runner was working in the business library, and that's how you met."

The waitress came by. "Hi. Can I get you folks anything?"

"Uh . . ." Terry asked Mandy with his eyes and she shrugged and smiled a yes. "Maybe a couple coffees," said Terry. "Got any pies?" To Mandy, "Want a piece of pie?"

Whoa. Hold on a minute. Time-out.

Mandy dropped the mentalist routine. She looked around the room for anything weird, from another time, another place, anything nutty. She looked at the waitress. It was the same one, with Lisa on her name tag.

Lisa looked back and said, "We have apple, blueberry, cherry, and pumpkin."

"Wait a minute," said Mandy with a side glance at Terry and Joanie. "Can you . . . ?"

Lisa perked an eyebrow, waiting.

"Can you . . . see them?"

"See who?"

Mandy pointed at Terry and Joanie so directly it was probably rude. "Them."

Lisa looked at her funny. "I don't get it."

Sigh, a little sad. "It's nothing. How about a piece of cherry?"

"Cherry it is." Then she looked at Terry.

"Apple," he said.

She wrote it down.

"Wait!" said Mandy.

"Apple," said Joanie.

"Wait," said Mandy. "You can see them?"

Lisa was flustered, detecting some kind of gag, but said, "I don't get it."

Mandy dug out her cell phone and checked the time. "What time is it?"

Lisa had a watch. "Eleven-oh-five."

Exactly what her cell phone said.

Terry smiled at her, his usual likable self. "I think we're all missing something here."

Mandy reached and gave his hand a little poke. Then she reached and poked Joanie, and finally Lisa.

"She's a magician," Joanie explained, now eyeing Mandy warily as if expecting the next routine.

"I . . ." Mandy couldn't see through them either. They looked as solid as they felt. She forced a nervous little laugh. "Well, uh . . . may I have some decaf coffee?"

"You got it," said Lisa. She left.

Joanie. Terry. Sitting right there, right in front of her, and the right ages for 2011.

"You all right?" Terry asked.

"You really are Terry and Joanie," she said. "I mean, it's, uh, it's the, the mentalism thing, I was playing around, I didn't know . . ." Struck speechless, stopped cold, she could only smile and give an apologetic shrug.

"Well," said Terry, "it was an amazing demonstration." He gave Joanie a comforting squeeze. "You were so accurate it was disconcerting."

Joanie was disconcerted, all right. "Is this . . . is what you did really a trick?"

Terry held her close. "Yes, of course it was." Then he smiled at Mandy to show he wasn't mad or anything. "I'm just amazed at the extent of homework you had to have done, and . . . I'll never figure out how you knew we'd meet you tonight. It's a real craft you have there!"

No! Mandy cried out inside. It wasn't a trick. She put her hands in her lap so the trembling wouldn't show. "Could . . ." Her voice trembled. She drew a breath to steady herself. "What can you tell me about the Mandy Whitacre you knew?"

Lisa brought coffee cups and filled them. Then she talked about the apple pie and how it was fresh from the oven, and then she talked about where they were from: Joanie, Terry, and Mandy were from the Spokane/Coeur d'Alene area; Joanie and Terry still lived in Coeur d'Alene; Lisa grew up in Hawthorne, Nevada, and was studying at the University of Nevada, Las Vegas.

Finally, Lisa left.

Where were they?

Joanie looked puzzled. "What do you want to know?"

Terry broke in, "I thought you were supposed to tell us."

Well . . . she could blow them out of the water by telling them, but that wouldn't prove Joanie and Terry were real friends from then, the life she couldn't possibly have lived but did somehow . . . *Oh, Lord, help me, don't let me freak out.*

"Sweetheart, are you all right?" Joanie asked.

What can I say, what can I say? "I . . . I might know you, I mean, kind of like a trick and kind of for real. It's hard to explain."

They looked at each other.

"Could you tell me . . . what was her father's name?"

Joanie tilted her head. "You don't know that?"

Terry said, "So . . . what? We're doing mentalism in reverse? How's this work?"

Oh, please, just tell me! She was desperate but wanted with all of her being not to look crazy. "Uh, okay, let's do this: let me try a little mentalism on Mandy and we'll see how I do."

They perked up, Terry ready to be amazed, Joanie still nervous about it.

"Uh . . . she . . . she . . ."

Lisa brought the pies. "Apple for you, apple for you, and cherry for you. Can I bring you anything else?"

Terry thought he might like some cream for his coffee. Lisa then recalled she had a cousin in Spokane but hadn't been up there to visit since high school. Was the weather still cold up there? Yes, that was why Terry and Joanie thought to spend some time in California and then Vegas. So, could she bring them anything else? No, they were fine.

"I know!" said Mandy. "Why don't you ask me some questions?"

"Ask you . . . ?" Joanie faltered.

"About Mandy, anything you want."

"Who'd she marry?"

Ohhh . . . Her mind froze. She didn't know the answer to that. She didn't want to know, she just couldn't bear it. "Sh-she got married?"

Lisa popped by again. "Oh, I forgot to ask: is this on separate tickets?"

Separate, they told her, Mandy on one, Joanie and Terry on the other.

Terry asked, "What was her favorite animal?"

Mandy was still working on the fact—was it a fact?—that she got married. "Uh, animal?"

Terry helped her out, "She had some pets."

"Doves?"

They affirmed that but didn't seem too impressed. Joanie countered, "She was a magician. Easy guess."

Mandy groped for the right suggestion, the right way. She finally tried, "Now, what if I asked you some questions?"

Terry said, "Well, how are we going to know whether you know our answers are right?"

Joanie offered, "Well, if we give a wrong answer and she says we're right, then we'll know she doesn't know."

He crinkled his face.

"Uh, back and forth, back and forth," said Mandy. "I'll ask one, you ask one. Let's try that."

"Okay," said Terry, "you asked what her father's name was. It was Arthur."

"Where did Mandy live?"

"No, you tell us," said Joanie.

"Hayden, on a ranch. What was the name of the ranch?"

"Wooly Acres. What did they raise there?"

"Llamas and some horses. What were the names of Mandy's doves?"

Joanie scrunched her face. "Um . . . Bonkers was one. What were the names of the others?"

"Lily, Maybelle, and Carson. What big, significant thing happened to Mandy in the ninth grade?"

Joanie balked a moment, then answered, "Her mother, Eloise, died of breast cancer. What was Mandy's favorite card trick in junior high?"

"Flipping the Aces. Who was Mandy's favorite Mouseketeer?"

Joanie was reeling from the question and from knowing the answer. "Cubby." Then, mustering strength, she sang an advertising jingle they learned in their childhood, "If you need coal or oil . . ."

"Call Boyle," Mandy sang back. "Fairfax eight-one-five-two-one."

Joanie's hands went to her face and she gazed over her fingers at Mandy. "My God!"

Yes, Mandy thought. Silence. It was her turn. "Um . . ." She didn't want to ask. "Is . . . is Arthur, Mandy's dad . . . is he . . . ?"

"You mean, is he alive?" asked Joanie.

"Yes."

Joanie seemed to sense the game was getting serious. She spoke as if bringing bad news to a friend. "He died from a heart attack in 1992. I think he was about eighty-three."

Mandy's hand went over her mouth. She shouldn't have asked.

She should have known she would believe the answer, that an old sorrow-in-waiting would take its opportunity.

Daddy . . .

This was not a dream she could wake up from, a delusion she could excuse away. There were no other worlds she could run to, no other places or times in which to hide. There was only this corner booth in the Claim Jumper restaurant at twenty-two after eleven, and all of it, including the couple sitting there, was real. She looked away as the tears came. She couldn't hold them back.

Game over.

Terry sighed. "Well, it's been very interesting." But Lisa had not brought their checks yet.

Mandy tried to recover, couldn't shake it, signaled she'd be okay—it was a lie—put a napkin to her eyes.

Joanie reached and touched her. "Sweetie, I don't know what just happened. Is there some way, any way I could understand this?"

What other way was there? "Joanie . . ."

Joanie stroked her shoulder to comfort her. "Just help me understand."

"I'm . . . What if . . ." She stepped off the precipice. "What if I really was Mandy? What if I really was born January fifteenth, 1951, and I really did go to school with you and we were friends and . . . well, what if that could really happen?"

Joanie's gaze lingered. Did she believe? Did she?

Terry fidgeted and looked for Lisa. Joanie . . .

Mandy could see her words had fallen to the ground. Joanie's eyes, though sorrowful, were perplexed and disbelieving. "Sweetheart, I'm sorry, but that just can't be. My friend Mandy . . . is dead."

Dane was back at the ranch where he could wake up in a plain and simple life, think without distraction, believe most everything he saw or heard, and live in the world as it was, not as it was dressed up to be. From this vantage point he could handle things with a reasonable perspective—things like the letter he got in the old-fashioned U.S. Mail from Jerome Parmenter instructing him to call Parmenter at such and such a time at such and such a number and be sure he called from a public pay phone of his own random choosing.

He chose the pay phone outside the Conoco Quik Stop on Highway 95, and for an added touch, he wore his cowboy hat and kept his coat collar turned up to obscure his face.

Parmenter got right to it. "I'm going to ask you a question from out of the blue, all right? Please don't ask me to explain it, it would take too long and I may be off my nut in the first place, all right?"

"All right."

"You've obviously seen Mandy time and time again as the young girl, we know that."

"Yes."

"But she was always quite real, solid?"

"Yes. She worked for me. I saw her shovel and move and clean things . . ." *I also kissed her.*

"Right, right, right. Now, was she always the same age?"

"What do you mean? She had a birthday in January." *I missed it.*

"No, no, uh, try a different age, a really different age, specifically . . . well, how old was she when she was in the accident?"

"Fifty-nine."

"Ever see her at fifty-nine?"

"You mean, after I met her again, after she, after I thought she'd died?"

"Yes. Thank you for the clarification."

"No, I . . ." Hold on.

"Hello?"

When it happened he thought it was a flashback or a drug reaction, but now his whole world was changing and another impossibility had to be reconsidered as possible. "I may have."

Now there was a pause at Parmenter's end. "You may have? Well, I need to know: did you or didn't you?"

"Well, that's been a pretty big question all along, hasn't it?"

"No, Dane, no! Now you know you aren't crazy, you aren't seeing things, so please be honest with me. Did you see Mandy at the age of fifty-nine?"

"I don't know what age she was. She was older. She looked pretty much the way she looked when I lost her."

"But you saw her after the accident; that's the first big fact I need to establish."

"Yes, it was after the accident."

"Where?"

"In my house."

"In your house?!" Parmenter's excitement-o-meter was actually beginning to register something. "When?"

"Well, a few months ago."

"No, no, not 'a few months.' I need to know the exact date and time, as close as you can get, down to the second if you can!"

Oh, brother. "I'll have to get back to you on that."

"Do. Find out, as precisely as you can, and get back to me. Do you know exactly where she was when you saw her?"

"Yes, I do know that. She was upstairs, looking out the east windows."

"Ahhh! Excellent! That's half the battle right there. Was she solid or transparent?"

"I would say she was solid. I could have touched her. I could smell her hair."

"Ohh!" He sounded as if he were having his own little Parmenter version of a fit. "All right, all right. Here's what I need you to do . . ."

This was where a stable mental platform was necessary. Sometimes—like now—Dane felt he was playing the clueless, cooperative sidekick to Parmenter's mad professor, shades of those old *Back to the Future* movies. He listened carefully, taking notes.

Date and time, date and time. Dane pored over the calendars on his kitchen wall, in his computer, in his cell phone, and on the wall in the loft, trying to remember. He saw her in the house right before he saw her running across his pasture, chased by the beat-up and mysterious Clarence. So when was that? Two weeks after Arnie took him to see Mandy—Eloise—perform at McCaffee's and he walked out on her. That was November 7.

Hold on. Did the fire department keep logs?

He got the number from the phone book and spoke with the dispatcher, a cheerful lady named Maureen. Yes, they did keep logs. He told her somewhere around mid-November, she looked, and bingo! There it was: "Okay, we got the call from the McBride Ranch—Dane Collins is listed as the caller—at ten-forty A.M. on Monday, November twenty-second."

"Bingo! That's it!" Then it hit him. "Huh. That's the date Kennedy was shot."

"Well, I guess you'd know," she said. "I wasn't born yet."

Right. Who was anymore?

So he called 911 at ten-forty; he called Shirley right before that, brought Mandy into the house before that, rescued her before that . . . saw her running in the pasture . . . right before that saw her standing at the window . . . couldn't have been more than twenty minutes. Okay: November 22, 2010, (close to) 10:20 A.M. PST. He wrote it down.

Now to call Parmenter. Hmm—which phone do I use this time?

chapter

43

Mandy closed her three-week run at the Orpheus on Wednesday, February 16. The next day, she arrived at the Spokane airport, where Seamus met her.

"I'm sorry I couldn't be there," he said as they drove I-90 eastbound through the city.

"I'm all right."

"You look like—"

"I said I'm all right."

"Well, if you need to unwind a day or two, that's no problem."

"Are you gonna help me or not?"

"Peace, peace. I've talked to the head of maintenance at the fairgrounds. He'll be there to let us in if that's what you want to do."

She let out a breath and tried to calm herself. "I'm sorry."

"It's okay. What you've been through . . . I leave you for just a few days and . . ."

"Yeah, I know. So how's the practice?"

"Oh, we're current. I have some court dates next week, have to do some depositions tomorrow. Pamela's helping me juggle everything, which reminds me: Vahidi and I talked yesterday and had a very nice conversation. They're offering the big room."

That news was as good as it was big and it did thrill her—to an extent. She had to crawl out from under her preoccupation to tell him, "That's wonderful, Seamus, it really is. I'll be more excited about it, I promise."

"He wants to open next month, but I want a bigger budget than they're offering. We're going to need a whole new sound track, and with that bigger stage you're going to need some stage extras and some movable sets, something eye-catching and classy."

She winced. "Are we going to have enough time for all that? We don't even have a show designed."

"Don't worry, your industrious manager is on it—but that's all for another day. We have today's business to think about."

The Spokane County Fairgrounds were a different sight on a cloudy day in February: dead quiet, deserted, coated with snow and slush. Only a quarter of the parking lot was plowed clear and in use for the three-day Home Design Show in the main exhibit hall.

Mr. Talburton, the maintenance guy, let them in through a gate in the fence and gave them two security passes to wear on lanyards. Apparently he and Seamus had already discussed the agenda for the visit and any applicable fees. Talburton produced a map of the grounds and marked key sites: the carnival area, the food court, the Rabbits and Poultry Building, and the Camelid Barn. He scribbled a phone number along the top of the map. "Here's my cell number if you have any questions."

They set out, braving two inches of slush between patches of bare pavement wherever they could find it. Mandy took Seamus's arm. "Thank you for doing this."

"You're very welcome. Try to talk to me. Tell me what you're feeling."

They were nearing the carnival area where Mandy, Joanie, and Angie overindulged on the stomach-turning rides. Except for the permanently built roller coaster and the shrouded carousel—Mandy could recall the music it played—there wasn't a ride in sight. The game pavilions were boarded up. There was a flat, slushy expanse where rows of craft and souvenir booths had stood. Mandy indicated a general area. "I bought an anklet from an old Indian guy right about there, and . . ."—she peered through a grove of trees to another empty space in front of the livestock barns—"over there, that's where the Great Marvellini was going to do his show at two. There was a stage and some bleachers . . ."

And now there was nothing. It was eerie, and brought back the same old fear she'd borne for months, that she was out of her mind, imagining things. Where she remembered carnival rides, there was nothing. The old Indian who sold her the anklet could have been a dream. The Great Marvellini? It was only her memory that placed a stage and bleachers in that spot.

"That would have been the North Stage," said Seamus, pointing at the map.

Mandy studied the map. The North Stage was there, at least. "I'm so glad."

"So there is a lot of fact here. There really is a fairgrounds, the locations are all the same."

"Yes, at least now, in this time, they are."

"But let me be sure now: what you've described so far took place . . . in 1970?"

She looked down at the snow, feeling so strange, so afraid.

"Come on, now, let's just work it through. Just show it to me. Go through the process. The point is to get it right out on the table where you can see it, own it, take charge of it. If it's yours, you can do what you want with it, but as long as you hide from it, it'll keep chasing you."

"It was September twelfth, 1970. Joanie and Angie and I were just about to start school again, our sophomore year at NIJC."

"And this was the same Joanie you met last Friday night?"

"Yes. And she was real. She was forty years older and she remembered all the same things I remembered from when we were growing up, so she had to be the same Joanie I was with that day, so that day had to have happened, right? She was here with me, she and Angie. We were just having fun at the fair, you know? My dad was showing his llamas over in the . . . well, there's a camelid building there now but it was another building then . . ."

They walked down a wide paved walkway spanning an empty field where rows of food booths on each side once formed a village of junk food eateries. "We didn't want to eat any of the junky stuff, especially Angie . . ."

They came to the end of the walkway, where two permanent buildings stood in the shadow of the grandstand. "This one here used to be the Spokane Junior League Booth. I bought a basket of chicken here, but Joanie and Angie wanted to get something else, so we were going to meet . . ."

The North Lawn was still there. The tables were gone, stored away; the trees were bare and gray against the winter sky. Mandy scanned the area first, imagining the tables, the people sitting at them, the crowd noise, and the pleasant heat of a lunchtime sun. The place looked so immensely different in September . . . of 1970 and 2010. The big honey locust tree was still where she remembered it. She walked through the snow to the thick trunk, touched the bark, and looked around to get her bearings.

"This is the spot," she said. "This is where I woke up and it was forty years later."

Seamus came to her side. "Right here?"

"Right here where I'm standing. I sat down and leaned against this tree in 1970, and the next thing I knew"—emotion choked her voice—"I was sitting in the same spot and the tree was bigger and it was 2010." She steadied herself against the tree and took in the North Lawn, the empty concession buildings, the vacant grandstand. "And I can't describe the feeling. Like being a little kid who's lost. You just don't know what to do."

She didn't know what to do now. She'd hoped that if she could go back to where it all started, some clue might reveal itself. Perhaps a feeling would occur, or a vision. Maybe a portal would open that would take her back.

But there was nothing here, only the cold, the quiet, the gloom of winter—in 2011.

"Do you remember what time it was?" Seamus asked.

"There was a clock on the corn dog booth right over there." The booth was gone; she pointed to where it was on that day. "It was one-oh-five. In 1970. In 2010 the corn dog booth and the clock weren't there anymore."

"That would have been Pacific Daylight Time . . ." Seamus took a pen and marked the location and time on the map. "Anything else? Just bring it out, envision it. Take command."

She described the people she saw before and after the jump in time and how things changed from one year to the other: the paint on the buildings, the clothing and hair styles, the sudden advent of strange little gadgets such as iPods and cell phones, the funny cultural shifts such as tobacco-free zones and hand-washing stations.

"And none of it was like a dream, you know what I mean? All the memories are of real things. I remember being in 1970 just as clearly, just as real, as looking up and seeing I had nothing but a hospital gown on and it was 2010."

Standing against a real tree in a real place, both of which confirmed a real memory, she discovered a new resolve and dared to say it to another person for the first time: "I think . . . I think there is no crazy woman standing here. It was real. All of it. I can't explain it, but somehow it was real. Everything I've seen, everywhere I've been, Joanie last week . . . it's all real."

She looked at him for his reaction, but there was no skepticism, no condescension in his eyes. He simply said, "Take hold of it. Own it, whatever it is."

She nodded and drank in the scene. It was hers. She'd really been here in both the recent and the distant past, and that was all there was to it. As for explanations . . .

"I need to find Joanie."

"You can use my car."

Parmenter's supersophisticated GPS-and-then-some arrived by FedEx, and Parmenter's enclosed list of instructions was clear enough. Dane went upstairs, stood in the exact spot where the mysterious vision of Mandy stood, and switched it on. The screen booted up, some numbers scurried across the LCD screen, and then it was ready. He pressed the Function button, then the Waypoint button, and in seconds he had the numbers.

This time he used the pay phone on the outside of a bank in Hayden and wore a hooded jacket.

"Very good, Dane, thank you very much."

"So what's this about?"

"Oh, it's probably nothing. Then again, it could be everything."

So close, so close to knowing! Mandy's hands trembled as she paged through the Coeur d'Alene phone book and found the number for Terry and Joanie Lundin—real names, a real number, proof that the couple she met in Vegas a week ago was not illusory—if the same Joanie answered the phone. *Oh, Lord, here goes.*

The same Joanie answered the phone, and the same Joanie answered Mandy's knock on her door. Mandy gave her a weak little smile, a face that said, *Well, here I am, can't help it, think you can help me?*

Joanie absorbed the sight of her, then stepped out and gave Mandy a sisterly hug. "I don't know who you are, kid, but any friend of Mandy's is a friend of mine."

They went into the quaint old house that Terry inherited from his parents and remodeled. On the hallway wall were pictures of their children and grandchildren. The kitchen was modernized; Joanie had a latte machine and took Mandy's request for a mocha.

As the machine ground and tamped the beans, Mandy had to marvel. "Wow."

"You've never seen one of these?"

"Oh, I have, but it seems like everybody has one now."

"Oh, they're the thing."

"All we had was one of those little coffeemakers with the paper filters."

Joanie caught the rich brew in a small cup. "So . . . you know about computers and cell phones and . . . ?"

"I got a cell phone. It still amazes me. And computers? *Guy*, it's unbelievable!"

Joanie handed her a mocha in a mug.

"Thank you!" It smelled heavenly.

Joanie reflected, smiled, and said, "*Guy!* I haven't said that in years. Where'd we ever get that, anyway?"

Mandy shrugged. "A take off on 'gosh' or 'golly'?"

"Do you . . ."

Mandy waited.

"Do you remember Mrs. McQuaig?"

Mandy cracked up and imitated how their third-grade teacher would get so involved in finishing a thought she'd run out of air. ". . . boys and girls, master these tables and they will always be at haaaannnnd . . ."

Which brought them around to Mrs. Goade, whose head-nodding mannerism was contagious so that the whole class started doing it.

"Whatever happened to Angie?" Mandy asked.

Joanie shook her head. "I don't know. Lost track of her after college."

They sat at the dining table, coffee mugs in hand, and neither seemed to notice how bizarre it was for a woman near sixty to be sharing old times and old names with a girl who'd just turned twenty: the Play Day race that Mandy won two years in a row; Joanie and Mandy doing a tap dance at the talent show in fourth grade; pretending to be Tennessee Walkers out on the playground; Steve Randall turning his eyelids inside out and chasing them; Mandy's magic act with interlocking rings in the talent show in sixth grade; Dave Leverson being a jerk from the first grade and all the way up through high school; Mandy being King Lear's daughter—what was her name?—in drama class, and Joanie being King Lear.

At last, Mandy drank down the settled chocolate from the bottom of her mug and asked, "So how are you taking this?"

Joanie thought a moment, gave her hands a little upturn, and said, "Just going with it."

Going with it. They used to use that term whenever things got freaky. "So am I."

"You never skip a beat. A lot of things you remember better than I do."

"Well, for me, they were just a few years ago."

"I'm not going crazy, am I?"

Mandy shook a pointed finger to emphasize, "No, you're not, not at all. I'm not crazy so I know you aren't."

"It's just that you being Mandy Whitacre is impossible. Other than that, I've got no problem."

"But that's the riddle I'm trying to solve. What am I doing here in 2011 when I should be back in . . . well now it would be 1971?"

"It's absolutely nuts."

"Well, what if we just pretended, kind of like we've been doing? What if we just assumed that I'm the real Mandy Whitacre?"

Joanie tilted her head thoughtfully and locked eyes with her. "So you were born . . . when?"

"January fifteenth, 1951."

"But now you're only twenty."

Mandy cringed. "Right."

"Watergate." That was all she said, and then she waited.

Mandy was puzzled.

"You don't remember that?"

"No."

"What about Karen Carpenter?"

Mandy sang a line of "Close to You."

Joanie wagged her head. It seemed being amazed was becoming a steady state for her. "So . . . you only remember things up until 1970."

"That's all the older I was, uh, am."

Now Joanie rubbed her face as if trying to clear her brain. "All right, let's pretend. How did you get here?"

"How . . . you mean—"

"How did you get from 1970 to 2011? You must have a story."

"Uhh . . . yeah . . ." Mandy steeled herself and went into it, recounting that sunny day in September 1970 at the Spokane County Fair. She listed the rides the three girls went on, the anklet she bought, their plans for lunch and seeing the Great Marvellini, the last time they saw each other: in line at the Spokane Junior League Chicken Basket concession.

At each and every step, Joanie reacted with increasing astonishment until her fingers were over her mouth and she was gawking, as if Mandy were Samuel or Elijah.

"And then," Mandy completed the story, "I woke up, I guess, and everything was different. I'd skipped ahead forty years, just like that, and I don't have the foggiest idea how or why, and I've been trying to find out ever since. Now, remember, we're pretending this is all true, okay? You don't have to believe it, just let me know if it checks out, tell me anything you can, I want to know. Were you with me at the fair that day?"

It was a stupefied, even fearful Joanie who answered "Yes."

"Do you remember—"

"Everything you said, yes. Some of it I'd forgotten until you told me about it, but now, yes, I remember it."

"So"—Mandy could feel a tinge of life and hope—"it happened, didn't it?"

Joanie nodded. "It happened. But you can't . . . how could you possibly be here?"

"I don't know."

Joanie thought a moment, her eyes watching the memories of that day. "So you never saw the Great Marvellini?"

"No. I never got there. I never saw you and Angie again."

Joanie looked at her. "But you were there."

Mandy didn't get that. "I was . . . ?"

"You were there with me and Angie when we saw the Great Marvellini."

It just didn't connect in Mandy's mind. How could . . . ? "But . . ."

"And he did a routine with doves. You don't remember that?"

Not in the slightest, though she tried. "No."

Joanie looked incredulous. "How could you not remember that?"

"I don't know! I wasn't there."

"But you *were* there!"

Mandy was getting flustered. "Well, let's just keep pretending . . . or something."

"All right, I'll play along, but listen, this is the truth. I was there, I saw it happen—and you'd better hang on for this one.

"Marvellini did a routine with doves. He'd throw out his arms and make some fire flash and there'd be a dove out of nowhere, and you were right there with him, really into it because you used to do the same trick with your doves. And then"—her eyes got a dreamy look—"one of the doves didn't fly back to Marvellini. It flew down to you. We were sitting right in the front row, and that dove just flew right down to you"—emotion choked her voice—"and you put out your hand and it landed on your finger like it knew you; it just perched right there."

Mandy knew doves, knew how it felt when such a fragile creature came to trust her. "You're not making this up?"

"Hey, I've gone along with you on this whole thing . . ."

"Right. Sorry. It's just so—"

"I know. But it happened. I was sitting right next to you. So then, Marvellini called you up onstage, and"—she broke into a smile, a silent laugh—"and you never did anything halfway. You did a dance step—it was a grapevine, I remember it—right across the stage and went up to him like you were some kind of paid, shapely assistant. The whole crowd went nuts. Angie and I about fell out of our seats we were laughing so hard. But then, you knew the moves. You just tossed that bird in the air like you knew what it would do, and it flew back to Marvellini like it was supposed to, and he was so impressed he told you to stick around, he wanted to talk to you after the show."

Then Joanie leaned over the table and delivered the rest of the story in hushed, tender tones. "And Marvellini had a stage assistant, stage manager, whatever you want to call it. And you don't remember, do you?"

Mandy shook her head sadly. "I don't remember anything after the tree in the North Lawn."

Joanie nodded, working with that. "There was this guy acting as Marvellini's assistant and it looked a little weird, a magician being assisted by another guy like they were, you know, gay or something. But he had that guy offer you his arm and escort you back to your seat, and that's how you and that guy met." She was holding out, teasing.

The longest time passed until Mandy had to ask, "What guy?"

"Have you ever heard of Dane Collins? He's a big-name magician now, or at least he was."

Mandy didn't hear the sentence after "Dane Collins." The name hit her like a blow to her chest, stole away her breath, carried away her thoughts. "Dane . . . ?" Even so, though Joanie's answer shocked her, it was the right answer. She couldn't have borne the sound of another name.

"That's how you met Dane Collins. Now tell me you don't remember that."

"I . . . met . . . Dane Collins?"

Joanie leaned back in her chair and just gave her a moment.

Mandy tried to imagine Dane as a young man but could see only the sixty-year-old escorting her back to her seat, getting her name, smiling at her, thanking her for coming, saying whatever it was he said, her fantasy of a reality that only Joanie was there to see. But if that was the day they met . . . "What are you saying?"

"You really don't remember?"

"No."

"This is heavy."

"Did I—"

"Marvellini offered you a job as his stage assistant and you took it, right there on the spot. We thought it was kind of a lame move, I mean, you were dropping out of college to go on the road with a nickel-and-dime magic act, but . . . we could see the little sparks between you and Dane and you know, he was one hunk of a guy. He was only nineteen, no older than we were, but he was cute, real cute!

"Anyway, you were Marvellini's stage assistant until he retired—or quit, just depends on which story you believe. He handed the whole show over to Dane and you, and by then you two were inseparable, so you got married"—she threw in a pause to let that sink in—"on June 19, 1971 . . . and you started up your act and you called it Dane and Mandy, and the rest is history."

Dane and Mandy. She remembered seeing, touching those names on all those crates in Dane's barn. All the dreams, all the years, all in the past. "I know Dane Collins!"

Joanie looked at her quizzically. "You know him? You mean, now?"

Mandy nodded.

"And how did this happen?"

"I worked for him! He coached me!"

"When? I thought you never met him."

"I did, but not back then!" Mandy tried to explain how the Gypsy Girl and then the Hobett met up with Dane Collins and became his protégée and worked on his place and learned how to put on a show, and how he never talked about his wife unless she asked him and didn't have any pictures of her in the house and how she just had to be around him and how she didn't know why she had to try on Mandy's costumes and dresses, she just had to, and by the time she got to that part she was in tears. She didn't say anything about their parting; she just couldn't.

Joanie dabbed her eyes with a napkin. "And let me guess: you're in love with him."

That was a question Mandy feared more than anything. She deflected it. "What did my dad think?"

"About?"

"About Dane and me . . ."

Joanie smiled. "He gave you away at the wedding. You know how the minister asks, 'Who gives this woman to be married to this man?' Your dad said, 'Her mother and I do,' and he put your hand into Dane's and just held it there for a while. He liked Dane. He told me, and I heard him say to other people, too, 'Eloise would have liked him.' I don't think he was ever worried about you." She laughed at another memory. "He helped you fix up the first house you rented, the one near Seattle. It was a rebuilt chicken coop. It didn't have any insulation and the water came from a spring up the hill." She shook her head at the memory. "I came by to see it once. Holy cow!"

"But we were happy?"

"It was like that line from *Fiddler on the Roof*, 'They're so happy they don't know how miserable they are.' You had all your money in that old moving van with your show gear in it, and, I tell you, you ran the wheels off that thing. You'd come through Spokane and Coeur d'Alene about twice a year, and every time your show was better. I knew you were going to outgrow the little county fairs and high school assemblies and I guess you did." Joanie found her a box of tissues, and Mandy pulled out several. "Come on, let's go on the Internet."

They went into the den where heads of deer, elk, and one bull moose stared into space from the walls. Joanie had a computer sitting on a desk in the corner. She placed a chair beside her own for Mandy, flipped open her Mac, and showed Mandy the steps to get online.

"Now you just type 'Dane and Mandy' into the search box up here . . ."

What came up was more than Mandy would be able to read in that one visit, but Joanie's mission for the moment was to find picture after picture of Mandy through the years, and the earliest ones . . . well, they were pictures of the Girl in the Mirror. Joanie hit the print command, and the printer zip-zip-zipped out hard copies.

"And let's see, if we go to the Social Security death index . . . and enter Arthur Whitacre . . ."

Daddy's name came up in the little boxes on the screen along with his Social Security number and the date of his death, March 12, 1992.

Tap tap. Zip-zip-zip.

"Can you bear to see more?"

By now Mandy felt numb, unable to fight or fathom it. She could only receive it, store it, let it season. "Please."

Joanie did a little more searching and brought up an obituary from the *Coeur d'Alene Press*. There was a photograph of Daddy, so much older than she remembered him. Joanie scrolled down to the part that read, "He is survived by his daughter, Mandy Eloise Collins . . ."

"That's you," said Joanie. "Do the arithmetic and you were . . .

forty-one when he died. And I remember you inherited the Wooly Acres Ranch, but there hadn't been any cattle or horses or llamas on the place for quite a while. Your dad got so he couldn't keep up with all that." Tap tap. Zip-zip-zip. "How're you doing? You okay?"

What could Mandy say? It was more than she could contain, and it all rang true. "What . . . what became of the ranch?"

"Uh, all I know is, you eventually sold it to a developer and now it's stores and parking lots."

Oh, that stung. *How could I?*

"You okay?"

Mandy couldn't say yes—she couldn't say anything—but she couldn't stop, either. She wordlessly asked for Joanie to go on.

"Okay then. Here's where the story ends. Here's the part I have to be honest about, just put it in front of you and hope you figure it out. I've been to this site plenty of times, printing out copies." She entered Mandy Collins, got a list of results, and scrolled directly to the one she wanted. It was a news story from the *Las Vegas Sun*:

FIERY WRECK KILLS MAGICIAN

Mandy Eloise Collins, best known as the witty and offbeat wife and partner of Dane Collins in the magical duo Dane and Mandy, was killed yesterday and her husband, Dane, injured when the Collins's car was sidestruck by another motorist, also killed in the crash. Dane Collins, riding in the passenger seat, escaped and was subsequently injured trying to rescue his wife from the burning vehicle . . .

Joanie printed a hard copy so Mandy could take all the time she needed to read it. "It's hard enough trying to explain how you weren't at the fair when you were, and you didn't see Marvellini when you did, and you didn't meet Dane when you did and you even married him. Now we have to explain how you can be sitting here right now when you're dead."

Mandy's head was spinning. When she met Dane he was a widower still mourning his wife, and now she was his wife? Were there two Mandys? Had one of the other Mandys she'd seen or become or even been, met Dane in 1970 while she, the Mandy sitting here, was wandering around the fairgrounds in a hospital gown . . .

Hospital gown.

She read more of the article and let out a gasp, then an audible whimper when she saw where Mandy Eloise Collins had died: ". . . rushed to the Clark County Medical Center, where she died of extensive burn injuries . . ."

Clark County Medical Center. She'd just recently visited those hallways, rooms, names, and faces she knew as if she'd been there a thousand times. Dr. Kessler knew her, too, that was plain to see.

"Mandy?" Joanie asked. "What is it?"

She scanned the copy looking for the date. "When did I die in the hospital? Is there a date anywhere?"

She found it at the top.

September 17, 2010.

She put her head down between her knees. Joanie ran for a glass of water.

She died in the Clark County Medical Center and awoke in a hospital gown at the Spokane County Fair on the same day.

chapter

44

Dane sometimes wondered if Parmenter would have been happier hiring a Pony Express rider to carry their messages back and forth. Four days—four days!—after their last phone conversation, Dane got another letter by U.S. Mail and made another call from a pay phone in Athol, Idaho, this time wearing a raincoat and a billed cap and feeling overtly melodramatic.

The phone call lasted half an hour, most of which Parmenter spent in backstory about a painter named Ernie and a hotel manager named Doris and preparatory remarks leading up to something dire that he never quite said but Dane could guess.

Dane finally cut him off. "All right, all right, you sold me twenty minutes ago, which is twenty minutes we just gave *them*. Give me specifics. I need locations, calendar dates, names of all the players, what kind of budget they're talking about, who's in charge . . ."

Parmenter responded, "How soon can you get down here?"

"I'll be there tomorrow."

Dane returned home, went straight up to his loft, and pulled some rolled-up drawings from a large round basket next to his drafting table. He hadn't even finished these—there had been some interruptions—but now they'd become important. He rolled the sheets out flat on the table, weighting the ends, and looked them over, mind open and fishing for ideas, any ideas.

A tight cocoon, a pod, a capsule . . . hoisted on a crane . . . wood construction might be better . . . But how would she ever get out of it?

"Eloise Kramer, may I introduce Emile DeRondeau. He's the best in the business."

Mandy extended her hand to a red-haired, red-bearded gentleman in unpretentious work shirt and jeans. His hand was rough, indicating that he not only designed award-winning magical effects, he also was closely involved in building them. "You can call me Mandy."

"That's her stage name," said Seamus, clarifying the obvious.

"Of course," he said with a smile. "I've seen your work. I love it."

"Thank you." She wanted to be more conversational, but the chatty neurons in her brain just weren't firing.

It was the first Wednesday in March. The sun was out, the temperature was getting comfy. Mandy, Seamus, and the Orpheus stage crew were having a concept meeting with Emile DeRondeau in the hotel's back parking lot, now blocked off and void of cars. While they watched from a safe distance, Big Max hooked a cable to an appropriately sized shipping crate, and a huge crane began hoisting it aloft.

"You might stick with the name by which I introduce you," Seamus whispered sideways to her.

"I prefer Mandy," was all she cared to whisper back. She shifted her focus to the ascending crate, trying to concentrate on one solitary thing without her mind spinning off in a hundred directions, reviewing, reliving, sorting, *fearing*. These people were planning her life, and it was all she could do to park herself in this meeting and pay attention.

Andy and Emile were watching the crate and noting where the sunlight was coming from.

"An afternoon show, definitely," said Emile.

Andy looked toward the south side of the parking lot. "We could place the bleachers over there. They'd be in the shade of the parking garage by about two, and the sun would be behind the audience."

Seamus leaned down. "Try cashing a check under that name. There's a reason you have the name Eloise Kramer and a reason I created it for you: survival. Mandy is not the answer, it's the problem. It's the name for everything you need to put behind you."

"Assuming it's all a delusion."

He half laughed with a roll of his eyes. "I thought you confirmed that with your 'old friend' who never met you before."

She took the rebuff, letting him have the last word. She'd led him to believe that her visit with Joanie had come to nothing, that it was no more than a same-name coincidence. Compared to the truth, it hardly seemed a lie. Besides, there was no aspect of her story that he wouldn't see as an excuse for an airheaded, career-threatening infatuation with a sixty-year-old man. If it took a lie to keep from going there . . . well, it did, didn't it?

She let it go and watched the crate, now looking very small as it neared the mast of the crane some 150 feet off the ground. The thought of being locked inside that thing gave her stomach a twist.

"What do you think?" Seamus asked Emile.

Emile squinted as he studied the crate, now stark against the sky. "Any higher and it'll be too small for the audience to see. You've got enough thrill for the money."

"Great. We can't afford a bigger crane."

Andy asked, "Ready to drop?"

Emile and Seamus exchanged a glance and then Seamus said, "Okay, let her go."

Andy signaled the crane operator. The crate came loose and dropped for an awesome stretch of time before smacking into the pavement and exploding into splinters.

"Doable?" Seamus asked Emile.

Emile nodded. "We can work with that."

Mandy checked out the tops of the buildings around the parking lot. The Orpheus was the tallest, but now it would be to the audience's right instead of behind the event. Not a problem, she supposed. "So then I rappel down that side?"

"Oh, no," said Seamus, "we're working the big room now. Big room, big stunt." He gave her a whimsical look, shot a side glance at Emile, then said, "You're going to hang-glide."

Her mouth dropped open, but she immediately liked the idea, looking up at the hotel, envisioning it.

"I have an instructor lined up. We can get you started on that right away."

"So . . ."

Seamus traced the imagined spectacle with his hand. "You're trapped in the crate, the clock is ticking, the time runs out, and the crate drops into the pit, BOOM! But then your doves appear, they circle to draw attention, then they fly up . . . up . . . to the top of the hotel, where you cast off from the roof on a hang glider with the doves flying in formation with you. You circle down, make a pass in front of the bleachers, you come in for a landing right in front of them, the doves land on your arms, ta-da! Big finish!"

She shook her head, but there was that twist in her stomach again. "*Guy*, you have a lot of confidence."

He put his arm around her. "Yeah. Yeah, I do. But it's all up to you. We're going to need all your thoughts, all your senses, everything you are, and everything you have directed this way and nowhere else. This is your career. You're on the rise now and you can be unstoppable if that's what you choose. You understand what I'm saying?"

She regarded the splinters of wood littering the parking lot and the dizzying height of the Orpheus Hotel. "Oh, I understand."

"Good, very good." As he walked away he looked back and pointed at her. "Eloise."

The lady who arrived at Priscilla's boardinghouse drove a Mercedes but her eyes were empty as if the soul were gone, and her clothing was plain, like any unknown person on the street. She introduced herself to Priscilla as Mandy Whitacre's Aunt Betsy. When Priscilla didn't quite buy it, she said, "Oh dear, yes, I forgot. She would probably use her real name here: Eloise Kramer?"

Priscilla let Aunt Betsy into the house, but only as far as Eloise Kramer's door. Aunt Betsy slipped a little pink envelope under the door, said thank you, and left.

* * *

That evening Mandy ducked into her room at Priscilla's like a rabbit evading a hawk. She locked the door behind her and leaned against it as if she could hold everything at bay and then stood there, eyes closed, breathing, just breathing, hoping for a break, just one tiny moment of respite from all that, that *stuff* out there.

Time out, she prayed. *Time out*, please.

Dane. I'm gonna call Dane and I'm just gonna tell him, I'm gonna tell him everything and I don't care what he thinks.

She reached into her shoulder bag . . .

There was an envelope at her feet. It was small and pink like the envelopes for thank-you cards or baby shower invitations. She cringed. Judging from the last time she saw an envelope like this, it wasn't good news. She picked it up and tore it open. Inside was a note, same handwriting as before.

Dear Ms. Whitacre:

    Though our personal acquaintance comes no closer than that moment in the hallway at Clark County Medical, I am familiar with the circumstances that have befallen you since September 17 and was, I regret to say, one of the instigators who brought them about.

    As such, let me settle some questions I'm sure have haunted you:

    Nothing you've seen or experienced is illusory or delusional, but the result of procedures performed upon my recommendation, but without your knowledge or permission, in the basement of Clark County Medical Center. It is all explainable and you are not mentally ill.

    You had nothing to do with Doris Branson's accident or Ernie Myers's injuries, nor are you in any way responsible for their deaths; those were *our* doing. The obituary I sent was to warn you, but I've since come to realize that neither I nor anyone else can stop what has already happened.

    I have kept something safe that belongs to you. If you will show this letter to the man whose address and phone number I have included, he will guide you to it.

    I have destroyed everyone and everything I desired to save, including you and lastly, myself. All that is left for me is to destroy the lie

I've become and hope the truth will help you put things together. I won't
ask you to forgive me. Maybe God will.

Yours truly,
Margo J. Kessler

The lady drove her Mercedes to a nice house on the west side,
brewed some tea, then spent an hour at her kitchen table finishing a
letter on her laptop. Leaving the letter open on the computer screen,
she printed a hard copy, then folded and concealed it in the old family Bible she had stored away in a box in the basement. The wrong
people were certain to find the letter on the computer; hopefully,
they would be content in destroying that. Someday the right people
would find the printed copy, and then the world would know.

Satisfied, she went to her bedroom, said a rosary, then injected
herself as she lay upon her bed.

It was cold enough to wear a jacket, dark enough to make street signs
and address numbers hard to read. Mandy used a penlight to consult
a map and Dr. Kessler's directions on the passenger seat and, after
one wrong and one missed turn, found her way to an ugly, bumpy
street on the outskirts of town. At this hour, her Bug was only one of
the occasional cars, so she shifted down a gear, eased off the pedal,
and carefully eyed the boxy, weathered-walled, single-story businesses she passed: USED FURNITURE, APPLIANCE LIQUIDATORS, RECYCLING
CENTER. She passed a vacant lot, a redneck bar, an old school with
plywood over the windows, and then came upon a high chain-link
fence with hundreds of hubcaps hanging on it. This had to be it.
Yep. There was a sign in customary black on yellow wired to the
fence next to the gate, J & J'S AUTO WRECKING. Mandy pulled up to
the sagging chain-link gate and beeped her horn, as Mr. Jansen had
instructed her.

He turned out to be not as scary as he sounded on the phone.
Sure, his voice was gruff, his coveralls were greasy, and the bill of his
"J&J all the way" cap was finger-smudged to a nearly even black, but
he had a friendly smile with all his front teeth still there; he didn't

chew and spit, at least in her presence; and his dog, a half lab and half everything else, was friendly, the licking sort.

"So you must be the one," he said, touching the bill of his cap. "Pardon my not shaking hands, I've been working." He showed her his hands.

No further questions. She gave a little bow and touched the brim of an imaginary hat. "Pleased to meet you, and I don't really know what this is about."

"Do you have the note from the doctor?"

She had it in her hand and gave it to him. He opened and read it with the aid of his flashlight, his face darkening with each line. "Holy cow." Then he asked, "What do you do for a living?"

"I'm a magician. I'm going to be opening a show at the Orpheus in three weeks."

He nodded, satisfied. "You're the one, all right." He handed the note back, now bearing his fingerprints. He pulled a rag from his hip pocket and wiped his hands. "And I don't know what this is about either, but let's get her done."

Using his flashlight, he led her through a meandering canyon of misshapen, dismembered automobiles piggybacked on either side. His dog, at home in this place, disappeared into the blackness ahead and occasionally looked back, retinas shining in the flashlight beam. Mandy, unsure of where she was stepping and kicking against rattly, tinny little things in the dark, pulled her own penlight from her pocket and put it to use. "The doctor had a hulk brought here," said Jansen. "It'd been in a wreck and I guess she bought it from the insurance company. They trucked it in on a flatbed and she's been paying me to keep it safe, keep anybody from touching it or crushing it until a lady magician comes looking for it. Guess that's you."

They rounded a corner and came to an open space near the back fence. Parked up against that fence were what Mandy assumed to be Mr. Jansen's keepsakes: a street rod with great paint but no engine; a mid-40s Dodge power wagon with no windshield or seat but with a winch on the front; a half-size yellow school bus . . . and the fire-ravaged, caved-in, cut-open remains of a BMW sedan, its paint seared away, its crooked body ashen gray.

"That's it," said Mr. Jansen, sweeping his light over it.

She knew he was waiting for her side of the story, her explanation, but all she could think of was the distance between herself and that twisted cage of metal and how afraid she was to cross it. *No*, she felt. *I'm safe over here, away from you. I'm alive. You have nothing to do with me.*

But, it seemed to say, *you want to be* her, *and I have everything to do with* her.

Your story . . . is her story? Mine?

Fear pressed her back, but longing pulled harder, drew her closer. The driver's door was gone forever, the driver's seat a blackened, metal outline with chunks of foam clinging like mold.

But I'm alive. This never happened to me.

Walk through, it said. *Find out. Know.*

Longing against fear, knowing against hiding. She went closer, her penlight playing over the soot-blackened windows. The rear passenger window on the driver's side was shattered. Someone must have tried to get in.

. . . Dane Collins . . . was subsequently injured trying to rescue his wife from the burning vehicle . . .

The frame on the driver's side was smashed in, the floor buckled, and the seats askew.

. . . when the Collins's car was sidestruck by another motorist . . .

She was *here?* The girl in the mirror, the dancer in the blue gown?

. . . Mandy Eloise Collins . . . wife . . . of Dane Collins . . . killed yesterday . . .

Mr. Jansen stayed alongside, holding his light for her. The covering on the dashboard was split open, peeled back, exposing yellow foam beneath. The center console had folded in upon itself, sagging, wrinkled, the gearshift a blackened stalk. She could smell the stench of burned cloth, leather, plastic . . . flesh? She knew that smell. She shied back.

This is death, where the story ends.

But how else can I ever live as me?

She made herself reach and touch. The metal was rough with paint blisters, rust, and corrosion. She felt like running but took hold of the doorframe so she would stay.

"Careful," said Mr. Jansen, pointing with his light. "That metal's sharp."

She ran her light along the tear in the roof. It was jagged, like a bread knife. She placed her foot on the bottom of the doorframe, her hand on the frame of the seat back.

"Whoa, here, wait a minute," said Mr. Jansen. He dashed to the street rod and brought back an old seat cushion. While she waited, he set it on the frame of the driver's seat and stepped away, holding his light for her.

In a slow and careful process, placing a hand here, a foot there, watching for sharp edges, she settled into the creaking skeleton of the driver's seat, into the center of the ashes and smell, steeling herself to look at the warped and bubbled instrument panel, the black crumbles of melted handles, buttons, and air vents on the seats and floor. In the beam of Mr. Jansen's light, she placed her hands on each side of the out-of-round, skeletal steering wheel and looked into the dark through a misshapen void that used to be the windshield.

A good space of time passed before Mr. Jansen said anything. "You all right?"

She was, and it bothered her. She tried to imagine the hood and grille of another car plowing into her left side faster than she could react, the scream of tires, the slam of metal, the flying particles of glass and the brain-jarring impact, how it must have sounded and smelled, how it must have felt to be trapped in this crumpled cooker while the smoke and flames roasted her alive. . . .

But she'd never been here. This was all part of another story she'd never lived.

"Well," she said at last, "it happened to somebody. That's a fact."

She would have climbed out, but Mr. Jansen stood on the ground immediately to her left and didn't move. He was shining his flashlight at the floor of the car, at the ashes and crumblings around her feet.

"What?" she asked.

He just wiggled the flashlight to draw her attention, so she looked.

With each wave of his light, something amid the ashes sparkled. Something pretty in the middle of all this ugliness? She bent over, reached for the sparkle, and felt a small, crusty chain between her fingers. At first it was just another forlorn piece of someone else's tragedy, but when she lifted it from the ashes and spread it across her palm . . .

A silver chain, stained by ash and smoke, the tiny links wilted by the heat, the ends broken and burned away, and in the center of its length . . . one indistinguishable lump of silver, and one intact silver dove.

"I saw it there when they first brought the car in," said Mr. Jansen. "But Dr. Kessler said, 'No, don't touch it, leave it right where it is.'" He tilted his light to study her face. "Looks like it was this that she was keeping for you."

chapter

45

Parmenter was driving the car. "Fortunately, it's after eight. The main crew's gone home and Moss is the only one there."

Dane was lying on the floor in the back. "What does he know about your contact with me?"

"Just about everything. I had to contact you first. You had knowledge of the past forty years, you already knew who Mandy was, you know who she is—with a little explanation, of course . . ."

"Of course."

"While Mandy is, or *was*, a young girl with no idea in the world that she'd been married to you for forty years, no way to fathom or believe what we would tell her. We needed you to help us contact and communicate with her, which meant contacting and communicating with you, which meant letting you in on all the pertinent details. That much he knows."

"Do you trust him?"

"Well, I—"

"Don't."

"Right. Don't. Okay, here we are."

"Just drive on in and act normal."

"Act normal. Riiight . . ."

Dane felt the car slow, then turn, then roll to a stop. Parmenter rolled down his window, and Dane could hear the beep from the card reader as Parmenter swiped his card through it. A faint mechanical whir told him a gate was opening.

They drove down a ramp to underground parking, the sound of the engine and tires reverberating off the concrete walls. Parmenter pulled into a parking lot and shut off the engine. He gave the area a quick 360-degree sweep, then said, "Okay. We'd better make it quick."

An entry door was only a few yards from where the car was parked. They ducked through, took an elevator up one floor, went down a bare hallway to a service door, stepped through that to another hallway that led to another door that Parmenter unlocked with his security card.

Inside that door was a cluttered office: a desk piled with blue-penciled computer printouts, stacks of binders and manuals against the wall, two whiteboards filled with incomprehensible formulas, and a computer system with three monitors side by side, each one showing a fluctuating display of columns, numbers, graphs, and vaporous, undulating shapes.

Parmenter rolled a chair from a corner. "Have a seat."

Dane settled in, appreciating all the scribblings on the whiteboard—even if Parmenter had faked all of it, it was still impressive.

"That's our bottom line, I suppose," the scientist said, waving a felt tip marker at the whiteboard. "I reworked it several times, from several directions, and every time I landed on one conclusion." He sighted down the marker at some scribblings in the lower right corner of the second whiteboard, some letters mixed with some numbers and a squiggle sitting on top of some other letters and numbers divided up with slashes and squiggles.

Dane ventured a guess. "Mandy's in deep soup."

"Well, we all are, but she is at the heart of the problem. Her reversion was so vast—forty years, several hundred miles!—that her gravitational leverage on the Machine is insurmountable. We can't counter it. She's controlling the Machine, using all its power and capability to perform her magic." He scanned the scribblings for help, but then just said it. "And to maintain her secondary timeline, the very thing that keeps her forty years behind the rest of us. But it's not without cost. The deflection necessary—"

The other door to the office opened and a younger man, with black curly hair, stepped in. Parmenter rose to make the introduction. "Dane Collins, may I introduce my associate and project manager, Dr. Loren Moss."

Dane rose and shook the man's hand. There were no smiles.

"Loren, I was just about to tell Dane about the deflection debt, how it forced retracings of the other subjects."

Moss nodded and addressed Dane. "Every reversion, every time we shift a timeline or create a new one, we bend space just a little more. It's like bending a spring; the more you bend it, the more it resists, until you just can't add any more strain without removing some first. We call that *deflection debt*. We can't place any more stress on the universe without relieving some first."

Parmenter continued, "The rats were so small and the reversion so brief, just a matter of minutes, that the deflection debt was negligible. Monkeys were larger and had greater mass, so they required a little more. The human subjects had far greater mass and required much longer reversions—some a day or two, the soldier—"

"Seven days," said Moss.

"One of our own staff—"

"Me," Moss offered. "Fourteen months."

"Followed by Ernie Myers who only required a three-hour reversion; we reverted him back to the instant he fell from his ladder so he'd remember the fall but not remember being injured. It worked—the first time. Doris Branson, the same thing. We reverted her to the moment of her car accident so the last thing she remembered was losing control of the car. That was four hours. But it was adding up. Our readings indicated a building imposition on the space-time fabric and we were wondering how much more strain we could impose before we reached our limit."

"I think Mandy put us there."

"Absolutely," said Parmenter, referring to the computer monitors. "Not that it's her fault, of course, but the deflections she imposed were so severe that the space-time fabric began to cast off the earlier deflections. I imagine that little toy block has retraced by now . . ."

"It's like a ship that's too heavy," said Moss. "If you still want to load more cargo you have to unload something else first."

"So our little toy car broke into pieces again, our restored pop can squashed again, the rats all retraced, and then the monkeys—" Parmenter leaned toward the monitors. "Wait, hold on."

Hold on? Dane was about to pounce with a question and now Parmenter was saying "Hold on"? Dane held his peace; it looked serious.

Parmenter tapped away at his keyboard, muttering computations to himself. Moss waited patiently, no doubt familiar with how Parmenter operated. At last, alarmed, Parmenter leaned back, blew out a breath, and said, "She's coming here."

Moss looked incredulous. "Coming here? You mean . . . ?"

Parmenter pointed to fields of numbers on the screen, explaining to Dane, "These are space-time axes with corresponding coefficients, designated Kiley, Baker, Delta, blah blah blah; anyway, by looking at the Machine's readouts I can closely estimate the gravitational influence Mandy is exerting or will be exerting on the Machine over a given span of time, and from that I can calculate her distance from the Machine, and in . . . forty-three minutes, five seconds, she and the Machine will be no more than two meters apart, which means she's going to be here in this lab, which means we—most especially *you*—are going to have some real convincing to do if we hope to save her life."

Those last three words! "I'm listening. You were talking about the monkeys."

"They retraced."

"What does that mean?"

Parmenter looked at Moss, who just looked back at him. Parmenter took it. "Retrace, retrace, uh, it means . . . in order to revert someone, we have to reverse them on their own timeline—rewind their life, so to speak. But if that's all we did, then they would simply retrace the same timeline and go through the same accident, injury, whatever, all over again. That's why we create a secondary timeline, one with an open future that hasn't been lived yet. When we place the subject on the new timeline, they effectively bypass whatever calamity befell them on their old timeline and continue living as if it never happened. That's the whole object."

"But you had to burn the monkeys."

Parmenter was a little surprised. "I suppose Mandy told you about that."

"She did."

"They died. Their reversions failed because their secondary timelines failed and they fell back into their original timelines and retraced."

"And that was largely due to the load Mandy placed on the space-

time fabric," said Moss. "Any secondary timelines prior to her reversion became unstable."

Parmenter spoke for his associate. "Loren's secondary timeline
was disrupted when Mandy came through the lab on a tertiary corridor—"

"We have less than forty minutes, Doctor," Dane reminded him.

"She's been here before—well, not completely here, maybe half
here and half wherever else she was. That's how she knows about the
monkeys." Parmenter rolled his eyes at his own verbal morass.

Moss stepped in. "Mandy can generate additional timelines and
pass into and out of them. It's how she can see and be in several
different places at the same time. It's how she levitates, how she
moves from one place to another and makes objects move and mul-
tiplies objects, including herself. I'm sure she doesn't know how she
does it."

"She's about to find out," said Parmenter, watching the monitors.

"But she does it. Anyway, she was riding a third timeline right
through the hospital when she bumped into my secondary timeline and dissolved it. I fell back to my original timeline, retraced it,
and now I'm dying of cancer again. But that's the same thing that
happened to our other experimental subjects, Corporal Dose, Doris
Branson, Ernie Myers. Mandy's built up such a load on the space-
time fabric that she's bumped the other subjects off their secondary
timelines and they've retraced."

Parmenter jumped in, "Which made every one of them a security
risk. They were starting to catch on, starting to ask questions, threatening legal action, and of course it was only a matter of time before
they started talking to each other—Myers and Branson had Mandy in
common, and all three had this hospital in common."

Dane put up a hand to stop them, then sat and processed, his fingers on his brow. "So . . . you're saying that these other three were . . .
eliminated? Rubbed out? Killed?"

Moss and Parmenter looked at each other as if afraid to use the
words. Parmenter finally offered, "It's what I was saying about control
and how the people now running this project will stop at nothing to
retain it."

"You mean DuFresne, Carlson?"

Parmenter nodded. "They've become the figureheads, top of the pecking order. DuFresne heads the medical interests, Carlson the technical, and both of them are answering to the military, who never show their faces at all."

"How much time?" Moss asked.

Parmenter consulted the monitors. "Thirty-four minutes, thirty-six seconds."

And Dane sat there looking at them.

"Are you . . . are you keeping up with all this?" Moss asked.

"I can panic or I can think," Dane said. "Question one: is Mandy a risk to this project and to the people running it?"

Both nodded. "Absolutely," said Parmenter. "She's not only demonstrating the Machine's capabilities before the public—thank God people think it's trickery—she's also controlling it."

"The Machine is like a computer that's crashed," said Moss. "We can monitor what's happening, we can access limited capabilities—"

"Like the toy block."

"But Mandy is essentially running away with our invention."

"All right," said Dane, talking slowly, evenly. "Question two: do you believe your scientist friends and government people will try to kill Mandy the same as they killed the others?"

That pained Parmenter. Moss took the question. "They would have killed her long before this, but that wouldn't have fixed the crash."

"What if she quit performing her magic, quit using the Machine?"

"That wouldn't fix the crash either," said Moss. "The Machine would still be down, inaccessible."

"So what if you just turned the Machine off, unplugged it?"

They chuckled at some inside knowledge. Parmenter seemed sheepish as he said, "It's not here in our time dimension so we can do that. The more it works for Mandy, the more it gets entangled in multiple dimensions."

Moss added, "Right now it's sitting in our time dimension but drawing power—it's plugged in—in another time about three and a half seconds behind ours and traveling close to the speed of light . . . somewhere."

Dane sighed in frustration.

"We've worked through a lot of these questions already," said Parmenter, pointing at the whiteboards.

"But you've brought me into it and blathered about some theory of yours, so I gather you've thought of *something*."

Again, the two seemed reticent and looked at each other. Parmenter ventured an answer. "They—we—need to recalibrate the Machine, completely reset it, and the only way we can do that is to find out exactly what the Machine did on September 17 so we can work backward through that process and undo whatever it did."

Moss added, "And the only way we can do that is to find out exactly where and when Mandy arrived after her reversion, how far we sent her in space and how far back in time."

"And only Mandy can tell us that."

"Which is the main reason she's still alive."

Dane mused on that a moment.

"Uh, twenty-nine minutes," said Parmenter.

"So you need me to persuade her to tell you?"

They nodded yes but weren't happy about it.

"And say she does. What happens to her?" They hesitated, and Dane didn't like the looks they gave each other. "You said you would have to work backward through the process and undo whatever the Machine did. Did I hear you correctly?"

Parmenter finally said it. "If we—if *they*—expect to regain control of the Machine, they would have to undo all past actions and start afresh. They would have to retrace her."

Dane knew what that meant, and now he had to sort his thoughts and feelings enough to contain more than disdain for these men and their project, he also had to hold back an animal rage.

Moss checked his watch. "Twenty-six minutes."

"*She can . . .*" Dane took a breath and controlled his tone. Even so, his voice was shaking. "She can walk in that door right now as far as I'm concerned. She can walk right up to you, and you can face her, and look her in the eye, and tell her yourself."

Parmenter spoke in gentle, perhaps timid tones, as if addressing a lion with bared claws. "Umm . . . we are hoping, of course, as you and I discussed, that we can find an alternative."

"And if we don't?"

"Uh, we—"

"*Say it!*"

Moss and Parmenter exchanged another look. Parmenter faced

up to it. "If we don't find an alternative, then the only way to reset the Machine and clear the deflection debt is to retrace Mandy . . . and she will burn to death all over again."

There was nowhere else to go and, from some inkling of intuition she couldn't explain but opted to trust, she knew something was brewing back at the hospital; she knew someone was there in that basement behind those big double doors who might not be glad to see her but was going to see her, like it or not, live or die.

She parked her VW in the visitor parking and, rather than risk being seen, remained inside the car, relaxing, immersing herself in the space around her, the streams, currents, ripples, and folds of other times and places. It was still a bizarre feeling, as easy as ever to mistake for madness or, at best, a dream state, but she'd grown used to it, even mastered it to the point that she could judge when she was "on," really in tune with it, or maybe a little "off," not quite finding her way. Tonight she was "on," *way* on, as if the layers of time and space were rose petals emanating in graceful arcs from a center, and she was very near, almost inside, that center. Finding, connecting, slipping through were easy, and in mere seconds she was *there*, in that alternate, overlaid space that took her from her VW to a subterranean hallway she'd visited before.

The rushing, invisible current grabbed at her again and would have carried her down the hall, but she was ready for it and planted her feet solidly on the tiles. Clunk! She was in the hall for real . . .

. . . and face-to-face with the steel double doors. AUTHORIZED PERSONNEL ONLY!

Immediately she felt it: terror was coming through that steel and knifing through her as if she were already on the other side wishing she could get out. Her feet wouldn't move, not toward the doors, not away from them. It was like standing at the top of her first escalator when she was four: she was frozen.

But that made her angry. *Mandy Whitacre, you're not four. You're not even twenty. You've been through enough, been bruised enough, been scared enough, you're old enough. Now you can either wimp out on this side of the doors until the dragon comes out and eats you anyway, or you can go in there, kill it, and be done with it.*

So that resolved that. She straightened her spine and held her head up. "I'm Mandy Whitacre," she told the doors, and with one quick reach into a quaking, tea-stained other world, she let the doors suck her in, pulling her body through the metal like a string of taffy.

She went spinning, all things around her blurring, she groped for the veil, the way out . . .

Clunk! She fell out on the other side, standing in a featureless hallway lit by can lights in the ceiling. There was that deep, electric hum again, so often a part of her other visions and journeys. She heard no voices, saw no one.

The fear would not go away. She sequestered it in a pocket of her mind, drew a deep breath, and took the first step. Other steps followed the first. She moved down the hall.

A steel door on her left taunted her with a big cold handle and red letters that shouted with authority, AUTHORIZED PERSONNEL ONLY— just like *Don't go out on the casino floor, you're underage!* "Oh, shush!" The latch clacked open for her and she ventured a peek inside.

She'd seen this place. It was a furnace room, a maze of water and steam pipes, aluminum ducts, catwalks and stairs all built around a furnace the size of a mobile home, and alongside the furnace, an iron box like a woodstove on a brick pedestal with a control panel and a heavy front door. She descended a flight of steel stairs and approached it, gripped the big handle, and creaked the door open. Inside was a gas-fired combustion chamber lined with ashes. An incinerator. This was where the monkeys burned.

One more proof I'm not crazy, she thought. A new boldness pushed the fear farther back inside her.

Double doors on the other side of the hallway looked like hospital doors that could lead to a ward or operating rooms. They didn't appear to be bolted shut; they were unmarked. She crossed the hall, pressed against the door on the right . . . it swung open. She stepped through.

In the first few seconds she was overwhelmed. It could have been a television studio with a stage built in the center, or a space flight control room with the launch pad in the middle. The room was about forty by forty with a high ceiling, windowless, all concrete, lit by fixtures suspended from an overhead grid like a soundstage. Rows of control consoles with dials, switches, keyboards, and monitors were arranged on three sides of the room, all facing the center, where a hexagonal enclosure of steel and glass about twelve feet across stood like a space-age gazebo, steel pillars at each corner, a flat canopy rigged with lights over the top. Electrical cables snaked from the platform across the floor, some taped down, some not, connecting the platform with every console, every steel cabinet marked DANGER HIGH VOLTAGE, every blinking panel.

For the next few seconds, she was stunned speechless and im-mobile.

On the right side of the room was a large console raised higher than the others, apparently the command control center. Behind that console, face illumined with blue light from a monitor, sat the man who'd come into McCaffee's with a computer and egged her into doing the levitation. Sitting next to him was the younger, Tom Hanks–looking guy she'd seen superimposed in her apartment.

In front of the console, rising to his feet as she came in, his eyes meeting hers unabashedly, was Dane Collins.

At the sight of him the fear left her, carried away in a sigh as her body eased, even teetered from relief. She couldn't imagine the story to explain why he was here, and where could she begin to tell hers? She could only find strength in the fact that he was here at all.

So in that long, face-reading, eye-meeting stretch of time, the electrons hummed through the cables and consoles, the panel lights blinked but drew no attention, the ventilation system rushed qui-etly . . . and no one said a word.

Dane looked up at the steel and glass enclosure, then back at her, his cue for her to take a look.

She walked, her sneakers making little squeaks that carried through the room, then climbed the seven steps to the enclosure for a closer look through the glass. The enclosure contained a bench the size of a hospital bed. The bench was draped with a sheet that hung crookedly over either side, as if arranged in haste. The sheet was soiled, stained brown . . . with blood?

The smell. It turned her nose, stung her spirit. Like singed hair, rotting flesh, something burning. She'd smelled it in her visions and interdims; she'd smelled it in the scorched car.

The two men exchanged a glance. Dane Collins propped an

elbow in the opposite hand, his fingers over his lips, his gaze strong and reassuring.

She descended the steps and walked toward the raised console, reaching into her pocket. Dane turned, and they stood facing the two strangers together. She drew out her hand.

In her palm was the half-melted, ash-encrusted anklet with one dove still intact.

She asked, "What have you done to me?"

chapter

46

Parmenter introduced himself and Moss, but Mandy did not feel cordial and did not offer her hand. He pulled up a chair for her behind the console and offered her some coffee. She requested a bottle of water and sat with Parmenter, Moss, and Dane to hear the other side of her story.

"You have unknowingly been involved in a government-funded experiment . . ." Parmenter began, and the story unfolded part by part.

". . . we'd never tested the process on burn injuries, so your case was an irresistible opportunity . . ."

". . . the bloodstains on the sheet are all that remained. Where you went and how far back your reversion was, we hadn't a clue . . ."

". . . the massive gravitational influence you have on the Machine is aberrant, totally unexpected . . ."

". . . what you're experiencing is alternate, parallel timelines woven through space, and what's astounding is how you've learned to create them at will . . ."

The audacity of these people was incomprehensible, enraging, tempered only by the fact that Mandy was still alive. Her anger made her bold, her questions and comebacks sharp-edged. Parmenter and Moss accepted and endured it, explaining, never defending. The meeting became a bilateral debriefing, the scientists as earnest to hear her side of it as she was to hear theirs. Mandy felt they could get along, but she wasn't ready to be friends.

They showed her the Machine.

"We haven't opened it, haven't touched or tampered with anything, including the soiled sheet . . . yes, I guess you could call it a crime scene: we didn't dare disturb anything until we had the uh, crime, solved.

"The bench contains the Machine's interdimensional core; it resembles a big black domino, about six feet long, ten inches thick, accelerated to ninety-five percent of the speed of light . . . oh, it's traveling that fast, all right, but in relation to an alternate dimension of time and space while maintaining a motionless foothold in ours. You could say it has its foot in the interdimensional door, holding it open so people and objects can pass through, which you've been doing on a regular basis. Every bouncing tennis ball, every levitation, every vanish passes through that core. Oh, and every journey through time and space, such as your encounter with Moss . . ."

They showed her the makeshift sleeping quarters where she surprised Moss during the night. It was just as she remembered it.

She remembered parts of the lab as well, in fragmented images of consoles, lights, shadowy faces, muffled conversations, like a continuous volley of déjà vu. She could remember and describe some of the rooms before they showed them to her.

Near midnight, they were seated around a table where the day crew took their breaks—three doughnuts left over from that day rested in a white box next to dirty coffee cups that never made it back to the kitchen. There was silence. In slow, awkward phrases and apologetic tones, Parmenter and Moss had described the final outcome, the bottom line of Mandy's future as they saw it.

She looked across the room at the Machine, looked again at them, tried to believe but couldn't. Hope as in, *This is just a bad dream and I'll wake up,* wasn't working so well for her anymore. She tried denial, expecting they would now tell her the *next thing,* the one bit of good news they hadn't told her yet, the way out. Maybe there would be a second opinion that it didn't have to be this way.

She looked at Dane and thought she saw a ray of hope. She could tell he believed it and yet . . . he'd thought of something. Yes, *surely* he'd thought of something! *Dane, speak up! Tell me, tell* them!

He was listening, watching, thinking.

She asked, "Does it have to happen?"

Parmenter had come across a writing pad and scribbled on it, apparently organizing his answers even as he spoke them. "Inexorable equilibrium. Theoretically, the universe must return to normal anyway. It can't stay stretched forever. That's the fatal flaw in all of this."

Moss inserted, "It's conceivable that the space-time distortion could last longer than your lifetime, meaning you would never retrace before you died naturally."

"But the administrators and financiers of this project aren't going to wait that long, not by any stretch of the imagination. They want the Machine back."

"They would really do that?" Mandy asked.

"They would do that." Parmenter prepared a moment, then said, "We told you about Dr. Kessler, and you recall meeting her in the hallway . . ."

"Did she take her life?" Mandy took Kessler's note from her pocket and handed it to him.

Parmenter read it and nodded. "She did, earlier today. She knew what would become of you but she couldn't stop it. I'm afraid Moss and I can't stop it either. A moral argument doesn't hold much weight against 'matters of national security.' But please . . ." He looked at Dane.

Dane laid his hand upon hers. "Before we despair, there might— *might*—be an alternative."

Don't tell me. There is a next thing?

Parmenter put down his pen and searched his mind for the right way to begin. "You recall, of course, your encounter with two thugs when you had the flat tire?"

"Yes."

"Do you recall"—he stopped, struggling for the question—"what your mental processes might have been immediately afterward?"

"My mental . . . I'm not sure what you're asking."

Dane said, "Remember running across my pasture, trying to get away from Clarence?"

She fervently wished she could. "I don't remember anything after they gave me that shot. I just remember waking up on your couch."

Parmenter pressed it. "You don't remember any kind of interdimensional transference, any contact with another timeline?"

Her mind was a blank. "No."

"No . . . longing, reaching, whatever it is you do to influence the Machine?"

Dane pitched in, "Right before I looked out my window and saw you running across my pasture, I saw you in my house."

Now, this was news. She wrinkled her brow and stared at him.

He continued, "Only, you were"—now he stumbled—"you were . . . older, the way you were before the accident."

"You don't remember that?" asked Parmenter, and then he shook his head at himself. "Well, how can you? It hasn't happened yet."

Mandy was frustrated. "Guys, try to make sense."

Parmenter regrouped with a little clap of his hands. "Okay. Here's my theory on this. Before all this began, before we started adding timelines, before anyone or anything was reverted, you had your timeline and the Machine had its timeline, and at that point everything was in balance, no space-time distortion. So the point is, if we dissolve all timelines secondary to the original two—yours and the Machine's—there would be no stress on the space-time fabric, and the two timelines would play themselves out in the natural order of things. It would be as if we never tampered with them."

"Which would be wonderful—for the *universe*."

Parmenter pointed his index finger upward, "Ahhh, but . . . *but*! Dane saw you in his home in Idaho at the age of fifty-nine *after* the accident, which suggests to me that somehow, in some way, you will exist as your chronologically correct self, intact and alive, subsequent to the accident, which suggests that somehow, in some way, you managed to circumvent the accident, and there's only one way I know of to do that and still allow the universe to remain in balance with no additional timelines."

Then he waited as if they might guess. They didn't. "Trade timelines. You take the Machine's timeline, it takes yours. It plays out your timeline and burns up, you play out its timeline and live out your life with the man you love—*if* the theory is sound, that is."

"But . . . why wouldn't it be sound?" she said to Dane, "You saw me alive in your house."

Parmenter countered, "All of this is theoretical, entirely contingent. Dane seeing you in his house—your house, the house—is one outcome that flashed through given the conditions at the time. Anything could change, any outcome could result."

"No promises, in other words."

"No, but if it *did* happen as Dane saw it, then it *could* happen if we can replicate it. Now, admittedly, there are problems. For one thing, the trade would mean the destruction of the Machine, which the other scientists and the government guys will never allow, which is almost moot in light of a bigger problem. The interdimensional mass of the Machine, that part of the Machine actually straddling time dimensions, is"—he scribbled it as he said it—"one thousand, six hundred and thirty-two pounds. And how much do you weigh?"

"A hundred and eight pounds."

"You see the problem."

"Not yet."

"It's like a pair of scales, like a teeter-totter. If you're going to trade timelines, the trade has to be weight for weight, mass for mass, the same on both sides, an even trade, and you don't weigh one thousand, six hundred and thirty-two pounds. That's a lot of candy bars." He rested his head on his hand. "Oh, and there's another problem: in order to force the trade, to make the Machine bump from its timeline to yours, yours would have to be the only other timeline available, which means we would have to dissolve your secondary timeline, the one you're living on right now, so that you fall back into your original, but of course, should you do that, you'll immediately retrace the original and come to your original end, the, uh, you'll perish, uh, in a fire."

She looked at Dane again. She could tell he was *really* thinking, his fist propped under his nose, his eyes like steel.

"Oh, and there's still the other problem," Parmenter continued. "The mental state, the reach, the method you used to generate that momentary linger on the Machine's timeline—that would be the moment you appeared in Dane's home as, uh, yourself. Whatever you did, however you felt, whatever method you used, it was an incredible fluke, an accident, but it put you ahead in time." He scurried over to the command console and came back with a three-ring binder full of notes and computer printouts. "I got the exact time and location of your appearance from Dane and extrapolated backward—well, actually, extrapolated the Machine forward in computer simulation, but at any rate, the readings show a major deflection in the Machine's timeline at that point, meaning an incursion of another timeline into its own. *If* the theory were sound, and *if* you'd weighed one thousand, six hundred and thirty-two pounds at that point, and *if* you'd occupied only your original timeline, you could have bumped the Machine from its timeline to yours and taken its place. You could have done it—if you had any idea how." He calmed, looking at his notes. "But, of course, you didn't weigh one thousand, six hundred and thirty-two pounds, you were occupying multiple timelines at the time and had no idea how you were doing what you were doing, and so . . . here you sit. Which brings us to the last problem."

"Are you sure?"

"No. It's just the last one I can think of at the moment."

"Go ahead."

"Your reversion, which we still don't understand, and all the manipulations you've imposed on the Machine since then have rendered it . . . well, it's all messed up, okay? We can't make any of this work until we recalibrate it, and we can't do that until we know the exact extent of your reversion, where you went and when you got there."

Dane clarified, "He needs to know where you were when you suddenly appeared in our time, and exactly what time and date it was. Do you remember?"

Of course she remembered. She and Seamus had verified it on site at the fairgrounds. Still, she held her peace, reading their faces.

"Oh!" said Parmenter. "Before you say anything, there's still one more problem, and it's only fair to tell you. Once you supply the information and we recalibrate the Machine, it will be fully controllable from this room, meaning anyone with access to the controls can dissolve your secondary timeline and retrace you. They will be able to end your life at will."

She almost laughed. She did smile at the inescapable cosmic joke being played on her, the pitiful sense of doom coursing through her. If this was sanity, being crazy made a lot more sense.

Parmenter said in conclusion, "So it comes down to whether we have your trust, I suppose."

She did laugh this time, but her laugh was bitter. "You gotta be kidding."

Parmenter looked at Dane, so she looked at Dane, and Dane began, "I've been working on a plan—"

She signaled stop with her hand. "No, no, just hold on a minute." Then she looked him over. "First, tell me who you are."

He met her eyes, but then he couldn't and looked away. The pain she saw all over him took her back to his bedroom when he stopped the dance and backed away . . . when he didn't dare look at her as she was leaving. "There's so much to think about right now, so much we just can't get wrong—"

"Mr. Collins"—only his last name felt safe—"at least give me that much. I've spent every minute of every day trying to figure out who I am, and before I give these guys the ability to fry me if they want, I need to know I'm right. I need to know who you are, and I need to know that *you* know."

He turned his gaze upon her and let his eyes rest there. They were filling with tears, but he blinked them away and spoke resolutely. "Mandy, I'm your husband. We were married June nineteenth, 1971."

Speaking of time, that stopped it. She explored his eyes, but in a different way now that she had permission, and for the first time since the county fair her world felt quiet, settled, unmoving. It was a sensation she wouldn't identify until later, that of her soul dropping anchor. "Okay," she said. "Let's hear the plan."

chapter

47

Dane unrolled the drawings on Preston Gabriel's dining-room table, and the white-haired magician took a long, careful look at his rendering of a cocoonlike pod. It was six feet tall, hexagonal, with six triangular panels at the bottom that opened like a flower and closed to a point. The pod was designed to be suspended—and then dropped—from a crane. The drawing showed a girl stuffed inside, head down.

"Explosive bolts?" Preston asked, pointing to the panels that composed the pod's lower end.

"We can conceal them in the seams and she can trigger them with her toes."

"So how do you protect her head and shoulders?"

They looked at a third man in the room, Emile DeRondeau. The designer/builder replied, "It's all in how the charges are mounted. We position them to blow outward."

"After which she has . . . ?"

Dane answered, "One second, two seconds at best. Think it's do-able?"

Preston shook his head trying to fathom it. "You'd better ask Mandy. The timing—"

"She said she'd find out."

"That's not the scary part," said Emile.

"All the parts are scary," said Preston.

Emile pointed at an escape hatch on the back of the cocoon, the side away from the audience. "For me, the scariest part is this packing bolt that locks her in."

No man had an argument there.

"But the point," said Dane, "is to keep her safe from beginning to end."

"What about the rigging in the costume?"

Dane whooshed a sigh. "We're going to need Keisha on that— which means she's in for some staggering news."

"How long do we have?" asked Preston.

"Mandy premieres in the big room at the Orpheus Friday, the twenty-fifth of March. This stunt happens in the rear parking lot at two that afternoon. That gives us just under three weeks."

"You could have come up with this a year ago," said Emile.

"Well," said Preston, eyebrows arched at the prospects, "that's why they call it magic."

"And if it works, it'll be the biggest stunt Mandy's ever done," said Dane.

"The Grand Illusion."

Dane looked at the drawing. "Not a bad name for it."

Jack Wright didn't care much for Vegas people. "I got two thousand acres and barely enough water thanks to you people down there, you and your politics and your money."

Loren Moss tried to explain that he had nothing to do with that. "I'm not a hotel owner or a developer. I'm a professor of astrophysics," he explained.

"So what are you doing in Vegas?"

"Well, that's what I came to talk to you about."

They were driving in Jack's old pickup across his ranch to a piece of ground that wasn't much use for grazing anymore and a safe distance from people, homes, or anything else breakable. When they were out of sight of any sign of mankind in any direction, Jack pulled to a stop, the desert dust blowing from the truck tires. "This what you had in mind?"

Moss climbed from the truck and looked in all directions. In the distance, a jackrabbit bounded out of sight among some rocks. There might have been some rattlesnakes around, maybe some leggy, venomous insects among the scrub brush, but that was all. "Yeah, yeah, Jack, this is just what I had in mind."

"So what are you doing, testing a bomb or something?"

Moss laughed. "Oh, no, no, it's just an experiment we didn't want to do in town. Depending on how things go, there could be an explosion, maybe a little fire."

Jack took that in stride, surveying the bleak surroundings from under the brim of his hat. "Well, you won't hurt anything out here."

"So we got a deal?"

"Soon's I get the money."

Moss handed Jack two thousand dollars in hundreds. "And by the way, you don't know anything about this."

"Never heard of you."

Eighteen days to Mandy's premiere . . .

Just standing on the ground harnessed to the hang glider got Mandy's adrenaline going. The wing quivered and tugged with any breath of wind; she could jump up and feel it grab the air as she came down. It was like Mary Poppins's umbrella, only for real, big enough to ride on the wind and take her and her instructor with it—which it did.

Hands on the control bar, face down the hill, start running into the breeze, control bar slightly forward . . .

Ooh! Wow! It still thrilled her the way the wing picked them up, just like that, and the hillside dropped away.

Feel it, feel it, feel it: pull the control bar from the direction you want to turn, push forward to nose up, pull back to nose down, don't overcorrect, anticipate where the wing is going, time it out, catch those updrafts . . .

Sailing through the air wasn't much different from sailing through time and space. In both environments you rode currents and waves, negotiated through surges and ripples. The mental discipline was exactly the same: *feel it, anticipate, don't overcorrect, get the rhythm.*

Her instructor was impressed with how fast she caught on, as if she'd done it before. *Well . . .*

Move over, birdies, Momma Dove's on the wing!

At dusk, in the middle of Jack Wright's most desolate acre, Mandy tried not to fidget as Parmenter affixed sensors to her forehead to monitor her brainwaves and advised her as she affixed some more to herself to monitor her vitals. Wires from the sensors led to an interface, the interface was connected to Parmenter's laptop computer, the computer was hooked up to a satellite receiver, and back at the lab, Loren Moss was monitoring the data at the Machine's central console.

This stuff was still mind-boggling.

They were set up under a shade canopy where Dane had neatly stacked exactly 35.76 concrete blocks with a combined weight of 1,520 pounds. They'd brought them in Loren Moss's pickup truck, each one carefully weighed and labeled, including a block they had to chip down to 0.76 of its original size and weight.

Parmenter checked the readings from the sensors on his computer and nodded satisfaction. "All right. Now, Mandy, if you'll take a seat on top of the blocks . . ."

She stepped carefully onto the blocks, holding the wires from the sensors so as not to snag or tangle them. Dane took her chair next to Parmenter's picnic table workstation to observe.

"Comfortable?" Parmenter asked.

"Just dandy," Mandy replied, secretly wishing she could sit on a pillow—Parmenter said she could have one, but if she did they would have to chip away some more of the 0.76 concrete block to allow for the added weight.

"All right," he said, tapping away at the computer keys. "You and your clothing and the concrete blocks should now total one thousand, six hundred and thirty-two pounds. You are wearing exactly the same clothes you wore when we weighed you?"

"Same clothes."

"Nothing new in your pockets?"

"Nope."

"Uh, what about that gum?"

"Oh." He put out his hand and she spit the gum into it.

"Very good." Parmenter gave the gum to Dane. "Now, according to Dane's best recollection and the cut of your later costumes, you weighed an additional four pounds at age fifty-nine, so we've factored that in."

She tried not to make a face—her face was always saying things she didn't mean to, always giving away her thoughts and feelings. How could that guy be so doggone clinical about this? She was not only going to gain four pounds in a matter of minutes if not seconds, she was also going to gain thirty-nine years and, if she couldn't stir up the magic feelings, thoughts, or vibes needed to pull this off, she was going to burn to death. *But hey, no sweat, no big deal. It might work, it might not, you win some, you lose some, but whatever happens, it'll be fascinating and educational.*

She stole a look at Dane, careful not to look too long, not to let her eyes place any obligation on him. As he tried to say, there were so many things to think about, so many things they couldn't get wrong. Their love was too big a question to tackle now, and for all they knew, the whole matter of Dane and Mandy and their bond of forty years was meant to end on September 17. So, of course, he was guarded and she understood, but one look, any look at him told her he was the same man, steady as a rock, the only thing she could be sure about.

Parmenter put on a headset and spoke via his computer to Moss back at the lab. "We are ready at this end."

In the solitude of the lab, Moss, headset in place and eyes on the monitors, replied, "Clear signal. Go ahead."

Parmenter scanned his computer screen, Mandy, the blocks, the sensor wires one more time. "All right. Now, this is all exploratory. We need to find out if you can include the mass of the blocks in your timeline with you. You were able to do that with the nurse's coat when you slipped out of the Spokane Medical Center."

Oh! Mandy thought. *I still need to return that!*

"You've done it with smaller objects in your magic act; you've managed to keep your clothes with you whenever you've traveled interdimensionally, so we know it's possible. If you can make yourself one unit of mass with the blocks in this test run, then you should be able to make yourself one unit with them when you default to your original timeline and attempt to swap timelines with the Machine. Is that all clear?"

Mandy ran it through her mind again, then asked, "So then, it would be Mandy and her blocks, one thousand, six hundred and thirty-two pounds of stuff, bumping out the Machine's one thousand, six hundred and thirty-two pounds of stuff and taking over its timeline?"

Parmenter gave a big nod. "So all you have to do is pull in those blocks. Go interdimensional and take them with you."

She drew a deep breath and sighed it out to ease her jitters. "Okay."

She looked down at the blocks, big, blah-looking, lifeless concrete things. It was hard to bond with them. No images came to her mind, no feelings to her heart. She could feel Parmenter and Dane watching her. "Am I supposed to make them move or something?"

"If that will help."

She stared at them again, but nothing happened. She and the blocks were in this time dimension, stable and benign, and it was tough to find a reason, a desire, to go elsewhere.

Parmenter suggested, "Well, why don't you try doing a magic trick with them? Yes, make them move."

She closed her eyes for a moment, stroked her forehead—

"Careful of those wires!" Parmenter butted in, shattering her concentration.

Can't find it. Can't find it.

Then Dane stood before her, leaned over the blocks, and touched her shoulder, looking into her eyes . . . just enough. "What if you thought about . . . Christmas? The dress you wore, the cake we enjoyed . . . how we danced."

Oh, no, was he going to go there, actually permit one small measure of belief that once, maybe still, they were in love? That she could really be . . .

She didn't want to cry but she did, from deep inside, from so long ago. ". . . sorry . . ."

"No," said Parmenter, eyes glued on his monitor. "Don't be sorry, these are good readings, very promising. You're deflecting the Kiley *and* the Delta!"

Mandy whispered, "Could you please get him to shut up?"

Dane looked at Parmenter, and the scientist got the message. Then Dane said, "Think of home."

And then he removed his touch and backed away.

No, don't go away! Don't leave me!

He kept backing away, then turned and walked across the darkening desert, not looking back.

Walking away . . . again. She felt it, the longing to go with him, to be where he was.

The earth moved and she felt she was floating above it. The blocks beneath her wavered, their cold gray turning to a tea-stain amber. She could smell that same old smell of something burning. She slipped *inside*, reaching, finding the waves, the currents, the invisible, nonmaterial handles that could carry her wherever her thoughts would take her. With longing and sorrow, she reached with a hand she didn't have and touched a block.

It leaped through the veil and became a solid gray block, part of her world.

She reached for another, then another, then felt herself expand into a *will* that had no shape, no size, just presence, surrounding and permeating those blocks. They all joined her, became real within her envelope. She hung on, learning the feeling, the effect. They weren't hula hoops, doves, or singing bottles and they were no fun to watch, but they were hers.

"I'm Mandy Whitacre," she heard herself say, "and I want to go home."

"Excellent!" Parmenter shouted. "Excellent!"

Wham! She was back under the canopy, sitting on the blocks. Her backside was getting sore without a pillow. They'd have to have a word with Parmenter about breaking her concentration.

Parmenter was on his feet, calling into his headset. "Did you get that?"

* * *

Moss was impressed, scanning the monitors. "I copy Delta thirty-two on thirty-two, Kiley twelve on twelve, Baker twenty-three on twenty-five, a little short but within limits. I would say we have a match."

Parmenter threw back his head in jubilation. "Ahhh! So far, the theory works!"

"So you got what you wanted?" she asked, feeling very tired.

"Phase one, complete! We've established that you can combine yourself with other objects to compose one unified mass! Very good. *Very* good! Now note that, remember that, remember how you did it."

Dane returned from the dark, stepping back under the canopy.

"I guess we got it," she told him.

He smiled at her. "I could feel it."

Fourteen days to Mandy's premiere . . .

Emile DeRondeau handed Dane a pair of safety glasses, a requirement for being on the main shop floor. "You should know, Seamus Downey's already here. He likes to keep his nose in everything."

"Oh. Oh, that's good," Dane replied, putting on the glasses. "The closer he's watching the better."

"Exactly."

Emile DeRondeau's company, EDR Theatrical Design and Effect, occupied an expansive building that used to be a major grocery store and was one of the backstage wonders of the showbiz world. Some of the most memorable and impressive set designs, stage effects, and convention displays originated in this place, conceived and constructed by Emile and his team of eight semi-eccentric dream builders. The place sounded like a factory, with the incessant whirring of drills, whining of saws, and growling of grinders and sanders.

Emile led the way through the main shop to Room C, tucked

away in a corner of the building and placarded against casual visitors. In the center of the room, the pod hung like a plumb bob from a ceiling hoist, suspended a foot off the floor. It was functional but still in the bare plywood stage until all the gimmicks and safety features were tested.

Standing next to it, getting a thorough briefing from one of Emile's builders, was Seamus Downey.

"Mr. Downey!" Dane called out, walking right up to him.

Mr. Downey's face tightened a moment, but he immediately put on a smile. "Well. This is a surprise."

Dane extended his hand.

Downey shook it and asked, "What are you doing here?"

Emile piped in, "It was my request, actually. Eloise needs a safety coach, Dane was the first one I thought of. Turns out they already knew each other!"

"Yeah," said Seamus, his smile crooked. "Small world."

Dane looked the pod over, allowing himself to come close to Seamus for a lowered-voice conversation. "Just so you know, you are her manager, Mr. Downey, and I respect that. I'm only here to assure her safety. It's a technical role."

"Looks to me like you couldn't stay away."

Dane smiled. "Well, we have our friendship, but we'd make a pretty odd-looking couple, don't you think?" He poked his head through the escape hatch, inspecting the pod's interior. "Just give her some time. As near as I can tell, you're definitely in the game. As for me, when the stunt's over, my job's over and I'm going home. But it's a privilege being here and I want to thank you."

Seamus eased a bit. "Okay. You're welcome. We all want Eloise to be perfectly safe."

Emile called, "Eloise, you ready?"

Mandy was perched on a chair against the wall, watching the little encounter between Dane and Seamus and reminding herself not to show any feelings about it. She was wearing navy sweats and a body harness and wrapping each ankle with a sport bandage to protect her from the shackles. One final wrap around her left ankle and she was ready.

Dane greeted her and talked only about the stunt. "Now, I know heights don't bother you much, but you're going to be upside down and hanging by your ankles a hundred and fifty feet off the ground, so we're going to do a little fear inoculation and step through this slowly."

Emile signaled the hoist operator. He raised the pod to where it aligned with an escape platform fifteen feet above the floor. With a quiet whirring, the six panels composing the bottom of the pod opened like a flower, and a second cable passing through the pod dropped back down.

A nasty-looking pair of leg shackles were laid out on a tumbling mat immediately below the pod. Mandy stepped up and a crewman clamped them around her ankles as Dane explained, "These shackles are safety-wired so they won't fall off and hit you on the chin and embarrass you in front of all those people. Make sure the safeties are in place before they hoist you up. Now, this cable hooks to your body harness . . ."

Dane kept explaining, she kept rehearsing and testing. With her ankles shackled and her hands cuffed to a chain about her waist, she lay down on the mat and the hoist took her up, feet first, until she was hanging upside down with her face even with Dane's.

"How you feeling?" Dane asked.

"Like a bat," she answered.

"Your weight should be on the harness, not your ankles."

Her ankles felt fine. "Good to go."

"Okay." Dane almost touched her. She couldn't touch him, she was handcuffed. He renewed his business-only face. "We'll see you upstairs." He said to the hoist man, "Up slowly."

The cable raised her. With her chin to her chest she could look up past her feet and see the pod about to swallow her like a man-eating plant. To one side she could see Dane hurrying up the scaffold stairs to meet her at the top.

An invisible guide wire kept her turned toward the rear of the pod and the escape hatch. Feet first, she slipped inside until her feet rested on the pod's ceiling. She hung the chain that bound her ankles on a hook in the ceiling, and a quick outward roll of her feet tripped the shackles open. "Legs are free," she said, then pressed a button with her toe to close the six petal doors. They whirred shut below her, a soft cradle came up against each of her shoulders, and she was sealed inside, in the dark.

She heard Dane's voice right outside.

"Okay, cuff release."

Bending her elbows triggered the cuffs—they slipped off.

"Hands on the grips," he told her. "Cable release when you're ready."

On either side of her, at shoulder level, was a short handgrip. She grabbed on. The grip on the right included a small lever she compressed with her hand. Click! "Cable free."

"Now drop your knees toward your chest . . ."

Her knees pressed against the panel in front of her but nothing happened. "Uh, am I doing this right?"

"Your knees should be pressing against the panel."

"They are."

"Oh, brother!" Dane yanked a packing bolt from the escape hatch locking mechanism. "Attention, everybody!" All the techs and observers on the floor looked up at him. He held up the bolt for them to see. "This packing bolt should only be in place during transport of the pod. Be sure to flag it and remove it before the stunt. Got it?"

They were embarrassed. Good thing. Seamus looked disgusted, but with good reason.

"Okay," he called to her, "knees against the panel."

She kneed the panel and it popped open. She pushed against the grips, lifting her body, and with one quick tumble, she was out on the platform. High fives.

"Is she out?" came Seamus's voice from below.

Mandy peered around the mirror system that would hide her escape and gave him a thumbs up. He looked astounded, then delighted.

Okay, so more than just the illusion was working.

* * *

Twelve days before Mandy's premiere . . .

Dane met with Preston Gabriel, Emile DeRondeau, and Keisha Ellerman in a tree-shaded picnic area behind an elementary school near Preston's house.

"Mandy's checked out in the pod," Dane reported. "All systems are go."

Emile asked, "Go? Going?"

Keisha told him, " 'All systems are go.' It's old astronaut talk."

"Ohhh."

Dane asked Preston, "Comfortable with the big room show?"

"It's coming together on schedule. Emile's building the sets and I'll bring up some effects from LA. We'll be ready for the premiere."

"So Keisha, what've you got?" Dane asked.

Keisha opened her sketchbook. "The Grand Illusion involves these two designs . . ." She flipped to the pages. "This one, in black leather with silver tunic, is in keeping with the macabre, medieval aspect of the stunt's opening. The cuff release is integrated into the waistband, and I'll include some extra banding around her ankles as she requested. It's cut with a little extra room to fit over this one . . ." The flowing, angelic costume in glimmering white got an immediate reaction. "This was her idea, something totally opposite the black outfit to express a metamorphosis from death to life, escaping this world and soaring to heaven. The train and the streamers fold up against her back inside the leather suit, and the quick change deploys in less than a second." Keisha loved the thought of it. "Like a butterfly from a cocoon."

"Weight?" Preston asked.

"Ten and one-half ounces."

He nodded with a smile and wrote it down.

"The harness is sewn into the gown in this waistband, in the sash, and in the bodice. And these slots running along the tops of the sleeves will hold the torso rigging and trapeze clamps."

"Those clamps are nearly ready," Emile told her.

"What about the rigging?" Dane asked Emile.

Emile looked at Preston, who shared his concern. "The weight turned out to be a problem. We'll have to go with a smaller-size filament. It'll handle the load but it's tougher to keep from tangling and obviously it's tougher to see."

"We're sewing it up right now," said Preston. "We'll test it tomorrow and give you a report."

"Fantastic."

"So how's she enjoying the hang gliding?"

Dane allowed himself a grim chuckle. "It's the only thing that doesn't make her nervous."

chapter

48

Ten days before Mandy's premiere . . .

Hands on the control bar and take off running. Feel that big kite lifting, pulling on the harness. Step off, ride on the air. You're a bird.

It was Mandy's second solo, and none too soon. She sailed close to the mountain slope, picking up speed, rocks and scrub blurring under her and looking close enough to tickle her belly. Down the slope was an SUV parked on a dirt road, its tailgate open, its cargo space filled with cages of doves. Preston Gabriel stood ready.

She'd reached through time and space and guided her doves plenty of times before, but never from a hang glider, and never quite as many.

Preston released the birds—twelve this time—and they fluttered from the SUV like tiny angels, wings flashing in the sun. They were circling, orienting, looking for her. She veered slightly left to keep them to her right.

"C'mon, birdies!" she called. She reached, wide awake, eyes open, much of her mind on her own flying.

There! She found Carson, her veteran, el primo. He responded right away, flying in the envelope of her invisible hand, power climbing to meet her. Maybelle and Lily followed him as they always did; Bonkers came around from one of his search circles, made eye contact, and came from behind. She had them, could feel them, and they could sense her, their Momma Dove. Now for the others. She'd worked with them on the ground and gotten them used to the effect. She hoped the training would stick in flight.

It did! First one, then two, then another one, then three more, then the rest all responded to her interdimensional touch—*Oops! Not that way, over here!*—and followed as she swooped past the SUV and Preston Gabriel waved.

She caught an updraft and could feel the sudden lift in her stomach. *C'mon, birdies, c'mon!*

They followed her in no particular formation, just flying along, playing a game.

Okay . . . Carson, take the lead. . . .

She reached and guided Carson to a point straight ahead of the wing, then set Lily and Maybelle wing-to-wing behind him. Bonkers happily slipped into the rear of the diamond formation.

Now for the point of the exercise: could she handle the rest of the birds and still have enough awareness to fly the glider? She still had envelopes around the others and extra copies of herself to keep track of things, so she and some other shes—she didn't count how many, she was too busy flying the glider—went to work putting this dove here, those two over there, arranging, arranging, holding in place, aligning—*wow, what a trip!* The doves seemed to like it. They certainly weren't alarmed. Maybe they felt sheltered, as if back in their nests.

The moment came. She got them into formation, the diamond out front, four wing-to-wing on the left in a swept-back line, four wing-to-wing on the right in a swept-back line, one big, graceful migratory V aligned perfectly with the glider's leading edge—and they were holding formation! She could feel, touch, guide each and every one of them, and they were letting her, easy and steady, just doing what birds do.

It was weird, but oh, so beautiful!

Eight days before Mandy's premiere . . .

Preston Gabriel had to strike a few deals and grease a few palms, but he got what he wanted: use of a rubble-strewn vacant lot where an old hotel had been imploded and a new one would soon be built. The lot was one of the few open areas left in town, and as luck and

Providence would have it, only one block from the Orpheus. Wearing orange reflective vests and hard hats to look like they belonged there, Preston and a crewman walked the empty ground and looked back at the Orpheus to get a compass bearing. According to the weather forecast, the winds should be light and favorable. A little prayer might help.

The day before Mandy's premiere . . .

VOOOOM!

Now, that was one impressive volcano. When the forty propane jets ignited and filled the crater with flame, the effect made Dane jump. He could feel the heat halfway up the bleachers. Andy the stage manager had warned all cast and crew to clear the stage for the burn, and with good reason. The heat was enough to singe their hair if not worse.

Emile, who sat beside him, asked, "What do you think?"

Dane had to force himself to look at Emile's creation, the conical top of a volcano about 15 feet across and 6 feet high, the right size to dominate center stage and incinerate a pod dropped down its throat from 150 feet. Had he the presence of mind he would have said it drew curiosity, looked big budget, created anticipation, would be fun to watch, brought thrill to the stunt . . . but he couldn't find the words.

He could see her through the blackening glass, crumpled over the steering wheel, the deflated airbag curling at the edges, melting into her face.

The volcano was setting afire the disposable fake trees near the crater's edge. The effect was meant to frighten and add an element of danger. It worked. Dane looked away from the flames. "Impressive, Emile. I mean, *really* impressive."

Emile had to speak up over the simulated, amplified roar of the eruption. "As good as I could do for the money. I told Vahidi it didn't have to be this big, but he's concerned about the other volcano in town. He wanted something that would compete. Are you okay?"

The heat, the sound, even the smell . . .

Her hair crinkling, vaporizing down to her scalp . . . steam and smoke rising through her blouse.

"Well, let's give it a go," he said, just wanting to get it over with.

Emile radioed the crane operator, "Let her go."

One hundred and fifty feet above the volcano, a dummy test pod hung from the cable. When the crane operator released the hook, the pod fell—it seemed to fall forever—and landed in the volcano with a carefully engineered crash and explosion that produced a ball of fire and a shower of fireworks. The pod was incinerated, just like that.

Just as planned, without a hitch. Dane felt sick. "Can you turn it off, please?"

"Sure." Emile spoke into his radio, "Okay, kill the volcano."

The volcano died with a smoky mutter, the shards and splinters of the fallen pod still flaming in its throat.

Here and there around the stage and bleachers, cast and crew applauded. Dane only wished he could have been stronger.

Emile must have read his face. "Dane. It's okay. It's going to work out."

Of course, he thought, *she won't be in the pod. She'll be long gone.*

They'd run everything, starting at two o'clock, and the whole show took twenty minutes from Mandy's magical appearance in the maw of the volcano—no fire at the time—to her soft-as-a-feather landing back on the stage in her hang glider, her doves circling about her. Turning on and testing the volcano came afterward just in case something unforeseen occurred that would have posed a danger. Nothing unforeseen happened.

Not that it couldn't.

Mandy, out of her costume and back in her jeans and jacket, came back on the stage. With an assist from Andy, she inspected the smoldering embers of the dummy pod in the volcano. When she looked up at Dane, he could tell it was for reassurance. He could only send her a thumbs-up and mouth Emile's words "It's going to work out."

They were ready to roll.

The night before Mandy's premiere . . .

Mandy returned with Parmenter to the canopy in the desert, the

35.76 concrete blocks, and Parmenter's preoccupied rattling about Bakers and Kileys and numbers that meant nothing to her. Dane was not there, on purpose. They all agreed, even though it pained her, that having him close quelled her tension, eased her longing, blunted that particular edge of unrest that she needed to . . . how did Parmenter put it?

"Remember," he said, helping her tape the sensors in place once again, "we need to reproduce as closely as we can the conditions of that day. Anything you can recall, any feelings you may have had, you need to bring those back because they are what brought you within reach of the Machine's timeline."

That day was the day she was ambushed but escaped and, in a drugged stupor, fled to Dane's ranch—at least that's what she understood to have happened. Having been in a drugged stupor, she just plain didn't remember it, and that was the problem—and yes, they had considered drugging her again to reproduce that condition; but decided that wasn't the prime condition, being ambushed and in danger of death was.

All she could do was her best, just try to be scared, as if a killer were chasing her. It sounded like Method acting, something she hadn't quite mastered.

"Now remember," Parmenter was saying, "until the Machine is recalibrated, you have primary control. It will change its settings to accommodate whatever you're doing. The real challenge will come during the retrace. The Machine will be recalibrated and you'll be on your original timeline, but you'll still have to control the Machine from there, which is going to be trickier."

"Got it," she said, not wanting to hear it all over again.

"We're ready." He said it again into his headset, as if Moss needed to be told separately, "Loren, we're ready."

Back in the lab, Moss was at his station, watching the graphs and readings on the monitors. "And . . . may we have a word in private?"

"Yes, I'm on the headset. Go ahead."

"I suppose her vitals are what we want: her blood pressure's up, her heart is racing. But I'm getting nearly flat readings from the Machine. She's not getting through."

"Any suggestions?"

"I suggest you stop yakking so much and just let the kid work it out."

"Oh. Yeah, you might be right."

Mandy stood facing the stack of blocks, trying not to calm down in any general sense, but in one particular sense. She had to have singleness of mind and will, but at the same time be agitated and, if possible, distraught. *Verrrry simple.*

Parmenter sat down and just smiled at her. "Go ahead. I'll be quiet."

One goal of tonight's session was to manipulate the blocks, all 35.76 of them, at the same time and see what that felt like, *if* she could even do it. She pretended they were doves and reached for the first block just as she reached for Carson while in flight. *There. That was easy.* As she and Parmenter watched, it lifted off the stack. It felt heavy to her, just like a big ugly concrete block, but it was floating, moving wherever she wished it to go, back and forth, turning on an axis.

Okay, now for the second one. No problem. She'd done this with hula hoops, microphones, bottles, spinning quarters, tennis balls.

She kept going, lifting three at once, then four, then five. Eventually she had ten of them circling the remainder of the stack like old movie Indians attacking a wagon train. Parmenter was excited as he watched, but he kept his promise and stayed quiet.

Thirty-two blocks all swarming around like bees was wild, very crowded, and scary enough to make Parmenter back away. The biggest trick was to keep them swarming without hitting each other, which got to be like that old rub-your-tummy-and-pat-your-head game, a lot to keep track of. It helped to keep splitting her mind into subminds that rode on the back of each block as if she, she, she, she, she, and all the other shes were driving ugly, 42.5-pound bumper cars.

After 32, then 35.76 were no bigger deal.

Now. Could she control all these blocks and be distraught? She kept driving the blocks and driving the blocks as she let one more thought come in, that of dangling at the end of a cable 150 feet off the ground. That didn't make her distraught, just nervous. She thought of Dane, the aspens, the white fence, the big ranch house on the hill . . .

Oh, brother. She could sense her Deltas and Bakers and Candlestick Makers falling off.

Yep. Parmenter was frowning as he watched his monitor and listened to his headset.

"No, no," said Moss, "she's holding steady on the accumulated mass, but her corridor isn't moving. She still has a discrete timeline."

"Should I say anything?" Parmenter asked.

"You could try saying 'Boo.'"

She tried remembering Clarence and Lemuel, how conniving they were, how much it hurt to be zapped with a taser and jabbed with a needle. That got her dander up, but that was anger more than fear. She thought of escaping from them and running back to the ranch—the ranch? Where'd the ranch go? She'd lost it.

"Umm . . ." Parmenter said. "Is there something I could do that would frighten you?"

The blocks broke free and clunked to the ground. Mandy bent in frustration, hanging her head. She felt so tired.

Parmenter got something from Moss through his headset. "Yes, right, I'm getting the same thing here."

Moss scanned his monitors once again, a curious smile on his face. "Well, she is getting there, she's a little closer each time."

Parmenter came back, "But how long can we keep this up? The others are . . ." He lowered his voice, apparently to keep Mandy from hearing. "You know the situation there. We can't keep DuFresne and his bunch on hold forever, and we certainly can't keep a lid on what we're attempting. Sooner or later it's going to come to light and we'll miss our chance entirely."

Moss nodded, smiling more broadly. "I know. I think you're right." He looked over his shoulder.

Immediately behind him, face lit by the monitors, was Dr. Martin DuFresne. He was hearing every word over a speaker and nodding in amused agreement with Parmenter's appraisal. Next to DuFresne was the man they all referred to as Carlson. The project team knew little or nothing about him except that he was the one who brought large sums of cash in a briefcase on a regular basis and acted as if he and the people he represented owned the whole project, which, for all practical purposes, they did.

Moss continued, "But I think she has enough on her mind right now. She has a premiere tomorrow. You can't expect her to handle all this tonight."

Parmenter nodded to Moss, who couldn't see him, then addressed Mandy. "You've done very well, just moving along step by step. Don't be discouraged. We'll get there."

"We'd better," she said as she peeled off the sensors.

Dane sat alone in Preston's dining room going over his checklist one last time, page . . . after page . . . after page. Every item was already verified and checked off twice by himself, Preston, and Emile, but if he wanted to sleep at all tonight, he would have to go over it one more time just in case that one little thing that slipped everyone's mind would come to his. By God's grace, if it was there he'd think of it before he fell asleep.

The doorbell rang. At nearly eleven P.M., that did not feel right. Preston was on the road somewhere between LA and Vegas, and of course he wouldn't ring the doorbell. Dane wondered if Preston kept any firearms in the house, but it was a little late to be thinking about that, and maybe a little paranoid.

He went to the door and looked through the peephole.

Well . . . !

He had to crack the door open and put his finger to his lips—Parmenter said the house might be bugged—but after that, he flung the door open and gave Arnie Harrington a hug.

* * *

It was Parmenter's turn to sleep overnight at the lab; he'd worked
and bargained and made offers to make it happen that way, and Moss
seemed only too happy to sleep in his own bed that night.

Well and good. Parmenter had things to do he didn't want anybody to see, such as weighing himself on a medical scale he'd borrowed from upstairs, then combing carefully through his office for
his notes, files, and hard drives, all the essential secrets of the Machine's development and how it worked. He put them all in a box,
then weighed himself holding the box.

Not quite.

He threw in a paperweight and two manuals.

Too much.

He took out the paperweight.

Okay. Within limits.

Just after midnight, two semitrucks exited the Las Vegas Freeway
and turned up a street one block from the Orpheus. They belched,
rumbled, and hissed onto the rubble-strewn vacant lot and parked
side by side. Preston Gabriel and two of his crew hopped down from
the cab of the first one; three more of his crew climbed down from
the cab of the other. They would sleep in the trucks that night, but
first they had a lot of prep to do.

Dane took Arnie for a walk through the neighborhood and told him
enough to keep him awake worrying. The rest, he supposed, would
have to wait until a day long after tomorrow when the story would
have an ending. With Arnie tucked in on the living room couch,
Dane turned in, easing into the big four-poster in Preston's guest
bedroom. He set the alarm for six in the morning, clicked off the
lamp . . .

And lay sleepless for a little while, dwelling on an image that
hovered in his mind—a snapshot that still existed in an album back
in Idaho: Mandy, not in a glimmering gown on a big stage, exulting
in the thrill and applause of her audience, but in pants and a top

she made herself on a portable sewing machine they took every-where with them on the road, standing at an outdoor picnic grill in a public park, cooking up their dinner. They had no roof over their heads other than a travel trailer, no future beyond a month or two of low-paying festivals, county fairs, or Grange hall gigs, and yet there she was, flipping burgers and boiling green beans, her heart chained to his for the distance. That was forty years ago.

Only the Lord God could have brought him such a woman. He never could have found her himself, never could have known hers would be the kind of love that would last so long and still be so te-nacious despite a gulf of age and memory. She was a kid who didn't even know who he was, but still she came looking.

He hadn't thought of it in these terms until now, but maybe this was why he always opened doors for her, let her take his arm when they walked, stood when she entered the room. Loving her had al-ways been easy, but somewhere along the way he just knew he had to honor her.

Mandy was numb with exhaustion, one blink away from sleep, but at long last she was alone and it was quiet, and after tomorrow nothing would matter the way it did now. She knelt by her bed.

"Dear Lord, I gave you my life a long time ago and I meant it, so whatever it is, or was—only you know—it's yours. Near as I'm allowed to know, most of it's already happened and it's like I missed it, so I hope you don't mind my praying backward—I figured I could since time is all messed up anyway—but I hope I lived my life well and you're pleased, and . . . whatever my life was—and you know and I don't, so I'm just saying this, just asking—if it's okay with you, could it really be true? Could I please have lived my life with Dane? Could I please have been his wife? That's the only way I can imagine it, and that's what Dane and everybody tells me, so I hope that's your way of seeing it, too. I hope we had a great life together.

"But even if I was never in love with him, and even if we were never together, thank you for letting me meet him and love him for just a little while, as weird as it was. I pray you'll always take care of him and reward him for being the wonderful man he is. He treated me really well. Just wanted to say so.

"Guess I'll see you tomorrow."

She climbed into bed and turned off the light.

chapter

49

At 5:00 A.M., March 25, Parmenter was at the command console of the Machine, running simulations of what might be to come and checking the readings that resulted. He could tell Mandy was still asleep. The monitors were void of activity and, apart from maintaining Mandy's secondary timeline, the Machine was at rest, allowing him a limited but sufficient access to its functions. This would be his only opportunity.

At 5:20, having double-checked his times, readings, and figures, he weighed himself, holding the box containing his notes, printouts, and hard drives. He'd lost one pound during the night, probably due to dehydration and elimination.

At 5:50 he accessed the Machine. The processing time was snail-paced but he got the input prompt he wanted and entered 14:24:09, two-twenty-four and nine seconds in the afternoon, today.

He added a book to the box and weighed himself and the box again. Within limits.

At 5:54, based on a conversation with Dane regarding when Dane planned to get up that morning, he entered some presets to initiate a function at precisely 6:00 A.M.

At 5:55 he went up the steps to the glass enclosure and, for the first time since Mandy's reversion, opened the door. The stench of the bloodied sheet brought back the gruesome memory of September 17, but Parmenter's disgust was mixed with a scientist's regret. To put forward a theory, these molecules staining the sheet—skin cells, fluids, blood—did not revert with Mandy because they no longer composed something living in the present and possibly because they were not part of the arrangement of molecules that composed the living Mandy in 1970. Under any other circumstances he would have devoted himself to testing the theory and confronting the plethora of riddles and questions that remained, but that was only the scientist side of him. The human side, prevailing, could only do the right thing.

He stepped inside the enclosure, closing the door behind him, then sat on the bench holding his box of knowledge and secrets. He waited.

At 6:00 A.M., Dane's alarm jolted him. He reached over and shut it off, then sagged back upon the pillow, waking up to the burden of this day and the visceral wrenching that left him only during his few precious hours of sleep.

Oh, Lord, is this day really happening? It's the stuff of bad dreams, not real life. If I don't get out of bed, maybe I'll wake up for real in a little while.

Such words, such thoughts. This day had to happen, as unavoidable as life always was. He flopped over on his back and stared at the real ceiling fan above him, still there just like everything else. He got up and got started.

At 06:00:00, March 25, the Machine awakened, the enclosure glowed an eerie blue, the interdimensional core beneath the bench hummed with energy. Parmenter sat still, letting the program run, recording his mass, his exact location, and exactly when in the course of time this event occurred. After five seconds, the program completed, the Machine went dark, and Parmenter found himself in a strange, non-typical state of mind: he'd just done the last thing he could have done.

By 7:30 A.M., Andy's stage crew was onsite, giving the bleachers a final cleanup and dressing up the stage, placing a few more artificial plants, trees, and stones to suggest a medieval, fairy-tale forest and replacing the burned trees around the volcano with fresh ones.

The sound man was running the sound effects and music cues, making sure they all lined up with the script, which they did. The ground-shaking rumble of a volcano, the explosive thud of a pod landing in the volcano's crater, the *whoooosh!* of a hang glider circling to earth, all playing against a thrilling musical sound track, were great people attractors. Curious tourists and passersby paused at the ribbon barriers around the parking lot to see what was going on, and from there could read the splashy signage telling them there would be a spectacle on this very spot at two that afternoon.

On the roof of the Orpheus, the three-man hang glider crew gave Mandy's glider one more preflight while monitoring the wind sock on the roof and the wind sock on the ground. So far so good, but even mild breezes boiled and swirled around and between the high structures on the Strip, and if the winds got too intense, Mandy would have to fall back on her rappelling routine.

One block away, Preston and his crew unfolded a sixty-foot platform that spanned the top of one truck and trailer, and on top of this they carefully laid out a foot-thick, sixty-foot-long cluster of fine fibers bound with Velcro loops. They had a wind sock as well, installed on the other truck's radio antenna. Right now it barely stirred, but that could change as the day warmed up.

By 8:00 A.M. Dane had made the rounds checking on everything and now stood with Emile on the stage, "preflighting" the pod prior to hoisting it aloft and second-guessing his own design. *I could have . . . maybe I should have . . . this is a little awkward, I could have put it over here . . .*

But the design, as it was, was sound and the escape hatch was functional. Given that, the greatest danger today, if any, would be human error.

Which put it all on Mandy, and if there'd been an easier way he would have taken it.

* * *

At 9:00, Mandy arrived with Seamus, and while Seamus oversaw everything and took videos, she squeezed into the pod for one last go-through with Dane and Emile.

While she squirmed inside the pod, testing the petal doors, shedding the shackles and cuffs and tripping the escape hatch, she remained detached and clinical, never suggesting through tone or action that there were any galactic-size issues overshadowing this whole day, never showing that there had ever been or would ever be a love between herself and Dane, the clearest and farthest opposite of the truth. Dane followed the same script, to the point that she hungered for assurance, for one moment when they could say something . . . anything.

Maybe when it was over. For now, with the clock ticking, there was only the Grand Illusion—the timing, the devices, the costume change, the winds, getting it right.

And, of course, there was Seamus.

At 10:05, Seamus called Mandy, Dane, and Emile together and suggested they run one more test flight of the hang glider. Mandy was agreeable, but given that it was the surprise ending for the stunt and that people were beginning to linger around the perimeter of the parking lot, they decided to forgo it. Everything else was ready. The pod was safe and sound with the stage crew keeping an eye on it, ready to hoist into position at the top of the show.

At 11:23, Parmenter and Loren Moss were seated at the command console, monitoring the readings as they had been doing for days on end, and of course, until the Grand Illusion actually took place, there wouldn't be much to monitor. At the moment, Mandy's readings were predictable: quivering, fluctuating, exerting small flashes and distortions on the space-time fabric as if she were troubled and nervous. Parmenter and Moss found it easy to stray to other topics of conversation. Two staff members, by now indifferent to this whole monotonous process, sat at the table eating some fresh doughnuts and talking about sports.

* * *

At 12:00 noon, as the signs and the newspaper and television ads all promised, the ribbons around the parking lot came down and folks were allowed to drift in, find a spot in the bleachers, get comfortable, and wait. They arrived in small trickles at first, but there was no doubt the trickle would turn to a flood as two in the afternoon approached.

Along with the people came the news trucks. Vahidi had seen to that. Mandy's Grand Illusion would be broadcast live on two stations and on the evening news on all of them, which was the greatest free publicity the Orpheus Hotel could ask for, and all the more reason to give them a real show.

At 12:30, Moss and Parmenter availed themselves of microwaved sandwiches from the kitchen and nibbled at them as they watched the monitors showing nothing interesting. One of the staff had brought in a television so they could watch the live broadcast, but right now the station was carrying a network show, six political pundits sitting around a table interrupting each other. When Parmenter turned down the sound, no one complained.

"What are we expecting, anyway?" Moss finally asked.

Parmenter had to think to come up with something. "I suppose we could be seeing the Machine approach its limits. From what I understand, this is going to be one heck of a stunt."

"Ohhh, that's for sure."

Moss's tone was a bit elevated when he said that. It made Parmenter wonder what he meant.

Moss piped up, "Bigger than what we're planning in the desert?"

What? Parmenter put up a hand of caution. "Not here."

Moss looked at the two staff members finding something to do at another station. "They can't hear us."

"We don't discuss it here."

"Well . . . maybe in cloaked terms . . ."

"Not in any terms!"

"But it does look promising."

Parmenter answered, if only to end the topic, "Yes. I would say the theory's working."

"But"—Moss looked all around the lab—"does it ever bother

you? Do you ever consider the cost in terms of the progress we've made? We would lose all of this."

"We've already lost it. We can't contain or control what this is, what it means, what it can do."

"What it can do. You can imagine how that looks through my eyes."

Parmenter nodded. "I realize—"

"Do you? I'm dying, and this"—he looked around the room at the amazing Machine—"this could have saved me . . . and come on, being realistic, of course I have to wonder if there isn't something we don't know yet, some tiny, hidden secret yet to be discovered that could change the rules."

Well, Parmenter thought, *it's happened.* "Loren, you do remember all the steps we went through where we talked just as you're talking now, and how those steps brought us to this pitiful point. *If* we hadn't stolen Mandy's body and reverted it without anyone's permission or knowledge; *if* we'd not tried a cover-up of Watergate proportions instead of admitting our error; *if* we hadn't, from the start, chosen the Machine over every human life we entangled with it; *if* we hadn't reached the point where we were actually plotting to retrace and kill an innocent young woman . . ."

"But you're fine with letting your own friend and colleague die."

Parmenter's heart sank. "It's more than your life and Mandy's. It's the nature of the Machine coupled with the nature of mankind. We've already demonstrated the results in this very lab, in our own choices and actions."

"I see it differently."

"I can understand that. I was expecting it, to be honest."

"Is that why you didn't trust me with Mandy's reversion data?"

Well, now we're getting down to it. "Loren, I would hardly trust myself, and it was an extreme act of trust for Mandy to do so. She trusted me with her life."

Just then the hallway door opened and several men came into the room. Parmenter recognized Martin DuFresne, Carlson, and three other physicians in DuFresne's camp—*speak of the devil!* There were three other men he'd seen maybe once before. They were the government interests who stayed deep in the background, unnamed, unseen, making things happen, definitely not to be trusted. Last through the door were two men he'd not seen before: one was dark, Mediterranean, perhaps Middle Eastern, the other blond, with a ruddy, pock-marked face.

He nodded at the men in greeting. They didn't nod back or say a word as they assembled in a rough line behind the command console, eyes unfriendly, wary.

Parmenter eyed them all, then Moss. "Don't tell me. You've changed sides."

Moss gave his hand a little turn upward. "It's my life, Jerry. If we keep going with the Machine recalibrated and Mandy no longer a factor, we might find a way to make a reversion stick."

"Yours, I take it."

Moss jerked his head in the direction of DuFresne and company. "They put me first in line."

Parmenter knew he had little or nothing with which to bargain. "I could never betray Mandy's trust. I can't give you the information."

Moss only smiled. "We have it."

Mandy let Seamus walk her to her dressing room—the new one above and behind the big room stage, the one with the rich carpet, mile-long makeup counter, huge, illuminated mirror, full bath with walk-in shower, and separate lounge area where she could relax, do interviews, entertain guests. He seemed particularly pleased to show her her name on the door, just the way she liked it: Mandy Whitacre.

Facing her, his hands on her shoulders, he told her, "This is it, sweetie. But don't think of this as an arrival; think of it as a beginning. This is where we place the bar and we rise from here."

"I hope I can do you proud," she said.

"I have every confidence that you will—"

She cut off his sentence with a kiss, then gave him a look she hoped would show her appreciation. "Gotta get ready."

He enjoyed the kiss, she could tell. "We'll all be waiting." He threw her a little salute and backed down the hall, keeping her in sight until she closed the dressing room door.

Once inside, she rushed into the luxurious, marble-floored bathroom and washed the kiss from her face.

* * *

Parmenter didn't have to ask; DuFresne seemed nearly bursting to tell him. "Seamus Downey was hired by our friends here, which meant he had all the inroads and connections with the government he could have needed. He got her a new identity so she'd blend into the system unnoticed, be able to work for a living and have as normal a life as possible, and most especially, confide in him when the time came."

Moss was allowed to finish the revelation. "When she visited the fairgrounds, he was there, taking note of the time, the date, and the exact location. We ran the information through the simulator and with a little finessing we got the numbers to jibe. We can recalibrate."

Parmenter pushed Moss to say it, maybe think it. "And then?"

"And then we recover full control of the Machine and a space-time fabric free of deflection, a blank slate. From there, we continue to explore, and I promise, we *will* work out the problems."

"You made no mention of what will happen to Mandy."

Moss only gave his head a dismissive tilt. "It's a foregone conclusion."

Parmenter looked at the gathering. "Or what will happen to me."

DuFresne spoke. "It would be impossible to ignore your immeasurable value to this project. We can only hope that, in time, you'll be able to put the greater good above these momentary difficulties. I can assure you, you'll be kept safe and the process will be painless."

"As a matter of fact," Moss added, "this is one way your invention can do you a world of good. When you wake up, you'll be a year younger, and as far as you'll remember, all this trouble never happened."

The thought of fleeing had no sooner entered Parmenter's head than a lightning bolt shot through his body and every motor nerve seemed to short out. He saw the pockmarked face above him and felt the prick of a needle in his neck, but he could do nothing about it.

At 12:54, Mandy sat alone at the oversize makeup counter where she really had to get going on her showbiz face and her showbiz hair, but had to be sure, had to try things first. Cradling her chin in one hand and keeping the other in her lap, she toyed with the lipsticks, makeup brushes, eyeliner, foundation, and blush, making them scoot about the counter like little bumper cars, each one independently controlled. A tube of mascara, an eyebrow pencil, and a lipstick brush did a drag race, popping wheelies at one end of the counter and zipping down the counter until the mascara spun out, the eyebrow pencil sputtered out, and the lipstick brush won, screeching around a tight victory circle and then dancing in victory. The foundation and a lipstick were doing a figure eight and about to collide in the middle; she made the lipstick jump over the foundation and continue on. She closed her eyes and placed herself aboard each little item as it scurried around the counter. This would have been a load of fun any other day.

As the makeup kept moving around the counter, she eyed a chair, reached invisibly, and lifted it, holding it in space. Beyond the chair, the three aspens jutted up through the floor and disappeared through the ceiling; the white paddock fence divided the room.

Sure would like to be there *right now.*

"Looks like our magician friend is rehearsing," said Moss, now in charge at the command console as his cohorts observed with unbroken attention. The monitors were showing small deflections as Mandy multiplied herself and made things move. "She is really good at this! She has twelve separate timelines working right now, each one controlling a different object."

DuFresne expressed the sentiments of all. "We have got to master this! We need to achieve this level of control."

"We will—or may I say, *I* will?"

"So what happens when we recalibrate? Will that kill her ability?"

"Now's when we find out." Moss entered the vital numbers. "We enter the ending point, 13:05:23, September 12, 1970, and have the Machine reverse-calculate from there back to 10:17:24, September 17, 2010. That should bring the Machine back to its original setting and we can regain control." He entered some more commands until the cursor blinked on the final field, Initiate. "Hang on to your hats." He hit the Enter key. The monitors filled with a flurry of numbers and graphic patterns moving faster than the eye could follow.

* * *

Clunk! The chair landed on the floor and toppled over. Mandy's mind went spinning away from the objects on the counter, and she could no longer see herself piloting each one. A lipstick and a makeup brush fell on the floor. The vision of the aspens and the fence dissolved. The room was deathly quiet, and Mandy felt as if she were totally, really there in the room, a solid floor beneath her, solid walls around her, no sense of drifting, no invisible currents and eddies swirling around her.

What happened?

She felt strangely awake, as if she'd been in a trance for the past several months. Was this how normal really felt? She forcefully blinked her eyes and looked about the room, just trying to perceive and understand it. *So this is where I am?* She could smell the newness of the carpet, the sweet smell of the makeup for the first time; there was no burning smell to cover it.

Is this normal? Maybe it is.

But . . . I can't have normal, not today.

She looked in the mirror and saw the same Mandy Whitacre she'd been since the county fair. That hadn't changed.

But something had.

50

The bleachers were filling up: a busload of bald and blue-rinsed retirees making a special stop, moms, dads, and restless kids, younger couples without kids, slightly seasoned couples away from their kids, single guys on a lark, single girls eyeing the single guys, older guys with younger women, tourists with all sizes and types of cameras. The crowd was buzzing, eyeing the stage, the whimsical forest, the volcano intermittently grumbling and burping smoke. The TV crews were setting up their cameras along the top of the bleachers, down on the ground, anywhere they could get a good shot, and Emile was advising them what would be happening and where.

Dane blended with the crowd, sitting on the top row of the bleachers but about to surrender his spot as the crowd pressed in. From here everything looked ready to roll, but he was making sure of the last few items on his checklist: cable cinch, tight; escape hatch packing bolt, removed; release hook, functional; stage clock—the oversize hourglass that ran for one minute—operative. The winds were favorable.

One thing still unchecked: the call he would have to get from Parmenter by 1:30 if, and only if, there was no need to go ahead. He checked his watch: 1:10.

In the makeshift sleeping quarters adjacent to the lab, Parmenter lay on the bed unconscious, his phone in his pocket.

In the lab, as Moss and DuFresne watched and the others wondered, streams and columns of numbers counted down and graphs jittered until finally, with an electronic warble, the Machine rebooted and the original control interface filled the screen, the fields clear.

With one victorious clap of his hands Moss announced, "Gentlemen, we are back online. I'll keep the fields open for her input and let her have control. We want her confident."

DuFresne spoke to Mr. Stone and Mr. Mortimer. "Let's get it done."

They hurried out the door.

He asked Moss, "So what if she tries to go interdimensional to escape?"

Moss wagged his head. "We won't give her that. The moment she's in the pod, we retrace." He puffed a little sigh of relief. "And with her total weight no more than 112, she won't have anywhere else she can go."

"Except the volcano," DuFresne suggested, amused at his own wit.

"What more could we ask for?"

One of the staff set a video monitor atop the console. "Seamus is sending video."

The monitor lit up and after some snow and flicker the picture appeared. Seamus was shooting from the parking lot, looking up at the bleachers, panning across the stage.

DuFresne donned a headset. "Seamus, can you hear me?"

Seamus, wireless earpiece in place, kept taking in the scene as he replied, "Loud and clear."

"Excellent," came DuFresne's reply. "Be advised, we have control of the room and the Machine is recalibrated. Stone and Mortimer are on their way."

"Very good," Seamus replied, giving them a view of the crane. "No problems here. They're going ahead with it."

Mandy stood in the middle of the dressing room, eyes closed, a silver, glimmering hula hoop in her hands, feeling the texture and weight, the curve of the circle, smelling the plastic. Her palms were sweating.

All right, now remember . . . remember!

She set the hoop against a chair, backed away, and tried to reach across space and time. The hoop just sat there, far away, untouchable, unreachable.

She looked at Bonkers, Carson, Maybelle, and Lily, perched peacefully in their cage, nibbling on seeds, preening. She tried to reach . . . she couldn't feel them, they didn't sense her.

What a fine fix to be in: she was normal, in the solid, real world, and *here* she was panicking. *Dear God, no! I've got to find it, I've got to find it—*

A gentle knock on the door. It opened.

Keisha, with costumes on hangers. "Hi. Guess it's time."

It was 1:20 when Dane stood beside the crane checking the zip line, the illusion's secret avenue back to the ground. From any angle of view the audience would have, it was obscured by the crane's boom and allowed the performer to descend to the ground unseen and finish the escape. The thing was a real pain to get right, but Emile managed. Dane's cell phone hummed on his belt.

"Yeah."

"Dane"—Mandy sounded troubled—"could you talk to me just a little bit?"

He sighed, and she probably heard it. He wanted to talk with her, touch her, open his heart more than anything else in the world, but would that achieve the effect they needed?

"Are you sure you should—"

"Dane, I just need . . ." She *was* troubled. "I need to see something, just *feel* something."

Oh, no. Not this late in the game. "Are you all right? Are you—"

"Tell me how we met."

He checked his watch. "Uh . . . you mean, at the fair?"

"Yes, tell me."

It would be all right to tell her, even the best thing he could do. He brought back the memory—not at all difficult, it was one of his favorites. "It was in the middle of Marvellini's dove routine. I was in the wings setting up the levitating table when I saw you in the front row—just you. Joanie and Angie were there, but the sunlight was on you, you were the one glowing. Your hair was like, well, like a sun-washed wheat field in summer, and the wonder in your eyes . . . I couldn't look away."

Keisha sat waiting, entirely patient.

Mandy sat on the edge of her chair, dabbing tears from her eyes, drinking in the sound of Dane's voice and every detail she wished she could remember.

"You loved those doves," he told her. "I could tell. You watched them more than Marvellini, and then . . . that dove—his name was Snickers—he must have picked up on that because he chose you over Marvellini. He came flying out of Marvellini's sleeve and headed straight for you. He landed on your finger like you already knew each other and he was really happy there. I think he would have stayed."

Dane could still feel what he felt that day, and it came through his voice. "It was my job to patch up the gaffes, so I ran down to get Snickers back, but when you stood up with that dove on your hand, and his little head right next to your cheek . . . I wished I had a camera, but that's okay, I can still see it, that image of you, just so perfect I had to get you up on that stage and . . ." A flood of emotion overtook him too quickly to disguise it, but maybe that was just as well. "When you danced across the stage and took a bow, I felt my future was determined from that moment. I felt, I knew, you were the one."

She'd have to do her makeup over again. But from somewhere, some part of her could feel him, even hear his voice without the phone. She looked across the room at the hula hoop and reached. It stood up, rolled back and forth, did a spin in place.

"Thank you, Mr. Collins." A quick, tear-blurred glance at ever-patient Keisha. "I gotta go."

*   *   *

Dane clicked off his phone and slipped it back on his belt. He cleared his eyes just as three people appeared on the stage: Seamus Downey and . . .

Dane edged behind the crane, out of sight. Remarkable. Shocking, actually. The other two were dressed in uniforms to make them look as if they were from the fire department. One carried a clipboard, and they seemed to be giving the stage an additional, last-minute once-over. The olive-skinned guy he was seeing for the first time, but the blond guy . . . he was wearing sunglasses and a fireman's dress hat, supposedly to hide his appearance, but his war-torn face Dane remembered vividly—he'd almost had a knock-down, drag-out fight with him back in his pasture in Idaho, and come to think of it, Mandy actually had.

Dane could see Emile in his control booth on the third level of the parking garage behind the bleachers. Dane got on his radio. "Emile, this is Dane."

"Emile. Go ahead."

"Who are those guys on the stage?"

"Fire inspectors."

"We've already passed inspection."

"Seamus called for it. He wanted to be sure."

"Oh, he did, did he?"

"I just got off the phone with the fire department. They didn't send them."

"I'll get right back to you."

So Seamus Downey, who miraculously produced a fifty-thousand-dollar settlement from the Spokane County Medical Center for hiring those two guys, was now in their company as they snooped around the effects. Bernadette Nolan was right: the hospital in Spokane never hired them.

But DuFresne and his government backers did, along with Seamus Downey, Mandy's bighearted manager who made it a point to find out exactly where and when Mandy's reversion placed her.

The three men were spending a noticeable amount of time checking out the pod.

Dane checked his watch. It was 1:30, and there had been no call from Parmenter. They all agreed that Parmenter would have to remain at his post for the plan to work, and the scientist said he had a contingency plan, but now Dane had to abide by Parmenter's final admonition, "If I don't call by 1:30, if you don't hear from me . . ."

He got on the radio again. "This is Dane. We have a go. Please acknowledge."

"This is Emile. We have a go."

"This is Preston. We have a go."

Atop the semi, Preston and three crewmen unfastened the Velcro loops from around the bundle of webbing and carefully lifted the top edge of what looked like a huge fishnet woven from fine, nearly invisible fibers.

In the lab, Moss and DuFresne received a quick message in their headsets from Mr. Stone. "All set."

By 1:30 Mandy had slipped on the white, angelic costume and then, with Keisha's help, folded and secured its flowing edges inside a black leather bodysuit.

Keisha closed up the last breakaway seam of the bodysuit and asked, "All right, how's that?"

Mandy did some stretches, went through a few dance moves, waved her arms about. "It's working."

"Looks good from here." Then she lowered her voice as if sharing a secret. "I allowed for a few extra pounds." She winked.

Mandy slipped a silvery tunic over the bodysuit and looked in the mirror, seeing once again Keisha's signature touch.

"Just like old times," Keisha said. "You look as marvelous as ever you did."

Mandy turned to face her. This was good-bye. "I wish I could have remembered you."

Keisha placed a hand on each side of her face. "I do earnestly hope to see you again."

At 1:40, Dane, Mandy, Emile, Max, Andy, and Carl met under the stage for a word of prayer. Mandy figured it was a prayer meeting one would only see in show business: she dressed in silver and black like a fantasy hero; Dane and Emile looking tense, still wearing radio head-sets; enormous Max dressed like an executioner, Mandy's shackles draped around his neck; Andy and Carl dressed like slithery hench-men from the dark side, Carl carrying Mandy's handcuffs. Dane and Mandy were the only Christian believers. Emile was agnostic, Andy was into Scientology, Max was searching and thinking his family ought to find a church somewhere, Carl didn't give religion much thought at all.

But they all prayed together because they were a team, and she could feel it: this was her moment, they'd all worked very hard to make it happen, and their hearts were with her.

Dane said the Amen and then let them know, "Gentlemen, it's been a privilege."

"Right on," "Same here," "Back at you," "Let's do it again some-time" . . . they dismissed to their stations.

"And lady," Dane said.

She gazed into eyes she needed time, precious time, to fully un-derstand. A moment, an eternity, passed, and there were no words. He finally looked to make sure they were alone and said quietly, "It's a go. God be with you." He turned his eyes away and without another word, walked out, leaving her alone in the semidark amid the panels and rigging and girders, alone to take hold, finish the show, and find her way back.

She sank onto a makeshift bench, her thoughts and feelings tending in one direction: *Lord, why me?* Then she smiled at herself, playing back a memory: Dane, the sorrow-worn widower, and she, the half-doped "hoper," in his living room, and she giving him a lecture about not giving up but living the rest of the life God had for him. Boy, was that big old shoe ever on the other foot now.

Except that—and how was this for weird humor?—the rest of the life God had for her might be no more than the next hour.

Andy and Carl brought in her hula hoop and let her know her doves were on their way to the third level of the parking garage. She thanked them and they left her alone again.

Alone. Ohh, she could feel it as if it were the story of her life, feel it so strongly it had to have been planned. By whom? She sighed. Same old answer: God—which brought a nice release: where was the point in giving up? If there was going to be a big old defeat, let it come from God, not her. It was better to take hold, finish the show, and find her way back . . . or die trying.

All right. That was settled.

She put the loneliness to work. *What I wouldn't give to see the ranch again, even fork up some hay and manure; have a mocha at the breakfast table; dance a waltz—no, some swing!—and I'd love to get back to that kiss we never finished.*

From where she sat she took hold of the hula hoop across the room and made it float in midair, turn, spin. She closed her eyes and petted her doves in their cages in the parking garage.

And for a moment she could see the aspens growing under the stage and a hint of the green pasture amid the girders in the dark.

At 1:51, Moss and DuFresne, fully aware of the eyes watching everything from behind them, maintained a confident air. Moss indicated the readings. "She's getting it back. We have a multiplicity of time-lines . . . weak at this point, but coming up to strength."

DuFresne asked, "Can you cut those timelines off?"

Moss nodded with confidence. "Just giving her some rope."

"Seamus, it looks good."

The video monitor showed a wide shot from the top of the bleachers, taking in the gathering crowd. The bleachers and a good half of the parking lot were full.

Just then, the television showed a live feed from the local station.

"Hey, turn it up!" said one of the Watchers.

DuFresne turned up the sound.

". . . on this sunny afternoon at the Orpheus Hotel Casino, live show business at its best, the Grand Illusion outdoor escape by up-and-coming magician and escape artist Mandy Whitacre. Hello everyone, this is Steve Kirschner . . ."

"And I'm Mark Rhodes."

"And this is a special, live edition of *Vegas Today*, your instant source for the latest entertainment news from the Entertainment Capital of the World."

* * *

Folks in the front reception area of Clark County Medical Center were paying half attention to the television in the corner while reading old magazines, texting on cell phones, and waiting.

Arnie Harrington, incognito in a jogging outfit, set aside a two-week-old *Time* magazine and paid full attention as the screen switched between a high angle of the bleachers and stage, a close-up of the stage, and a traveling handheld taking in any key point of interest.

Whatever happened, he'd know.

At 2:00 P.M., Emile, in the control booth with headset in place, cued the music. A fanfare sounded, the trees onstage began to sway, the volcano rumbled and belched white smoke. The crowd cheered and whistled, here to have a good time and already into it.

For Mandy, being under the stage was like being inside a huge, cartoonish clock striking noon. Valves were hissing, hydraulics gushing, levers jerking, pulleys spinning, all just above her head. She cowered a bit, pulling her tunic around her. Seeing Emile's marvelous brain-child from the bleachers was one thing; seeing it from inside was entirely something else and no less frightening.

Max, Carl, and Andy took it in stride. In the middle of all that busyness they hurried under the stage to their posts, Max and Carl onto the hydraulic lift, and Andy to the control panel to wait for the strains of creepy music, their cue. When the music played, Max and Carl gave a little wave, Andy hit the Up button, and up they went. The audience began to boo.

Dane eased over to the edge of the crowd at stage right and watched as Max and Carl, decked out and masked in black leather, popped out of the swaying forest and gave the booing crowd disdainful wave-offs like "bad guy" world wrestlers. They swaggered over to the pod, went through the motions of rigging it to the cable, then signaled the crane operator—once again, one had to overlook the incongruity of a monstrous, modern construction crane in a medieval setting. At least the crane itself was hidden behind a leafy, woodsy screen with only the huge boom to ignore.

The crane operator, nonchalantly sipping a cup of coffee, eased the lever back and the pod lurched skyward, shrinking, gently swinging on the end of the cable, tantalizing the audience with things to come. After a dizzying, neck-straining ascent it reached its highest point, 150 feet above the ground and directly above the volcano, a thin cable stretching down from inside the pod to the stage, another harbinger of future thrills.

Max and Carl swaggered into the trees to remain out of sight until needed.

Mandy arranged her tunic about her and took her place on the hydraulic lift immediately below the mouth of the volcano. From here she could look up and see the sky, clear and blue, the home of birds, of angels. Maybe hers, too.

"You okay?" Andy asked.

That brought her back to business. She crouched slightly to allow the effects that would happen above her and steeled herself. "Let's give 'em a show."

Andy threw some levers, actuated some valves.

To the delight of the crowd, the music turned bold and magical and, to the delight of every eye, a huge bubble slowly rose out of the volcano and perched with a soapy quiver in the volcano's mouth. It filled with smoke, making it look like a huge white marble, and then, with a puff of fireworks, it popped, the smoke cleared away, and there was Mandy Whitacre on a circular, silver platform, holding a glimmering silver hoop to frame her body and face.

Applause!

She'd never seen this big an audience in one place in the daylight, in front of her on the bleachers, to either side of her on the ground. For an instant she could identify with a trained whale at one of those big sea aquariums, holding a hoop, surrounded by laughing, applauding people in sunhats and sunglasses, sitting row upon row in the sun.

The music cue. Time for her routine. *Okay, here we go, let's do it!*

She went into dance moves, twirling the hoop above her head, making it spin like a coin atop her fingertips, then—*Come on, grab hold!*—setting it spinning like a wheel, wobbling a few degrees off axis for the cool look of it, suspended above her. The folks were with her, loving it.

She stepped out of the volcano and onto the stage, the hoop moving out before her until it hung in the air, wobble-spinning perpendicular to the bleachers, its silver coating flashing in the sun.

Now for the birdies!

She found, could *feel* Carson, Maybelle, Lily, and Bonkers as they launched from their handlers on the third level of the parking garage. Such troupers, day after day, aiming to please and all for a cuddle and some treats! *Celery leaves all around when this is over, guys and gals!*

She went to them on the waves of time and space, flew with them, guided them, and by now they understood her gentle proddings. They flew abreast in a wide formation over the audience, then fell into single file as they circled down and flew loop after loop through the hoop. Loop the Hoop!

The folks loved it.

On command, the doves broke out of the loop and flew a horizontal circle high above the stage while Mandy let the hoop flop sideways and wobble down to her waiting hands. As she held the hoop in outstretched arms to frame her body and face, the doves came down to rest, two on each arm, a charming portrait inside the hoop.

Ta-da! The crowd was hers.

Too bad it couldn't last. The "bad guys"—now Andy made three—came back onstage, emerging from the woods. The audience booed again. With a sorrowful face—only half acting—she sent the doves back to their handlers and dropped the hoop so that she stood within its circle. She tossed off her tunic and tried to *appear* ready. The music dropped to an ominous low drone signaling *Oh-oh, be careful, look out, this is dangerous . . .*

Tell me all about it.

Getting into the restraints wasn't the scary part. Max clamped on the leg irons with the same care he always used; Carl cuffed her hands with every regard for her comfort and safety. Andy brought the cable and hook over with the same caution and attention. They'd been through stunts like this many times before.

It was the pod, that tiny little box way up there. As she lay on the stage and Andy fixed the hook to her shackles and body harness, she could see straight up into that cavity no bigger than she was and not see the end of the darkness inside.

She'd never gotten used to that thing, never felt right about it, and concrete blocks out in the desert were fine, she could handle them, but this . . . it brought back every trapped feeling she'd ever had.

Her legs were bound. She couldn't move her hands. This time it scared her.

Use it!

"Ready?" Andy whispered.

The truth? *No,* she thought but couldn't say. *No, wait, I can't find it, I can't, I can't think . . .*

She was hanging upside down. The crowd, every face upside down, was dropping away below her. The blood was pounding into her head. She was gasping, clenching her fists, trying not to.

It's a go, he said. It's a go.

I'm not going to get out of there! I'm not ready! Oh, God, don't let them . . .

There was no way Dane could put aside the fear, not with her so small up there, arms and legs bound, hooked and dangling like a help-less fish. All he could do was stay put and stay steady, keep his mind on the details, make sure things happened when they should.

Fifty more feet to go, and then . . .

It was so far to fall.

She looked up past her feet. The pod was a predator with jaws wide open. A breeze played over her. She felt herself gently swinging, getting sick. The crowd was buzzing, stirring up. She could see straight down the volcano. It was huffing, smoking. Pilot flames burned inside the rim.

From a block away, Preston and his crewmen could see Mandy rising toward the pod, a flea on a thread with no appeal to turn back, slow down, find another way. History, her life, Dane's, theirs, the Grand Illusion, were relentlessly moving forward. All they could do was keep up.

Preston and three men were ready at their stations on the platform atop the semi, Preston holding one end of the net, a crewman holding the other end, and two crewmen evenly spaced along the length, supporting the middle. Two crewmen remained on the ground, waiting for Preston's signal.

She tried once more to reach for her birds, to touch them—

Her feet passed within the open petal doors, then her legs, her waist, her shoulders. Her shackled feet came up against the ceiling of the pod. She hesitated, let her head flop, and looked down. It was a sunny day. People were ant-size and alive down there, looking up at her through sunglasses, from under visors and sunhats. Kids were pointing. Big Max, now a tiny round spot of black, stood by the oversize hourglass, waiting to turn it over.

The volcano, a gaping, smoking orifice, was waiting.

It's a go.

She hung the shackles on their hook and tripped them open, then pressed a button with her toe to close the petal doors. They closed around her head and shoulders much tighter than she remembered, shutting out the world where the sun shined and life was happening. She was encased in the dark.

On the stage, with a growl and an impressive display of muscle, Big Max hefted the hourglass and flipped it upside down. As the deep rumble of an impending eruption came over the sound system, he, Carl, and Andy feigned panic and ran from the stage only seconds before the propane jets opened wide and the volcano sent up a tower of flame, igniting the fake trees. It was as frightening as anyone could ask for. Everybody screamed.

The sand in the hourglass was running: Mandy had one minute.

It was hard to breathe.

She could hear and feel the rumble below her, faintly discern the excited cries of the people. Less than one minute. *Think, girl, think.*

Bend your elbows! The cuffs opened, fell aside.

Reach. Reach. Control, now. Be there, touch them, guide them . . .

Nothing.

So dark, so tight, she couldn't move, could only muster one thought: *Oh, God, let me out of here!*

Her hands, shaking, went for the grips. She squeezed the lever on the right grip and felt the hoist cable click free.

What if . . . what if I can just . . .

She bent her knees against the escape hatch. *Maybe. Maybe. Oh, please . . .*

The hatch was a wall. It didn't budge.

The realization hit her like a punch in the stomach. The packing bolt. Someone did exactly what Dane expected they would do and there was no turning back. She wasn't ready to believe it. Her heart was racing, beating against her sternum. She cried, then screamed and kneed the hatch again. *Again.*

Sealed tight.

chapter

51

It was now 14:16:23 local time.

"Go, go, go!" said Preston.

His crewmen on top of the semi stretched the netting tight and above their heads. With the netting stretched, thicker strands were visible, running in courses across the net at sixteen-inch intervals, strands just the right size to be clutched by . . .

The two crewmen on the ground flung the big trailer doors open. Inside each ventilated trailer was a living, bustling, cooing *hive* of white doves perched like beads on row upon row of aba-cuslike frames—not hundreds of doves, *thousands*, startled by the opening of the doors and the sunlight beaming into the trailer's depths. Hundreds and hundreds took to wing and rushed out the trailer doors like a blizzard, white wings flashing. They rose into the air as one body, then scattered, swirled around in every di-rection, alighted on the roofs of the trailers, settled on the ground to look for grit or goodies, landed on the fence that bordered the lot, flew across the street to land on window ledges, streetlights, signs, the sidewalk. They stopped traffic, wowed the pedestrians, perched on anything and everything, flitted, preened, strutted, and bobbed . . .

But that was all they did. As for the thousands still perched in the trailers, they didn't seem to know what to do other than perch there.

Preston and his men stared blank-faced at the doves and then looked at each other.

In the lab, as DuFresne, Carlson, and the Men of Power watched, Loren Moss initiated the retrace with one keystroke. The whole room lurched enough to throw those standing off balance. They recovered, hands on chairs, the wall, a table, mindful to remain icy, ruthless, in charge.

Moss whistled in thrilled amazement, eyes on the monitors.

Mandy had only an instant to take back control of her situation, to shed the panic and see it through. She pressed her hands against the confining walls of the pod to steady herself. She breathed evenly, prayed . . .

Come on, girl, be cool, think, finish the show—

Ohh!

Mandy felt the pod lurch as if hit by a gust of wind and at that moment *awoke* from being in the pod, in the dark, so hemmed in she could hardly move to being in the pod, in the dark, so hemmed in she could hardly move, but *different*, as if she'd stepped out of the universe for an instant, then stepped back into the same place to find the place had changed. It was weird, far from normal, and yet . . . she'd felt this before. Where?

Something was rubbing, tickling her ears and neck. She thought her angel costume had popped out at her shoulders. She checked with her fingers . . .

Her hair was long and straight, hanging into the narrowing cavity below her. The realization stunned her, tightened her insides: the fairgrounds, under the tree, that's where!

Dane ran around the edge of the crowd, looking for any change, any indication. He got on the radio. "Preston, anything?"

* * *

Preston, his men, and their birds were becoming nuisances but that was all. "I've got nothing! No control whatsoever."

I've gone back, Mandy realized. *I'm starting over. I'm going to die in here.*

The pod was so tight she couldn't spread her arms from her body, could not bend her knees enough to kick. A scream only bounced back in her face, as trapped in here as she was.

"Look at that," said Moss, indicating a monitor. "She's stuck. No activity."

"Like an interdimensional flatline," DuFresne mused. "Dead to time and space." He looked over his shoulder. "Finally." The Watchers were pleased.

"Oh, Dane," she cried out loud, "I'm so sorry. It could have worked, it should have worked . . ."

Dane.

He was still in her mind like a permanent resident, a dear, clear thought when no other thought would come. *Let him be your starting point*, she told herself. *Tell me again, Dane. Tell me how we met, the name of the dove . . . Snickers, that was it. He flew down and landed on my finger . . .*

She gasped, the sound bouncing from the confining walls.

She could *see* Snickers landing on her finger, fluttering as he got a grip, folding his wings, looking at her as the crowd laughed. She could *see* the crowd, the stage, the poultry pavilion behind the stage, the trees, the fairgrounds.

She *remembered*!

She let the memory—yes, the *memory*!—play in her mind: Angie and Joanie giggling, Marvellini—he had black hair parted in the middle, an oversize handlebar mustache, a baggy tux with tails—playing it for laughs: "Snickers! He's quite the ladies' man, you know!"

And then a young man stood before her, his face the most pleasant thing in the world to look at, his eyes laughing and kind. He didn't try to recover Snickers from her hand, he just said, "Hi. What's your name?"

And she looked into those eyes and told him, "Mandy."

She could feel the grip of Snickers's hot little feet on her finger, the nap of his feathers . . .

Bonkers. Somewhere far outside herself, she could feel *his* feet—and by his reaction she knew he could feel her touch. Maybelle? Yes! Maybelle was there, too, listening. Lily popped into her awareness—she could see the little dove looking right at her.

DuFresne noticed one small, jittery bar appearing on a graph. "What's that?"

Carson popped into her consciousness, as if he didn't want to be left out. She stroked their necks, loved them up. She was with them.

Up in the parking garage, the four doves could not sit still. They chirped, fluttered, bobbed, and bowed in their cages until their handlers turned them loose. They flew over the audience and straight for the pod, circled it as if looking for something, then alighted on the top of the crane boom like little watchmen.

Now she found others . . .

"Preston!" said a crewman.

A dove was flying back. Two others, perched on a building ledge, alerted, fidgeted, then took to the air, returning. Four from a streetlight followed, heading for the trucks.

Were they just flying on an impulse, or . . . ?

Preston and his men held the net ready.

* * *

More bars appeared on the graph.

"Wait, wait, what's happening?" DuFresne wanted to know.

Moss tapped frantically at the keyboard. "She's creating time-lines."

"What!?"

"Hang on, I'll cancel them."

"She's supposed to be retraced!"

"She hasn't *completed* the retrace. She can still influence the Machine."

"Well, *fix* it!"

Moss tapped at the keys. A line dropped off the graph.

She lost two doves. *Oh, no, you don't! You come back here.* She found them again, with ten others.

She remembered Marvellini asking, "Young lady, how would you like a job?"

Forty others.

She could still hear the young man say, "Oh, by the way, my name's Dane."

And now she could see herself on the back of each dove, envision her arms about its neck. What a ride!

Dane's radio crackled. Preston's voice. "Dane, we might have something."

The monitor in the lab was coming alive with bars on the graph, interdimensional intensity waves, deflection vectors.

"What is going on?" DuFresne demanded, and now the Watchers were stepping up for a closer look.

"I'm canceling, I'm canceling!" Moss countered.

DuFresne watched the monitors. It didn't look like it.

She'd found it. The feel, the intuition, was different, like driving on the wrong side of the road or writing with the wrong hand, but she'd found it. Some of her reaches were dropping out for no reason, but she just had to feel around to find them again, along with a couple hundred others.

Yes! She could remember when Dane told her, "Hey, Mandy, guess what: Marvellini's calling it quits. He's offering us the business if we want it."

DuFresne was losing his cool. "I thought you were canceling!"

Moss was losing his as well. "She keeps resetting!"

"Dane," Preston radioed, "it's working! She has them!"

The doves were returning in droves, bursting from the trailers, lining up in wing-to-wing formations, one formation behind the other, formation on formation, descending toward the net like waves breaking.

Hundreds of horizons reeled, rocked, and raced before the eyes of Mandy's mind as each bird climbed, banked, dropped, lined up wing-to-wing with forty-four others, and descended behind other lines of doves toward the trucks, the four men, the net. She placed herself on the back of each bird to guide, prod, love it along, feeling the wind streaming over each dove's head, the violent beating of the wings, the muscles driving like pistons. *Okay, drop down, level out, you see that cord running across the net? Grab on, grab on. . . . That's it! Now climb, baby, and pull! PULL!*

Preston and his men had planned for this, envisioned it, hoped for it beyond all reason, but absolutely nothing came close to standing there and seeing it. Line upon line, wave upon wave, the birds took hold of each horizontal course of webbing and pulled it skyward, lifting the next course for the next line of birds who came in as one, grabbed hold, and lifted. With each additional line of birds lifting, the net rose faster, opening up more courses for more lines of doves to grab, until lines were coming in by the fives, tens, twenties, grabbing their courses and pulling, pulling toward the sky. The last hundred courses reeled off in a blur.

It was the most amazing thing these men had ever seen.

A gasp moved like a wave over the audience, from the folks in the bleachers and then the folks on the ground as heads turned toward the south. What was this, a cloud, a huge white banner? What could it be? Surely it wasn't what it looked like: a glimmering, sparkling, living magic carpet . . . made of . . . were those *birds*?

People in the bleachers rose to their feet as the usual *ooohhhs* and *aahhhs* ebbed to a stupefied silence and the silence broke into a cacophony of cries, questions, exclamations. This couldn't be. It just couldn't be.

They'd never seen anything like it.

Neither had Dane. He wanted to drop to his knees in awe and gratitude, but . . . not yet, and not where he'd be seen. He headed for the crane, the main point of vulnerability.

Moss fell back from the keyboard, overwhelmed by the numbers and the blinding speed with which every setting, every indication, every prediction was changing.

"Seamus!" DuFresne shouted into his headset. "What's going on?"

Seamus stammered trying to answer, his video camera sweeping, blurring, searching.

The announcers on the television were going berserk. The cameras zoomed in on a huge white banner flying toward the Orpheus. "What is that?" they shouted. "No, I don't believe it! I have never, ever seen anything like this!"

Seamus got his camera pointed and zoomed, but the shot was too shaky.

The television cameras zoomed in closer, stabilized.

DuFresne was on his feet, nose inches from the television screen. "Are those . . . are those *doves*?"

Moss couldn't think of which key to press. He could only read the monitors. "Exactly four thousand, eight hundred and sixty-four—on that many timelines."

She remembered!

The wedding cake was half gone by the time they left the reception . . . their travel trailer was a Terry and had a propane furnace . . . they kept the original Bonkers, Lily, Maybelle, and Carson on the windowsill next to the dinette . . . she cooked dinner on a barbecue stand in Brentwood Park in Minot, North Dakota, because they couldn't afford restaurants . . . they hauled and stored all their gear in the vanishing trunk Dane built.

And she really was Mandy Collins, riding a zillion doves and marveling at the view below each bird's pounding wings. In countless minds, through countless eyes flying free, she could see the pod dangling just below the boom of the crane.

Inside the pod, her body was racing through different hairstyles and lengths; her fingernails were growing out, jerking short again, growing out, jerking back. She may have had a few colds in the last second or two.

Okay, guys, steer for the pod . . . this way, this way . . .

Only a few seconds and they would be overflying the stage.

The TV announcers were on their feet.

"Like a flying carpet—literally!" cried Kirschner.

"At least a hundred feet long, sixty, eighty feet wide, made up entirely of white doves!" Rhodes shouted, his voice high-pitched, his mike distorting.

At the hospital, Arnie had to move up close to see around the people crowding the television.

"An unbelievable precedent in the world of entertainment!" cried the announcer. "Impossible to believe, but there it is, folks, and we guarantee, what you are seeing, we are seeing."

People around the lobby—patients, nurses, doctors, administrative staff—were running over to see, scrambling to find another television, spreading the word: "You've got to see this!" They were stunned, totally engaged, astounded.

And Arnie had to laugh. "Dane, you old trickster!"

Back in the vacant lot, Preston and his men had folded up the platform, the wrapping, the Velcro strips, and loaded them into a trailer. Now, with stacks rapping and diesel smoke belching, the two semis drove out of the vacant lot while they had the chance.

"Cancel those timelines!" DuFresne roared. "Get rid of those birds!"

"There isn't time!" Moss shouted back. "It takes at least one second to cancel each timeline, that's—she's way ahead of us!" Then, in all his number crunching, he discovered something that hit him like a blow to the stomach. "Oh, no . . ."

"What? What now?"

"Four thousand, eight hundred and sixty-four doves . . . the girl, the costume, that, that rigging, whatever it is . . . no wonder!"

All eyes went to the video screens now filled with synchronized doves connected by a nearly invisible grid with something—ribbons? flags?—trailing on thin threads beneath it.

DuFresne didn't take his eyes away as he prodded, *"What?"*

Moss pounded the console. "She has gravitational equivalence with the Machine. Equal mass, one thousand, six hundred and thirty-two pounds!"

DuFresne needed no further explanation. "Stone! Mortimer! Drop the pod!"

Moss objected, "No! Not before the retrace is complete!"

"Drop it *now*!"

Mr. Stone, out of his fireman's uniform and back in his basic black, was at the controls of the crane. Mr. Mortimer, also back in style, was just behind the crane, pouring out the remainder of the crane operator's "medicated" coffee and making sure the man's "fainting spell" would look convincing. Stone had been waiting for the hourglass on-stage to run out before triggering the release, the point being to make the show appear to go as planned even while the girl's retraced body incinerated in the volcano. The cloud layer of birds doing a fly-by under the crane's boom forewarned him there could be a change in plan. He replied, "Roger that," and reached for the red button.

Another hand yanked his back! Now somebody—oh, no, not the old magician!—dropped on top of him.

Not that Dane had any choice but to throw himself into it, but he did have some advantages. He outweighed Stone and, as luck had it, was the guy on top. The crane cab was a tight place with little room for wrestling or hauling back for a punch, and all Dane really had to do was keep Clarence or whatever his name was crunched into that chair and away from the controls. Sure, it was going to hurt—Clarence nailed him in the side of the head, knocking off his headset—well, that hurt more than he expected.

Mandy, trapped in the pod *and* flying outside with the doves, could see the stage and the flaming volcano passing a hundred feet below. Some of the doves were spooking at the heat and flames—she couldn't blame them, it was more than enough to spook her—but they followed their buddies and kept flying straight and level, fifty feet beneath the pod and a hundred over the heads of the crowd.

To those on the ground, 4,864 pairs of wings flying in tight forma-tion put out a sound as awesome as the sight, a rushing clamor like a stadium-size crowd applauding in a heavy rainstorm. People's mouths hung open, kids clung to their parents, cameras blinked, clicked, and flashed, and voices across the entire crowd clashed in a corporate, involuntary drone of wonder and astonishment.

* * *

Atop the hotel, the hang glider crew had been waiting for Mandy to arrive and get harnessed up, but now they stood like ornamental statues on the edge of the hotel roof, the only ones granted a view of the birds from above.

"Emile . . ." the leader radioed.

"Uh, roger, stand by," Emile came back. "We have traffic in the area."

Clarence kept swinging and Dane kept trying to grab his arms to keep him from swinging, which worked only half the time. He dug his knee into Clarence's groin and got some mileage out of that, though it was purely accidental.

Mandy grabbed two tabs, one on each shoulder of her leather costume, and yanked downward. In less than a second she went from medieval warrior princess to glimmering angel.

Next—there was no way to think or plan it, she just had to bring all her minds and selves and doves together and agree on the timing, speed, and placement, that one precise point in time that was . . . *now*!

She squeezed her eyes shut, plugged her ears, braced herself, hit a button with her toe . . .

Everyone heard the noise, like a short string of firecrackers all popping at once. A puff of smoke and fire from the pod caught their eyes. The petal doors had blown open. They cheered, *shrieked*, as . . .

Mandy dropped out of the pod into blinding sunlight, spreading her arms and legs like a sky diver as the rush of air unfurled streamers and a long train from her costume. The doves were like a cloud deck below her. They filled her vision and disoriented her a moment—she felt as if *she* were rushing backward and they were standing still. She was floating.

* * *

The crowd saw an angel with a glimmering, silken comet's tail free-falling.

An apparatus like a trapeze trailed just behind and below the doves, suspended from the grid by wires so fine they had to be assumed more than seen, and slowed by flags of silk to keep it trailing, in the clear. Before anyone had time to complete the thought: *Uh-uh, never, no way . . .*

As Dane took another blow to his body that sent his radio flying but managed to land a punch of his own, bloodying Clarence's nose . . .

As the hourglass trickled down to its last grains of sand . . .

As Moss and DuFresne were just realizing they'd missed their chance to cover up the retrace . . .

Mandy brought one more object into her realm of control, that trapeze behind and below her. The birds kept moving, she kept dropping, it appeared she would fall right into the last several rows of birds . . .

She stretched her arms out front. Feather-light, composite clamps—Dane's brainchild, Emile's craftsmanship—shot out of her sleeves like open claws.

Her hair was curled now, fluttering above her head. She had this style when she and Dane did the Carson show in 1989—she was thirty-eight.

The last row of doves slipped under her and she fell past, body flattening out, arms extended. She could see the maw of the volcano, larger now, a circle filled with flames. Heat struck her face.

The trapeze rigging was racing past, the lines marked with fluorescent stripes for her reference, counting down, counting down, getting closer.

She tucked her chin to see the trapeze. Here it came . . .

Oh, Lord, if I'm to live . . .

A microsecond early. She lowered her arms six inches—

The trapeze slammed into the clamps, her hands fell free, she dropped below the trapeze, the trapeze yanked the harness lines out of the slots in her sleeves until they terminated at the torso harness sewn into her costume and went taut. The jerk was mushy but enough to pull her arms and legs down into a crawling position, enough to make the birds sink a little from the added weight, but the birds recovered, she straightened into a graceful flying pose, and . . .

She was flying under their wings, trailing a long train and streamers of silk.

A fluttering to her right caught her eye. She grinned. Bonkers and Lily, wings beating, were flying their own formation with her. She looked to her left. Carson and Maybelle.

Well, where Momma Dove went, they went. That's just the way they were.

Dane didn't see the ultimate payoff of his design, but he heard the roar of the crowd, and it was not the sound of horror at something gone tragically wrong; it was the frenzied, jumping-up-and-down jubilation at something that had gone incredibly right.

Well, Clarence could drop the pod now.

The other guy—Lemuel. Dane only saw a peripheral corner of him when a lightning bolt hit him in the back of the neck. The next thing he knew, he was on the asphalt beside the crane. He couldn't move, but he could look up.

An angel was flying by, suspended under a cloud of doves.

Maybe I'm dead, he thought. *Maybe I'm in heaven.*

Emile was just about to order the drop . . .

Mr. Stone had his orders. He lunged for the button.

* * *

The pod dropped, the open petal doors causing it to invert like a shuttlecock on the way down. Only half the audience saw it fall, but all heard the explosion when it hit and saw the fireball. Wow!

Emile went back to watching Mandy and her doves make a climbing turn, circling around to make one more pass by the bleachers and over the crowd.

In the background of Mandy's mind it was her fortieth birthday. She opened Dane's gift to her: the most beautiful diamond wedding ring she ever saw. Dane said, "It's about time you had a really nice one." That was 1991.

In 1992 she was in his arms, weeping at the news he'd brought: her father, Arthur, had passed away suddenly, a failed aortic valve.

The rest of her mind was on her doves—*Easy now, right turn, that's it, stay together, let's give 'em a show*—and where in God's universe she was going to find and join up with the Machine. That timeline, that certain fold in space, was like an elusive word on the tip of her tongue, something she knew she knew but couldn't remember. What happened that day? She was afraid, she was drugged, she ended up in Dane's pasture, then his living room . . . how? *What did I do?*

In 1995 her periods became sporadic, her life became pointless, applause irritated her, and Dane couldn't do anything right—and right now she was having a hot flash.

Moss and DuFresne had a debacle in front of them and deadly power in high places pressing in from behind.

"As I was trying to tell you," said Moss, "if we kill her short of the retrace we'd have to rework the numbers manually. It would take years."

DuFresne shot back, "But if she finds the Machine's timeline with that much mass . . ."

Silence.

An idea. Moss ventured, "Can we, can we cripple her? Wound

her so she can't think clearly, so she can't do . . . whatever it is she does?"

DuFresne barked into his headset. "Stone! Mortimer!"

Stone and Mortimer had just slinked away from the crane and into the crowd when they heard the order. They looked skyward, reached inside their jackets.

52

L ocal time: 14:18:47.
     Mandy and her doves were half a lap around, slowly climb-
ing. Far below to her right were the parking lot and bleachers filled
with ant-size people; to her left, beyond the flat roofs of a retail center, was the vacant lot. She'd visited that site and knew how to find it,
but it sure looked small from here, and a long way to go.

     She could feel the years passing. Her hair was shorter now, in the
style she settled on somewhere in her late forties. Her costume was
feeling tight.

Stone and Mortimer left their guns concealed. Not here, around all
these people. They'd have to follow her, look for a chance.

Dane watched her circle back around, the doves blending into one
huge wing, making a beautiful fly-by for all the folks with all their
cameras. Now it made sense, and didn't bother him, why nobody
noticed him lying there on the pavement shorted out like one big
funny bone.

     "Dane! You okay?"

     It was Andy and Big Max. Of course, they could never stay hidden
behind the stage, not with Mandy giving the world a show it would
never forget. They grabbed him and yanked him to his feet without

looking at him, and he didn't look at them either. As the sight and the incredible sound passed directly overhead they let go of him and he almost collapsed but grabbed on. "Did you see those two guys?"

"What two guys?" Andy still wasn't looking anywhere but up.

Dane held on to Andy, waiting for his legs to remember they were there. He swept the area.

Oh, brother. There they were, running after Mandy as she turned south.

He tried to run after them—his legs didn't know how to do that. He returned to the pavement, hobbled back to his feet—his feet had to be down there somewhere—limped after Clarence and Lemuel as they cleared the parking lot and dashed into the street, stopping and slowing traffic, weaving through.

Mandy's brain was like a city coming out of a blackout; lights were coming on everywhere. She knew so many friends, recalled so many shows . . .

Below her, two doves flew down toward the rooftops, then four more . . . five more. How did she lose them?

Mind on the doves! Stay with them!

Reach for the Machine. Feel that day. Run for the ranch.

She passed over the street, over the retail center even as she saw herself on Robin Hill Road in the shadow of the aspens, looking up that long driveway toward that beautiful house, building the rehearsal stage, unpacking the crates of illusions in the barn . . .

I helped *pack* those crates!

But the *Machine!* That timeline was ungraspable, like a rainbow backing away.

She was gasping for breath and so were the doves.

What did I do that day? If I could only remember.

One thing she did remember: the Horizons Hotel. It was her and Dane's last gig before . . .

They were going to drive to Idaho.

Moss leaned toward the monitor. "Oh, don't tell me. Are we getting lucky?"

DuFresne and the others could see the same thing: fewer bars indicating deflection of time and space, a shrinking number of time-lines.

"She's losing it," Moss reported. "More retrace, less deflection, less influence on the Machine."

"How long does she have?" DuFresne asked.

"Not very."

Dane was getting his legs back as he stepped off the sidewalk and into the traffic, got one car to stop, then another—the bumper tapped him off balance; he put his hand on the hood to recover. A Corvette almost ran him over, but the guy behind the Corvette stopped and waved him through. He made it to the other side, looked up just in time to see Mandy's flying carpet disappear over a women's clothing store. The two guys had just dashed around a corner—a distant corner. He ran again, pushing against his age, like running uphill. He might never catch them, but he would try. If he caught up they might kill him, but at least he'd be keeping them busy.

He rounded the corner. There they were, still running, looking for a chance.

The rubble-strewn lot looked much bigger because she was nearly over the top of it, but also because the birds were tiring, starting to sink. Five or six more peeled off the rigging and flew toward the ground, obviously exhausted and just wanting to set down somewhere. She'd lost them, couldn't find them, couldn't call them back. Was this going to mess up the weight thing?

Take hold, girl! Finish the show, find your way back.

She steered her remaining doves onward, toward the empty lot. Some of them were getting confused, just following their buddies. The ground was coming up.

She remembered.

The dove anklet. She wore it the morning of their trip because it had come to symbolize new beginnings, God's hand in their lives.

That morning, Dane was still finishing his coffee and toast as they walked to the car.

"I'll drive," she said.

He tossed her the keys to the BMW.

Local time: 14:23:19.

What Dane wouldn't give for some oxygen! He couldn't draw enough breath, couldn't get his legs to hurry anymore. He made it to the sidewalk across from the vacant lot. Clarence and Lemuel had already made it to the other side and were positioning themselves amid the rubble, looking for a chance.

She was sinking toward the bricks, brown dirt, crumbled foundations. The Machine . . . still so far away. The memory of that frightening, dopey, wonderful day seemed far away too, as good as lost.

Oh, sweet love, I wanted so much to see Idaho again, to start the new season of our lives. I couldn't wait.

She remembered driving the BMW, seeing Las Vegas for the last time—and then . . .

A disturbance, a ripple in space, made her look down. Two men were running amid the rubble, looking up at her.

Faces she would never forget.

The Machine hummed so loudly it turned Moss's and DuFresne's heads. The whole room resonated, quivered with the tone. The monitor went crazy with colors, waves, graphs. The deflection figures shot to a new high.

Dane got across the street just as the dark guy, Lemuel, reached for his gun. Dane hollered—gasped, mostly—"Stop! Don't you . . . do that!"

Clarence rolled his eyes, plainly fed up as he positioned himself to block anything Dane might try.

Oh, great.

Lemuel had his gun in hand and was aiming.

Dane kept running. What else could he do?

She saw Lemuel aim at her, then a puff of smoke. A dove fell through the rigging and spiraled behind her. She felt it struggle, die, and slip from her hold.

No! Every muscle tensed, her hands trembled. Her eyes darted everywhere, but of course she was wide open with nothing she could do, no place she could hide.

The doves shuddered, out of sync.

Don't lose the doves! She reached, held, tried to keep the fear at bay. *God, help me!*

She remembered.

The gravel against her face as they held her down. The stab of the needle. The tire iron in her hand.

Animal terror.

Moss's hands were poised above the keyboard, but everything was happening so fast. "Convergence," he said.

"What?" DuFresne asked.

Was the guy deaf? "*Convergence!* Her timeline, the Machine's timeline!"

"Stone! Mortimer! Shoot her!"

Dane had to get to Lemuel before he could line up another shot.

Clarence held his hand up. "Now, take it easy, old man! There's nothing you can do."

Well, nothing that would actually *work*. Head down, Dane charged into Clarence, who easily sidestepped and threw him aside.

Dane! Dane was down there! She saw him go tumbling and another puff of smoke from Lemuel's gun. She was with the dove, guiding it, when the bullet took off its wing, she felt its agony, and lost hold. It fell past her in death, spinning toward the ground.

Dane got up again, went for Lemuel, trying to stop him, trying to save her . . .

The white paddock fence became so vivid she could touch it. In clear, crystalizing memory she half climbed, half leaped over it. The pasture grass whipped against her legs as she ran for the ranch house, for home, for *him*, reaching, *reaching* . . .

Lemuel caved in Dane's guts with his elbow and Dane fell backward, losing awareness, his vision darkening.

Moss was pounding keys, trying to cancel the timeline and normalize deflection. The Machine pushed back, canceling his commands, directing energy toward the timeline, increasing deflection.

He was arm-wrestling with the girl!

Clarence was cocky enough to turn his back. Dane landed a kick that bent Clarence's knee and made him buckle, if just for an instant. In that instant he went for Lemuel again.

Lemuel pointed the gun at him.

In mind, spirit, memory, Mandy was running forever and ever . . . longing, reaching, looking up through drug-darkening eyes at a man and a woman in the window of that beautiful house . . . together . . . where she wanted to be . . . where she belonged . . .

As she fell into the grass . . .

As she fell toward the broken bricks and concrete . . .

She reached so hard a shudder went through the birds . . .

Through Dane.

* * *

Through the Machine.

And Dane was *somewhere else*. No Lemuel, no vacant lot, no noise, no pain . . . no body? He rode on waves of colors, fell into shadowy crevasses, passed through brightness, darkness, sounds from his memory he heard all at once, far away. He was floating, suspended . . . *in between. . . .*

A warning flashed on the monitor, catching Moss's eye. Mandy's collective mass now exceeded that of the Machine by 185 pounds.

"*Yes!*" Moss exclaimed, getting everyone's attention. He answered the question in their eyes. "She's yanked Collins into her collective mass, trying to save him. She's ruined the gravitational equivalency!"

"Meaning?" DuFresne demanded.

"Meaning no timeline trade today, folks! She's just killed herself and her husband." Moss leaned back, relieved. "Too bad Parmenter didn't see that one coming—"

But then, at that instant, the Machine's clock indicated 14:24:09, and Moss and everyone else saw the adjustment the Machine made— by prior programming.

Jerome Parmenter was no longer lying on the bed in the next room. With a flash he appeared in the Machine, sitting on the bench holding a box, and he was looking out through the glass with a strange, gotcha kind of smile.

The monitor proclaimed it: gravitational equivalence had been restored. The masses were balanced.

Lemuel spun, looked, pointed the gun in all directions as if he still had an enemy, but he didn't. He looked up. Engulfed in an eerie, tea-stained atmosphere, Mandy and her doves hovered, wavering as if seen through heat waves, their sound slowed and muffled, the motion of the wings hardly discernible.

* * *

The Machine, with Parmenter inside, was distorting like rubber, bending, twisting, warping. The deep HUMMMM was shaking the floor.

Moss leaped from the console. *"Run! Get out! Get out!"*

Mr. Stone and Mr. Mortimer just stood there. They'd never seen anything like it.

There was little about the collision Mandy could have remembered. She didn't see the other car plowing through the intersection against the light. Her head hit the airbag before she had any awareness of an impact.

But she did remember entering the intersection.

The last thing the Machine's monitor indicated was a unity of timelines.

And then the room filled with flames, flashing and flying about the room like spirits, converging in spirals on the Machine, enveloping the platform, the bench, the glass, the cables—as Parmenter sat inside and watched.

DuFresne made it out first. Moss and Carlson were blocked by the other men crowding the door. Carlson was in the doorway and Moss was only a few feet inside the room when the shock wave hit.

In the hospital lobby, the floor heaved and then dropped under Arnie's feet, depositing him across a couch and in the lap of a gentleman fortunate enough not to be standing. Everyone else ended up on the floor. The magazines hopped off the coffee table, the phones and monitors flew off the reception desk, plants fell over, pictures came off the walls, and people screamed, covering their heads, covering each other, crawling for cover. The place was in chaos.

The television fell on its side but the picture still worked. Arnie stared at the screen, aghast. It was like seeing the space shuttle *Challenger* blow up all over again.

*   *   *

The crowds at the Orpheus were on their feet, their mood gone from awe and jubilation to wide-eyed, drop-jawed shock. First there was that wondrous sight, the magic flying carpet made entirely of white doves, and then . . . a flash, a fireball, and a sonic boom that shook the ground, rattled and echoed through the hotels, and hit the crowd hard enough to knock some of them over.

Even if Mr. Stone and Mr. Mortimer survived the blast that flattened them into the ground, they did not rise to flee before a shower of flaming metal, shards of glass, blazing lumps of plastic, and smoldering circuitry came down on them like a shower of meteors, burning, melting, blackening the ground, and spewing smoke.

Emile was spellbound, watching through binoculars. Like everything else this day, planning and expecting this were one thing; seeing it was far, far beyond that.

As the last burning shred of metal hit the ground, he got on his radio. "Dane? Dane, come in. Dane, do you read me?"

Nothing.

Dane awoke with a start, lying in bed in Preston's home. Daylight streamed through the windows. What on earth?

With horror and disbelief he saw the time: 2:25—in the afternoon! How could he have overslept that long? Why didn't anyone call him? Where was everybody?

And why was he lying in bed fully clothed, the keys to Preston's car still in his pocket? He even had his shoes on.

Whatever happened at the hospital—earthquake, gas explosion, terrorist attack—everyone agreed it happened under the building. The fire department was on its way. Four security personnel streamed down the NO ADMITTANCE stairways to a locked door, used clearance badges to get through, and stepped cautiously into the hallway.

No smoke. No apparent damage.

The big double doors appeared intact. AUTHORIZED PERSONNEL ONLY.

"Okay," said the chief of security, "heads up." He went to the keypad.

For the other three, this was scary but tantalizing. Even though they had access to every other part of the building, none of them had ever been allowed down here.

The chief swiped his card through the slot, and the doors opened.

They hit the floor, arms covering their faces, sure they were goners . . .

. . . as hundreds of white doves exploded into the hallway, panicked and flapping, bouncing off the walls and ceiling, careening down the hallway.

Dane sat on the steps that led from the house into the garage, the keys to Preston's Lexus in his hand. He distinctly remembered parking the car in this garage the night before, but now it wasn't there. Stolen? Arnie took it? Preston came and got it?

Then . . . the next strange thing: he remembered getting up that morning, driving to the Orpheus, checking the pod, running through the routine with Mandy, deciding not to rehearse the hang glider.

So how did he get here?

Emile got a mike from the sound crew. "Thank you so much for being a part of our amazing show today with the one and only Mandy Whitacre! Please walk to the nearest exit and have a great day here in the Entertainment Capital of the World!"

He gave the mike back to the sound guy, put on a different hat and jacket than he'd been wearing, and slipped away through the crowd.

Vahidi was collaring anyone he could find. "Where is she? What happened? Where's Downey?"

Everyone was still in shock, with no answers. He never found Seamus Downey. He never would.

Dane went back into the house, walking slowly, dazed by the memories spontaneously popping up and replaying in his brain. Mandy flying under all those birds. The volcano, and then there was a fight—

Ouch! Somebody hit him while he was standing in the hallway. He looked around—*Oof!* Another blow, and it hurt. No one was there but he remembered: *Clarence! He beat the snot out of me!*

Zap! He went numb, then his feet hurt, his knees complained, he was out of breath . . . *Oh! That car almost ran over me!*

By the time he got to the living room he'd suffered more pain and bruises and a blow to his stomach that put him on the floor. But he remembered where it all came from, right up to the point when Lemuel pointed a gun at him.

So this is what it's like. *Mandy, you are one incredible trouper!*

But what's happened? What'd I miss? As he lay on the floor dabbing blood from his mouth and thinking he might throw up, he recalled, *The TV stations were there!*

He crawled to the entertainment center, grabbed the remote, and brought the big screen to life.

The cameras were focused on the nearly empty bleachers, the crowds milling around and leaving, the stage with the dead and silent volcano.

Kirschner and Rhodes were still there, talking it up.

". . . and we're still trying to find out exactly what happened. This, pardon me, but this does not look like part of the act, Mark."

"No, Steve, it sure doesn't. There's damage, fire, no sign of Mandy Whitacre the magician."

A remote, handheld camera was circling the burning wreckage. Fire trucks and firemen were there, hoses dousing the flames.

Kirschner went on, "You all saw it, that incredible flight of thousands—it had to be thousands—"

"Oh, at least," said Rhodes.

"Thousands of doves and Mandy Whitacre suspended, flying beneath them, and now . . . we can only guess that this wreckage is all that's left of the secret mechanism by which that illusion was accomplished."

"And something went terribly wrong."

"But we don't know what, and it could be some time before we do know."

The two announcers kept talking away, describing what was plainly visible on the screen and telling everyone they didn't know anything.

Then Kirschner interrupted himself. "And as we look across the— Oh, my God!" Pause, some mike noise. "You won't believe this. We've just been informed there's been a major explosion at the Clark County Medical Center. Fire crews are on the site now, and . . . hang on to your hats: there are . . . thousands of *doves* in the building!"

It hurt to run again, but Preston also had his Jeep Wrangler in the garage, and Dane had the key.

He parked and limped from three blocks away, past curious onlookers, police cars with lights flashing and radios squawking, fire trucks standing by with nothing much to do and, as he came within a block of the hospital, doves, more doves, and all the more doves the closer he got, as thick as soapsuds in the trees, on the sidewalks, on the overhead wires, on the street signs, fence railings, everywhere. The firemen and police were working around them, wading through them, with no apparent plan as yet what to do with them all. News crews were arriving, cameramen were leaping from their vans. Hospital personnel in uniforms, coveralls, candy striper outfits, even scrubs, stood around, ambled around, clustered in little groups to watch and guess what had happened. Some played with the birds, all of which were notably tame around people.

Police were stretching out their yellow tape, but Dane went to some candy stripers and let his bruises and bleeding speak for him. The candy stripers helped him along, slipping through the barrier and directing him to one of the hastily set up first aid stations. From there he directed himself into the milling crowds, scanning, jumping to see over heads, picking up information from conversations on every side.

There had been no major damage—things were knocked over,

spilled, and broken, but nothing a mop or broom couldn't handle. There was no fire, no loss of electrical power, the patients were all safe and were not going to be evacuated. The birds were the biggest problem as far as anyone could see.

The going story was that something had happened in the basement. The rumors included a gas explosion, a mental patient with a bomb, a terrorist with a bomb, a boiler explosion, a localized earthquake, a faulty foundation, and a sinkhole. No one knew for sure because the basement levels were restricted, only people with the right clearance could go down there, and those people weren't saying anything.

Of course, the main question spreading all over the campus was the birds and how they got there. The name "Mandy Whitacre" and the words "Grand Illusion" were popping up.

The main door was open. Orderlies and janitorial staff were herding and shooing doves out the door with brooms.

"Dane!" a voice whispered behind him. A hand on his shoulder jerked him around. It was Arnie, wearing a jogging outfit and a billed cap. He immediately took off the cap and jammed it down on Dane's head, the bill so low it blocked Dane's eyes. "What are you doing here?"

"I woke up back in my bed in Preston's house, back where I was at six this morning."

"Don't look around, just walk! This way!"

"It had to be Parmenter. He must have known I was going to get pulled into Mandy's collective mass. He had the Machine spit me out someplace safe—more than nine hours ago."

"No, I mean, what are you doing *here*? Are you crazy?"

"Have you found her?"

Arnie walked him under the ribbon and toward the trees on the edge of the visitor parking. "Oh, yeah, right, we had a lovely reunion in the lobby while all hell was breaking loose. You kidding? The place is nuts right now. They've blocked off the basement, all the doors, everything."

"We've got to find her."

"No, *you've* gotta get out of here, that's what *you've* gotta do. The place is crawling with cops and cameras and everybody's asking questions. And the two of you seen together? Eeesh! Why don't you just hang a sign on her? What are you thinking?"

They ducked on the other side of a tree, keeping their faces toward it.

"We were wondering what happened to you. One minute you're there, the next minute—man, what *did* happen to you? You look like you had a scrape with somebody."

Dane nodded. "Twice."

"Ehh. Figures. Nothing halfway about you."

Dane tried to look around the tree, but Arnie yanked him back. "Hey! Stick with your own plan. If she's here, we'll find her."

"She's got to be here." He nodded toward the doves. "They made it."

Arnie chuckled and wagged his head. "I hope to shout they did, and not a feather out of place." And then, just taking in all the doves, he had to laugh. "Dane, you always were the idea man, I gotta tell ya!"

"Thank Parmenter." Dane smiled, not in joy but in hope. "And Preston must have called in a thousand favors." His attention lingered on some doves perched in the branches above them.

"Well let's get you out of town. I've already gotten some calls, people wondering if you were mixed up in this." Arnie noticed Dane staring. "What?"

There were four doves perched side by side. They were fidgeting, nodding, and bobbing in Dane's direction, as if they knew him. He spread his arms out straight.

They flew down and perched on his arms, two on the left, two on the right.

Arnie did a jaw drop—then stood in front of Dane and the birds, trying to hide them. "What do you say we get 'em out of here?"

"They'll let you hold them."

Cradling a bird in each hand, they stole away.

On the far side of the hospital, as firemen, police, animal control people, and hospital maintenance personnel hurried through a loading door with a variety of fish, bird, and butterfly nets, a maintenance lady in coveralls and billed cap walked by them carrying a broken lamp. She dropped the lamp into a Dumpster beside the loading dock, then continued toward the street, not looking back.

chapter

53

Rancher Jack Wright never heard from or saw the weird scientists again, which was fine with him; it was part of the deal. As for the 35.76 concrete blocks, they also were part of the deal. He hauled them away to use in a new pigsty, leaving that isolated little piece of his ranch looking as if no one had ever been there—if anyone even cared to look.

On Saturday evening at about seven, Dane stepped through the back door into his kitchen. The place was quiet.

"Hello?" he called, but there was no answer.

He walked through the house, checking the living room, the downstairs guest room and bath, the rooms upstairs. He stopped by his closet where Mandy's costumes and wardrobe still hung neatly, touching the sleeve of the blue gown. Passing by his dresser, he studied a recent photo portrait; she was still so lovely.

He checked his answering machine. No messages. Well, that was part of the plan, cell and land phone silence until they knew which way the winds were blowing, whether the bad guys were listening.

He drove to the Quik Stop on Highway 95 to use the pay phone. Somewhere in Las Vegas, in a hotel room, a rented office, perhaps the home of one of Arnie's friends, a telephone rang, but no one answered. He rechecked the number Arnie gave him and dialed again. Still no answer. He returned the receiver to the cradle less than gently, then sighed, resigning himself to a little more waiting, a little more not knowing.

He returned to the ranch, carried in his luggage, and then brought in Mandy's four doves in their cage. They were tired, ready to sleep, so he set them in the utility room with the light off so they could call it a night.

Shirley had left all his mail in a pile on the kitchen counter and a note catching him up on the spraying she'd done, getting a new drive belt for the lawn mower, replacing the bulbs in the shop with the brighter wattage he wanted, having Susan the housekeeper skip a week and . . . blah blah blah, *thank you, Shirley*, he was too tired, too edgy to read the rest.

He fixed himself a bowl of oat flakes, something quick and easy, and settled in front of his computer to see if he could get any news.

The EPA had taken immediate interest in the "hazardous waste spill" in that vacant lot. A remediation crew showed up within an hour, cordoned off the area, and worked through the night to sanitize it, replacing six inches of topsoil and hydroseeding grass. The agency also took over the subbasement of the hospital, declaring those floors an environmental hazard and sealing them off. Dane had to wonder why a hospital was allowed to remain open sitting on top of an environmental hazard, but of course there was no explanation.

Public outcry prevented any killing of the doves, so they were being captured to be sold on the Internet, distributed to pet stores, employed by local magicians, adopted by bird lovers from all over the country. White doves were free for the catching and selling dirt cheap in Las Vegas.

As for deaths, casualties, missing persons, even what became of Mandy Whitacre, the newspeople had nothing, and the government was strangely, silently uninvolved.

Dane sighed and let his head drop. He didn't know, would probably never know, what Parmenter's "contingency plan" was, but if Dane threw Mandy's collective mass off, there would have been only one way to counterbalance it. He probably would never see the venerable scientist again.

The Orpheus Hotel Casino had already booked another act for the big room in the aftermath of the great and mysterious tragedy:

Gabriel's Magic, featuring the famous television magician Preston
Gabriel, who just happened to have some time available. Well, that
worked. The Orpheus got a spike in name recognition no amount of
money could buy and a great show besides. Now Dane didn't feel
quite so bad.

He closed the computer and rubbed his eyes, so very tired. To
stay out of airports where he might be seen or looked for, he'd driven
Preston's Wrangler from Vegas to Salt Lake City, where he slept in a
cheap room, then drove all day Saturday to get home . . . to an empty
house, and no word.

He tried to sleep that night and finally dropped off. The telephone let him sleep; it never made a sound.

Sunday morning the weather was cheerful, a rare occurrence for
March in Idaho. It helped. There wasn't a swelling bud or a new blade
of grass in sight, but it helped. Dane checked the answering machine
again—it was a little irrational, but he might have missed something.
No messages.

All right. He'd take another trip down to the Quik Stop and try
the number again. He grabbed his coat from the closet—

A cooing from the utility room stopped him. *Oh, brother. Can't
it wait?*

Well . . .

If all things were ordinary, he would have left them there until
he got back, but these were not just four little doves among many,
these were Bonkers, Carson, Lily, and Maybelle. They were stars, ultimate aviators, and most of all, heroes. He saw them fly with Mandy
through the whole thing and it tugged at his heart like crazy. However things turned out, he owed them.

And, of course, there was Mandy. She'd want them well taken
care of.

He brought them into the kitchen and they were glad to see
him, sidestepping back and forth on their perches, chirping, bobbing around. He gave them some breakfast—fresh seeds, water, celery tops from the refrigerator—and leaned on his elbows watching
them scarf it all down. "I wonder if you guys even have a clue what
you did."

They just kept eating, cooing, and chirping.

He shrugged. *All in a day's work. Another day, another seed, another leaf of celery.*

They needed to get out of this cage. It seemed to Dane like living in a hotel room, out of a suitcase. They needed to be home in their coop, where they had plenty of room to move and fly around. "Okay, guys, let's go."

The dove coop was a temporary and adequate installation inside the shop building, just the right home for the doves until spring warmed things up and they could spend more time outside. The shop building was just a short walk down the path toward Mandy's Meadow.

The morning sun made it a pleasant walk—warm colors, warmth on Dane's south shoulder, the snow all gone, and a little steam coming off the barn roof. Some crocuses were coming up. The doves were fluttering, looking all around, excited.

He opened the door to the shop and went inside.

"Wow! You remember this place, don't you?" They were really hopping and chirping, more agitated than he expected. *They must really be glad to be home.*

The cage door flipped open.

"*What?* Hey, whoa, whoa, don't—!"

They crowded through it, jostling, bumping, climbing over each other.

In all his effort to keep them in their cage he didn't notice he'd left the shop door open.

"No! No no no no no!"

If it had been a movie with somebody else climbing the walls and grabbing the air trying to catch four ultimate aviators, Dane would have gotten the biggest laugh out of it, but it wasn't and he wasn't. He could have sworn they were working as a team, faking him out until they all got out the door.

The door. Why didn't I just close the door?

Stupid. No, preoccupied. I've been through a lot.

No, stupid.

He stepped through the door and, for the sake of his own dignity and self-worth, closed it after him. The doves were up by the house aviating, making wild circles and loops over the driveway, showing off, having the time of their lives. "Yeah, rub it in."

The phone rang in the kitchen.

"*Oohhh!*" When it rained, it poured. Loose doves *and* the phone ringing. If Dane had been sitting on the toilet right now the morning would have been perfect.

He ran up the pathway, all stops out, pedal to the metal, his legs still sore from the last big run, and got to the kitchen door as the answering machine picked up. "Hi, this is Dane. Please leave a short message . . ."

Who? Who is it?

The doves were soaring high, heading down the driveway, as good as gone.

He almost went inside to hear the message but stopped on the threshold.

"Hi, this is Jack Lewis . . ." Arnie's code name! "Just want you to know that your order is still in process"—they hadn't found Mandy yet—"but be advised the, uh, the means of shipping is, uh, unavailable . . . well, it's gone, we can't find it." They couldn't locate her blue Volkswagen. "However, if you have any information you can get back to us at . . ."

Arnie was leaving a new number to call, but Dane was watching the doves circle down toward the front gate, then perch, hop, and fly in short bursts along the top of the paddock fence, following . . .

A blue Volkswagen, rolling, jostling, whirring up the driveway. Arnie hung up, and Dane didn't care. He stepped into the driveway, wanting only to see who was behind the wheel. When the little car came near the house and into the winter-thin shade of the aspens, he could see through the windshield.

It was . . .

What world was he living in now? Had he fallen from the real world into another madness, or from one madness, one dream, into another? Could he really believe what he was seeing, or was another reality or illusion or goofy deflection in the space-time watchama-callit going to horn in and change everything again? He wanted to believe, but he couldn't. He thought he'd be ready and could handle it, but all he could do was stand there.

When she'd stopped the Bug, set the brake, and turned off the engine, she looked at him through the car window for the longest time, as if she were having the very same questions, as if that pane of glass could shield her from answers she couldn't bear.

She was glad he remained so still, so everyday human with his bruises, tousled morning hair, and confounded expression. She needed a good, reassuring look at him before she opened the car door—and maybe he needed that kind of look at her.

He looked like the man she remembered, as real as ever he'd been. *She* looked like . . .

She stole a look at herself in the rearview mirror.

Do you remember, my love? All the years, all the seasons, all the changes we went through? These are what brought us to this day, this is who we really are, and this is where we belong. Do you see it that way?

Dane approached as the doves lit on the car roof, their feet tap-tap-tapping on the metal. He gazed at her through the window, put his fingertips on the glass. She placed her fingertips against his from the other side. They had the time, so they took it to look at each other.

She was alive. Beautiful and unafraid.

He placed his hand on the door handle. The latch clicked. He eased the door open, she swung her feet out, and then she stood with no glass, no door, no barrier between them.

She'd made it to Idaho.

"Well . . ." he said, drinking in the sight of her. This was she, the woman he'd loved for forty years.

Six-oh, she thought. *Of course.* He was supposed to be sixty and now it didn't seem one bit strange to her. She was feeling kind of sixtyish herself and it wasn't so bad, just a month or two older than she was before. It fit.

"Well . . ." she said back with a little smile, but thought, *Go ahead, touch me.*

* * *

He extended his hand. Maybe she'd touch him and see he was real, or he'd touch her . . .

She took his hand in hers and covered it with her other hand.

She was real, as real as ever she'd been.

They embraced, and from there they got to know each other again, taking it slow, feeling it new, savoring the hours as on their very first night.

chapter

54

Her soul at peace, Mandy slept until midday, then rose, showered, and slipped into Dane's blue robe. It was warm and comfortable, and there was just something commemorative about it: she'd worn it right after he rescued her the first time. The thrill of it was, she didn't have wet clothes in the dryer and, just as on their first day married, she would never have to leave.

Dane must have heard her stirring about. As she emerged from the bedroom he came up the stairs carrying a latte for himself and a mocha for her, brewed in their same old trusty coffeemaker.

"Oh, thank you, kind sir."

"But of course."

He'd pulled on his jeans and a pair of slippers. She took a second look at him, something she'd been doing since she got here.

"What?" he asked.

"You are so hairy!"

"Why, thank you."

"When we first got married you had maybe two hairs on your chest."

He shrugged and sipped from his latte. "Have you seen my ears lately?"

He settled into a chair in the loft. There was a sweeping view of the valley behind him, but he wouldn't stop looking at her.

She went to the east windows, admiring the view, recalling raking and sweeping out the barn, cleaning out the shop, *all the work on this place . . . and all the snow, Lord have mercy!* She certainly had the energy back then.

"So," she ventured, "what are we going to do? I mean, how do we tell the world I'm alive again?"

He put on a very typical deep-in-thought expression. "Well, we could borrow from Mark Twain and say the reports of your death were greatly exaggerated."

She smiled, enjoying the smell of the mocha beneath her nose. "I suppose."

He smiled back and sipped from his coffee. "I'm making a list."

"I still have a coat I borrowed from a nurse in the Behavioral Health Unit. We need to put that on the list, get that back to her."

"That'll be the easy part."

Okay. She felt better. "Oh, and I've been meaning to say"—he waited, clearly enjoying the sight of her—"it sure means a lot to me that you didn't fall for a younger woman."

She could see the twinkle in his eye before he said it. "And go through menopause all over again?"

She could have given him a slick comeback, but something caught her eye . . .

A girl running through the pasture toward the house, staggering, falling, getting up again, reaching desperately.

"What is it?" he asked, but then he froze at the sight of her just as she remained transfixed by the sight out the window. "Ohhh, man. Déjà vu. You see her, don't you?"

It was . . . well, of course. It was the girl who'd been *looking in* the mirror, the child who so desperately wanted to be her. "Oh, keep running, little one. Keep running."

Dane stood beside her, put his arm around her. "Don't you worry. She's going to be just fine."

The image in the pasture dissolved like a wisp of steam, and then it was just the two of them.

a note from the author

Of course I've been asked, "What's the book about?" and it's never been quite enough to answer, "A love story about two illusionists who are separated by death but not really, not yet, and their quest to find each other and be reunited." That's a nice encapsulation, but it doesn't express the heart of the story.

A better answer would be found in the symbolism and thematic elements:

- Being lost in this weird and sinful world, trying to discover who we are and where we belong;

- The deception and lure of this world that we overcome as we reach for heaven, our home;

- The comforting presence of the Holy Spirit and His quiet assurances that we have a place in this world as well as a holy and eternal destination;

- Our longing and lifelong quest as the bride of Christ to be united with Jesus, our bridegroom.

And I need to add a personal, heart-level reflection: For me, the story is about Barb, my dear wife and best friend for forty years, and the mystery, tenacity, beauty, and wonder of our love from the day we met until now. Building the story and developing its themes were a matter of mind and creativity, but it was our love that drove it, that gave it life. Thinking about Dane and Mandy, I thought about us, and not only that, I also found a new appreciation for what our marriage symbolizes. After all, what is the Gospel if not the story of our savior wooing us to Himself and that relentless, unutterable longing that makes us reach across our years and through our limitations to find Him? For me, that's the *heart* of it. That's where I live.

So I suppose this tale is a fictional tribute to love as God made it, and by that, an illustration of how beautiful the love between ourselves and our Lord can be. It's a story worth telling, always. Thank you for sharing it with me.

Blessings.
Frank E. Peretti

acknowledgments

Every time I do a novel, there are friends around to help me with the details. It's fun to see such learned and professional people dive headlong into making up and telling a story, and I always get an education in the process.

Special thanks to . . .

Dr. Paul Brillhart, a wonderful brother in the Lord and an avid storyteller himself, who has enthusiastically helped me injure, kill, hospitalize, treat, and heal a host of characters in believable ways in two novels so far.

Teirza Bristow, a genuine emergency room nurse who talked me through every detail of ER procedure in a case like Mandy's.

Dr. James Kirby, who gave me a fascinating telephone tour of a real behavioral health unit and provided an abundance of details on how a case like Mandy's might be handled. Of course, the people and facility Mandy encounters in the story are fictionalized and have to be passive bad guys. Dr. Kirby, his staff, and their facility are a lot nicer!

The one and only Tony Brent, magician and comedian, who gave me so much of his valuable time to talk about the performance and business of magic. Keep an eye out for him, Google him, be sure to catch his show; he'll keep you amazed and in stitches at the same time. All the best, my friend!

Look for the eBook editions of
the bestselling classics
This Present Darkness,
Piercing the Darkness, and *Prophet*

By FRANK PERETTI